MARCHIN'S FINGER TIGHTENED ON THE FIRING STUD.

A burst of flame leaped across the gap, bathing the robot in fire but actually merely splattering impotently against the impassable barrier that was the force screen.

The metal creature, unharmed by the deadly blast, waited impassively. Almost a minute slipped by while Marchin hopelessly continued to direct his fire at the barrier that shielded the robot's patient bulk. Then, seeing he was accomplishing nothing, Marchin cursed vividly and in a quick bitter gesture hurled the blaster across the room at the stiffly erect robot.

The weapon clanged off the creature's chest and fell to one side.

The robot laughed. The laugh was unmistakably the laugh of Ben Thurdan.

Marchin howled an imprecation, and began to run.

For a moment at first Mantell thought he was going to try to dash out the door, but that was not Marchin's intention, apparently. Instead he ran straight toward the robot in a mad suicidal dash.

He traveled ten feet. Then the robot lifted one ponderous arm and discharged a bolt of energy from grids in its fingers. The flare caught Marchin in the chest with such impact that it lifted him off the ground and hurled him backward the whole distance he had covered in his dash.

He tottered, clawed at his throat, and staggered into a swirly screen at a table behind him. He fell and didn't get up.

THE PLANET STORIES LIBRARY

STRANGE ADVENTURES ON OTHER WORLDS
AVAILABLE EXCLUSIVELY FROM PLANET STORIES!

FOR AUTHOR BIOS AND SYNOPSES,
VISIT PAIZO.COM/PLANETSTORIES

Publisher's Cataloging-In-Publication Data
(Prepared by The Donohue Group, Inc.)

Silverberg, Robert.
 The chalice of death : three novels of mystery in space / by Robert Silverberg ;
cover illustration by Kieran Yanner.

 p. ; cm. -- (Planet stories ; #33)

 Stories originally appeared in the Ace Double novel series.
 Chalice of death originally issued as: Lest we forget thee, Earth. [S.l.] : Agberg,
c1958.
 Shadow on the stars originally issued as: Stepsons of Terra. [S.l.] : Agberg,
c1958.
 "September 2011."
 Contents: Introduction -- The chalice of death -- Starhaven -- Shadow on the
stars.
 ISBN: 978-1-60125-377-4

 1. Interplanetary voyage--Fiction. 2. Science fiction, American. 3. Adventure
stories, American. 4. Short stories, American. I. Yanner, Kieran. II. Title. III.
Title: Lest we forget thee, Earth. IV. Title: Stepsons of Terra. V. Title: Chalice of
death. VI. Title: Starhaven. VII. Title: Shadow on the stars.

PS3569.I472 A6 2011c
813/.54

PLANET stories

COVER ILLUSTRATION BY KIERAN YANNER

THE CHALICE OF DEATH
THREE NOVELS OF MYSTERY IN SPACE

BY ROBERT SILVERBERG

Thirty thousand years ago, Earth reigned as the supreme force for law and order in the galaxy. Now her mighty star empire lies vanquished and long forgotten, and Earthman Hallam Navarre must seek out and recover his ancestors' secret weapon—or be doomed to suffer the fate of the lost homeworld he's never seen.

Interplanetary fugitive Johnny Mantell flees authorities to the artificial pirate world of Starhaven, sanctuary for the criminals and misfits of space. There he hopes to find a new home for himself—if only he's willing to submit to the space station's iron-fisted dictator and his potentially mind-shattering psychprobe.

Deep-space colonist Baird Ewing travels to Earth for the first time in the thousand years since his ancestors last departed, seeking aid against the aliens who have set out to destroy his colony. But the weapon he finds upon the ancient Earth can save only one planet, and Ewing must decide which homeworld will live and which will be utterly annihilated.

PLANET STORIES is published bimonthly by Paizo Publishing, LLC with offices at 7120 185th Ave NE, Ste 120, Redmond, Washington, 98052. Erik Mona, Publisher. Pierce Watters, Senior Editor. Christopher Paul Carey and James L. Sutter, Editors. Michael Kenway, Editorial Intern. *The Chalice of Death: Three Novels of Mystery in Space* © 2012 by Agberg, Ltd. Introduction © 2011 by Agberg, Ltd. *The Chalice of Death* © 1958, 1986 by Agberg, Ltd. (original title: *Lest We Forget Thee, Earth*). *Starhaven* © 1958, 1986 by Agberg, Ltd. *Shadow on the Stars* © 1958, 1986 by Agberg, Ltd. (original title: *Stepsons of Terra*). Planet Stories and the Planet Stories planet logo are registered trademarks of Paizo Publishing, LLC. Planet Stories #33, *The Chalice of Death*, by Robert Silverberg. January 2012. PRINTED IN THE UNITED STATES OF AMERICA.

Introduction

This is the second of two omnibus volumes collecting the science-fiction novels that I wrote for the Ace Double Novels series back in the early years of my career, more than fifty years ago. The other omnibus is called *The Planet Killers: Three Novels of the Spaceways*; and before I discuss the three books in this one, I want to recapitulate part of the introduction to the other collection, by way of setting the historical context for Ace Books and my involvement with their Double Novels program.

I was a college sophomore in the fall of 1953, hoping in a rather desperate way to become a professional science-fiction writer some day, when the first Ace Double Book appeared. In those days it was possible to buy all the science fiction that was published, even on a college sophomore's budget, because there really wasn't very much of it—four or five magazines a month, and one or two paperbacks at most—and so I snapped it up.

It was an unusual-looking book. For 35 cents—five or six dollars in today's purchasing power—you got a short, thick paperback containing A. E. van Vogt's novel *The World of Null-A*. But if you turned the book over, flipping it from top to bottom in the process, you discovered a second van Vogt novel on the back—*The Universe Maker*. Two for the price of one—182 pages of small type for *Null-A*, and 138 more for *Universe Maker*! And, though the greatly ballyhooed *World of Null-A* was plainly the main event here, one could not actually consider one book to be the lead novel and the other its backup, because each was printed upside down in relation to the other, so that the volume had neither "front" nor "back," just two novels in one binding, each with its own cover and each inverted vis-à-vis its companion.

As I examined it I don't think I allowed myself the fantasy of having some book of mine published in the Ace Double series just yet. It would have been much too far-fetched. I still hadn't managed to sell even one short story, though just a couple of months earlier I had had an article on science-fiction fandom accepted by one of the professional s-f magazines. That sale had brought me $30, but to me an article was a somewhat lesser thing than a story, and I would not think of myself as a real science-fiction writer until I had sold a story or two. Selling novels, perhaps, would come later, but I tried to keep my adolescent fantasies as plausible as I could.

So I bought the van Vogt Ace Double Book more as an avid collector of science fiction than as a potential author of Ace Doubles. Indeed there was no other reason then for me to have bought the book, for I had read *World of Null-A* three or four years before, in almost complete bewilderment, in its original magazine version, and, though I didn't know it at the time, I had already read *The Universe Maker* too. (It had previously been published under a different title in a 1950 issue of the pulp magazine *Startling Stories*.) But there was no indication of that in the double volume, since the title of the shorter novel was unfamiliar and the book gave a copyright date of 1953 for it. Ace Books, I was to learn, was never very fastidious about copyright information or book titles. But, as I've said, I had bought the book mainly as a collector's item, for the novelty of its back-to-back format.

A month later came a second Ace Double: Leigh Brackett's *The Sword of Rhiannon* bound with Robert E. Howard's *Conan the Conqueror*. I bought that too. I realized that these odd little Ace Doubles were something I wanted to collect as a series.

Once again, I had read the two books before. The famous Robert Howard novel was plainly labeled as a reprint. The Brackett was palmed off as an original novel, copyright 1953, but the text looked familiar, and for good reason: I had read a slightly shorter version of it, under the title of "Sea-Kings of Mars," in the June, 1949 *Thrilling Wonder Stories*.

The months went by, and nearly every one brought a new Ace Double: more van Vogt, an Eric Frank Russell novel, works by L. Sprague de Camp, Murray Leinster, Jack Williamson, Isaac Asimov, Clifford D. Simak. I had learned by now that the editor of the series was Donald A. Wollheim, a veteran figure whose experience in science fiction went back almost to its earliest days. The authors, that first year, were all long-established writers of the field, no newcomers among them, and the books were either reprints of hardcover novels or else reissues of recent magazine serials, disguised by new titles and copyright dates. Ace did not seem to be a market for previously unpublished fiction, not even from well-known pros.

I had by now sold a couple of stories to the lesser s-f magazines and was in the process of selling a young-adult novel to a hardcover firm, but at that early date I saw no likelihood of ever having a book of my own in the Ace series. Things changed. In the summer of 1955 one of the Ace Doubles included a novel that had never been published before, by a relatively new young writer named Philip K. Dick who had broken into the field just a couple of years earlier with a lot of short, clever stories for the pulp magazines. Then came a novel by another recent arrival on the scene, Gordon R. Dickson, and a second one by Dick. The Ace Doubles series was starting to turn into a market for new work by younger writers.

In the summer of 1955, too, though I was still in college, I broke into professional writing in a big way, with stories sold to *Astounding Science Fiction*, *Amazing Stories*, *Fantastic*, and three or four other magazines. Even though these stories rarely rose above the level of minimal professional competence, there were a lot of them, a *lot*, and my productivity alone was earning me a great deal of attention, just as theirs had done for Philip K. Dick and Robert Sheckley a couple of years before. And at the World Science Fiction Convention in New York in September, 1956, my prolific output won me recognition with a Hugo Award as Best New Writer of the Year.

That evening, after the award ceremony, Don Wollheim came up to me and said, "Do you think you'd be interested in writing novels for us at Ace?"

Ah, it was a wondrous thing to be 21 years old, three months out of college, standing there with a shiny new Hugo in my arms, and having Donald A. Wollheim inviting me to write for him, only three years after I had bought that first van Vogt/van Vogt Ace Double!

A week or so later I was having lunch with Wollheim at Steuben's Tavern, a German restaurant down the block from his midtown Manhattan office. He suggested that I send him an outline and the first three chapters of a book. That afternoon I spent an hour or so staring at the Dick and Dickson books, and one by Charles L. Harness, and a couple of Leinsters, as if merely by studying the close-packed typeface of those books I would form a Platonic-ideal notion of what an Ace Double Book ought to be. I did, in fact, have some idea of that already: just about all of them that had been published thus far were books of 40,000–50,000 words, fast-paced, heavy on color and action, rich in science-fictional wonderment. Brackett, van Vogt, Leinster, Williamson— these, I thought, correctly, were the prototypical Ace authors whose work I should emulate. One could have chosen worse role models than those.

I began to sketch an outline for a book that I called *Years of the Freeze*. I gave the outline to Wollheim the following week and he bought it right away and I wrote it that fall in one breathless rush, using a flimsy bridge table as my desk in my still mostly unfurnished new post-college apartment. He called it *The Thirteenth Immortal* when he published it in the Ace Double series in May of 1957. (Wollheim almost always changed my titles. He did it to almost everybody else, too.) It was printed back-to-back with James Gunn's *This Fortress World*, a reprint of a novel I had read and admired when it was first published in 1955. I had spent quite some time talking with Gunn at the 1955 World Science Fiction Convention, telling him of my aspirations as a writer.

So there I was, an author of Ace Doubles. And sharing a volume with James E. Gunn. Decades later, the Science Fiction Writers of America would name us both as Grand Masters, but I had no fantasies of such exalted future status back then. I was more than content just to have sold a book to Ace.

By the time *The Thirteenth Immortal* came out, I had already written and sold Wollheim a second book, published a few months later in 1957 as—his title again—*Master of Life and Death*. (My original title was the feeble *Gateway to Utopia*.) My back-to-back companion this time was the Anglo-Irish writer James White, with *The Secret Visitors*. When I met White that month at the

London science-fiction convention, we posed for photos back-to-back, though we weren't able to manage the reciprocally inverted configuration of an Ace Double.

Then came *Invaders from Earth* in the spring of 1958 (for once Wollheim kept my original title; the book was paired with *Across Time* by "David Grinnell," a pseudonym for Wollheim himself) and *Lest We Forget Thee, Earth* just a month later (the companion was *People Minus X* by Raymond Z. Gallun, a writer who had been famous in the field before I was born), and *Stepsons of Terra* (my title: *Shadow on the Stars*) still later the same year, bound with Lan Wright's *A Man Called Destiny*. In the spring of 1959 came *Starhaven*, under the pseudonym of "Ivar Jorgenson," this one a reprint of a previously published hardcover book. It was doubled with *The Sun Smasher* by Edmond Hamilton, another of my early literary heroes. Like Philip K. Dick and Poul Anderson and Murray Leinster and A. E. van Vogt, I had become one of the Ace regulars.

Áll three of my 1958–59 Ace books had their origins in work I did for Larry T. Shaw's magazine *Science Fiction Adventures*. Shaw, an old-time s-f fan, might have had a splendid career as an editor if he had ever found a major publisher to back him, for his taste was superb and he had the useful knack of coaxing writers to do their best work without seeming actually to be nagging them; but it was his fate always to work for marginal companies in low-budget ventures. *Infinity* was his special pride, a low-budget magazine that ran high-budget-type stories by the likes of Arthur C. Clarke, Isaac Asimov, James Blish, Damon Knight, C. M. Kornbluth, and Algis Budrys. It even published Harlan Ellison's first science-fiction story. I was a regular contributor to *Infinity* and many of my best short stories appeared there. The companion magazine, *Science Fiction Adventures*, was a blood-and-thunder operation done strictly for fun by everybody involved, featuring space-opera novellas of interstellar intrigue and blazing ray-guns in the mode of the beloved old 1940s pulp, *Planet Stories*. I was a regular contributor to *SFA*, too: in fact, I practically wrote the whole magazine. As I look through my file copies, I see a long story or two by me (often under some pseudonym) in virtually every issue. I loved writing these melodramas of the spaceways, and the readers evidently enjoyed them too, for my stories (under whatever pseudonym) were usually the most popular offerings in each issue, according to the reader letters that Shaw received.

The original format of *SFA* provided "Three Complete Action Novels" (actually, novelets of 15,000 to 20,000 words in length) in each issue, plus a few short stories and features. In the fall of 1956, when the magazine was just a couple of issues old and I was already established as its main writer, editor Shaw had the idea of running a series of related novellas, since the series story had long been a favorite of s-f readers. (E. E. Smith's "Lensman" novels, Clifford Simak's "City," Robert A. Heinlein's "future history" series, Henry Kuttner's mutant stories, etc., etc.) I was invited to dream up a three-part series for the magazine, and swiftly obliged.

The first of the three, "Chalice of Death," which I wrote in December, 1956, ran in the fourth issue, dated June, 1957. I worked off the tried-and-true theme of a galaxy so widely settled by humanity that the location of Earth itself had been forgotten, and ended the story with the rediscovery of decadent old Earth and the prospect of a revival of its ancient galactic hegemony. Shaw ran it under a pseudonym I had already been using elsewhere, "Calvin M. Knox," since there had been novellas under my own name in the previous two issues. After taking time out to do a couple of unrelated pieces for *SFA*, I wrote the sequel to "Chalice," called "Earth Shall Live Again!", in March, 1957, and Shaw published it in the December, 1957 *SFA*. (Which also contained the lead novella, "Valley Beyond Time," under my own name, so that I was responsible for about three-quarters of that issue's fiction content.) I finished the trilogy in June, 1957 with a novella that bore the gloriously pulpy title of "Vengeance of the Space Armadas," which ran in the March, 1958 issue and saw Earth properly restored to its preeminent place in galactic affairs.

By no coincidence at all, the three novellas added up exactly to the right length for an Ace Double Novel, and in October, 1957 I gathered up a set of carbon copies and sold it to Don Wollheim, my fourth Ace sale, right on the heels of my sale to him of *Invaders from Earth*. He published *Invaders* in April, 1958 under the Silverberg byline and brought out the "Chalice" stories just a month later as by "Calvin M. Knox." I had called the book *The Chalice of Death*, but Wollheim did his customary title-changing thing and released it under the title, *Lest We Forget Thee, Earth*, a name which I never admired and which I have replaced, for this new edition, with my original one.

By then, steaming right along in my wildly prolific ways, I had helped Larry Shaw with a couple of further experiments in editorial policy at *Science Fiction Adventures*. He wanted to vary the three-novella format that he had been using since the beginning, and asked me to write an extra-long work that he could hype as a "Book-Length Novel," to be backed up by a few shorter stories. In May, 1957, I obliged with "Thunder Over Starhaven," a 28,000-worder that Shaw ran in the October, 1957 issue. Because both Silverberg and "Knox" were appearing all over the place in the magazine, Shaw rang in yet a third pseudonym for me and put out "Starhaven" under the name of "Ivar Jorgenson."

A word or two about that "Jorgenson" byline is necessary here. My use of it wasn't entirely kosher. "Ivar Jorgensen"—note the spelling—had made his debut in 1951 in a pulp magazine called *Fantastic Adventures* with a rather nice Viking fantasy called "Whom the Gods Would Slay." Other "Jorgensen" stories followed, and gradually word leaked out that they were the work, not of a swaggering Scandinavian bard, as claimed, but of Paul W. Fairman, a mild-mannered staff writer for *Fantastic Adventures* and its companion magazine, *Amazing Stories*. When Fairman moved along to become the first editor of a magazine called *If*, he took "Jorgensen" along with him, and still later, in 1955, he wrote still more "Jorgensen" stories for William L. Hamling's *Imagination*.

The bibliographical problems began in 1957 when Hamling decided that "Jorgensen" was a house pseudonym that could be applied to the work of any of his authors. I had become part of Hamling's writing staff by then, along with my collaborator of the time, Randall Garrett, and Hamling hung the name on some stories that Garrett and I turned in. Which of them I wrote and which

Garrett did and which we did together is something I no longer can tell, but it is certain, at any rate, that those stories, eight or nine of them, weren't written by Paul Fairman!

The next move came when Larry Shaw of *Science Fiction Adventures* chose to capitalize on what he imagined to be the popularity of the Jorgensen name by having me write three long stories for him under that name. The first was "This World Must Die!", which became *The Planet Killers*. I followed it two months later with *Thunder Over Starhaven*, which took up almost an entire issue and shortly thereafter appeared in book form as *Starhaven*. The third, "Hunt the Space-Witch!", came out in his other magazine, *Infinity*, a couple of months after that.

Either through my carelessness or Larry's, though, the byline on those three was spelled "Ivar Jorgenson," with an "o" in the last syllable. Collectors of my work would be entitled to think that although Fairman wrote most but not all of the "-sen" stories, I was the author of all the "-son" ones, except for the ugly fact that in 1953, in his own magazine, *If*, Fairman had used the "-son" ending on a story that he had written for himself. There is also the nasty case of a little story called "A Pause in Battle," published in the May, 1957 issue of Hamling's *Imaginative Tales*, that gets the "Jorgensen" spelling on the contents page and the "Jorgenson" spelling with the story itself. I don't know who wrote it: perhaps Garrett, or maybe Fairman. I didn't. Nor did I write any of the paperback novels by "Ivar Jorgensen" that I am sometimes asked to autograph. My one and only "Jorgenson" novel is *Starhaven*. It was only after it was published that I learned that Fairman was annoyed at the appropriation of what had once been his personal pseudonym by other writers, and I stopped using it.

With "Thunder Over Starhaven" standing at 28,000 words, I needed to add only fifty pages or so of copy to have a manuscript the length of an Ace book, and I lost no time doing the expansion and turning it in to Wollheim, calling it, simply, *Starhaven*. To my amazement and dismay, he rejected it—the first rejection I had ever had from him. I'm not sure why he turned it down, but my best guess, as subsequent events would seem to confirm, is that he simply had too many of my books in his inventory and wanted to slow things down a little.

My reason for thinking that is that I salvaged the rejected manuscript on my hands by selling it in January, 1958 to Avalon Books, a small hardcover house that distributed its product mainly through lending libraries. Avalon paid very little for its books, but that pittance—$350—was better than nothing, I figured. Imagine my surprise when, some months later, Avalon turned around and sold paperback reprint rights to *Starhaven* to Don Wollheim of Ace Books! I suppose he had used up his Silverberg inventory by then and was ready for a new one, even one that he had rejected not long before. His reprint edition came out in the spring of 1959. (It was the sixth book of mine that Ace had published.) Wollheim's odd maneuver cost me $150, no small sum in those days: had he bought the book when I submitted it to be an Ace original, I would have earned $1000 for it, but instead I got $350 from Avalon and $500 from Ace, because Avalon was contractually entitled to keep fifty percent of the proceeds from any paperback reprint sale.

Having successfully experimented with a longer lead novella, Larry Shaw now wanted to try another innovation: filling virtually an entire issue of *Science Fiction Adventures* with *one* novel. Again he turned to me, and again I was quick to comply.

This time it was agreed that the story would appear under my own byline, since it was by now a better-known name than any of the pseudonyms I had been using in the magazine. And, since the story would bear my own name, I was a trifle less flamboyant about making use of the pulp-magazine tropes that the magazine's readers so cherished. There would be no hissing villains and basilisk-eyed princesses in this one, no desperate duels with dagger and mace, no feudal overlords swaggering about the stars. Rather, I would write a straightforward science-fiction novel, strongly plotted but not unduly weighted toward breathless adventure.

"Shadow on the Stars" is what I called it, and that was the name it appeared under in the April, 1958 issue of *Science Fiction Adventures*. The cover announced in big yellow letters, "A COMPLETE NEW BOOK—35 cents" and indeed it did take up most of the issue, spanning 112 of the 130 pages and leaving room only for two tiny short stories and the feature columns. Mainly it was a time-paradox novel—a theme that has always fascinated me—but there was at least one concession to the magazine's traditional policy, a vast space battle involving an "unstoppable armada" of "seven hundred seventy-five dreadnoughts." I chose to handle the big battle scene, though, in a very untraditional underplayed manner, as you will see, and I did a bit of playful stuff with the ending, too, providing two endings, in fact, and two final chapters that had the same chapter number.

The readers loved it. The next issue was full of letters of praise, including one that said, "Silverberg is becoming a really disciplined artist," and asserted that "Shadow on the Stars" seemed somehow to synthesize the previously antithetical traditions of Robert A. Heinlein and E. E. Smith. I have never been one to spurn the praise of my readers, but I confess I did have my doubts about calling the author of "Shadow on the Stars" an "artist," and the Heinlein/Smith comparison struck me as a bit grandiose. (Actually, I thought the novel owed more to A. E. van Vogt.)

And then came the depressing news that *Science Fiction Adventures* was going out of business, for reasons unconnected with the quantity of material I was contributing to it. A lot of magazines folded in 1958, including a few that I never wrote for at all. What had done them in was the sudden collapse that summer of the American News Company, the giant (and allegedly mob-controlled) distributing company that was responsible for getting most of the science-fiction magazines of the day to the newsstands. When ANC went under, nearly all of the magazines in the s-f field died with it.

But Ace Books was still thriving, and I lost no time getting a slightly expanded version of "Shadow on the Stars" over to Don Wollheim, who bought it in April, 1958 and published it five months later under, of course, a different title—*Stepsons of Terra*. I didn't like it much, but arguing with Wollheim about titles was a little like arguing with God about the weather. You took what you got, and that was that. This time around, though, I have restored my original title. Don isn't here to say no, and my bibliographers will be able to figure things out.

There you have the story behind these three books. I went on writing books for Ace for another few years, but with decreasing frequency, because the death of most of the science-fiction magazines had led me to move out of s-f into a host of other fields of work. And by 1964, with my twelfth Ace book, *One of Our Asteroids Is Missing*, my career as a writer of Ace Double Books came to its end. I was finding new strengths as a writer, by that time, and was ready to move on to larger and better-paying publishing houses like Doubleday and Ballantine with books of a more complex sort. (Other writers Wollheim had developed, such as Philip K. Dick, John Brunner, and Samuel R. Delany, were beginning to move along also, and he was, with some justification, resentful of our departures from his list, but we were all young and ambitious and couldn't remain Ace authors forever.)

One of Our Asteroids Is Missing appeared ten years and two months from that day in the fall of 1953 when, as a starry-eyed apprentice with dreams of selling a story some day running through his head, I had picked up that very first Ace Double science-fiction volume, the back-to-back van Vogt book. In that decade I had run the whole course from reader and collector to novice writer to successful professional, and my relationship with Ace and its editor Don Wollheim, was an essential step along the way. I'm pleased to see these early novels of mine, so important in my evolution as a writer, returning to print now after these many decades.

Robert Silverberg
January, 2010

The Chalice of Death

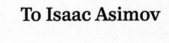
To Isaac Asimov

Chapter One

It was midday on Jorus, and Hallam Navarre, Earthman to the Court, had overslept. He woke with an agonizing headache and a foul taste in his mouth. It had been a long night for the courtier, the night before—a night filled with strange golden out-system wines and less strange women of several worlds.

I must have been drugged, Navarre thought. He had never overslept before. *Who would do something like that?* As the Overlord's Earthman, Navarre was due at the throne room by the hour when the blue rays of the sun first lit the dial in Central Plaza. Someone evidently wanted him to be late, this particular day.

Wearily, he sprang from bed, washed, dabbed depilatory on his gleaming scalp to assure it the hairlessness that was the mark of his station, and caught the ramp heading downstairs. His head was still throbbing.

A jetcab lurked hopefully in the street. Navarre leaped in and snapped, "To the palace!"

"Yes, sir."

The driver was a Dergonian, his coarse skin a gentle green in color. He jabbed down on the control stud and the cab sprang forward.

The Dergonian took a twisting, winding route through Jorus City—past the multitudinous stinks of the Street of the Fishmongers, where the warm blue sunlight filtered in everywhere, and racks of drying finfish lay spread-winged in the sun, then down past the temple, through thronging swarms of midday worshippers, then a sharp right that brought the cab careening into Central Plaza.

The micronite dial in the heart of the plaza was blazing gold. Navarre cursed softly. He belonged at the Overlord's side, and he was late.

Earthmen were *never* late. Earthmen had a special reputation to uphold in the universe. Navarre's fertile mind set to work concocting a story to place before the Overlord when the inevitable query came.

"You have an audience with the Overlord?" the cabbie asked, breaking Navarre's train of thought.

"Not quite," Navarre said wryly. He slipped back his hood, revealing his bald dome. "Look."

The driver squinted flickeringly at the rear-view mirror and nodded at the sight of Navarre's shaven scalp. "Oh. The Earthman. Sorry I didn't recognize you, sir."

"Quite all right. But get this crate moving; I'm due at court."

"I'll do my best."

But the Dergonian's best wasn't quite good enough. He rounded the Plaza, turned down into the Street of the Lords, charged full throttle ahead—

Smack into a parade.

The Legions of Jorus were marching. The jetcab came to a screeching halt no more than ten paces from a regiment of tusked Daborians marching stiffly along, carrying their blue-and-red flag mounted just beneath the bright purple of Jorus, tootling on their thin, whining electronic bagpipes. There were thousands of them.

"Guess it's tough luck, Sir Earthman," the cabbie said philosophically. "The parade's going around the palace. It may take hours."

Navarre sat perfectly still, meditating on the precarious position of an Earthman in a royal court of the Cluster. Here he was, remnant of a wise race shrouded in antiquity, relict of the warrior-kings of old—and he sat sweating in a taxi while a legion of tusked barbarians delayed his passage.

The cabbie opaqued his windows.

"What's that for?"

"We might as well be cool while we wait. This can take hours. I'll be patient if you will."

"The hell you will," Navarre snapped, gesturing at the still-running meter. "At two demiunits per minute I can rent a fine seat on the reviewing stand up there. Let me out of here."

"But—"

"*Out!*"

Navarre leaned forward, slammed down the meter, cutting it short at thirty-six demiunits. He handed the driver a newly-minted semiunit piece.

"Keep the change. And thanks for the service."

"A pleasure." The driver made the formal farewell salute. "May I serve you again, Sir Earthman, and—"

"Sure," Navarre said, and slipped out of the cab. A moment later he had to jump to one side as the driver activated his side blowers, clearing debris from the turbo-jets and incidentally spraying the Earthman with a cloud of fine particles of filth.

Navarre turned angrily, clapping a hand to his blaster, but the grinning cabbie was already scooting away in reverse gear. Navarre scowled. Behind the superficial mask of respect for the Earthmen, there was always a certain lack of civility that irked him. He was conscious of his ambiguous position in the galaxy, as an emissary from nowhere, as a native of a world long forgotten and which he himself had never seen.

Earth. It was not a planet any longer, but a frame of mind, a way of thinking. He was an Earthman, and thus valuable to the Overlord. But he could be replaced; there were other advisers nearly as shrewd.

Navarre fingered his bald scalp ruminatingly for a moment and flicked off his hood again. He started across the wide street.

The regiment of Daborians still stalked on—seven-foot humanoids with their jutting tusks polished brightly, their fierce beards combed. They marched in an unbreakable phalanx round and round the palace.

Damn parades anyway, Navarre thought. Foolish display, calculated to impress barbarians.

He reached the edge of the Daborian ranks. "Excuse me, please."

He started to force his way between two towering, haughty artillery men. Without breaking step, a huge Daborian grabbed him by the scruff of his neck and threw him back toward the street. An appreciative ripple of laughter went up from the onlookers as Navarre landed unsteadily on one leg, started to topple, and with a wild swing of his arms and three or four skipping steps, barely managed to remain upright.

"Let me through," he snapped again, as a corps of tusked musicians came by. The Daborians merely ignored him. Navarre waited until a bagpiper went past, one long valved chaunter thrust between his tusks and hands flying over the electronic keyboard. Navarre grabbed the base of the instrument with both hands and rammed upward.

The Daborian let out a howl of pain and took a step backward as the sharp mouthpiece cracked soundly against his palate. Navarre grinned, slipped through the gap in the formation and kept on running. Behind him, the bagpiping rose to an angry wail, but none of the Daborians dared break formation to pursue the insolent Earthman.

He reached the steps of the palace. There were fifty-two of them, each a little wider and higher than the next. He was better than an hour late at the court. The Overlord would be close to a tantrum, and in all probability Kausirn, that sly Lyrellan, had taken ample advantage of the opportunity to work mischief.

Navarre only hoped the order for his execution had not yet been signed. There was no telling *what* the Overlord was likely to do under Kausirn's influence.

He reached the long black-walled corridor that led to the throne room somewhat out of breath and gasping. The pair of unemotional Trizian monoptics who guarded access to the corridor recognized him and nodded disapprovingly as he scooted past.

Arriving at the penultimate turn in the hall, he ducked into a convenience at the left and slammed the door. He was so late already that a few moments more couldn't aggravate the offense, and he wanted to look his best when he finally did make his belated appearance.

A couple of seconds in front of the brisk molecular flow of the Vibron left him refreshed, and he stopped panting for breath. He splashed water on his face, dried off, straightened his tunic, tied back his hood.

Then, stiffly, walking with a dignity he had not displayed a moment before, he stalked out and headed for the throne room.

The annunciator said, "Hallam Navarre, Earthman to the Overlord."

Joroiran VII was on his throne, looking, as always, like a rather nervous butcher's apprentice elevated quite suddenly to galactic rank. He muttered a few words, and the micro-amplifier surgically implanted in his throat picked them up and tossed them at the kneeling Navarre.

"Enter, Earthman. You're late."

The throne room was filled to bursting. This was Threeday—audience day—and commoners of all sizes and shapes thronged before the Overlord, desperately hoping that the finger of fate would light on them and bring them forward to plead their cause. It was Navarre's customary job to select those who were to address the Overlord, but he observed that today Kausirn, the Lyrellan, had taken over the task in his absence.

Navarre advanced toward the throne and abased himself before the purple carpet.

"You may rise," Joroiran said in a casual tone. "The audience began more than an hour ago. You have been missed, Navarre."

"I've been employed in Your Majesty's service all the while," Navarre said. "I was pursuing that which may prove to be of great value to your Majesty—and to all of Jorus."

Joroiran looked amused. "And what might that be?"

Navarre paused, drawing in breath, and prepared himself for the plunge. "I have discovered information that may lead to the Chalice of Life, my Overlord."

To his surprise, Joroiran did not react at all; his mousy face revealed not the slightest trace of animation. Navarre blinked; the whopper was not going over.

But it was the Lyrellan who saved him, in a way. Leaning over, Kausirn whispered harshly, "He means the Chalice of *Death*, Majesty."

"Death . . . ?"

"Eternal life for Joroiran VII," Navarre said ringingly. As long as he was going to make excuses for having overslept, he thought, he might as well make them good ones. "The Chalice holds death for some," he said, "but life for thee."

"Indeed," the Overlord said. "You must talk to me of this in my chambers. But now, the audience."

Navarre mounted the steps and took his customary position at the monarch's right; at least Kausirn had not appropriated *that*. But the Earthman saw that the Lyrellan's tapering nest of fingers played idly over the short-beam generator by which the hand of fate was brought to fall upon commoners. That meant Kausirn, not Navarre, would be selecting those whose cases were to be pleaded this day.

Looking into the crowd, Navarre picked out the bleak, heavily-bearded face of Domrik Carso. Carso was staring reproachfully at him, and Navarre felt a sudden stinging burst of guilt. He had promised to get Carso a hearing today; the burly half-breed lay under a sentence of banishment, but Navarre had lightly assured him that revokement would be a simple matter.

But not now. Not with Kausirn wielding the blue beam. Kausirn had no desire to have an Earthman's kin plaguing him here on Jorus; Carso would rot in the crowd before the Lyrellan chose *his* case to be pleaded.

Navarre met Carso's eyes. *Sorry,* he tried to say. But Carso stared stiffly through him. Navarre knew he had failed him, and there was no gainsaying that.

"Proceed with your tale," Joroiran said.

Navarre looked down and saw a pale Joran in the pleader's square below, bathed in the blue light of chance. The man glanced upward at the command and said, "Shall I continue or begin over, Highness?"

"Begin over. The Earthman may be interested."

"May it please the Overlord and his advisers, my name is Lugfor of Zaigla Street, grocer and purveyor of food. I have been accused falsely of thinning my measure, but—"

Navarre sat back while the man droned on. The time of audience was coming to its end; Carso would go unheard, and at twenty-fourth hour the half-breed would be banished. Well, there was no helping it, Navarre thought glumly. He knotted his hands together and tried to follow Lugfor's whining plea of innocence.

A t the end of the session, Navarre turned quickly to the Overlord, but Kausirn was already speaking. "Majesty, may I talk to you alone?"

"And I?" Navarre put in hastily.

"I'll hear Kausirn first," Joroiran decided. "To my chambers. Navarre, attend me there later."

"Certainly, Sire."

Navarre slipped from the dais and headed down into the dispersing throng. Carso was shuffling morosely toward the exit when Navarre reached him.

"Domrik! Wait!"

The half-breed turned. "It looks like you'll be the only Earthman on Jorus by nightfall, Hallam."

"I'm sorry. Believe me, I'm sorry. I just couldn't get here in time, and that damned Lyrellan grabbed control of the selections."

Carso shrugged moodily. "I understand." He tugged at his thick beard. "I be only half of Earth, anyway. You'll not miss me."

"Nonsense!" Navarre whispered harshly.

The half-breed nodded gravely. "My writ commands me to leave the cluster. I'll be heading for Kariad tonight, and then outward. You'll be able to reach me there if you can—I mean—I'll be there a sevennight."

"Kariad? All right," Navarre said. "I'll get in touch with you there if I can influence Joroiran to revoke the sentence. Damn it, Carso, you shouldn't have hit that innkeeper so hard."

"He made remarks," Carso said. "I had to." The half-breed bowed and turned away to leave.

The throne room was nearly empty; only a few stragglers remained, staring at the grandeur of the room and probably comparing it with their own squalid huts. Joroiran enjoyed living on a large scale, beyond doubt.

Navarre sprawled down broodingly on the edge of the royal purple carpet and stared at his jeweled fingers. Things were looking bad. His sway as Joroiran's adviser was definitely weakening, and the Lyrellan's star seemed to be the ascendant. Navarre's one foothold was the claim of tradition: all seven of the Joroiran Overlords had had an Earthman as adviser, and the current Overlord, weak man that he was, would scarcely care to break with tradition.

Yet the Lyrellan Kausirn had wormed himself securely into the monarch's graces. The situation was definitely not promising.

Gloomily, Navarre wondered if there were any other local monarchs in the market for advisers. His stay on Jorus did not look to be long continuing.

Chapter Two

After a while, a solemn Trizian glided toward him, stared down out of its one eye, and said, "The Overlord will see you now."

"Thanks." Navarre allowed the monoptic to guide him through the swinging panel that led to Joroiran's private chambers, handed the creature a coin, and entered.

The Overlord was alone, but the scent of the waxy-fleshed Lyrellan still lingered. Navarre took the indicated seat.

"Sire?"

Perspiration beaded Joroiran's upper lip; the monarch seemed dwarfed by the stiff strutwork that held his uniform out from his scrawny body. He glanced nervously at the Earthman, then said, "You spoke to me of a Chalice today, as your reason for being late to the audience. This Chalice . . . is said to hold the secret of eternal life, is that not so? Its possessor need never die?"

Navarre nodded.

"And," Joroiran continued, "you tell me you have some knowledge of its whereabouts, eh?"

"I think I do," said Navarre hoarsely. "My informant said he knew somebody whose father had led an earlier expedition in search of it. An unsuccessful expedition, but a near miss." The statement was strictly from whole cloth, but Navarre reeled it off smoothly.

Joroiran looked interested. "Indeed. Who is he?"

Sudden inspiration struck Navarre. "His name is Domrik Carso. His mother was an Earthman, and you know of course that the Chalice is connected in some legend-shrouded way with Earth."

"Of course. Produce this Carso."

"He was here today, Sire. He searched for pardon from an unfair sentence of banishment over some silly barroom squabble. Alas, the finger of fate did not fall on him, and he leaves for Kariad tonight. But perhaps if the sentence were revoked I could get further information from him concerning the Chalice, which I would most dearly love to win for Your Majesty . . ."

Joroiran's fingers drummed the desktop. "Ah, yes—revokement. It would be possible, perhaps. Can you reach the man?"

"I think so."

"Good. Tell him not to pay for his passage tickets, that the Royal Treasury will cover the cost of his travels from now on."

"But—"

"The same applies to you, of course.

Taken aback, Navarre lost a little of his composure. "Sire?"

"I've spoken to Kausirn. Navarre, I don't know if I can spare you, and Kausirn is uncertain as to whether he can handle the double load in your absence. But he is willing to try it, noble fellow that he is."

"I don't understand," Navarre stammered.

"You say you have a lead on the whereabouts of this Chalice—correct? Kausirn has refreshed my overburdened memory with some information on this Chalice, and I find myself longing for its promise of eternal life, Navarre. You say you have a lead; very well. I've arranged for an indefinite leave of absence for you. Find this man Carso and together you can search the galaxies at my expense. I don't care how long it takes, nor what it costs. *But bring me the Chalice, Navarre!*"

The Earthman nearly fell backward in astonishment. Bring Joroiran the Chalice? Dizzily, Navarre realized that this was the work of the clever Kausirn: he would send the annoying Earthman all over space on a fool's mission, while consolidating his own position securely at the side of the Overlord.

Navarre forced himself to meet Joroiran's eyes.

"I will not fail you, my Lord," he said in a strangled voice.

He had been weaving twisted strands, he thought later in the privacy of his rooms, and now he had spun himself a noose. Talk of tradition! Nothing could melt it faster than a king's desire to keep his throne eternally.

For seven generations there had been an Earthman adviser at the Overlord's side. Now, in a flash, the patient work of years was undone. Dejectedly, Navarre reviewed his mistakes.

One: He had allowed Kausirn to worm his way into a position of eminence on the Council. Allow a Lyrellan an inch and he'll grab a parsec. Navarre now saw—too late, of course—that he should have had the many-fingered one quietly put away while he had had the chance.

Two: He had caroused the night before an audience day. Inexcusable. Someone—an agent of Kausirn's, no doubt—had slipped a sleep drug into one of his drinks. He should have been on guard. By hereditary right and by his own wits he had always chosen the cases to be heard, and in the space of a single hour the Lyrellan had done him out of *that*.

Three: He had lied too well. This was something he should have foreseen; he had aroused weak Joroiran's desire to such a pitch that Kausirn was easily able to plant the suggestion that the Overlord send the faithful Earthman out to find the Chalice.

Three mistakes. Now, he was on the outside and Kausirn in control.

Navarre tipped his glass and drained it. "You're a disgrace to your genes," he told the oddly distorted reflection on the wall of the glass. "A hundred thousand years of Earth-man labor to produce what? *You?* Fumblewit!"

Still, there was nothing to be done for it now. Joroiran had given the word, and here he was, assigned to chase a phantom, to pursue a will-o'-the-wisp. The Chalice! Chalice, indeed! There was no such thing.

He tossed his empty glass aside and reached for the communicator. He punched the stud, quickly fed in four numbers and a letter.

A blank radiance filled the screen, and an impersonal dry voice said, "Citizen Carso is not at home. Citizen Carso is not at home. Citizen Car—"

Navarre cut the contact and dialed again. This time the screen lit, glowed, and revealed a tired-looking man in a stained white smock.

"Jublain Street Bar," the man said. "You want to see the manager?"

"No. Is there a man named Domrik Carso there? A heavy-set fellow, with a thick beard?"

"I'll look around," the barkeep grunted. A few moments later, Carso came to the screen; as Navarre had suspected, he was indulging in a few last swills of Joran beer before taking off for the outworlds.

"Navarre? What do you want?"

Navarre ignored the belligerent greeting. "Have you bought your ticket for Kariad yet?"

Carso blinked. "Not yet. What's it to you?"

"If you haven't bought the ticket yet, *don't.* How soon can you get over here?"

"Couple of centuries, maybe. What's going on, Navarre?"

"You've been pardoned."

"*What?* I'm not banished?"

"Not exactly," Navarre said. "Look, I don't want to talk about it at long range. How soon can you get yourself over here?"

"I'm due at the spaceport at twenty-one to pick up my tick—"

"*Damn* your ticket," Navarre snapped. "You don't have to leave yet. Come over, will you?"

Navarre peered across the table at Domrik Carso's heavy-shouldered figure. "That's the whole story," the Earthman said. "Joroiran wants the Chalice—and he wants it real hard."

Carso shook his head and exhaled a beery breath. "Your damnable glib tongue has ruined us both, Hallam. With but half an Earthman's mind I could have done better."

"It's done, and Kausirn has me in a cleft stick. If nothing else, I've saved you from banishment."

"Only under condition that I help you find this nonexistent Chalice," Carso grunted. "Some improvement that is. Well, at least Joroiran will foot the bill. We can both see the universe at his expense, and when we come back—"

"We come back when we've found the Chalice," said Navarre. "This isn't going to be any pleasure jaunt."

Carso glared at him sourly. "Hallam, are you mad? There is no Chalice!"

"How do you know? Joroiran says there is. The least we can do is look for it."

"We'll wander space forever," Carso said, scowling. "As no doubt the Lyrellan intends for you to do. Well, there's nothing to do but accept. I'm no poorer for it than if I were banished. Chalice! *Pah!*"

"Have another drink," Navarre suggested. "It may make it easier for you to get the idea down your gullet."

"I doubt it," the half-breed said, but he accepted the drink anyway. He drained it, then remarked, "A chalice is a drinking cup. Does this mean we seek a potion of immortality, or something of the like?"

"Your guess weighs as much as mine. I've given you all I know on the subject."

"Excellent; now we both know nothing! Do you at least have some idea where this Chalice is supposedly located?"

Navarre shrugged. "The legend's incomplete. The thing might be anywhere. Our job is to find a particular drinking cup on a particular world in a pretty near infinite universe. Unfortunately, we have only a finite length of time in which to do the job."

"The typical short-sightedness of kings," Carso muttered. "A sensible monarch would have sent a couple of immortals out in search of the Chalice."

"A sensible monarch would know when he's had enough, and not ask to rule his system forever. But Joroiran's not sensible."

They were silent for a moment, while the candle between them flickered palely. Then Carso grinned.

"What's so funny?"

"Listen, Hallam. Why don't we assume a location for the Chalice? At least it'll give us a first goal to crack at. And it ought to be easier to find a planet than a drinking cup, shouldn't it?"

Navarre's eyes narrowed. "I don't follow you. Just where will we assume the Chalice is?"

There was a mischievous twinkle in the half-breed's dark eyes. He gulped another drink, grinned broadly, and belched.

"Where? Why, Earth, of course!"

Chapter Three

On more-or-less sober reflection the next morning, it seemed to Navarre that Carso had the right idea: finding Earth promised to be easier than finding the Chalice, if it made any sense to talk about relative degrees of ease in locating myths.

Earth.

Navarre knew the stories that each Earthman told to his children, that few non-Earthmen knew. Even though he was a half-breed, Carso would be aware of them too.

Years ago—a hundred thousand, the legend said—man had sprung from Earth, an inconsequential world revolving around a small sun in an obscure galaxy. He had leaped forward to the stars, and carved out a mighty empire for himself. The glory of Earth was carried to the far galaxies, to the wide-flung nebulae of deepest space.

But no race, no matter how strong, could hold sway over an empire that spanned a billion parsecs. The centuries passed; Earth's grasp grew weaker. And, finally, the stars rebelled.

Navarre remembered his mother's vivid description. Earthmen had been outnumbered a billion to one, yet they kept the defensive screens up, and kept the home world untouched, had beaten back the invaders. But still the persistent starmen came, sweeping down on the small planet like angry beetles.

Earth drew back from the stars; its military forces came to the aid of the mother world, and the empire crumbled.

The withdrawal was to no avail. The hordes from the stars won the war of attrition, sacrificing men ten thousand to one and still not showing signs of defeat. The mother world yielded; the proud name of Earth was humbled and stricken from the roll call of worlds.

What became of the armies of Earth no one knew. Those who survived were scattered about the galaxies, seeded here and there, a world of one cluster, a planet of another.

Fiercely the Earthmen clung to their name. They shaved their heads to distinguish themselves from humanoids of a million star-systems—and death it was to the alien who offered himself as counterfeit Earthman!

The centuries rolled by in their never-ending sweep, and Earth herself was forgotten. Yet the Earthmen remained, a thin band scattered through the heavens, proud of their heritage, guarding jealously their genetic traits. Carso was rare; it was but infrequently that an Earthwoman could be persuaded to mate with an alien. Yet Carso regarded himself as an Earthman, and never spoke of his father.

Where was Earth? No one could name the sector of space, but Earth was in the hearts of the men who lived among the stars. Earthmen were sought out by kings; the bald-heads could not rule themselves, but they could advise those less fitted than they to command.

Then would come a fool like Joroiran, who held his throne because his father seven times removed had hewed an empire for him—and Joroiran would succumb to a Lyrellan's wiles and order his Earthman off on a madman's quest.

Navarre's fists stiffened. *Send me for the Chalice? Aye, I'll find something for him!*

The Chalice was an idiot's dream; immortal life was a filmy bubble. But *Earth* was real; Earth merely awaited finding. Somewhere it bobbed in the heavens, forgotten symbol of an empire that had been.

Smiling coldly, Navarre thought, *I'll find Earth for him.*

Unlimited funds were at his disposal. He would bring Joroiran a potion too powerful to swallow at a gulp.

Later that day he and Carso were aboard a liner of the Royal Fleet, bearing tickets paid for by Royal frank, and feeling against their thighs the thick bulge of Imperial scrip received with glee from the Royal Treasury.

"Ready for blasting," came the stewardess's voice. "We depart for Kariad in fifteen seconds. I hope you'll relax and enjoy your trip."

Navarre slumped back in the acceleration cradle and closed his eyes. In a few seconds the liner would spring into space. The two hunters for the Chalice would have begun their quest.

His heart ticked the seconds off impatiently. *Twelve. Eleven.*

Nine. Six.

Two. One.

Acceleration took him, thrust him sharply downward as the liner left ground. Within seconds, they were high above the afternoon sky, plunging outward into the brightly dotted blackness speckled with the hard points of a billion suns.

One of those suns was Sol, Navarre thought. And one of the planets of Sol was Earth.

Chalice of Life, he thought scornfully. As Jorus dwindled behind him, Navarre wondered how long it would be before he would again see the simpering face of the Overlord Joroiran VII.

Kariad, the planet nearest to the Joran Empire in their cluster, was the lone world of a double sun. This arrangement, economical as it was in terms of cosmic engineering, provided some spectacular views and made the planet a much-visited pleasure place.

As Navarre and Carso alighted from the liner they could see that Primus, the massive red giant that was the heart of the system, hung high overhead, intersecting a huge arc of the sky, while Secundus, the smaller main-sequence yellow sun, flickered palely near the horizon. Kariad was moving between the two stars in its complex and eccentric hour-glass orbit, and, in the light of the two suns, all objects acquired a strange purple shimmer.

Those who had disembarked from the liner were standing in a tight knot on the field while Kariadi customs officials moved among them. Navarre stood with arms folded, waiting for his turn to come.

The official wore a gilt-encrusted surplice and a bright red sash that seemed almost brown in the light of the double suns. He yanked forth a metal-bound notebook and began to scribble things.

"Name and planet of origin?"

"Hallam Navarre. Planet of origin, Earth."

The customs man glared impatiently at Navarre's shaven scalp and snapped, "You know what I mean. What planet are you from?"

"Jorus," Navarre said.

"Purpose of visiting Kariad?"

"I'm a special emissary from Overlord Joroiran VII; intent peaceful, mission confidential."

"Are you the Earthman to the Court?"

Navarre nodded.

"And this man?"

"Domrik Carso," the half-breed growled. "Planet of origin, Jorus."

The official indicated Carso's stubbly scalp. "I wish you Earthmen would show some consistency. One says he's from Earth, the other—or are you not an Earthman, but merely prematurely bald?"

"I'm of Earth descent," Carso said stolidly. "But I'm from Jorus, and you can put it down. I'm Navarre's traveling companion."

The customs officer riffled perfunctorily through their papers a moment, then handed them back. "Very well. You may both pass."

Navarre and Carso moved off the field and into the spaceport itself.

"I could use a beer," Carso said.

"I guess you've never been on Kariad, then. They must brew their beer from sewer-flushings here."

"I'll drink sewer-flushings when I must," Carso said. He pointed to a glowing tricolored sign. "There's a bar. Shall we go in?"

As Navarre had expected, the beer was vile. He stared unhappily at the mug of green, brackish liquid, stirring it with a quiver of his wrist and watching the oily patterns forming and re-forming on its surface.

Across the table, Carso was showing no such qualms. The half-breed tilted the bottle into his mug, raised the big mug to his lips, drank. Navarre shuddered.

Grinning, Carso crashed the mug down and wiped his beard clean.

"It's not the best I've ever had," he commented finally. "But it'll do in a pinch." Shrugging cheerfully, he filled his mug a second time.

Very quietly, Navarre said, "Do you see those men sitting at the far table?"

Carso squinted and looked at them without seeming to do so. "Aye. They were on board the ship with us."

"Exactly."

"But so were at least five of the other people in this bar! Surely you don't think—"

"I don't intend to take any chances," Navarre said flatly. "Finish your drink. I want to make a tour of the spaceport."

"Well enough, if you say so." Carso drained the drink and left one of Overlord Joroiran's bills on the table to pay for it. Casually, the pair left the bar.

Their first stop was a tape shop. There, Navarre made a great business over ordering a symphony.

The effusive, apologetic proprietor did his best. "*The Anvils of Juno*? I don't think I have that number in stock. In fact, I'm not sure I've ever heard of it. Could it be *The Hammer of Drolon* you seek?"

"I'm fairly sure it was the *Juno*," said Navarre, who had invented the work a moment before. "But perhaps I'm wrong. Is there any place here I can listen to the *Drolon*?"

"Surely; we have a booth back here where you can experience full audiovisual effect. If you'd step this way, please . . ."

They spent fifteen minutes sampling the tape, Carso with a prevailing expression of utter boredom, Navarre with a scowl for the work's total insipidity. The symphony was banal and obvious—a typical Kariadi hack product, churned out by some weary tone-artist to meet the popular demand. At the end of the first fifteen-minute movement Navarre snapped off the playback and rose.

The proprietor came bustling up to the booth. "Well?"

"Sorry," Navarre said. "This isn't the one I want."

Gathering his cloak about him, he swept out of the shop, followed by Carso. As they re-entered the main concourse of the terminal arcade, Navarre saw two figures glide swiftly into the shadows—but not swiftly enough.

"I do believe you're right," Carso muttered. "We're being followed."

"Kausirn's men, no doubt. The Lyrellan must be curious to see which way we're heading. Or possibly he's ordered my assassination, now that I'm away from the Court. But let's give it one more test before we take steps."

"No more music!" Carso said hastily.

"No. The next stop will be a more practical one." Navarre led the way down the arcade until they reached a shop whose front display said simply, *Weapons*. They went in.

The proprietor here was of a different stamp than the man in the music shop; he was a rangy Kariadi, his light blue skin glowing in color-harmony with the electroluminescents in the shop's walls.

"Can I help you?"

"Possibly you can," Navarre said. He swept back his hood, revealing his Earthman's scalp. "We're from Jorus. There are assassins on our trail, and we want to shake them. Have you a back exit?"

"Over there," the armorer said. "Are you armed?"

"We are, but we could do with some spare charges. Say, five apiece." Navarre placed a bill on the counter and slid the wrapped packages into his tunic pocket.

"Are those the men?" the proprietor asked.

Two shadowy figures were visible through the one-way glass of the window. They peered in uneasily.

"I think they're coming in here," Navarre said.

"All right. You two go our the back way; I'll chat with them for a while."

Navarre flashed the man an appreciative smile and he and Carso slipped through the indicated door, just as their pursuers entered the weapons shop.

"Double around the arcade and wait at the end of the corridor, eh?" Carso suggested.

"Right. We'll catch them as they come out."

Some hasty running brought them to a strategic position. "Keep your eyes open," Navarre said. "That shopkeeper may have told them where we are."

"I doubt it. He looked honest."

"You never can tell," Navarre said. "Hush, now!"

The door of the gun shop was opening.

The followers emerged, edging out into the corridor again, squeezing themselves against the wall and peering in all directions. They looked acutely uncomfortable now that they had lost sight of their quarry.

Navarre drew his blaster and hefted it thoughtfully. After a moment's pause he shouted, "Stand still and raise your hands," and squirted a bolt of energy almost at their feet.

One of the pair yelled in fear, but the other, responding instantly, drew and fired. His bolt, deliberately aimed high, brought down a section of the arcade roofing; the drifting dust and plaster obscured vision.

"They're getting away!" Carso snapped. "Let's go after them fast!"

They leaped from hiding and raced through the rubble; dimly they could see the retreating pair heading for the main waiting room. Navarre cursed; if they got in there, there would be no chance of bringing them down.

As he ran, he leveled his blaster and emitted a single short burst. One of the two toppled and fell; the other continued running, and vanished abruptly into the crowded waiting room.

"I'll go in after him," Navarre said. "You look at the dead one and see if there's any sort of identification on him."

Navarre pushed his way through the photon-beam and into the spaceport's crowded waiting room. He caught sight of his man up ahead, jostling desperately toward the cab-stand. Navarre holstered his blaster; he would never be able to use it in here.

"Stop that man!" he roared. "Stop him!"

Perhaps it was the authority in his tone, perhaps it was his baldness, but to his surprise a foot stretched out and sent the fleeing spy sprawling. Navarre reached him in an instant, and knocked the useless blaster from his hand. He tugged the quivering man to his feet.

"All right, who are you?"

He punctuated the question with a slap. The man sputtered and turned his face away without replying, and Navarre hit him again.

This time the man cursed and tried fruitlessly to break away.

"Did Kausirn send you?" Navarre demanded, gripping him tightly.

"I don't know anything. Leave me alone."

"You'd better start knowing," Navarre said. He drew his blaster with his free hand. "I'll give you five to tell me why you were following us, and if you don't speak up I'll burn you right here. One . . . two . . ."

On the count of three Navarre suddenly felt hands go round his waist, other hands grabbing at his wrist to immobilize the blaster. He was pulled away from his prisoner and the blaster wrenched from his hand.

"Let go of him, Earthman," a rough voice said. "What's going on here, anyway?"

"This man's an assassin," Navarre said. "He and a companion were sent here to kill me. Luckily my friend and I detected the plot, and—"

"That's enough," the burly Kariadi said. "You'd all better come with me."

Navarre turned and saw several other officers approaching. One bore the blaster-charred body of the dead assassin; the other two pinioned the figure of the furiously struggling Domrik Carso.

"Come along, now," the Kariadi said.

Chapter Four

A good beginning to our quest," Carso said bitterly. "A noble start!"

"Quiet," Navarre told him. "I think someone's coming to see us."

They were in a dungeon somewhere in the heart of Kariad City, having been taken there from the spaceport. The surviving assassin had been placed in another cell.

But someone *was* coming. The door of the cell was opening, and a yellow beam of light began to crawl diagonally across the concrete floor.

A slim figure entered the cell. Light glinted off a bald skull; the visitor was an Earthman, then.

"Hello. Which of you is Navarre?"

"I am."

"I'm Helna Winstin, Earthman to the Court of Lord Marhaill, Oligocrat of Kariad. Sorry our men had to throw you down here in this cell, but they weren't in any position to take chances."

"We understand," Navarre said. He was still staring without believing. "No one told me that on Kariad the Earthman to the Court was a *woman*."

Helna Winstin smiled. "The appointment was but recent. My father held the post until last month."

"And you succeeded him?"

"After a brief struggle. Milord was much taken by a Lyrellan who had served as Astronomer Royal, but I'm happy to say he did not choose to break the tradition of an Earthman adviser."

Navarre stared at the slim female Earthman with sharp respect. Evidently there had been a fierce battle for power—a battle in which she had bested a Lyrellan. *That was more than I managed to do,* he thought.

"Come," she said. "The order for your release has been signed, and I find cells unpleasant. Shall we go to my rooms?"

"I don't see why not," Navarre replied. He glanced at Carso, who looked utterly thunderstruck. "Come along, Domrik."

They were led through the corridor to a liftshaft and upward; it was evident to Navarre now that the dungeon had been in the depths of the royal palace itself.

Helna Winstin's rooms were warm and inviting looking; the decor was brighter than Navarre was accustomed to, but beneath the apartment's obvious femininity lay a core of surprising toughness that seemed repeated in the girl herself.

"Now then," she said, making herself comfortable and motioning for the men to do the same. "What have you two done that brings you to Kariad with a pair of assassins on your trail?"

"Has the man confessed?"

"He—ah—revealed all," Helna Winstin said. "He told us he was sent here by one Kausim, a Lyrellan attached to the Joran court, with orders to make away with you, specifically, and your companion, too, if possible."

Navarre nodded. "I suspected as much. Can I see the man?"

"Unfortunately, he died under interrogation. The job was clumsily handled."

She's tough, all right, Navarre thought appreciatively. She wore her head shaved, though it was not strictly required of female Earthmen; she wore a man's costume and did a man's job, and only the rise of her bosom and the slightness of her figure indicated her sex.

She leaned forward. "Now, may I ask what brings the Earthman of Joroiran's court here to Kariad?"

"We travel on a mission from Joroiran," Navarre said. "We seek the Chalice of Life for him."

A tapering eyebrow rose. "How interesting! Joroiran has become a student of mythology, then! Or does the Chalice really exist?"

"'It might," Navarre said. "But our target is only indirectly the Chalice." In terse, clipped sentences he told her the whole story of their search for Earth. A strange look crossed her face when he finished.

"Lord Marhaill is all too likely to side with your friend Kausirn in this matter," she said. "And if I help you it may mean the loss of my post here—if not all our lives. But the prize is great—Earth herself!"

"You'll help us, then?"

She smiled slowly. "Of course."

The main library of Kariad City was a building fifty stories high and as many more deep below the ground, and still it could not begin to store the accumulated outpourings of a hundred thousand years of civilization on uncountable worlds.

"The open files go back only about five hundred years," Helna said, as she and Navarre entered the vast doorway, followed by Carso. "Everything else is stored away somewhere, and hardly anyone but antiquarians ever bothers with it."

Navarre frowned. "We may have some trouble finding what we want, then."

An efficient-looking Dergonian met them at the door. "Good day, Sir Earthman," he said to Helna. Catching sight of Navarre and Carso, he added, "And to you as well."

"We seek the main index," Helna said.

"Through that archway," said the librarian. "May I help you find your information?"

"We can manage by ourselves, thanks," Navarre said.

The main index occupied one enormous room from floor to ceiling. Navarre blinked dizzily at the immensity of it. He watched as Helna coolly walked to a screen mounted on a table in the center of the index room and punched out the letters *E-A-R-T-H*. She twisted a dial and the screen lit.

A card appeared in the center of the screen. Navarre squinted to read its fine print:

> EARTH: legendary planet of Sol system (?)
> considered in myth as home of mankind
> See: D80009.1643, Smednal, *Creation Myths of the Galaxy*
> D80009.1644, Snodgras, *Legends of the First Empire*.

Helna looked up doubtfully. "Shall I try the next card? Should I order these books?"

"I don't think there's any point to it," said Navarre. "These works look fairly recent; they won't tell us anything we don't know. We'll have to dig a little deeper. How do we get to the closed shelves?"

"I'll have to pull rank, I guess."

"Let's go, then. The real location of Earth is somewhere in these libraries, I'm sure; you just can't *lose* a world completely. If we go back far enough we're sure to find out where Earth was."

"Unless such information was carefully deleted when Earth fell," Carso pointed out.

Navarre shook his head. "Impossible. The library system is too vast, too decentralized. There's bound to have been a slip-up somewhere—and we can find it!"

"I hope so," the half-breed said moodily, as they left the index room and headed for the library's administration office to ask for a closed-file permit.

Track fifty-seven of the closed shelves was as cold and as desolate as a sunless planet, Navarre thought bleakly, as he and his companions stepped out of the dropshaft.

A Genobonian serpent-man came slithering toward them, and the chittering echo of his body sliding across the dark floor went shivering down the long dust-laden aisles. At the sight of the reptile, Carso reached for his blaster; Genobonians entered this system infrequently, and they were fearsome sights to anyone not prepared for them.

"What's this worm coming from the books?" Carso asked loudly. His voice rang through the corridors.

"Peace, friends. I am but an old and desiccated librarian left to molder in these forgotten stacks." The Genobonian chuckled. "A bookworm in truth, Earthman. But you are the first to visit here in a year or more; what do you seek?"

"Books about Earth," Navarre said. "Is there a catalog down here?"

"There is, but it shan't be needed. I'll show you what we have, if you'll be careful with it."

The serpent slithered away, leaving a foot-wide track in the dust on the floor. Hesitantly, the three followed. He led them down to the end of a corridor, through a passageway dank-smelling with the odor of dying books, and into an even mustier alcove.

"Here we are," the dry voice croaked. The Genobonian extended a skinny arm and yanked a book from a shelf. It was an actual book, not a tape.

"Handle it with care, friends. The budget does not allow for taping it, so we must preserve the original—until the day comes when this track must be cleaned. The library peels away its oldest layer like an onion shedding its skin; when the weight of new words is too great—*whisht!* and track fifty-seven vanishes into the outworlds."

"And you with it?"

"No," said the serpent sadly. "I stay here, and endeavor to learn my way around the new volumes that descend from above. The time of changing is always melancholy."

"Enough talk," Navarre said brusquely, when it seemed the old serpent would maunder on endlessly. "Let's look at this book."

It was a history of the galaxy, arranged alphabetically by subject matter. Navarre stared at the title page and felt a strange chill when he saw that the book was more than thirteen thousand years old.

Thirteen thousand years. And yet Earth had fallen millennia before the time of the printing of this book.

Navarre frowned. "This is only the volume from *Fenelon to Fenris*," he said. "Where's Earth?"

"Earth is in an earlier volume," the Genobonian said. "A volume which we no longer have in this library. But look at this book; perhaps it may give you some information."

Navarre stared at the librarian for a long moment, then asked, "Have you read all these books?"

"Many of them. There is so little work for me to do down here."

"Very well, then. This is a question no Earthman has ever asked of an alien before, and if I suspect you give me a lying answer, I'll kill you here among your books and your dust."

"Ask away, Earthman," the serpent replied. He sounded unafraid.

Navarre moistened his lips. "This we should know before we pursue our search further. Tell me, *did Earth ever exist?*"

There was silence, broken only by the prolonged echoes of Navarre's voice whispering the harsh question over and over down the aisles. The serpent's bright eyes glittered. "You do not know yourselves?"

"No, damn you," Carso growled. "If we did, why would we come to you?"

"Strange," the serpent mused. "But yes—yes, Earth existed. You may read of Earth in this book I have given you. Soon they will send the book far away, and it will no longer be possible for us on Kariad to prove Earth's existence. But till then—yes, there was an Earth."

"Where?"

"I knew once, but I have forgotten. It is in that volume, that earlier volume that was sent away. But look, Earthmen. Read there, under *Fendobar*."

Navarre opened the ancient History with trembling fingers and found his way through the graying pages to *Fendobar*. He read aloud:

> FENDOBAR. The larger of a double-star system in Galaxy RGC18347, giving its name to the entire system. It is ringed by eight planets, only one inhabited and likewise known as Fendobar.
>
> Because of its strategic location, just eleven light-years from the Earth system, Fendobar was of extreme importance in the attack on Earth (which see). Starships were customarily refueled on Fendobar before . . .
>
> . . . coordinates . . .
>
> . . . the inhabitants of . . .

"Most of it's illegible," Navarre said, looking up. "But there's enough here to prove that there *was* an Earth—and it was only eleven light-years from Fendobar."

"Wherever Fendobar was," Helna said.

There was silence in the vault for a moment. Navarre said to the librarian finally, "There's no way you can recall the volume dealing with Earth, is there? In it we could find Earth's coordinates and everything else. Our quest would be shortened if—"

He stopped. The Genobonian looked at him slyly. "Do you plan to visit your homeland, Earthmen?"

"Possibly. None of your business."

"As you wish. But the answer is no; the volume cannot be recalled. It was shipped out with others of its era last year, sometime before the great eclipse, I believe—or was it the year before? Well, no matter; I remember not where the book was sent. We scatter our excess over every eager library within a thousand light-years."

"And there's no way you could remember?" Carso demanded. "Not even if we refreshed your memory?" The half-breed's thick hands shot around the Genobonian's scaly neck, but Navarre slapped him away.

"He's probably telling the truth, Domrik. And even if he isn't, there's no way we can force him to find the volume for us."

Helna brightened suddenly. "Navarre, if we could find this Fendobar, do you think it would help us in the quest for Earth?"

"It would bring us within eleven light-years," Navarre said. "That's a goodly jump toward finding Earth. But how? The coordinates are illegible!"

"The Oligocrat's scientists are shrewd about restoring faded books," the girl said. She turned to the Genobonian. "Librarian, may we borrow this book a while?"

"Impossible! No book may be withdrawn from a closed track at any time!"

Helna scowled prettily. "But if they only rot here and eventually are shipped off at random, why make such a to-do about them? Come; let us have this book."

"It is against all rules."

Helna shrugged and nodded to Navarre, who said, "Step on him, Carso. Here's a case where violence is justified."

The half-breed advanced menacingly toward the Genobonian, who scuttled away.

"Should I kill him?" Carso asked.

"Yes," said Helna instantly. "He's dangerous. He can report us."

"No," Navarre said. "The serpent's a gentle old creature who lives by his rules and loves his books. Just tie him up, Carso, and hide him behind a pile of rotting books. He won't be found till tonight—or next year, perhaps. By which time, we'll be safely on our way."

He handed the book to Helna. "Let's go. We'll see what the Oligocrat's scientists can do with these faded pages."

Chapter Five

The small ship spiraled to a graceful landing on the massive planet.

"This might well be Kariad," Helna said. "I am used to the sight of double stars in the skies."

Directly overhead, the massive orb that was Fendobar burned brightly; further away, a dim dab of light indicated the location of the huge star's companion.

"Even this far away," Navarre said, "it seems like home. The universe remains constant."

"And somewhere eleven light-years ahead of us lies Earth," grunted Carso.

They had traveled more than a billion light-years, an immensity so vast that even Helna's personal cruiser, a warp-ship which was virtually instantaneous on stellar distances of a few thousand light-years, had required a solid week to make the journey.

And now, where were they? Fendobar—a world left far behind out of the main currents of galactic history, a world orbiting a bright star in a galaxy known only as RGC18347. A world eleven light-years from Earth.

The Oligocrat's scientists had restored the missing coordinates as Helna had anticipated, and the three of them had said an abrupt good-bye to Kariad. They had swept out into space, into the subwarp and across the tideless seas of a billion light-years. They were driving back, back into humanity's past, into Galaxy RGC18347—the obscure galaxy from which mankind had sprung.

They had narrowed the field. Navarre had never thought they would get this far.

"We seek Earth, friend," Navarre told the aged chieftain who came out supported by two young children to greet the arriving ship.

"Earth? Earth? What be this?"

The old man's accents were strange and barely understandable. Navarre fumed. "This is Fendobar, isn't it?"

"Fendobar? The name of this world is Mundahl. I know no place called Fendobar."

Carso looked worried. "You don't think we made some mistake, do you, Hallam? The coordinates in that old book—maybe they weren't interpreted right. Maybe—"

"We'll see. Names change in thirty thousand years, don't forget." Navarre leaned close to the oldster. "Do you study the stars, old man?"

"Not I. But there is a man in our village who does. He knows many strange things."

"Will you take us to him?" asked Navarre.

The astronomer proved to be a withered old man who might have been the twin of the chieftain. The Earthmen entered his thatched hut and were surprised to see many shelves of books, tapes, and an unexpected, efficient-looking telescope.

He tottered forward to greet them.

"Yes?"

"Bremoir, these people search for Earth. Know you the place?"

A slow frown spread over the astronomer's wrinkled face. "The name has a familiar sound to it. Let me search my charts." He unrolled a thin, terribly fragile-looking sheet of paper covered with tiny marks.

"Earth is the name of the planet," Navarre said. "It revolves around a sun called Sol. We know that the system is some eleven light-years from here."

The ancient astronomer pored over his charts, scowling in concentration and scratching his leathery neck. After a while he glanced up.

"There is indeed a sun-system at the distance you give. Nine planets revolve about a small yellow sun. But those names . . . ?"

"Earth was the planet's name. Sol was the sun."

"Earth? Sol? There are no such names on my charts. The star's name is Dubihsar."

"And the third planet?"

"Velidoon."

Navarre looked away. *Dubihsar. Velidoon. In thirty thousand years, names change.*

But could Earth forget its own name so soon?

There was a yellow sun ahead. Navarre stared at it hungrily through the fore viewplate, letting its brightness burn into his eyes.

"There it is," he said. "Dubihsar. *Sol.*"

"And the planets?" Carso asked.

"There are nine." Navarre peered at the crumbling book the old astronomer had found for him finally, after long hours of search and thought. The book with the forgotten names of the worlds. Navarre counted off: "Pluto, Neptune, Uranus, Jupiter, Saturn, Mars, Venus, Mercury. And *Earth.*"

"Earth," Helna said. "Soon we'll be on Earth."

Navarre frowned broodingly. "I'm not so sure I actually want to land, now that we've found it. I know what Earth's going to be like—just like Fendobar. It's a dreadful thing when a world forgets its own name."

"Nonsense, Hallam!" Carso was jovial. "Earth is Earth, whether its people know it or not. We've come this far; let's land, at least, before turning back. Who knows? We may even find the Chalice!"

"The Chalice," Navarre repeated quietly. "I had almost forgotten the Chalice." Chuckling, he said, "Poor Joroiran will never forgive me if I return without it."

Nine planets. One spun in an eccentric orbit billions of miles from the small yellow star; three others were giant worlds, unlivable; a fifth, ringed with cosmic debris, was not yet solidified. A sixth was virtually lost in the blazing heat of the sun.

There were three remaining worlds—Mars, Venus and Earth, according to the book. The small craft fixed its sights on the green world. Earth.

Navarre was first from the ship; he sprang down the cat-walk and stood in the bright warm sunlight, feet planted firmly in sprouting green shoots nudging up from brown soil. Carso and Helna followed, leaving the ship a moment later.

"This is Earth," Navarre said. "We're probably the first from the main stream of galactic worlds to set foot here in thousands of years." He squinted off into the dense thicket of trees that ringed them. Creatures were appearing.

They looked like men—dwarfed, shrunken, twisted little men. They stood about four and a half feet tall, their feet bare, their middles swathed in hides. Yet despite their primitive appearance, in their faces could be seen the unmistakable light of intelligence.

"Behold our cousins," Navarre murmured. "While we in the stars scrupulously kept our genes intact, they have become *this*."

Unafraid, the little men filed toward them, grouping themselves around the trio and their ship.

"Where be you from, strangers?" asked a flaxen-haired dwarf, evidently the leader.

"We are from the stars," Carso said. "From the world of Jorus, he and I, and the girl from Kariad. But this planet is our homeworld. Our remote ancestors were born on Earth."

"Earth? You mistake, strangers. This world be Velidoon, and we be its people. You look naught like us, unless ye be in enchantment."

"No enchantment," Navarre said. "Our fathers lived on Velidoon when it was called Earth, many thousands of years past."

How can I tell them that we once ruled the universe? Navarre wondered. *How can it be that these dwarfs are the sons of Earth?*

The flaxen-haired little man grinned and said, "What would you on Velidoon, then?"

"We came merely to visit. We wished to see the world of our long-gone ancestors."

"Strange, to cross the sky merely to see a world. But come; let us take you to the village."

I n a mere hundred thousand years," Helna murmured, as they walked through the forest's dark glades. "From rulers of the universe to scrubby little dwarfs living in thatched huts."

"And they don't even remember the name of Earth," Carso added.

"It isn't surprising," said Navarre. "Don't forget that most of Earth's best men were killed defending the planet, and the rest—our ancestors—were scattered all over the universe. Evidently the conquerors just left the dregs on Earth itself, and this is what they've become."

They turned past a clear, fast-flowing brook and emerged into an open dell, in which could be seen a group of huts not unlike those on Fendobar.

The yellow sun shone brightly and warmly; overhead, an arbor of colorful birds sang, and the forest looked fertile and young.

"This is a pleasant world," Helna said.

"Yes. Life here has none of the strain and stress of our system. Perhaps," Navarre suggested, "it's best to live on a forgotten planet."

"Look," Carso said. "Someone important is coming."

A procession advanced toward them, led by the little group who had found them in the forest. A wrinkled gray-beard, more twisted and bent than the rest, strode gravely toward them.

"You be the men from the stars?"

"I am Hallam Navarre, and these are Helna Winstin and Domrik Carso. We trace our ancestry from this world, many thousands of years ago."

"Hmm. Could be. I be Gluihn, leader of this tribe." Gluihn stepped back and scrutinized the trio. "It might well be," he said, studying them. "Yes, it could indeed. You say your remote fathers lived here?"

"When the planet was called Earth, and ruled all the worlds of the skies."

"I know nothing of that. But you look much like the Sleepers, and perhaps you be of that breed. They have lain here many a year themselves."

"What Sleepers?" Navarre asked.

"All in good time," said Gluihn. He squinted at the sky. "It was a nice day for your coming here. The sky is good."

"What of these Sleepers?" Navarre demanded again.

The old man shrugged. "They look to be of your size, though they lie down and are not easy to see behind their cloudy fluid. But they have slept for ages untold, and perhaps . . .

Gluihn's voice trailed off. Navarre exchanged a sharp glance with his companions.

"Tell us about these Sleepers," Carso growled threateningly.

Now the old man seemed frightened. "I know nothing more. Boys, playing, stumbled over them not long ago, buried in their place of rest. We think they be alive."

"Can you take us there?"

"I suppose so," Gluihn sighed. He gestured to the flaxen-haired one. "Llean, take these three to look at the Sleepers."

H ere we are," the dwarf said.

A stubby hill jutted up from the green-carpeted plain before them, and Navarre saw that a great rock had been rolled to one side, baring a cave-mouth.

"Will we need lights?"

"No," said Llean. "It is lit inside. Go ahead in; I'll wait here. I care little to have a second look to see what lies in there."

Helna touched Navarre's arm. "Should we trust him?"

"Not completely. Domrik, stay here with this Llean and keep an eye on him. In case you hear us cry out, come running, and bring him with you."

Carso grinned. "Right."

Navarre took Helna's hand and hesitantly they stepped within the cave-mouth. It was like entering the gateway to some other world.

The cave's walls were bright with some form of electroluminescence, glowing lambently despite the fact that there was no visible light-source. The path of the light continued straight for some twenty yards, then snaked away at a sharp angle beyond which nothing could be seen.

Navarre and Helna reached the bend in the corridor and turned. A metal plaque of some sort was the first object their eyes met.

"Can you read it?" she asked.

"It's in an ancient language—no, it isn't at all. It's Galactic, but a terribly archaic form." He blew away the dust and rapidly scanned the inscription. He whistled.

"What does it say?"

"Listen:

> "'Within this crypt lie ten thousand men and women, placed here to sleep in the two thousandth year of Earth's galactic supremacy and the last year of that supremacy.
>
> "'Each of the ten thousand is a volunteer. Each has been chosen from the group of more than ten million volunteers for this project on a basis of physical condition, genetic background, intelligence, and adaptability to a varying environment.
>
> "'Earth's empire has fallen, and within weeks Earth herself will go under. But, regardless of what fate befalls us, the ten thousand sealed in this crypt will slumber on into the years to come, until such time as it will be possible for them to be awakened.
>
> "'To the finder of this crypt: the chambers may be opened simply by pulling the lever at the left of each sleeper. None of the crypts will open before ten thousand years have elapsed. The sleepers will lie here in this tunnel until the time for their release, and then will come spilling out as wine from a chalice, to restore the ways of doomed Earth and bring glory to the sons of tomorrow.'"

Navarre and Helna remained frozen for an instant after the final echoing words died away. In a hushed whisper he said, "Do you know what this is?"

She nodded. "'As wine from a chalice . . .'"

"Beneath all the legends, beneath the shroud of myth—there *was* a Chalice," Navarre said fiercely. "A Chalice holding immortal life—sleepers who would sleep for all eternity if no one woke them. And when they were awakened—eternal life for doomed Earth.'"

"Shall we wake them now?" Helna asked.

"Let's get Carso. Let him be with us."

The half-breed responded to Navarre's call and appeared, dragging the protesting Llean with him.

"Let the dwarf go," Navarre said. "Then read this plaque."

Carso released the squealing Llean, who promptly dashed for freedom. When the half-breed had read the plaque, he turned gravely to Navarre.

"It seems we've found the Chalice after all!"

"It seems that way," Navarre said.

He led the way and they penetrated deeper into the crypt. After about a hundred yards he stopped.

"Look."

A wall had been cut in one side of the cave and a sheet of some massively thick plastic inserted as a window. And behind the window, floating easily in a cloudy solution of some gray-blue liquid, was a sleeping woman. Her eyes were closed, but her breasts rose and fell in a slow, even rhythm. Her hair was long and flowing; otherwise, she was similar to any of the three watchers.

A lever of some gleaming metal projected about half a foot from the wall near her head. Carso reached for it, fingering the smooth metal questioningly. "Should we wake her up?"

"Not yet. There are more down this way."

The next chamber was that of a man, strong and powerful, his muscles swelling along his relaxed arms and his heavy thighs. Beyond him, another woman; then another man, stiff and determined-looking even in sleep.

"It goes on for miles," Helna murmured. "Ten thousand of them."

"What an army!" Carso said. He seemed to be staring down the long bright corridor as if peering ahead into the years to come. "A legacy from our ancestors: the Chalice holds life indeed. Ten thousand Earthmen ready to spring to life." His eyes brightened. "They could be the nucleus of the Second Galactic Empire."

"A bold idea," Helna said. "I like it."

"We could begin with Earth itself," Carso went on. "With these couples we could repopulate the planet with warriors. Then, conquer Kariad, Jorus—and that would be just the beginning!"

"*No,*" Navarre broke in, quietly but firmly. "We are forgetting the experience of the old days. We—you—talk of building a Second Empire in a riotous suicidal mushroom of expansion. It's fool's talk to think of an Empire."

"What do you mean?" Carso asked in surprise.

"Earth carved out a galactic empire once," Navarre said. "You see the result. No; no Empire-building for us. We should be content to rebuild Earth alone, to have her take her place as a free and independent member of the galaxy. No more than that." Navarre grinned broadly. "Enough of this. Domrik, Joroiran will be proud of us! He sent us to find the Chalice, and we succeeded!"

Chapter Six

Coming home to a planet that wasn't home was a bleak, painful business, Hallam Navarre thought. The Earthman stood alone in the midst of the crowd at the Jorus City Spaceport, letting the familiar colors and smells of Jorus become part of him again. He wondered just how much had changed in his year's absence.

One thing was certain: Kausirn had solidified his position with Joroiran. Perhaps, thought Navarre, the Lyrellan had been making ready against the eventual return of Navarre from his wild quest. He would soon find out.

He hailed a jetcab.

"To the palace," he said.

The driver shot off toward the main district of Jorus City. They took the chief highway as far as the Street of the Lords, swung round into Central Plaza, and halted outside the palace.

"One unit and six," the driver said. Navarre handed the man a bill and two coins and sprang out. He paused for a moment at the approach to the palace, looking up.

A year had gone by since the scheming Lyrellan had contrived to send him off on the fool's errand of searching for the Chalice. It had been a busy year.

Eight thousand of the reborn Earthmen from the Chalice Navarre had left on Earth, instructing them to marry and bring forth children. The remaining two thousand he had transported to the neighbor system of Procyon.

His plan was that the years would pass, and children would be born, and children's children. And a restored race of Earthmen would spring up to reunite their shattered home-world of thirty thousand years before.

Navarre smiled. If only he could keep his plan a secret for a few years, until they were ready . . .

Well, he thought, he would manage. But he was apprehensive about the sort of reception he would get in the Overlord's palace, where once he had been the power behind the man on the throne.

The place hadn't changed much, physically. There were still the accursed fifty-two steps to climb, still the black-walled corridor guarded by bland monoptics from Triz. But he became conscious of the first change when he reached the Trizians.

He chucked back the hood that covered his scalp, and, his status thus revealed, he started to go past. But one of the Trizians thrust out a horny palm and said, in a dull monotone voice, "Stop."

Navarre glared up angrily. "Have I been forgotten so quickly?"

"State your name and purpose here, Earthman."

"I'm Hallam Navarre, Earthman to the Court. I've just returned from a long mission on behalf of His Majesty. I want to see him."

"Wait here," the Trizian said. "I'll check within."

He waited impatiently. After a few moments the Trizian returned, followed by two armed members of the Overlord's personal guards—Daborians, tusked, vicious-looking seven-footers.

"Well?" Navarre demanded.

"I was unable to reach His Majesty. But the Lord Adviser wishes you brought to him for interrogation."

Navarre tensed. The Lord Adviser, eh? That undoubtedly meant Kausirn; the Lyrellan seemed to have coined a shiny new title for himself in Navarre's absence.

"Very well," he said resignedly. "Take me to the Lord Adviser."

Kausirn was sitting behind a desk about ten feet wide, in a luxuriously-appointed office one level beneath the main throne room. His pale, ascetic face looked waxier than ever—a sign of health among the Lyrellans, Navarre knew.

The Daborian guards at either side of Navarre nudged him roughly.

"Kneel in the presence of the Lord Adviser, Earthman!"

"That'll be all right," Kausirn said stiffly. He gestured dismissal to the guards with one dizzying wave of a ten-fingered hand. "Hello, Navarre. I hadn't expected to be seeing you so soon."

"Nor I you, Kausirn. Or is it Milord I should address you as?"

The Lyrellan smiled apologetically. "In your absence, Navarre, we thought it wise—the Overlord did, I mean—to consolidate your post and mine into one more lofty rank, and so the office of the Lord Adviser was created. Joroiran handles little of the tiresome routine of state now, by the way. He spends his days in contemplation and profound study."

That was a flat lie, Navarre thought. If ever a man had been born less fitted for a life of contemplation and profound study, that man was Joroiran VII, Overlord of Jorus.

Aloud he said, "I suppose you'll be happy to have some of the governmental burden lifted from your shoulders, Kausirn. I mean, now that I'm back."

The Lyrellan sighed and inspected his multitude of fingers. "This must yet be decided, Navarre."

"What?"

"The workings of our government have been quite smooth in the time you have not been with us. Perhaps His Majesty will not see his way clear to restoring you to your past eminence, inasmuch as you've failed to bring him that which he sent you forth to find. I speak of the Chalice, of course, and the immortality he so greatly desires."

"And what makes you so sure I failed to find the Chalice?" Navarre demanded bluntly. "How do *you* know?"

A faint smile crossed Kausirn's cold face. "Obviously you were not successful. The Chalice is a myth—as both you and I knew before you undertook your little pleasure cruise around the universe." He leaned forward, eyes narrowing. "Besides, if you *had* found the Chalice, would you bring it back for Joroiran, Earthman? No! You'd keep it for yourself!"

Navarre shrugged. "As you say, Kausirn. I found no Chalices for His Majesty. Still, I don't doubt but that he'll welcome me back to his service. The Overlords of Jorus have always found the advice of an Earthman useful to them."

Stern frigidity replaced the mocking warmth in Kausirn's eyes. "He has no need of you, Navarre."

"Let *him* tell me that. I demand to see him!"

"Today is Fourday," Kausirn said quietly. "His Majesty holds public audiences on Threeday, as you should be well aware . . . unless you've forgotten. I suggest you return next week. If fate should fall upon you, you'll have ample chance to plead your case before His Majesty and myself at that time."

Unbelievingly, Navarre said, "You *forbid* me to see him? You want me to come like a commoner to seek his ear at a public audience? You must be mad, Kausirn!"

The Lyrellan shrugged humbly. "His Majesty is deep in meditation. I wouldn't dare break in on his contemplations—particularly since he made a point of telling me only last week that government was much simpler for him, now that he had but one adviser. You seem to be superfluous, Navarre."

The alien had done his job well, Navarre thought grimly. He started forward. "I'll see Joroiran with or without your word, Lyrellan! I don't need—"

Kausirn's fingers flickered almost imperceptibly. Suddenly Navarre felt thick Daborian fingers clutch each of his arms. He was drawn backward, away from the Lyrellan.

"Take the Earthman out of the palace," Kausirn commanded. "And don't let him back in."

There was nothing to be gained by resisting; these Daborians would cheerfully break his arms at the first sign of struggle. Navarre scowled darkly at the Lyrellan and let himself be hustled out of the Lord Adviser's office, up the stairs, and out into the open.

End of plan one, Navarre thought bitterly, as he sat on a broad bench in the plaza facing the Palace.

He had hoped to regain his old position as Joroiran's right-hand adviser, with the eventual intention of making use of the Joran fleet as the nucleus of the reborn Terran space navy.

But Kausirn had moved swiftly and well, pushing Navarre completely out of influence.

He had to gain the ear of the Overlord. But how, if Kausirn governed all approaches?

Navarre looked up as a vendor came by, hawking confections.

"One for you, Sir Earthman? A sweet puff, perhaps? A lemon tart?"

Navarre shook his head. "Sorry, old one. I don't crave sweets now."

He glanced down at his shoes, but the old vendor did not go away. He remained before the Earthman, peering intently at him as if deeply interested.

Navarre sat patiently for a moment or two, and then, exasperated, said, "I told you, I don't want anything. *Will* you go away, now?"

"You are Hallam Navarre," the old man said softly, ignoring the Earthman's impatient outburst. "Returned at last!" The vendor dropped down on the bench alongside Navarre. "For weeks I have tried to see the Lyrellan, Kausirn, to plead my case. I have always been turned away. But now you have come back to Jorus—and justice with you!"

Navarre eyed the old man curiously. "You have a suit to place before the Overlord?"

"Nine weeks I have come to the Palace on Threeday, and nine times I have been passed over. I try—"

Navarre held up one hand and said sadly, "I'm afraid my help would be doubtful at the moment. I have my own troubles with the Lyrellan."

"No!" The old man was pop-eyed with astonishment. "Even you! The many-fingered one weaves a tight web, then. I fear for Jorus, Earthman. I had hoped, seeing you . . ." His voice trailed off hopelessly.

"Not a word of this to anyone," Navarre cautioned. "But I have a private audience arranged with Joroiran for later this day. Perhaps things will improve after that."

"I hope so," the vendor said fervently. "And then will you hear my suit? My name is Molko of Dorvil Street. Will you remember me?"

"Of course."

Navarre rose and began to stroll back toward the palace. So, he thought, even the people were discontented and unhappy over the role the Lyrellan played in governing Jorus? Perhaps, Navarre reflected, I could turn that to some advantage.

And as for the "private audience with Joroiran" he had just invented, possibly that could be brought about after all. Navarre pulled up his hood to shield his bald scalp from view, and walked more briskly toward the palace.

Chapter Seven

Seven generations of Navarres had served seven generations of the Joroiran Overlords of Jorus. The relationship could be traced back three hundred years, to brave Joroiran I, who, with Voight Navarre at his side, had cut his empire from the decaying carcass of the festering Starkings' League which had succeeded Earth's galactic empire.

The Joroiran strain had weakened, evidently; the seventh of the line had allowed himself to be persuaded by an opportunistic Lyrellan to do without an Earthman's advice. And so Navarre had been sent forth on the quest of the Chalice. But he knew he could use his seventh-generation familiarity with the palace surroundings to find his way back in.

Hooded, cowled, deliberately rounding his shoulders, Navarre shuffled forward down the flowered path to the service entrance of the Overlord's palace.

Bowed diffidently, Navarre touched the entrance buzzer, then drew back his hand in mock fright. A televisor system within was, he knew, spying on him; he had put the practice into operation himself to ward off would-be assassins.

A window in the door pivoted upward; a cold Joran face appeared—an unfamiliar face.

"Yes?"

"I am expected within." Navarre constricted his throat so his voice would be little more than a choked whisper. "I am Molko of Dorvil Street, vendor of sweets to His Majesty. I wish to see the Royal Purchase Officer."

"Hmm. Well enough," the guard grunted. "You can come in."

The burnished door hoisted. Navarre groaned complainingly and moved forward step by step, as if his legs were rotted by extreme age.

"Get a move on, old man!"

"I'm coming . . . patience, please! Patience!"

The door clanged down hard behind him. He pulled his cowl down tighter around his ears. The Purchasing Office was on the third level, two flights upward, and the liftshaft was not far ahead.

"I know the way," he said to the guard. "You needn't help me."

He tottered along the corridor until he reached the liftshaft, stepped in, and quickly pressed the stud labeled 2. A moment later he nudged the adjoining stud, the one marked 3.

The liftshaft door slid noiselessly shut; the tube rose and stopped at the second level. Navarre stepped out, stepped back in, and pressed 7.

Knowing the system was an immeasurable advantage to him. The stops of the liftshaft could be monitored from the first level; thus, if the old vendor were to claim to be going to 3 and should go to 7 instead—the Overlord's floor—there would be cause for immediate suspicion. But he had carefully thrown confusion behind him, now. There was no certain way of knowing who it was who had seemed to enter the liftshaft on the second level.

He waited patiently while the door opened and shut on the third level; then it went up to the seventh.

Navarre emerged, shuffling wearily along the character of the old vendor. He knew precisely where Joroiran's private study was located, and, more, he knew precisely how to get there. He counted his steps . . . eleven, twelve, thirteen. He paused thirteen steps from the liftshaft, leaned against the wall, waited.

Counterweighted balances sighed softly and the wall swung open, offering a crevice perhaps wide enough for a cat to pass through. Navarre was taking no chances. He squeezed through and kicked the counterweight, sealing the corridor wall again.

Now he found himself in an inner corridor. A televisor screen cast an invisible defensive web across the hall, but again Navarre had the considerable benefit of having devised the system himself. He neatly extracted a fuse from a concealed panel in the dark stone of the corridor wall, and walked ahead in confidence.

Joroiran's study door was unmarked by letter or number. Again, Navarre's doing. He huddled deep into his robes, listened carefully for any sound of conversation coming from within, and, hearing none, knocked three times, then once, then once again. It was a signal he had used with the Overlord for years.

Silence for a moment. Then: "Who's there?" in the hesitant, high-pitched voice of the Overlord.

"Are you alone, Majesty?"

Through the door came the petulant reply: "Who are you to ask questions of me? Speak up or I'll summon the guards to deal with you!"

It was Joroiran in his most typically blustery mood. Speaking in his natural voice Navarre said, "Have you forgotten this knock, Majesty?"

He knocked again.

Suspiciously, from within: "Is this a joke?"

"No, Majesty. I have come back." He threw back his hood and let Joroiran's televisors pick up his face and shaven scalp.

After a moment the door opened perhaps half an inch.

"Navarre!" came the whisper from within. The opening widened, and Navarre found himself face to face with his sovereign, Joroiran VII of Jorus.

The year had changed Joroiran, Navarre saw. The Overlord wore a shabby gray lounging-robe instead of his garments of state; without the elaborate strutwork that puffed out his frame when he appeared in public, he looked vaguely rat-like, a little bit of a man who had been thrust into a vast job by some ironic accident of birth.

His eyes were ringed with dark shadows; his cheeks were hollower than Navarre remembered them to have been. He said, "Hello, Navarre," in a tired, husky voice that had none of the one-time splendor of an Overlord.

"I'm happy to be back, Sire. My journey was a long and tiring one. I hope I didn't disturb your meditations by coming to you this way . . ."

"Of course not."

"Oh. Kausirn said you were too busy to be seen just now." Navarre chose his words carefully. "He told me you had recently said I was superfluous."

Joroiran frowned. "I don't recall your name having come up in discussion between us for the better part of a year," he said. "I recall no such decision. You've always been a valuable adjunct to the Court." The sudden pose of regality slipped away abruptly, and in a tired voice the Overlord said, "But then what I recall doesn't matter. Navarre, I should never have sent you away from the court."

Despite himself Navarre felt a sense of pity for the defeated-looking monarch. Evidently Kausirn had usurped more of the Overlord's power than Navarre had suspected.

"A year has passed since I was last here," Navarre said. "In that time—"

"In that time," Joroiran said mournfully, "Kausirn has taken increasing responsibility upon himself. About my only remaining official duty is to hold the Threeday audiences—and if he didn't fear the force of public opinion he'd soon be doing that himself."

Navarre's face took on an expression of shock. "You mean that while I've been gone he's seized some of the regal power?"

"I'm little more than a prisoner in the palace these days, Navarre."

"He said you spent your time meditating, in serious contemplation," Navarre began.

"I?" Joroiran pointed to the endless rows of books lining the walls. "You know as well as I, Navarre, that I never touch these books. I stare at them day after day. They haunt me with their memories of the past—of Overlords who ruled, instead of being ruled themselves." Joroiran flushed. "But I talk on too much. I sent you on a mission. What of it?"

Anticipation gleamed in the Overlord's sallow face.

"Failed," Navarre said bluntly, at once.

"Failed?"

"The Chalice is a hoax, a legend, a will-o'-the-wisp. For a year I pursued it, searching trail after trail, always finding nothing but dreams and phantasms at the end. After a year of such pursuit I decided I could be of better use to Your Majesty back here on Jorus. I returned—and found *this*."

Joroiran's face was bleak. Disappointment was evident. "I had hoped you might find the Chalice. But to live forever? Why? For what, now that—" He shook his head. "But you have come back. Perhaps things will change."

Impulsively Navarre seized the Overlord's hand. "I feared Kausirn's encroachments, but there was no way of pointing out the pattern of things to Your Majesty a year ago. Now that I have returned—and the shape of events is clearer to all—I can help you. You let Kausirn poison your mind against me."

"A fool's error," Joroiran said bitterly.

"But not of permanent harm. The Lyrellan will certainly not be able to defy you openly once you restore me—"

The sudden sound of clicking relays made the Earthman whirl. He spun to see the Overlord's door fly open. Kausirn stepped into the chamber.

"Away from that traitor, Sire!"

Navarre stared into the snout of a sturdy blaster held firmly in the Lyrellan's polydactyl hand.

Kausirn strode swiftly to the center of the room and ordered Navarre to one side with a brusque gesture. The Earthman obeyed; it was obvious that Kausirn would relish an opportunity to use that blaster.

Suddenly Joroiran drew himself up with a pale semblance of regality and said, "Why the gun, Kausirn? This is most unseemly. I have reinstated Navarre. As of this moment he is your fellow Adviser. I won't tolerate your uncivil behavior in here."

Good for him, Navarre thought, smiling inwardly. At least he had succeeded in winning Joroiran over, then. But would it matter, with Kausirn armed?

Turning, the Lyrellan chuckled gravely. "I mean no disrespect, Sire, but I took the liberty of listening outside Your Majesty's door for some moments. He told you, did he not, that he had failed to find the Chalice?"

"He told me that," the Overlord admitted. "What of it? The Chalice is only a legend. It was foolish of me to send him chasing it. If I hadn't listened to you—"

"The Chalice exists," the Lyrellan said tightly. *"And Navarre would use it as a weapon against you!"*

"He's insane," Navarre snapped. "I spent a year tracing the Chalice and found nothing but false trails. It was all a trick of his to get me from Jorus, Sire, but—"

"Silence," Kausirn ordered. "Majesty, the Chalice is a crypt, located on the ancient planet Earth. It contained ten thousand sleepers—men and women of Earth, suspended since the days of Earth's empire. I tell you Navarre has wakened these sleepers and plans to make them the nucleus of a re-established Terran empire. He intends the destruction of Jorus and all other worlds that stand in his way."

Dumbstruck, Navarre had to fight to keep his mouth from sagging open in astonishment. How could Kausirn *possibly* know?

"This is incredible," Navarre protested. "Sleepers, indeed! Sire, I ask you—"

"There is no need for discussion," said Kausirn. "I have the proof with me."

He drew a gleaming plastic message-cube from his tunic pocket and handed it to the Overlord. "Play this, Sire. Then judge which one of us betrays you and which seeks your welfare."

Taking the cube, Joroiran stepped to one side and converted it to playback. Navarre strained his ears but was unable to pick up more than faint murmurs. When the message had run its course, the ruler returned, glaring bitterly at Navarre.

"I hardly know which of you to trust less," he said somberly. "You, Kausirn, who has made a figurehead of me—or you, Navarre." He scowled. "Earthman, you came in here with sweet words, but this cube tells me that every word was a lie. You would help overthrow Kausirn only to place yourself in command. I never expected treachery from you, Navarre."

He turned to Kausirn. "Take him away," he ordered. "Have him killed. And do something about these ten thousand awakened Earthmen. Send a fleet to Earth to destroy them." Joroiran sounded near tears; he seemed to be choking back bitter sobs before each words. "And leave me alone. I don't want to see you any more today, Kausirn. Go run Jorus, and let me weep."

The little monarch looked from Kausirn to the stunned Earthman. "You are both betrayers. But at least Kausirn will allow me the pretense of ruling. Go. Away!"

"At once, Sire," said the Lyrellan unctuously.

He jabbed the blaster in Navarre's ribs. "Come with me, Earthman. The Overlord wishes privacy."

Chapter Eight

The lower depths of the Overlord's palace were damp and musty—intentionally so, to increase a prisoner's discomfort. Navarre huddled moodily in a cell crusted with wall-lichens, listening to the steady pacing of the bulky Daborian guard outside.

Not even Kausirn had cared to kill him in cold blood. Navarre had not expected mercy from the Lyrellan, but evidently Kausirn was anxious to observe the legal formalities. There would be a public trial, its outcome carefully predetermined and its course well rehearsed, followed by Navarre's degradation and execution.

It made sense. A less devious planner than Kausirn might have gunned Navarre down in a dark alcove of the palace and thereby rid himself of one dangerous enemy. But by the public exposure of Navarre's infamy, Kausirn would not only achieve the same end but would also cast discredit on the entire line of Earthmen.

Navarre cradled his head in his hands, feeling the tiny stubbles of upshooting hair. For a year, he had let his hair grow; the year he had spent in the distant galaxy that held Earth and Procyon. But at the end of the year, when the seeding of Procyon was done and already half a thousand new Earthmen had been born, Helna and Domrik Carso and Navarre had come together, and they had decided the time had come for them to return to the main starways.

"It's best," Carso had growled. "You stay away too long and it's possible Joroiran may decide to trace you. You never can tell. If we remain here, we may draw suspicion to the project. I vote that we go back."

Helna had agreed. "I'll return to Kariad, you to Jorus," she told Navarre. "We can enter once again the confidences of our masters. Perhaps we can turn that to some use in the days to come."

Now, trapped in a cell, Navarre wondered how Kausirn had found out his plans, how the Lyrellan had known that a new race of Earthmen was rising in Galaxy RGC18347. It was too accurate to be a mere guess. Had they been followed this past year?

Navarre frowned. Somehow his defenseless ten thousand would have to be warned. But first—escape.

He squinted through the murk at the Daborian guard who paced without. Daborians were fierce warriors, thought Navarre, but the species was not overlong on brains. He eyed the tusked one's seven-foot bulk appreciatively.

"Holla, old one, your teeth rot in your head!"

"Quiet, Sir Earthman. You are not to speak."

"Am I to take orders from a moldering corpse of a warrior?" Navarre snapped waspishly. "Fie, old one. You frighten me not."

"I am ordered not to speak with you."

"For fear I'd befuddle your slender brain and escape, eh? Milord Kausirn has a low opinion of your kind, I fear. I remember him saying of old that a Daborian's usefulness begins below the neck. Not so, moldy one?"

The Daborian whirled and peered angrily into Navarre's cell. His polished tusks glinted brightly. Navarre put a hand between the bars and tugged at the alien's painstakingly combed beard. The Daborian howled.

"It surprises me the beard did not come off in my hand," Navarre said.

The Daborian grunted a curse and jabbed his fist through the bars; Navarre laughed, dancing lightly back. Mockingly he offered three choice oaths, from the safety of the rear of his cell.

The Daborian, he knew, could rend him into four quivering chunks if he ever got close enough. But that was not going to happen. Navarre stationed himself perhaps a yard from the bars and continued to rail at the guard.

Maddened, the Daborian reversed his gun and hammered at Navarre with the butt. The first wild swing came within an inch of laying open the Earthman's skull; on the second, Navarre managed to seize the slashing butt. He tugged with sudden strength. He dragged the rifle halfway from the guard's grasp, just enough to get his own hands on the firing stud.

The bewildered Daborian yelled just once before Navarre dissolved his face. A second blast finished off the electronic lock that sealed shut the cell.

Fifteen minutes later Navarre returned to the warm sunlight, a free man, in the garb of a Daborian guard.

Verru, the wigmaker of Dombril Street, was a pale, wizened little old Joran who blinked seven or eight times as the stranger slipped into his shop, locking the door behind him and holding a finger to his lips for silence.

Wordlessly, Navarre slipped behind the counter, grasped the wigmaker's scrawny arm, and drew him back through the arras into his stockroom. There he said, "Sorry for the mystery, wigmaker. I feel the need for your services."

"You are not a Daborian!"

"The face belies the uniform," Navarre said. He grinned, showing neat, even teeth. "My tusks don't quite meet the qualifications. Nor my scalp." He lifted his borrowed cap. Verru's eyes widened. "An *Earthman*?"

"Indeed. I'm looking for a wig for—ah—a masquerade. Have you anything in Kariadi style?"

The trembling wigmaker said, "One moment."

He bustled through a score or more of boxes before producing a glossy black headpiece.

"Here!"

"Affix it for me," Navarre said.

Sighing, the wigmaker led him to a mirrored alcove and sealed the wig to his scalp. Navarre examined his reflection approvingly. In all but color, he might pass for a man of Kariad.

"Well done," he said. Reaching below his uniform for his money-pouch, he produced two green bills of Imperial scrip. One he handed to the wigmaker, saying, "This is for you. As for the other—go into the street and wait there until a Kariadi about my size comes past. Then somehow manage to entice him into your store, making use of the money."

"This is very irregular. Why must I do these things, Sir Earthman?"

"Because otherwise I'll have you flayed. Now go!"

The wigmaker went.

Navarre took up a station behind the shopkeeper's door, clutching his gun tightly, and waited. Five minutes passed.

Then he heard the wigmaker's voice outside, tremulous, unhappy.

"I beg you, friend. Step within my shop a while."

"Sorry, wigmaker. No need for your trade have I."

"Good sir, I ask it as a favor. I have an order for a wig styled in your fashion. No, don't leave. I can make it worth your while. Here. This will be yours if you'll let me sketch your hair style. It will be but a moment's work . . ."

Navarre grinned. The wigmaker was shrewd.

"Well, if it's only a moment, then. I guess it's worth a hundred units to me if you like my hair style."

The door opened. Navarre drew back and let the wigmaker enter. Behind him came a Kariadi of about Navarre's general size and build.

Navarre brought his gun butt down with stunning force on the back of the Kariadi's head, and caught him as he fell.

"These crimes in my shop, Sir Earthman—"

"Are in the name of the Overlord," Navarre told the quivering wigmaker. He knelt over the unconscious Kariadi and began to strip away his clothing.

"Lock your door," he ordered. "And get out your blue dyes. I have more work for you."

The job was done in thirty minutes. The Kariadi, by this time awake and furious, lay bound and gagged in the wigmaker's stockroom, clad in the oversize uniform of Joroiran's Daborian guard. Navarre, a fine Kariadi blue in color from forehead to toes, and topped with a shining mop of black Kariadi hair, grinned at the grunting prisoner.

"You serve a noble cause, my friend. It was too bad you had to be treated so basely."

"Mmph! Mgggl!"

"Hush," Navarre whispered. He examined his image in the wigmaker's mirror. Resplendent in a tight-fitting Kariadi tunic, he scarcely recognized himself. He drew forth the Kariadi's wallet and extracted his money, including the hundred-unit Joran note the wigmaker had given him.

"Here," he said, stuffing the wad of bills under the Kariadi's leg. "I seek only your identity, not your cash." He added another hundred-unit note to the wad, gave yet another to the wigmaker, and said, "You'll be watched. If you free him before an hour has elapsed, I'll have you flayed in Central Plaza."

"I'll keep him a month, Sir Earthman, if you command it." The wigmaker was green with fright.

"An hour will be sufficient, Verru. And a thousand thanks for your help in this matter." Giving the panicky old man a noble salute, Navarre adjusted his cape, unlocked the shop door, and stepped out into the street.

He hailed a passing jetcab.

"Take me to the spaceport," he said, in a guttural Kariadi accent.

As he had suspected, Kausirn had posted guards at the spaceport. He was stopped by a pair of sleek Joran secret-service men—he recognized the tiny emblem at their throats, having designed it himself at a time when he was more in favor on Jorus—and was asked to produce his papers.

He offered the passport he had taken from the Kariadi. They gave it a routine look-through and handed it back.

"How come the look-through?" he asked. "Somebody back there said you were looking for a prisoner who escaped from the Overlord's jail. There any truth in that?"

"Where'd you hear that story?"

Navarre shrugged innocently. "He was standing near the refreshment dials. Curious-looking fellow—he wore a hood, and kept his face turned away from me. Said the Overlord had captured some hot-shot criminal, or maybe it was an assassin. But he got away. Say, are Jorus' dungeons so easily unsealed?"

The secret-service men exchanged troubled glances. "What color was this fellow?"

"Why, he was pink—like you Jorans. Or maybe he was an Earthman. I couldn't see under that hood, of course, but he might very well have been shaven, y'know. And I couldn't see his eyes. But he may still be there, if you're interested."

"We are. Thanks."

Navarre grinned wryly and moved on toward the ticket booths as the secret-service men dashed down toward the direction of the refreshment dials. He hoped they would have a merry time searching through the crowd.

But the fact that he was effecting a successful escape afforded him little actual joy. The Lyrellan knew of his plans, now, and the fledgling colonies of Earthmen in Galaxy RGC18347 were in great danger.

He boarded the liner, cradled in, and awaited blast-off impatiently, consuming time by silently parsing the irregular Kariadi verbs.

Chapter Nine

Customs-check was swift and simple on Kariad. The Kariadi customs officers paid little attention to their own nationals; it was outworlders they kept watch for. Navarre merely handed over his passport, made out in the name of Melwod Finst, and nodded to the customs official's two or three brief questions. Since he had no baggage, he obviously had nothing to declare.

He moved on, into the spaceport. The money-changing booths lay straight ahead and he joined the line, reaching the slot twenty minutes later. He drew forth his remaining Joran money, some six hundred units in all, and fed it to the machine.

Conversion was automatic; the changer clicked twice and spewed eight hundred and three Kariadi credit-bills back at him. He folded them into his pocket and continued on. There was no sign of pursuit, this time.

Deliberately he walked on through the crowded arcades for ten minutes more. Then, all seeming clear, he stepped into a public communicator booth, inserted a coin, and requested Information.

The directory-robot grinned impersonally at him. "Yours to serve, good sir."

"I want the number of Helna Winstin, Earthman to the Court of Lord Marhaill."

His coins came clicking back. The robot said, after the moment's pause necessary to fish the data from its sponge-platinum memory banks, "Four-oh-three-oh-six K Red."

Quickly Navarre punched out the number. On the screen appeared a diamond-shaped insignia framing an elaborate scrollwork *M*. A female voice said, "Lord Marhaill's. With whom would you speak?"

"Helna Winstin. The Earthman to the Court."

"And who calls her?"

"Melwod Finst. I'm but newly returned from Jorus."

After a pause the Oligocrat's emblem dissolved, and Helna Winstin's head and shoulders took their place on the screen. She looked outward at Navarre cautiously; her face seemed paler than ever, the cheekbones more pronounced. She had shaved her scalp not long before, he noticed.

"Milady, I am Melwod Finst of Kariad West. I crave a private audience with you at once."

"You'll have to make regular application, Freeholder Finst. I'm very busy just now. You—"

Her eyes went wide as the supposed Finst tugged at his frontmost lock of hair, yanking it away from his scalp sufficiently far enough to show where the blue skin color ended and where the pale white began. He replaced the lock, pressing it down to rebind it to his scalp, and grinned. The grin was unmistakable.

"I have serious matters to discuss with you, Milady," Navarre said. "My seedling farm is in serious danger. The crop is threatened by hostile forces. This concerns you, I believe."

She nodded. "I believe it does. Let us arrange an immediate meeting, Melwod Finst."

They met at the Two Suns, a refreshment place not too far from the spaceport. Navarre, who was unfamiliar with Kariad, was not anxious to travel any great distance to meet Helna; since he was posing as an ostensible Kariadi, an undue lack of familiarity on his part with his native world might seem suspicious.

He arrived at the place long before she did. They had arranged that he was to find her, not she him; not seeing her at any of the tables, he took a seat at the bar.

"Rum," he said. He knew better than to order the vile Kariadi beer.

He sat alone, nursing his drink, grunting noncommitally any time a local barfly attempted to engage him in conversation. Thirty minutes and three rums later, Helna arrived. She paused just inside the door of the place, standing regally erect as she looked around for him.

Navarre slipped away from the bar and went up to her.

"Milady?"

She glanced inquisitively at him.

"I am Melwod Finst," he told her gravely. "Newly come from Jorus."

He led her to a table in the back, drew a coin from his pocket, and purchased thirty minutes of privacy. The dull blue of the force-screen sprang up around them. During the next half hour they could carouse undisturbed, or make love, or plot the destruction of the galaxy.

Helna said, "Why the disguise? Where have you been? What—"

"One question at a time, Helna. The disguise I needed in order to get off Jorus. My old rival Kausirn has laid me under sentence of death."

"How can he?"

"Because he knows our plan. Kausirn's spies are more ingenious than we think. I heard him tell the Overlord everything—where we were, the secret of the Chalice, our eventual hope of rebuilding the civilization of Earth."

"You denied it, naturally."

"I said it was madness. But he had some sort of documentary evidence he gave the Overlord, and Joroiran was immediately convinced. Just after I had won him over, too." Navarre scowled. "I managed to escape and flee here in this guise, but we'll have to block them before they send a fleet out to eradicate the settlements on Earth and Procyon. Where's Carso?"

Helna shrugged. "He's taken cheap lodgings somewhere in the heart of the city while he waits for word from you that his banishment is revoked. I don't see much of him these days."

"Small chance he'll get unbanished now," Navarre said.

"Let's find him. The three of us will have to decide what's to be done."

He rose. Helna caught him by one wrist and gently tugged him back into his seat.

"Is the emergency *that* pressing?" she asked.

"Well . . ."

"We've got twenty minutes more of privacy paid for—should we waste it? I haven't seen you for a month, Hallam."

"I guess twenty minutes won't matter much," he said, grinning.

They found Carso later that day sitting in a bar in downtown Kariad City, clutching a mug of Kariadi beer in his hand. The half-breed looked soiled and puffy-faded; his scalp was dark with several days' growth of hair, his bushy beard untrimmed and unkempt.

He looked up in sudden alarm as Helna's hand brushed lightly along his shoulder. "Hello," he grunted. Then, seeing Navarre, he added, "Who's your friend?"

"His name is Melwod Finst. I thought you'd be interested in meeting him."

Carso extended a grimy band. "Pleased."

Navarre stared unhappily at his erstwhile comrade. Filthy, drunken, ragged-looking, there was little of the Earthman left about Carso. True enough, Carso was a half-breed, his mother an Earthwoman—but now he seemed to have brought to the fore the worst characteristics of his nameless, drunken Joran father. He was a sad sight.

Navarre slipped in beside the half-breed and gestured at the bowl of foul Kariadi beer. "I've never understood how you could drink that stuff, Domrik."

Carso wheeled heavily in his seat to look at Navarre. "I didn't know we were on first-name terms, friend. But—wait! Speak again!"

"You're a bleary-eyed sot of a half-breed," Navarre said in his natural voice.

Carso frowned. "That voice—your face—you remind me of someone. But he was not of Kariad."

"Nor am I," said Navarre. "Blue skin's a trapping easily acquired. As is a Kariadi wig."

Carso started to chuckle, bending low over the beer. At length he said, "You devil, you fooled me!"

"And many another. There's a price on my head back on Jorus."

"Eh?" Carso was abruptly sober; the merriment drained from his coarse-featured face. "What's that you say? Are you out of favor with the Overlord? I was counting on you to have that foolish sentence of banishment revoked and—"

"Kausirn knows our plans. I barely got off Jorus alive; even Joroiran is against me. He ordered Kausirn to send a fleet to destroy the settlement on Earth."

Carso bowed his head. "Does he know where Earth is? After all, it wasn't easy for us to find it in the first place."

"I don't know," Navarre said. He glanced at Helna. "We'll have to find the old librarian who gave us the lead. Keep him from helping anyone else."

Carso said, "That's useless. If Kausirn knows about the Chalice and its contents, he also knows where the crypt was located and how to get there. At this moment the Jorus fleets are probably blasting our settlements. Here. Have a drink. It was a fine planet while it lasted, wasn't it?"

"No Joran spacefleet has left the Cluster in the last month," Helna said quietly.

Navarre looked up. "How do you know?"

"Oligocrat Marhaill has reason to suspect the doings on Jorus. He keeps careful watch over the Joran military installations, and whenever a Joran battlefleet departs on maneuvers we are apprised of it. This information is routed through me on its way to Marhaill. And I tell you that the Joran fleet has been absolutely quiet all this past month."

Reddening, Navarre asked, "How long has this sort of observation been going on?"

"Four years, at least."

Navarre slammed the flat of his hand against the stained table top. "Four years! That means you penetrated my alleged defensive network with ease . . . and all the time I was trying to set up a spy-system on Kariad, and failing!" He eyed the girl with new respect. "How did you do it?"

She smiled. "Secret, Navarre, secret! Let's maintain the pretense—I'm Earthman to Marhaill's Court, you to Joroiran's. It wouldn't be ethical for me to speak of such matters to you."

"Well enough. But if the fleet's not left yet, that means one of two things—either they're about to leave, or else they don't know where to go!"

"I lean toward the latter," said Carso. "Earth's a misty place. I expect they're desperately combing the old legends now for some hint."

"If we were to obtain three Kariadi battlecruisers, and ambush the Joran fleet as it came down on Earth . . ." Helna mused aloud.

"Could we?" Navarre asked.

"You're in Kariadi garb. What if I obtained an appointment in our space navy for you, Navarre? And then ordered you out—with a secondary fleet on—ah—maneuvers? Say, to the vicinity of Earth?"

"And then I tell my crewmen that war has been declared between Jorus and Kariad, and set them to destroying the unsuspecting Joran fleet!" Navarre went on.

"Not destroying," said Helna. "Capturing! We make sure your battle wagons are equipped with tractor-beams—and that way we add the Joran ships to our growing Terran navy."

Carso gave his approval with a quick nod. "It's the only way to save Earth. If you can handle the appointments, Helna."

"Marhaill is a busy man. I can take care of him. Why, he was so delighted to see me return after a year's time that he didn't even ask me where I had been!"

Navarre frowned. "One problem. Suppose Kausirn *doesn't* know where Earth is? What if no Joran fleet shows up? I can't keep your Kariadi on maneuvers forever out there, waiting for the enemy."

"Suppose," said Helna, "we make sure Kausirn knows. Suppose we *tell* him."

Carso gasped. "I may have been drinking, but I can't be *that* drunk. Did you say you'd tell Kausirn where our settlements are?"

"I did. It'll take the suspense out of the pressure of his threat. And it'll add a Joran fleet to a Kariadi one to form a nucleus of the new Terran navy—if the space battle comes out properly."

"And what if Kausirn sends the entire Joran armada out against your puny three ships? What then?"

"He won't," said Navarre. "It wouldn't be a logical thing to do. Earth is known to be defenseless. Kausirn wouldn't needlessly leave Jorus unguarded by sending out any more ships than he needs for the job."

"I still don't like the idea," Carso insisted, peering moodily at the oily surface of his beer. "I don't like the idea at all."

Chapter Ten

F our days later Navarre, registered as Melwod Finst at the Hotel of the Red Sun, received an engraved summons to the Oligocrat's court, borne by a haughty Kariadi messenger in red wig and costly livery.

Navarre accepted the envelope and absently handed the courier a tip; insulted, the messenger drew back, sniffed at Navarre, and bowed stiffly. He left, looking deeply wounded.

Grinning, the Earthman opened the summons. It said:

> By These Presents Be It Known
>   That Marhaill, Oligocrat of Kariad, does on behalf of him-
> self and his fellow members of the Governing Council invite
>   MELWOD FINST
> of Kariad City to Court on the seventh instant of the current
> month.
>   The said Finst is therein to be installed in the Admiralty of
> the Navy of Kariad, by grace of private petition received and
> honored.

The invitation was signed only with the Oligocrat's monogram, the scroll-work *M* within the diamond. But to the right of that, in light pencil, were the initials *H. W.*, scrawled in Helna's hand.

Navarre mounted the document on the mantel of his hotel room and mockingly bowed before it. "All hail, Admiral Finst! Melwod Finst of the Kariadi navy!"

C ourt was crowded the following day when Navarre, in a rented court costume, appeared to claim his Admiralty. The long throne room was lined on both sides with courtiers, members of the government, curious onlookers who had wangled admission, and those about to be honored.

Marhaill, Oligocrat of Kariad, sat enthroned at the far end of the hall, sprawled awkwardly with his long legs jutting in different directions. At his right sat Helna, befitting her rank as Earthman to the Court and chief adviser of Marhaill. On lesser thrones to both sides sat the eight members of the Governing Council, looking gloomy, dispirited, and bored. Their functions had atrophied; Kariad, once an authentic oligarchy, had retained the forms but not the manner of the ancient government. The Governing Council's only value was decorative.

It was an imposing tableau.

Navarre stood impatiently at attention for fifteen minutes, sweating under his court costume—and praying fervently that his dye would not run—until the swelling sound of an electronic trumpet called the assemblage to order.

Marhaill rose and made a brief but highly-charged speech, welcoming all and sundry to court. Then Helna surreptitiously slipped a scroll into his hands, and he began to read, in a deep, magnificently resonant voice which Navarre suspected was his own, and not simply an artificially, magnified tone produced by a microamplifier embedded in his larynx.

Navarre counted. His name was the sixty-third to be called; preceding him came three other new admirals, four generals, seven ministers plenipotentiary, and assorted knights of the realm. Evidently Marhaill believed in maintaining a goodly number of flashily-titled noble gentry on Kariad. It was a method for insuring loyalty and service, thought Navarre.

Finally:

"Melwod Finst. For meritorious service to the realm of Kariad, for abiding and long-standing loyalty to our throne, for generous and warm-hearted qualities of person, and for skill in the arts of space. We show our deep gratitude by bestowing upon him the rank of Admiral in our space navy, with command of three vessels of war."

Navarre had been carefully coached in the procedure by Helna. When Marhaill concluded the citation, Navarre clicked his heels briskly, stepped out of the audience, and advanced toward the throne, head back, shoulders high.

He gave a crisp military salute. "Thanks to Your Grace," he said, kneeling.

Marhaill leaned forward and draped a red-and-yellow sash over Navarre's shoulders.

"Rise, Admiral Melwod Finst."

Rising, Navarre's eyes met those of Marhaill's. The Oligocrat's eyes were deep, searching—but were they, he wondered, searching enough to discover that the new admiral was a shaven Earthman, renegade from Jorus? It didn't seem that way.

The shadow of a smile flickered across Navarre's face as he made the expected genuflection and backed away from the Oligocrat's throne. It was a strange destiny for an Earthman: an admiral of Kariad. But Navarre had long since learned to take the strange in stride.

He knelt again before Helna, thus showing the gratitude due his sponsor, and melted back into the crowd, standing now in the colorfully-sashed line of those who had been honored. Marhaill called the next name. Navarre adjusted his admiral's sash proudly, and, standing erect, watched the remainder of the ceremony with deep and abiding interest.

The military spaceport closest to Kariad City was the home base of the Fifth Navy, and it was to this group that Helna had had Navarre assigned.

He reported early the following morning, introducing himself rather bluntly to the commanding officer of the base and requesting his ships. He was eyed somewhat askance; evidently such prompt action was not expected of a political appointee in the history of the Kariadi navy. In any event, a sullen-looking enlisted man drove Navarre out to the spaceport itself, where three massive first-class battle cruisers stood gleaming in the bright morning rays of Secundus, the yellow sun.

Navarre nearly whistled in surprise; he hadn't expected ships of this order of tonnage. He watched, delighted, as Kariadi spacemen swarmed over the three ships, getting them into shape for the forthcoming battle maneuvers. They weren't expecting an actual battle, but from their enthusiasm and vigor Navarre knew they would be grateful for the unexpected opportunity of experiencing actual combat.

"Very nice," he commented, whenever any of the base officers asked his opinion of his command ships. "Excellent ships. Excellent."

He met his staff of under-officers, none of whom seemed particularly impressed by their new commander. He shook hands coldly, rather flabbily. Since they all knew he was a political appointee, he was determined to act the part fully.

At noon he ate in the officers' supply room. He was in the midst of discussing his wholly fictitious background of tactical skills when a frightened young orderly came bursting in.

"What's the meaning of this disturbance?" Navarre demanded in a gruff voice.

"Are you Admiral Finst? Urgent message for Admiral Finst, sir. Came in over top-priority wires from the palace just now."

"Hand it over, boy."

"Finst" took the sealed message, slid it open, read it. It said, *Come back to palace at once. Treachery. Serious danger threatens. Helna.*

"You look pale, Admiral," remarked an officer nearby.

"I've been summoned back to the palace," Navarre said brusquely. "Urgent conference. Looks very serious, I'm afraid. They need me in a hurry."

Suddenly all eyes swung toward the political appointee, who had in a moment revealed that he was actually a person of some importance.

"What is it, Finst? Has war been declared?"

"Sorry, I'm not at liberty to say anything now. Would you have a jet brought down for me? I must get to the palace at once."

Helna was pale and as close to tears as Navarre had ever seen her. She paced nervously through her private apartments in the palace as she told the story to him.

"It came in through my spy-web," she said. "We were monitoring all calls from Kariad to Jorus, and they taped—this!"

She held out a tape. Navarre stared at it. "Was it always standard practice to tape every call that goes through?"

"Hardly. But I suspected, and—here! Listen to it!"

She slipped the tape into a playback and activated the machine. The voice of an operator was heard, arranging a subspace call from Kariad to Jorus, collect.

Then came the go-ahead. A voice Navarre recognized instantly as that of the Lyrellan Kausirn said, "Well? This call is expensive. Speak up!"

"Kausirn? Carso here. I'm on Kariad. Got some news for you, Kausirn."

Navarre paled. *Carso?* Why was the half-breed calling Kausirn? Suspicion gnawed numbly at him as he listened to the unfolding conversation.

"What do you have to tell me?" came the Lyrellan's icy voice.

"Two things! The location of Earth, and something else. The first will cost you twenty thousand units, the second thirty thousand."

"You drive a hard bargain, Carso. We have our own clues about the whereabouts of Earth. Fifty thousand credits is no small amount for such information."

"You've heard the price, Kausirn. I don't really care, you know. I can manage. But you'll feel awful foolish when Navarre pulls what he's going to pull."

"Explain yourself."

"Fifty thousand credits, Kausirn."

A moment's silence. Then: "Very well. I'll meet—your terms. Give me what you have to tell me."

Carso's heavy chuckle was heard, deep-throated, confident. "Cash first, talk later. Wire the money to the usual place. When it reaches me, Lord Adviser, I'll call back—collect."

The Lyrellan's angry scowl was easy to imagine. "You'll get your filthy money!"

Click!

Helna said, "That's all we transcribed. The conversation took place at about 100 this morning. It takes approximately two hours to wire money from Jorus to Kariad. That means Carso won't be calling back for a half hour yet."

"I can't believe it," Navarre muttered. He clenched his blue-stained fists. "But yet I heard it. Carso—selling us out!"

"He was only a half-breed," Helna said. "He didn't have the pure Terran blood. You heard him: he didn't care. It was just a chance to get money. All the time he journeyed with us to Earth, he was doing it simply as a lark, a playful voyage. The man has the morals of a worm!"

Broodingly Navarre said, "He was banished for killing an innkeeper in a fit of drunken rage. And if we hadn't stopped him he surely would have killed the old Genobonian librarian. Everything in his character was sullen and drunken and murderous, and we let him fool us! We thought he was a sort of noble savage, didn't we? And now he's sold us out to the Lyrellan!"

"Not yet. We can still stop him."

"I know. But obviously he's the one who betrayed us to Kausirn while I was on my way back to Jorus last month; heaven knows why he didn't give Kausirn the coordinates for Earth while he was at it. I guess he was holding out for a higher price—that's the only sensible explanation. Well, now Kausirn's met his price."

Navarre glanced at the clock. "Order a jetcab for me, Helna. I'm going to pay Carso a visit."

Carso's lodgings were close to the center of Kariad City, in a dilapidated old hotel that might have seen its best days during the long-gone time of the Starkings' League. There was something oppressively ancient about the street; it bore the numbing weight of thousands of years.

Navarre kept careful check on the passage of time. Helna's astonishingly efficient spy system was now monitoring the influx of wired cash from Jorus to Kariad. She would arrange that the fifty thousand units en route from Kausirn would be delayed in reaching Carso at least until 1300. The time was 1250 now.

Navarre left the cab half a block from Carso's lodging house, and covered the rest of the distance on foot. A tired-looking Brontallian porter slouched behind the desk in the lobby, huddled over a tattered yellow fax-sheet. When Navarre entered, still imposingly clad in his admiral's uniform, the porter came to immediate attention,

Navarre laid a blue five-credit note on the desk. "Is there a Domrik Carso registered here?"

The porter squinted uncertainly, pocketed the five, and nodded obsequiously. "Yes, Admiral."

"His room?"

Another five. "Seven-oh-six, Admiral."

Navarre smiled mildly. "Very good. Now give me the pass-key to his room."

Bristling, the porter protested, "Why, I can't do that, Admiral! It's against the law! It's—"

A third time Navarre's hand entered his pocket. The porter awaited a third five-credit note, but this time a deadly little blaster appeared. The Brontallian, dismayed, cowered back, clasping his webbed, gray-skinned hands tightly in fear.

"Give me the key," Navarre said.

Nodding profusely, the porter handed Navarre a square planchet of copper with the Kariadi numerals 706 stamped on it. Navarre smiled and gave the terrified Brontallian the third five. Turning, he moved silently toward the elevator.

If anything, the residence floors of the building were seedier and less reputable-looking than the lobby. Evidently, luminopanels had been installed in the corridor ceilings some time in the past century, but they were dull and flickering things now, giving little light. The air-conditioning system was defective. It was a dismal place.

Navarre waited, poised outside Room 706, blaster cupped innocently in the hollow of his palm. He had, it seemed, arrived at just the proper moment. He could hear Carso's voice. The half-breed was in the act of trying to put through a collect call to Kausirn.

Minutes passed; Navarre heard the operator's voice through the door, but the sound was barely audible. Once a drunk came out of 703, stared inquisitively at Navarre, and reeled toward him with flustered determination and a fierce expression.

"Eavesdropper, eh? You know what we do—"

Navarre took three quick steps forward and caught the man by the throat, shutting him up. He tightened his grip; the drunk's pockmarked face went bright red. Navarre let go of him, tapped him sharply in the stomach, caught him as he toppled, and dragged him back into his room. The entire encounter had taken but a few seconds. Carso was still expostulating hotly with the operator when Navarre returned to his post outside the door.

More than a minute passed, and then Navarre heard the distinct syllables, "Go ahead, Kariad. We have the hookup."

"Carso here."

A familiar thin voice responded, "I take it you've received the money."

"It came," Carso rumbled. "And I'm delivering my end of the deal. Listen, now: Navarre planted settlements on Earth—now called Velidoon by its inhabitants, by the way—and on Procyon IV, which used to be called Fendobar and is now called Mundahl. These worlds are located in Galaxy RGC18347. The coordinates are—"

Navarre listened as Carso offered a full and detailed set of instructions that would enable the Joran fleet to reach Earth. He tensed; timing now would be of the utmost importance. The bait had been cast. He had to stop Carso before the half-breed told Kausirn how to avoid the hook.

Navarre touched his borrowed key to the plate-stud of the door, and it swung back, revealing Carso squatting before the televisor.

"Now, as to this second bit of information, Kausirn. It's simply this: Navarre and—"

Navarre threw the door open with a noisy slam. Carso was taken totally by surprise. He sprang up, muttering. But Navarre raised his blaster and put a quick bolt through the televisor, cutting off an impatient expostulation on the part of Kausirn.

Hefting the blaster speculatively, Navarre looked at Carso. "You've greatly disillusioned me, Domrik. I clung to certain outmoded beliefs that Earthmen had a certain higher loyalty, even half-breeds. Even the insignificant drop of Terran blood in their veins would—"

"What the devil are you talking about, Navarre? And what's the idea of busting in here and wrecking the visor. I'll have to pay—"

Navarre tightened his grip on the gun. "Don't try to bluff out of it. I listened to your whole conversation with Kausirn. I also overheard your earlier talk with him this morning. You sold us out, Domrik. For a stinking fifty thousand credits you were willing to hand Earth and Procyon over to Kausirn's butchers."

Carso's eyes were angrily bloodshot. He had obviously been drinking heavily—to soothe his troubled conscience, perhaps.

He said, "I wondered how long it would take you to find out about me. Damn you and your pure blood lines, Navarre! You and all your Earthmen!"

He came barreling heavily forward.

Navarre swung the blaster to one side and met Carso's charge with his shoulder. Carso grunted and kept on coming; he was a stocky man, easily fifty or sixty pounds heavier than Navarre.

Navarre stepped back out of the way and jabbed the blaster sharply into the pit of Carso's stomach.

"Hold it, Domrik. Stand where you are or I'll burn you open!"

Carso ignored him and swung a wild roundhouse aimed at Navarre's chin; the Earthman jumped back and fired in the same instant. For a moment, Carso stood frozen in the middle of the room, knees sagging slightly. He glared at Navarre as if in reproach, and dropped.

"I still don't believe it," Navarre said quietly. He tossed a blanket over Carso's body, slipped the blaster back into its holster, and left, locking the door behind him.

Chapter Eleven

In the control cabin of the Kariadi grand flagship, *Pride of Kariad*, lurking just off the spectacularly ringed world that was Sol VI, Admiral Melwod Finst, otherwise the Earthman Hallam Navarre, sat behind a coruscating sweep of bright screens.

"Any sign of the Joran ships yet?" he asked.

From Rear Observation Channel came the reply: "Not yet, sir. We're looking."

"Good."

He switched over to Master Communications and ordered a direct-channel hookup with his number two ship, *Jewel of the Cluster*, lying in wait just off the ecliptic orbit of Procyon VII.

"*Jewel* to *Pride*. What goes?"

"Admiral Finst speaking. Any sign of a Joran offensive yet?"

"Not a one, sir. We're keeping the channel open to notify you of any attack."

"Right."

Navarre paced the length of the cabin and back. The constant inaction, now that they were actually here in the Sol system, was preying on his nerves.

They were eight days out from Kariad. Navarre had taken his fleet out on the hop in due order, two days after the killing of Carso; even the mighty field generators of the three battle cruisers had required six days to bring the ships' across the billion-light-year gulf through hyperspace.

He had stationed one ship off the Procyon system, and his other two remained in the Sol group, waiting for the Joran fleet to appear. The men knew they were to fight Jorus; they were primed for battle, keen for it. The communications network was kept open round the clock. Whenever the ships of Jorus chose to make their appearance, Navarre and his fleet would be ready.

Helena had remained on Kariad, controlling operations from that end. Her spies had reliably reported that Kausirn had sent a fleet out to Earth. Navarre awaited it.

On the fifth day, the radar operator reported activity. They're emerging from hyperspace at the very edge of the Sol system, Sir. Four billion miles out, intersecting the orbit of Sol IX."

"Order battle stations," Navarre snapped to his Kariadi aides. Flipping the master channel, he sent an order riffling along subspace to the *Jewel*: "Get here at once—or faster!"

The *Jewel* hopped. A passage of a mere eleven light-years was virtually instantaneous; within minutes a compact wedge of three Kariadi ships waited off ringed Sol VI for the oncoming Jorans.

"We're looking to capture, not to destroy," Navarre repeated. "Our defensive screens are to be mounted and in use at all times. No shots are to be fired unless a direct order to do so comes from Control Center."

Two of Navarre's aides exchanged silent glances as he delivered this order. Navarre knew what they were thinking. But they would never dare to question his order, no matter how absurd it appeared; they were men of discipline, and he was their commanding officer.

The fleet shifted into defensive position.

Navarre ran a final check on the network of tractor-beams. All reported in working order at maximum intensity.

"Okay," he said. "The Jorans are heading inward toward us on standard ion-drive. Formation A, at once."

Formation A was a basket arrangement, the three ship swinging high into a synchronized triangular interlock and moving downward on the unsuspecting Joran ships. At that angle, the tractor-beam network would be at its greatest efficiency.

Navarre himself remained at the master-communication screens. He leaned forward intently, watching the dull black shapes of the three—only three!—Joran ships moving forward through space like a trio of blunt-snouted sharks homing in on their prey.

"*Now!*" he cried.

The bleak night of space was suddenly lit with the flaring tumult of tractor-beams; golden shafts of light lanced across the black of the void, crashing down on the Joran ships; locking them instantly in a frozen grip.

The Jorans retaliated: their heavy-cycle guns swung into action, splashing forth megawatts of energy. But Navarre had ordered out full defensive screens; the Joran guns were futile.

Navarre directed that contact be made with the Joran flagship. After some minutes of negotiation the link came through. Joran Admiral Drulk, eyes blazing with rage, appeared on the screen.

"What does this mean? You Kariadi have no jurisdiction in this sector of space—or are you looking to touch off a war between Jorus and Kariad?" He paused. "Or is there such a war already in progress—one that we don't know about?"

"Jorus and Kariad are at peace, Admiral."

"Well, then? I demand you release us from traction at once!"

"Impossible. We need your ships for purposes of our own. We'll require your immediate surrender."

Drulk stared at him. "Who *are* you?"

"Admiral Melwod Finst of Kariad." Grinning, the Earthman added, "You knew me at the court of Joroiran as Hallam Navarre."

"The Earthman! But—"

"No buts, Admiral. Will you surrender—or do we have to tow your ships into the sun?"

Chapter Twelve

Hallam Navarre stood at the edge of the city—the busy, humming, growing city they called Phoenix.

It was hardly a city yet, by Galactic standards. On Jorus, he thought, a settlement of this size would hardly rate the designation of a village. But city it was, and like the phoenix of old it rose from its own ashes.

The city rested between two upsweeping chains of hills; it lay in a fertile valley that split the heart of the great continent where the Chalice had been. All around him, Navarre saw signs of activity—the rising buildings, the clack of carpenters' tools, the buzz of the paving machines as they extended the reach of the city's streets yet a few hundred yards farther.

Women, big with child; men busy, impatient for the time when Earthmen would cover their own planet again. The six great captured spaceships stood in the sun, nucleus of the Terran navy-to-be. He saw Jorans and blue Kariadi working alongside the Earthmen—the captive crews of the spaceships, men to whom Navarre had given the choice of remaining on Earth as free men and workers, or of dying on the spot. The people of the old-young world had no time to waste in guarding prisoners.

It was slow work, Navarre thought, this rebuilding of a planet. It took time.

And there were so many enemies in the stars.

He began to walk through the city, heading for the Administration Building at its center. They greeted him as he passed—everyone knew Hallam Navarre, of course. But despite the warmth of their greetings he felt curiously ill-at-ease in their presence.

They were the true Earthmen, sleepers for thirty thousand years, untouched by the three hundred decades that intervened between the time of the beginning of their sleep and the time of Navarre's birth. They were full of the old glories of Earth, the cities and nations and the billions of people.

All gone, now; all swallowed by the forest.

Navarre recognized the difference between himself and the real Earthmen. He was as alien to them as the dwarfish, stunted beings who had come to inherit the Earth after the downfall of the empire, the little creatures who watched with awe as their awakened ancestors rebuilt their city.

Navarre was the product of an older culture than that of these sleepers from the crypt, and an alien culture as well. Earth blood was in his veins, but his mind was a mind of Jorus, and he knew he could never truly be a part of the race that was springing up anew on Earth and around Procyon.

But that did not mean he would not devote his life to their safety.

He entered his office—bare, hardly furnished—and nudged open the communicator stud. The robot operator asked for his number, and Navarre said, "I want to talk to Mikel Antrok."

A moment later he heard Antrok's deep voice say, "You want me, Hallam?"

"Yes. Would you stop off at my office?"

Antrok arrived ten minutes later. He was a tall, wide-shouldered Terran with unruly blond hair and warm blue eyes; he had served as leader of the Terran settlement during Navarre's absence on Jorus and Kariad.

He entered the office and slouched informally against the door. Navarre noticed that Antrok was covered with mud and sweat.

"Working?"

"Extending the trunk lines on the central communicator circuit," Antrok said. "That's how you reached me so fast. I was tapping into the lines when your call came along. Sweaty work it is, too—but we have to keep pace with the expansion of the city. What's on your mind?"

"I'm leaving. For Jorus and Kariad. And I probably won't be back."

Antrok blinked suddenly and straightened up. "*Leaving*, Hallam? But we're in the midst of everything now—and you've helped us so much. I thought you were staying here for good."

Navarre shook his head. "I can't, Mikel. Earth's not safe yet."

"But we have six ships—"

"Suppose Jorus sends sixty?"

"You don't expect a further attack, do you? I thought you said—"

"Whatever I might have said at the Council meetings," Navarre interrupted, "was strictly for the sake of morale. Look here, Mikel: it's seven months since the time we captured those three Joran ships. That's more than enough time for Jorus to start wondering what happened out here. And Kariad may wonder whatever became of their phony Admiral Finst and *his* three ships."

"But we're building more ships, Hallam."

"It takes two years to build a starship, and you know it. We have three in progress. That's still not enough. If Kausirn succeeds in working up enough imperial wrath against us, we'll have the whole Joran fleet down on our necks. So I'm going back to Jorus. Maybe I can handle the situation at close range."

"We'll miss you here," Antrok said.

Navarre shrugged. "Thanks. But you know it's not really true. You can manage without me. By the Cosmos, you *have* to manage without me! The day Earth finds that just one particular man is absolutely indispensable to its existence is the day you all might as well crawl back into the Chalice and go back to sleep."

Antrok nodded. "When are you leaving?"

"Tonight. I waited this long only because I wanted to get things shaped up."

"Then you won't even stay for the election?"

"There's no need of that. You'll win. And I've prepared a memorandum of suggestions for your use after you officially take over again."

Antrok looked doubtful. He said, "Of course I'm expecting to win the election, Hallam. But I'll admit I was counting on you to be here, to—"

"Well, I won't be. I'll be doing more important work elsewhere. But you know my general plans. As soon as the settlement's population reaches twelve thousand, detach two thousand and start building the second city—as far from this one as possible. That's the important thing to push right now— spreading out over Earth. Keep that starship factory intact, of course—and have the new city set to work building ships as soon as it's practical. You know the rest. Constant expansion, strengthening of government, close contact with the outfit on Procyon." Navarre grinned. "You can get along without me, Mikel. And if I'm lucky, I'll be back."

"And if you're not lucky?"

Navarre's expression darkened. "Then you'll know about it, Mikel. When the galactic fleet gets here to blast the settlement to atoms."

He left that night, in the small Joran ship that had originally carried him across space on the quest for the Chalice, more than two years before. Just before blasting off he sent a subradio message to Helna, at the court of Marhaill, to warn her that he was on his way back.

Even by hyperdrive, the trip took days, so great was the gulf separating Earth and its island universe from the star-cluster containing the Joran and Kariadi solar systems. Navarre was stale and weary by the time the mass indicator told him that Kariad, his destination, was in range.

He dropped down toward the Kariadi system, rapidly setting up the coordinates on the autopilot as the warpship lurched back into normal space; the journey would be completed on ion-drive.

Navarre fed in the coordinates for a landing at the main spaceport. He was aware that the Kariadi detector-net was too accurate for a craft such as his. He would never be able to slip unnoticed onto the planet's surface.

But he expected no trouble. It was seven months since he had last been in this galaxy, and he had let his hair grow; instead of an Earthman's traditional shaven scalp, he now presented a crop of wavy dark-brown hair. Anyway, he hoped that the search for Hallam Navarre had died down, on Kariad at least if not on Jorus.

He brought the ship down lightly on the broad concrete landing-apron of the spaceport and radioed Main Control for his clearance. It came promptly enough. He left the ship and joined the long line passing through the customs building.

He handed over his passport—a fraudulent one that had been drawn up for him on Earth. The document declared that he was one Nolliwar Strumo, a manufacturer of interplanetary space-vessels who was vacationing on Kariad.

The customs official was a weary-looking little Kariadi whose dark blue skin was streaked with bright rivulets of sweat; he had been passing people perfunctorily, without bothering to ask them more than the routine few questions. Waiting, Navarre scanned the line; he saw plenty of Kariadi, of course, and also the usual scattering of alien beings.

But no Jorans. That was queer.

Why, he wondered?

The customs man took his passport, scanned it boredly, and recited the standard question: "Name and planet of origin?"

"Nolliwar Strumo," Navarre said. He started to add, *Of Jorus,* but the words died lamely as he saw the cold expression on the official's face. The man had come suddenly awake.

"Is this a joke?" the official asked hoarsely.

"Of course not. My name is Nolliwar Strumo of Jorus. My papers are in order, aren't they?"

What's happened while I was away? he wondered. *What mistake could I have made?*

"In order?" the man repeated sardonically. He chuckled harshly and gestured to several nearby spaceport guards. Navarre tensed himself for a break-away, but realized he'd never make it. "Your papers in order? Well, not exactly. You just brought a small ship down on Kariad and thought you could march in with a passport like this?"

"I've been traveling quite a while," Navarre said. "Is there some change in the procedure? Is there a visa required now?"

"Visa! Friend, this passport's dated five weeks ago. I don't know where you got it or who you are, but the passport's obviously fake and so are you."

"I—"

The little man glared triumphantly at Navarre. "You may or may not be aware of it, but Kariad and Jorus severed diplomatic relations six months ago. We'll probably be at war with them within a month. This is a hell of a time for you to decide to take your vacation on Kariad, Mr. Nolliwar Strumo of Jorus—or whoever you are!"

He signaled to the guards. "Take him away and shut him up until Security can investigate his background. I wonder if he thought I was a fool? Next, please!"

Chapter Thirteen

Navarre sat in a windowless box of a room far below the surface level of the spaceport, breathing shallowly to keep the foul taste of the exhausted air from reaching the depths of his lungs, where it would linger for hours. He wondered what had gone wrong.

A state of war imminent between Jorus and Kariad, after hundreds of years of peace. And he had picked just this time to try to masquerade as a Joran citizen visiting Kariad! Why, it would have been safer to attempt to bluff his way through under his own identity, he realized. Or perhaps even to assume his false Kariadi guise and become, once again, Melwod Finst, Admiral of the Navy of Kariad.

He heard footsteps and straightened up. The interrogators were coming at last.

The positronic relays of the cell-door lock whirred momentarily; the door swung smoothly back into its niche, and Navarre blinked at the sudden bright stream of light that came bursting in. When he could see clearly again, he found himself confronted by the stout, stubby bore of a Kariadi blaster.

There were two interrogators, a large fat one and a small wizened one. Security interrogators always worked in teams of somatic opposites; it was part of the vast body of technique accumulated for the purpose of keeping the prisoner off-balance.

"Come with us," said the small one with the blaster, and gestured.

Navarre pushed himself up off the cot and followed. He knew resistance was out of the question now.

They led him up a long dreary cell-block, past a double door, and into a glass-doored room somewhat larger than his cell, brightly lit, with glowing luminescent panels casting a soft, pleasant radiance over everything.

Pointing to a large chair in the center of the room, the small one said, "Sit there."

Navarre sat.

The interrogators took seats against the walls, at opposite sides of him. He glanced from one to the other. They were dark blue in color, but otherwise they had little in common. The small man was dried and wrinkled like a prune; glittering, fast-moving eyes glinted at Navarre out of a mousy face. As for the other, he must have weighed nearly four hundred pounds; he slumped relievedly in his chair, a mountain of blue flesh, and dabbed futilely at the rivulets of sweat that came dribbling down from his forehead and bushy eyebrows and lost themselves in the wilderness of his many successive chins.

"Very well," the fat one began, in a patient, friendly voice. "You say you are Nolliwar Strumo of Jorus. Your passport says so also. Who are you?"

"Nolliwar Strumo, of Jorus," Navarre said.

"Highly doubtful," the heavy man remarked. "I must remind you that it's within our designated authority to make use of any forms of interrogation we may deem necessary in order to obtain information from you. We are nearly in a time of war. You claim to be a representative of a planet with whom we do not currently have diplomatic relations." He smiled coldly. "Now, this may or may not be true. But if you persist in claiming to be from Jorus, we'll have to treat you as if such is actually the case—until we find out otherwise."

While he was speaking, the character of the luminescent panels had been changing steadily. The pastel greens and gentle oranges had faded, and were gradually replaced by harsher tones, more somber ones, blues, violets. It was part of the psychological approach to interrogation, Navarre knew; the room color would get less friendly as the interview went on.

The small man said, in a dry rasping voice, "Your passport is obviously a forgery. We have laboratory confirmation on that. Who are you?"

"Nolliwar Strumo of Jorus." Navarre was determined to be stubborn as long as possible.

The fat man scowled mildly. "You have the virtue of consistency, at least. But tell us this: if you're from Jorus, as you insist, why are you here on Kariad? And why did you foolishly take no precautions to conceal your planet of origin when you must have been aware that traffic between Jorus and Kariad is currently prohibited? No, it doesn't stand up. What's your game?"

"I sell spaceships," Navarre said blandly.

"Another lie. No Nolliwar Strumo is listed in the most recent munitions directory published on Jorus."

Navarre smiled. "You've been very clever, both of you. And busy."

"Thank you. The identity of Nolliwar Strumo is obviously false. Will you tell us who you are?"

"No."

"Very well, then. Place your hands on the armrests of your chair, please," the fat man ordered.

"If I don't?"

"We'll place them there for you. If you want to keep all your fingers, do it yourself."

Navarre shrugged and grasped the armrests. The fat man jabbed a button on a remote-control panel in his hands, and immediately metal clamps sprang out of the Earthman's chair and pinioned him firmly.

The fat man touched another knob. A shudder of pain rippled through Navarre's body, making him wince.

"Your pain threshold is abnormally high," the fat one remarked conversationally. "Eight-one-point-three on the scale. No other Joran we've tested has run higher than sixty-six. Would you say he was a Joran, Ruiil?"

The small Kariadi shook his head. "On the basis of that, highly doubtful."

"You've had a sample, Nolliwar Strumo. That was just a test. The chair is capable of producing pain more than eighteen degrees above even your extraordinary threshold—and I can guarantee you won't enjoy it." He touched his hands lovingly to the control panel. "You understand the consequences. Now, tell us your name, stranger."

A bolt of pain shot up Navarre's left leg; it felt as if his calf muscle had been ripped from his living leg. He waited until some of the pain had receded, and forced a smile.

"I am not Nolliwar Strumo," he said. "The passport is forged."

"Ah! A fact at last! But who *are* you, then?"

Another lancing burst of pain racked him—this time, as if fleshy fingers had grasped the delicate chambers of his heart and squeezed, gently enough, but numbingly. Navarre felt torrents of sweat come dribbling down his face.

"Who I am is not for your ears," he said.

"Eh? And for whose, then?"

"Marhaill's. And the Oligocrat will roast both of you when he learns what you've done."

"We simply carry out a job," remarked the smaller man. "If you have business with Marhaill, you should have spoken up about it earlier."

"My business is secret. But I'd be of no use to him dead or mad from torture, which is why I'm letting you know this now."

The interrogators glanced at each other uncertainly. Navarre held his breath, waiting, trying to blot out the lingering after-effects of the pain. Interrogators were probably accustomed to this sort of wild bluffing, he thought.

"You are not from Jorus?"

"I'm an Earthman," Navarre said. "With my hair worn long." Cautiously he asked, "Is Helna Winstin still adviser to Lord Marhaill?"

"She is."

Navarre nodded. He had got into trouble once, by making incorrect assumptions about the status quo; from now on he was going to verify every point.

"Tell Helna Winstin that a long-haired Earthman is in the interrogation chambers, and would speak to her on urgent business. Then see if she allows your quiz game to continue any further."

The interrogators looked doubtful. "If we waste her time, stranger—"

"If you fail to call her, and somehow I survive your gentle handling," Navarre promised, "I'll see to it that your fat is stripped away layer by layer, blubbery one, and that your tiny companion is smothered in it!"

There was a moment's pause. Finally the small man, the one named Ruiil, stood up and said, "There's no harm checking. I'll call upstairs. Okay?"

"Okay."

Ruiil disappeared. He returned five minutes later, looking pale and shaken.

"Well? What's the word?"

"We're to free him," he said. "There's been some sort of mistake. The Earthman wants to see him in her chambers immediately."

With consummate punctiliousness, the two interrogators helped Navarre out of the torture chair—he was a little wobbly of footing on the left leg, which had borne the force of the chair's neural bolt—and paused a moment as he straightened up.

They led him back down the corridor, into a large and well-furnished room complete with a lavish bar. The interrogators live well down here, Navarre thought, as they drew a pale amber drink for him.

He gulped it. "Your hospitality is overwhelming. I'm impressed."

"Please don't hold this against us," the fat man said. The resonance was gone from his voice, now. He was whining. "We do our jobs. You must admit we had cause to interrogate you—and you said nothing! If you had only spoken up earlier . . ."

"I'll spare you," Navarre declared magnanimously. "Take me to Earthman Winstin, now."

They escorted him to a glide-channel furnished in clinging soft brown damask and shot upward with him toward the surface. A dull blue landcar waited there, and the fat interrogator scribbled an order on a stylopad and handed it to the waiting driver,

"Take him to the palace. The Earthman wants to see him quickly."

Navarre glanced back once and saw the tense, anxious faces of the interrogators staring at him; then he turned his head, and promptly forgot them. The day was warm, and both suns were in the sky, the red and the yellow.

Fifteen minutes later he was at the sumptuous palace of the Oligocrat, and just five minutes after that he was being shown through a widening sphincter into the private chambers of Helna Winstin, Earthman to the Court of Lord Marhaill.

She was waiting for him, a slim, wiry figure in glittering platinum-cloth and red tights, looking graceful and delicate and as resilient as neofoam webwork. Her scalp was bare, in Earthman fashion

"I was worried about you," she said.

"I ran into some snags when I landed. How was I supposed to know there was feuding going on between Jorus and Kariad? I posed as a Joran, and naturally the customs men collared me."

"I sent you a message about it," she said. "As soon as I received yours. But there are lags in subspace communication; you must have left too soon. Still, no damage has been done; you've arrived."

No damage, thought Navarre wryly, except for one throbbing leg and an uneasy ache in the area of the chest. He dropped down wearily on a richly upholstered divan and felt the faint soothing caress of the massage-cells as they went to work on his fatigued thighs and back.

"How is it on Earth?" she asked.

"Everything is fine."

Briefly, he described the status of the settlement as of the time he had left. She nodded approvingly when he was finished.

"It sounds encouraging. Do you think Antrok will win the election?"

"He's a logical choice. The boy's a natural leader. But what's this little storm brewing up between Jorus and Kariad?"

She smiled secretively. "You may remember that Admiral Melwod Finst left Kariad seven months ago on maneuvers, with three first-line ships at his command."

"And a Joran fleet of the same size departed about that time for points unknown, under the command of the excellent Admiral Hannimon Drulk."

"Exactly. Now, it became necessary in time for me to account for the whereabouts of Admiral Finst and his fleet. I could hardly reply that Admiral Finst was in reality an Earthman named Navarre, whose appointment to the Kariadi Admiralty I had obtained by coldly bamboozling my good Oligocrat Marhaill. So I took the alternate path of action and caused the maneuver of a subspace dispatch from the noted Admiral Finst saying he had been set upon in deep space by three unidentifiable starships, and was in the midst of a fierce battle."

Grinning, Navarre said, "I begin to see."

"Likewise," she went on, "I caused to be filtered into the hands of my tame Joran spy a report that Admiral Drulk's fleet had been destroyed in action somewhere in deep space. Then it was a simple matter to let Jorus accidentally find out about the similar fate that befell Admiral Finst."

"And so both Marhaill and Joroiran concluded that there had been a pitched battle between fleets of Kariad and Jorus in some distant sector of space," Navarre said. "Which led each of them to suspect that the other had some nefarious designs on him. And which kept both of them from guessing that their ships were perfectly safe, and were now serving as the main line of defense for the hated enemy Earth!"

Navarre leaned forward, suddenly serious. "So Jorus and Kariad are at the edge of war over six ships that they think were destroyed. Do you think it's a wise move to let such a war take place."

Helna said, "Of course not. But if I can keep them at the *verge* of war—if I can foment constant uneasy friction between the two systems—it'll keep their minds off Earth. Marhaill's a weak man; he'll listen to me. And he fears Jorus more than he does Earth. I knew I had to drive a wedge between him and Kausirn, and I succeeded."

"Kausirn's in charge, then?"

"Evidently. Joroiran is hardly seen in public any more. He's still alive, but completely in the power of the Lyrellan. Marhaill's aware of this."

Navarre clenched his fists angrily. He still had a mild liking for Overlord Joroiran, spineless, incompetent ruler that he was. And he disliked the Lyrellan intensely.

"Why did you came back, now?" Helna asked.

"I was afraid Kausirn might be stirring things up to send a Joran fleet to Earth. Six ships couldn't hold off the full force of the Joran navy any better than six sheep could. But if Jorus and Kariad are going to go to war with each other—"

Helna shook her head quickly, an expression of inward doubt appearing on her face. "Don't be too confident of that."

"What do you mean? I thought—"

"The public attitude is an unhealthy one. But I think Kausirn suspects that he's being hoaxed. I know he's been negotiating with Marhaill for top-level talks, face to face."

"Well? Can't you take advantage of your rank to head such talks off?"

"I don't know. I've warned Marhaill against a possible Joran assassination plot, but on this one thing he doesn't seem to listen to me. I think it's inevitable that he and Kausirn will get together and compare notes despite me. And then—"

"And then what?"

"And then Jorus and Kariad will undoubtedly sign a treaty of mutual harmony," Helna said. "And send a combined fleet out to crush Earth."

Chapter Fourteen

Two weeks later, Navarre left Kariad at night, in a small ship bearing the arms of the Oligocrat Marhaill. His pilot was a member of Marhaill's Secret Service, hand-picked by Helna herself. No one had been on hand to see him off; no one checked to see his passport, no one asked where he was going.

His flight clearance papers bore the code inscription XX-1413, signed by Marhaill, countersigned by Helna. That was enough to get him past any bureaucrat on Kariad; the translation of the double-X was, *Special Secret Ambassador for the Oligocrat, do not interfere.*

Navarre chuckled every time he had occasion to glance at his image in the ship's mirror, during the brief journey between the worlds. He could hardly recognize himself, after the job Helna had done.

His youthful crop of brown hair had been shaven once again; to his bald scalp had been affixed a wig of glossy black Kariadi-type hair, thick-stranded and oily. His normally high cheekbones had been lowered by an overlay of molding plastic; his eyebrows had been thickened, his lips built up into fleshiness and his jaw-contour altered, his ears drawn back and up by a simple and easily repairable bit of surgery.

He weighed twenty pounds more than he had the week before. His skin-color was bright blue.

He was Loggon Domell, Ambassador from the Court of the Oligocrat Marhaill to the Court of Joroiran VII, and only a skilled morphologist could have detected the fact that behind the outer layer that called itself Loggon Domell was one Hallam Navarre, Earthman.

This was the second time he had masqueraded as a Kariadi, but Helna and her technicians had done an infinitely more painstaking job than he had, earlier, when he had passed himself off as Melwod Finst. "Finst" had simply looked like Navarre with his skin died blue and his scalp wigged; Domell was an entirely different person.

It had all been remarkably simple. Helna had persuaded Marhaill that it would be well to send an ambassador to Jorus to discuss the galactic situation with Joroiran and with Kausirn; Marhaill, busy with his *drak*-hunting and his mistresses, had agreed, and asked Helna to suggest a man capable of handling the job.

"I have just the man," she had said. "One Loggon Domell, of this city. A wise and prudent man who will serve Your Majesty well."

Marhaill had nodded in agreement. "You always are so helpful, Helna. Send this Domell to Jorus!"

The little ship landed in midday at the Jorus City spaceport. By prior arrangement, a government car was there to meet him at the edge of the landing apron. A high-ranking Joran named Dilbar Loodig had been chosen as the official greeter.

Navarre knew this Loodig; a hanger-on at court, a man with a high hereditary title and little else to commend him. Loodig's boast was that he knew everyone at court by the slope of their shoulders and the angle at which they held their necks; Navarre wondered whether Loodig's ability would stand him in good stead now. It would cost the courtier his life if unhappily he were to recognize Navarre.

But Loodig gave no outward sign of recognition, and the Earthman knew he was not clever enough to have masked his true feelings had he detected Navarre behind the person of "Domell." Navarre presented his papers to the courtier; Loodig riffled through them, smiled ingratiatingly, and said, "Welcome to Jorus. Is this your first visit to our planet?"

"Hardly," Navarre replied smoothly. "In the old days before the present difficulties I spent many happy holidays here. I once had a summer cottage in the highlands of Veisk, overlooking the river." The microscopic distorter in his throat did curious things to the sound of his voice, making it lighter in texture, supplying a deep gravelly rasp as well. He spoke in pure Joran, but with a slight lilting inflection and a distinctly alien shift of the full vowel values.

"Indeed?" Loodig said, as they entered the car. "The highland country is some of our most beautiful. You must have enjoyed your stay there."

"I did," Navarre said gravely, and repressed a snicker. The car threaded its way rapidly through the city, onward to the palace. He noticed an escort evidently following; they were taking good care of the alleged Kariadi ambassador, it seemed.

At the palace, Navarre was ushered speedily through the outer rooms.

"Will I be able to see the Overlord shortly?" he asked.

"I've notified him that you're here," Loodig said. "The Overlord is not a well man, these days. He may not be able to see you immediately."

"Oh. How sad!"

"He's been in poor health quite some length of time now," said the courtier. "We here are all extremely worried about him."

I'll bet you are, Navarre thought. *If something should happen to Joroiran, Kausirn would jump at the chance to name himself regent for the heir apparent. The boy is only eight, now.*

Loodig excused himself, disappeared for a moment, and returned shortly after, smiling.

"The Overlord will see you, I'm happy to report. Please come this way."

Loodig led him down the narrow winding passages toward the smaller throne room Joroiran customarily used for private audiences. It was not nearly as magnificent a hall as the main throne room, of course, but it did serve amply well to awe visitors. Periscopic viewers allowed Security men to observe the course of the Overlord's audiences and protect him from harm.

They reached the door. Loodig knelt, making ceremonial gestures, while Navarre remained erect as befitted his rank as ambassador.

"His Excellency, Loggon Domell, Ambassador Plenipotentiary from Kariad," Loodig announced.

"Let him enter," Joroiran responded, in a pale, almost timid voice.

Navarre entered.

The Overlord was plainly showing the effects of his virtual captivity. A small, ineffectual man to begin with, he had hardly bothered to take the steps he once took to cover his deficiencies; instead of the magnificent framework-robe that provided him with his regal public stature, he wore only an embroidered cloth robe that added little to his appearance. He had looked poorly the last time Navarre had seen him, nearly a year before; now, if anything, he looked worse.

Navarre made the ambassadorial bow, unfolded the charter of credentials Marhaill had given him, and offered them to Joroiran. The Overlord scanned them briefly and put them aside. Navarre heard the door slide gently closed behind him, leaving him alone with Joroiran.

There was no indication that the Overlord recognized him; instead, Joroiran fixed his gentle, washed-out eyes on a point somewhere above Navarre's left shoulder and said, "It pleases me that I can speak with someone from Kariad. This present friction has long distressed me."

"No more so than it has troubled the sleep of Marhaill," Navarre said. "It seems that groundless enmity has sprung up between our worlds. I hope my visit will aid in restoring harmony."

Joroiran smiled feebly. "Yes. Indeed." He seemed to be at a loss for his next words. Finally he burst out, "My adviser—Kausirn—he should be here, now. We really should wait for him. He's made a much closer study of the situation than I have."

It was pathetic, Navarre thought. Kausirn had so puppetized the Overlord that Joroiran seemed totally incapable of conducting the business of the realm without the Lyrellan. But it was just as well. Navarre knew it was necessary to have Kausirn on hand when he made his play.

"The Lord Adviser is a man I've heard much about," Navarre remarked. "He seems to be a gifted administrator. He must take much of the burden of government from Your Majesty's weary shoulders."

Joroiran seemed to flinch at the telling thrust. He nodded tiredly. "Yes, he is a great help to me. A ruler has so much to think about—and Kausirn is indispensable to me."

"I've often heard Lord Marhaill say the same about his adviser—an Earthman. He finds her an absolute necessity in the operation of the government."

"*I* had an Earthman adviser once," said Joroiran distantly. "I thought he was loyal and trustworthy, but he betrayed me. I sent him on a mission . . . but he failed me. His name was Navarre."

"I often dealt with him when he served Your Majesty," Navarre said. "He seemed to me to be utterly loyal to Jorus. This comes as a great surprise to me."

"It was a blow to me, too. But luckily, when Navarre left me I had one such as Kausirn to take his place. Ah, he comes now!"

The door opened. Kausirn entered, smiling coldly. The deathly pallor that stamped his race lent contrast to the richness of his robes. Indeed, he was more finely dressed than Joroiran himself; the Lyrellan bore himself confidently, as if he and not the other sat on the throne.

"Your pardon, Majesty. I was unavoidably detained." Kausirn turned to Navarre and said, "You are Marhaill's ambassador? I give you welcome. I am Kausirn, Adviser to the Overlord."

"Greetings, Kausirn."

The Lyrellan's twenty fingers curled and uncurled tensely; his eyes seemed to be boring through the layers of plastic that masked Navarre, to expose the Earthman who skulked beneath.

"Let us go to the Council room," Kausirn suggested. "There we three may talk."

It took them perhaps ten minutes of uneasy verbal fencing in the small, well-lit room before they actually came to grips with the subject at hand. For first they were obliged to exchange pleasantries in true diplomatic fashion, approaching the topic circuitously, leading up to it in gradual and gentle manner.

Navarre let the Lyrellan control the flow of discussion; he had learned never to underestimate Kausirn, and he feared he might give himself away if he ventured to steer the conversation in some direction that might appear characteristic of Hallam Navarre.

He toyed with the drink-flask at his right hand, parried Kausirn skillfully, replied with grace to the inane questions of Joroiran. Neither of them seemed to suspect his true identity.

At length the Lyrellan leaned forward, spreading his ten-fingered hands wide on the burnished cupralloy meeting-table. With the tiny flicker of his eyelids that told Navarre he was choosing his words with particular care, Kausirn said, "Of course, the chief item of curiosity is the encounter that presumably took place between three Joran ships and three of Kariad, some eight months ago. Until the vaguer aspects of this matter are satisfactorily resolved, I hardly see how we can discuss any reaffirmation of ties between Jorus and Kariad."

"Of course," added Joroiran.

Navarre frowned thoughtfully. "You imply, then, that your three ships and three ships of Kariad fought a battle in space?"

Kausirn quickly shook his head. "I draw no such implications! But there *are* persistent rumors."

"May I ask just where the three Joran ships were supposedly stationed at the time of their alleged destruction, Lord Adviser?"

The Lyrellan nibbled a thin lip. "This infringes on highly secret information, Ambassador Domell."

Navarre rose swiftly from his seat, saying, "In that case, Adviser Kausirn, I fear we haven't much else to talk about today. If on this essential matter secrecy is to be maintained between our worlds, I hardly see how we can come to agree on any other major topics of current dispute. Of course—"

Smoothly, Kausirn said, "Again you seem to have drawn an unwarranted implication, Ambassador Domell. True, these matters are highly secret, but when did I say I would withhold knowledge of them from you? On the contrary: I summoned an ambassador from Kariad for the very purpose of revealing them."

He's falling into the trap, Navarre thought joyfully. He took his seat once again and glanced expectantly at the Lyrellan.

Kausirn said, "To begin with, there was a traitorous Earthman in this court once, a man called Hallam Navarre. This Navarre has been absent from this court for several years. He's a dangerous man, Milord, and a clever one. And he has rediscovered Earth!"

Navarre's eyes widened in mock astonishment. "No!"

"Unfortunately, yes. He has found Earth and established a belligerent settlement there. His intention is to conquer the galaxy—beginning with Jorus and Kariad!"

"And why, then, were we not informed of this?"

"Patience, good sir. When we of Jorus learned of this, we immediately dispatched a punitive mission to Earth—three ships, under the command of our Admiral Drulk. A preventive measure, you might say. We intended to wipe out the Terran settlement before they could make their attack on our systems."

"A wise move."

"But," said Kausirn, "our ships vanished. So far as we know, they reached the region of Earth, but that's the last we know of them."

"No dispatches whatsoever from them?"

"None."

"Strange," Navarre mused.

"Now," Kausirn went on, "we learn that the Grand Fleet of Kariad suffered an oddly similar loss—three ships vanished without trace while on maneuvers."

"And how was this fact learned?" Navarre asked, a trifle coldly.

Kausirn shrugged apologetically. "Let us cast diplomacy aside, shall we? I'll tell you quite frankly: our spy network brought us the word."

"I appreciate frankness," Navarre said.

"Very well, then. Jorus sends three ships out to destroy Earth; the same month, Kariad sends three ships out on maneuvers to points unknown. By some coincidence none of these ships is ever heard from again. The natural conclusion is that there was a battle between them, and all six ships were destroyed. Now, Milord, Jorus has no hostile intent against Kariad. Our fleet was on its way to Earth when the incident occurred. I can only conclude that, for reasons beyond us, Kariad has committed an unprovoked act of war against Jorus."

"Your logic is impeccable," Navarre said, looking at Joroiran, who had been following the interchange like a bemused spectator at a kinetics match. "But faulty, nonetheless. Why should Kariad attack Jorus?"

"Exactly the question that troubles us. Now, the rumor is rife that such an attack was made on our ships by Kariad. To be frank, again—our spy network can find no possible motive for the attack. We have no reason to suspect Kariad." Kausirn paused and drew a deep breath. "Let me present my *real* conclusion, now. The Joran ships were not destroyed by your fleet. Instead, *both* fleets were destroyed by Earth! The Earthmen have concealed strengths; we sent a ridiculously small contingent and it met destruction. Perhaps your fleet on maneuvers blundered accidentally into Terran territory and was destroyed as well."

Navarre said nothing, but stared with deep interest at the Lyrellan.

Kausirn continued, "I prefer this theory to the other, less tenable one of unprovoked assault on our fleet by yours. Therefore, I wish to propose that we end quickly the animosity developing between our worlds—an animosity engendered by baseless rumor—and join instead in an alliance against Earth, which obviously is stronger than we suspected."

Navarre smiled blandly. "It is an interesting suggestion."

"You agree, then?"

"I believe not."

"*What?*"

"Such an alliance," Navarre said, "would involve the necessity of our denying that our fleet had attacked yours. This, we are not in a position to do."

Kausirn looked genuinely startled. "You *admit* the attack, then? It was Kariad and not Earth who destroyed our ships?"

Smiling, Navarre said, "Now you draw the unwarranted implications. We neither affirm nor deny that our fleet and yours had an armed conflict provoked by us."

"Your silence on the subject amounts to an admission of guilt," Kausirn said stonily.

"This does not concern me. I act under instructions from Oligocrat Marhaill. I am not empowered to enter into any sort of alliance with Jorus."

For the second time, he rose from the table. "We seem to have reached an impasse. You boast of your spy system, Adviser Kausirn; let it discover our motives, if it can. I feel that I would not accomplish anything further by remaining on Jorus. Would you see that I am conveyed to the spaceport?"

Kausirn was glaring at him in glassy-eyed bewilderment. It was the first time Navarre had ever seen the Lyrellan truly off balance. And small wonder, he thought: Kausirn had hardly been expecting the Kariadi ambassador to reject the chance of an alliance in favor of what amounted to a declaration of war by implication.

"We offer you alliance against Earth," Kausirn said. "Earth, who may be the deadliest enemy your planet or mine will ever have. And you refuse? You prefer to let the cloud of war hover over Jorus and Kariad?"

Navarre shrugged. "We have no choice. Good day, Your Majesty. Adviser Kausirn, will you arrange transportation for me?"

With sudden shock he realized he had spoken the last words in his natural voice, not the false one of Loggon Domell. The throat-distorter had failed!

He froze for an instant, seeing the surprise on Kausirn's face give way to abrupt recognition.

"That voice," the Lyrellan said. "I know that voice. You're Navarre!"

He fumbled at his belt for a weapon, but the Earthman had already dashed through the opening doors of the Council room and was racing down the long corridor that led to an exit from the palace.

Chapter Fifteen

It had almost worked, he thought bleakly, as he sped down the corridor. If only the distorter hadn't conked out, he could have passed himself off as the Kariadi ambassador and prevented any alliance from forming between Jorus and Kariad by the puzzling, noncommital character of his responses. Well, he thought resignedly, it had been a good idea, anyway

The *splat* of an energy-gun brought down mortar over his head. He heard Kausirn's angry voice shouting, "Catch that man! He's a spy! A traitor!"

Navarre whirled round a corner and came face-to-face with a surprised Daborian guard. The huge being took a moment to consider the phenomenon that had materialized before him, and that moment was too long. Navarre jabbed a fist into his stomach, kicked him as he fell, and kept running. The skirt of his ambassadorial garb was hindering him, but he made a good pace anyway. And he knew his way around the palace.

He crossed the narrow passageway that led to the kitchen quarters, spiraled down a helical staircase, jumped across a low railing, and found himself outside the palace. Behind him came the sound of confused yelling; there would be a fine manhunt under way any minute.

The car was waiting, though. He forced himself to adopt a calm pace and walked toward it.

"Back to the spaceport," he ordered. Turbos thrummed and the car glided rapidly into the streets.

The trip to the spaceport seemed to last forever; Navarre fretted impatiently as they passed through crowded streets in the center of Jorus City, finally emerging on the highway that led to the port. Once at the spaceport, he thanked the driver, got out, flashed his credentials, and hastily made his way to the waiting Kariadi spaceship.

For the first time since the beginning of his flight, he paused for breath. He was safe, now Kausirn would never dare to fire publicly on a vessel bearing the royal arms of Kariad.

Once the ship was in space he called Helna via subradio and signaled for her to scramble. After a moment the transmitter emitted the bleeping sound-pattern that told him the scrambler was on.

"Well?" she asked. "How'd it go?"

"Fine—right up until the end I had everything wrapped up until the distorter went dead and Kausirn recognized me by my voice."

"Oh!"

"I was on my way out by then. Kausirn woke up too late. I'm in space and not being pursued, as far as I can tell. He can't very well attack me now."

"But the mission's a failure, then?"

"I'm not so sure of that," Navarre said. "I had him fooled into thinking Kariad *had* actually destroyed those ships, and not Earth. Now, of course, he knows it was all a hoax. There'll probably be an alliance between Jorus and Kariad after all, once Kausirn contacts Marhaill and lets him know the real identity of his ambassador "

"Will he do that?"

"I don't doubt it. Kausirn's deathly afraid of Earth. He doesn't want to tackle the job of destroying the settlement himself; he wants to rope Kariad in, just in case Earth turns out to be too much for Jorus' fleet alone. So naturally he'll do his best to avoid a war with Kariad. He'll get in touch with Marhaill. You'd better not be on Kariad when that happens."

There was silence for a moment. Then Helna said, "You're right. It isn't going to be easy to explain to Marhaill just how I accidentally happened to send a disguised Earthman out as his special ambassador to Jorus. We'd better go to Earth."

"Not me, Helna. You."

"And where will you go?"

"I've got a new idea," Navarre told her. "One that can make use of the fact that Jorus and Kariad are going to ally. Tell me, can you think of a *third* world that's likely to be scared by such an alliance?"

"Morank, of course!"

"Right. So I go to Morank and offer the Polisarch some advance information on the coming alliance. If I handle it right this time, the Moranki ought to fall right in line. Meantime you go to Earth and explain the shape of things to Antrok. I'll keep you posted on what happens to me."

"Good luck," she said simply.

He forced an uneasy laugh. "It'll take more than luck. We're sitting ducks if Kausirn ever launches the Grand Fleet against our six ships."

Navarre broke the contact and turned away from the myriad dials and vernier controls of the subradio set. Behind him was a mirror, and he stared at his false Kariadi face.

That would have to be changed. From now on, he would sail under his own colors; there was nothing to be gained by further masquerade.

He moved down the companionway to the washroom of the little ship, nudged the control pod that widened the sphincter, and stepped in, sealing the room behind him. A bottle of neohexathyl was in the drug cabinet; he broke the seal, poured a handful of the cool green liquid over his face and shoulders, and stepped under the radiating field of the Vibron.

He felt the plastic layers covering his face sag; with a quick twisting gesture he ripped them away—and his own features, strangely pale, appeared. He had grown accustomed to the face of Loggon Domell; seeing Hallam Navarre burst forth suddenly was startling.

A second treatment with the dissolving fluid and the Kariadi wig came off—painfully, for his own hair had grown somewhat underneath it. He stripped and rubbed neohexathyl over his body, seeing the blue stain loosen and come away under the molecular flow of the Vibron. Within minutes, all that remained of Loggon Domell, Kariadi Ambassador, was a messy heap of blue-stained plastic lying on the washroom floor.

Navarre cleaned himself, depilated his scalp, and dressed again. He grinned at himself in the mirror, and scooping up the lumps of plastic, dumped them cheerfully in the disposal unit.

So much for Ambassador Domell, he thought. He drew the blaster at his hip, squinted into the charge-chamber for an instant to assure himself that the weapon was functioning. The tiny yellow indicator light within was glowing steadily and evenly.

He reholstered the weapon and left the washroom, feeling clean and fresh now that he was able to wear his own identity again.

Up ahead, the ship's pilot was lounging in his cabin; the ship was on hyper-drive, now, and no human hand could serve any purpose in guiding it. The silent ultronic generators would bring the ship unerringly through the noth-ingness of hyperspace; the pilot's job was strictly that of emergency stand-by, once the ship had entered warp.

Navarre returned to his own cabin, switched off the visual projector on his communicator, and buzzed the pilot. There was a pause; then the screen lit, and Navarre saw the man, dressed in off-duty fatigues, trying to conceal a look of sour impatience.

"Yes, Ambassador?"

"Pilot, are you busy just now? I'd like you to come to my cabin for a moment if you're not."

The pilot's square-cut blue face showed a trace of annoyance, but he said evenly, "Of course, Ambassador. I'll be right there. Is anything wrong."

"Not exactly," Navarre said.

Navarre waited. A moment later the annunciator-light atop his door flashed briefly. The Earthman depressed the enameled door-control and the door pivoted inward and away. The pilot stood there, arms folded, just outside in the corridor.

"You called me, Ambassador? I—*who are you?*"

Navarre's hand tightened on the butt of his blaster. "Hallam Navarre is my name."

"You're—you're an Earthman," the pilot muttered, backing away. "What happened to the Ambassador? How did you get aboard the ship? And what are you going to do?"

"Much too many questions for one man to answer at once," Navarre returned lightly. "The Ambassador, I regret to inform you, is dead. And I fear I'll need the use of your ship."

The Kariadi was wobbly-legged with fear. He half-fell into Navarre's cabin, but the Earthman, suspecting a trick, moved forward swiftly, caught the man by the throat, and propped him up against the left-hand bulkhead.

Through a constricted throat, the man asked, "What are you going to do to me?"

"Put you to sleep and drop you overboard in one of the escape capsules," Navarre told him. "And then I'll pursue a journey of my own."

He drew a dark violet ampoule of perredrin from his jacket pocket and flicked the safety off the spray-point with his thumb. Quickly he touched the tip of the ampoule to the man's arm and squeezed; the subsonic spray forced ten cubic centimeters of narcotic liquid into the pilot's blood stream instantly.

He turned gray-faced and crumpled forward within the space of three heartbeats; Navarre caught him and slung him over one shoulder. The pilot's mouth hung slackly open, and his chest rose and fell in a steady, slow rhythm, one breath-intake every fifteen seconds.

The escape-capsules—there were two of them aboard the ship—were situated aft, just above the drive compartment, in a womb-like alcove of their own. They were miniature spaceships, eleven feet long, equipped with their own precision-made drive unit. Navarre stuffed the slumbering Kariadi in head-first, making sure he was caught securely in the foam webwork that guarded against landing shock, and peered at the navigating dial.

For the convenience of laymen who might need to use the escape-capsules in a hurry, and who had no notion of how to astrogate, the engineers of Kariad had developed a shortcut; a number of possible orbits were preplotted, and the computer was equipped to select the most effective one and fit it to whatever destination the escaping passenger chose.

Navarre tapped out *K-A-R-I-A-D* on the dial, and the computer unit signaled acknowledgment and began clicking out the instructions for the drive. Navarre stepped back, slammed shut the automatically-locking hood of the capsule, and yanked down on the release lever.

The capsule quivered momentarily in its moorings; then the ship's cybernetic governor responded to the impulse and cut off the magnetic-field that held the capsule in place. Slowly, it glided down the passageway toward the outer skin of the ship. Photonic relays opened an airlock for it as it approached; Navarre watched the capsule with its sleeping voyager vanish through the lock and out of the ship, bound on an orbit of its own.

Some days later, the slumbering, pilot would be awakened by a gentle bump. He would discover he had made a perfect landing somewhere on Kariad.

Navarre turned away and made his course frontward to the ship's control center. Altering the ship's course was not so simple as merely punching out a destination on an escape-capsule's computer.

He dropped into what had been the pilot's chair, and, lifting stylus and slide rule, addressed himself to the considerable task of determining the quickest and most efficient orbit to the planet of Morank.

Morank was the fourth world of a red super-giant sun located eight light-years from Kariad, ten light-years from Jorus. Morank itself was a large and well-populated world, a busy commercial center, and, in the old days of the Starkings' League, Morank had fought a bitter three-cornered struggle with Jorus and Kariad for trade rights in their cluster.

That had been more than five hundred years before. The Starkings' League had endured ten thousand years, but it was dying, and its aggressive component worlds were beginning to thrust up their own noisy claims for independence. Morank, Jorus, and Kariad—the three most powerful worlds of their cluster, the richest, the best-situated—were foremost in the fast-rising revolt against the powerless Starkings.

Still nominally federated into the League, the three worlds jockeyed for position like so many racing animals readying themselves for a break from the post. After two hundred years, the long-overdue break finally came; Joroiran I and his bold Earthman cohort, Voight Navarre, rebelled from the dying League and declared the eternal independence of the Jorus system. Morank had come right after, and then Kariad.

Three hundred years—but for the last hundred of that time, an uneasy friendship had existed among the three powerful planets, each watching the other two warily, none making any too-overt motions toward extending its sphere of control.

Navarre smiled. An alliance between Jorus and Kariad was sure to open some eyes on Morank.

His little ship blinked back into space within landing distance of the planet. In the sky the vast bulk of Morank's feeble red sun, Draximoor, spread like an untidy octopus, tendrils of flame extending thread-like in all directions.

Navarre fed the landing coordinates into the computer. The ship plunged planetward.

And this is Earth's last chance, he thought. If Morank allows itself to be pushed in the right direction, we may yet survive. If not, there'll be no withstanding the combined fleets of Jorus and Kariad.

A landing field loomed below. The ship radio sputtered and came to life; a voice spoke, in crisp syllables of the local *lingua spacia*.

"This is Central Traffic Control speaking from the city of Ogyglan. If you intend to effect a landing on Moranki territory, please respond."

Navarre flashed the answering signal. A moment later there came the okay, and with it was relayed a set of field coordinates, supplementing those he had, already computed. He acknowledged, punched the new figures into his tape, and sat back, tensely, awaiting the landing.

Chapter Sixteen

The Grand Spaceport at Ogyglan was a dazzling sight: to offset the dimness of the vast, pale red sun, batteries of photo-flood illumino-screens had been ranked along the areaway that led from the space-port buildings to the land field itself. To Navarre it seemed as if the entire planet was glowing, but it was a muted radiance that brightened without interfering with vision.

Three burly chisel-faced Morankimar waited for him as he clambered down the catwalk of his spaceship and strode across the field.

The Morankimar were humanoid aliens, cut to the general biological pattern of the humanoid type, but approximating it not quite so closely as did the Jorans and the Kariadi. They were heavy-set creatures, nearly as broad as they were wide, with dish-like oval eyes set lemur-like in independent orbital sockets, rotating with utter disregard for each other. Their skins were coarse-grained and pebbly, a dark muddy yellow in color and unpleasant of texture. Fleshy protuberances dangled beard-fashion from their extremely sharp chins. They were sturdy, durable, long-lived creatures, quick-witted and strong.

As Navarre approached them he observed much anguished rotating of eyes. Finally, the foremost of the aliens, a bleak-visaged oldster whose skin had long since faded to a pale chartreuse, rumbled in *lingua spacia*, "Your ship bears the royal arms of Kariad. Are you perhaps the Oligocrat's Earthman?"

"Hardly," Navarre replied, in Joran. He understood the Morankimar tongue, but it was a jawbreaking agglutinating language for which he held little fondness; only a lifelong speaker of it could hope to handle its maddening irregularities with success.

"I'm Hallam Navarre, formerly Earthman to the Court of Overlord Joroiran of Jorus. I've come to Morank bearing an important message for the Polisarch."

"A message from Joroiran?" asked the alien, in a thickly accented version of Joran.

"No," said Navarre. "A message *about* Joroiran. And about Oligocrat Marhaill. I think the Polisarch would be interested in what I have to say."

"We will take you to him."

A car was summoned; they left the spaceport and drove at a steady unflagging clip through the enormous metropolis of Ogyglan, toward the local residence of the Polisarch of Morank.

At length they came to a building that seemed to have no foundation; it drifted ten feet above the ground, terminating in a smooth glassy undersurface, mirror-bright, jet-black. The building itself was a square untapering tower, a solid block of masonry.

"This is the residence of the Polisarch," Navarre was told.

The Earthman looked upward at the shining rectangle that hovered before him. Sleek, handsome, its sides icy blue and gleaming, it was a handsome sight.

He frowned. "What holds it up?"

"A hundred million cubic feet of graviton repulsors. The Polisarch must never touch Morankimar soil—nor may his residence."

Navarre nodded. It was a fact he had forgotten.

A drawbridge descended from the lip of the building and they rose, the bridge rising behind them and tucking itself invisibly into place.

Navarre found himself in a wide, cream-colored marble anteroom. The shining floor was a solid slab of milky obsidian.

Two Morankimar clad in violet robes appeared from a concealed alcove and requested Navarre's blaster. Without protest he handed it over, and also, upon request, the slim curved blade beneath his vest. The palace guards evidently had monitored him by fluoroscreen.

Finally he was ushered into a vestibule that opened on an extensive drape-hung hall.

Navarre felt a curious tremor of anticipation as he crossed the threshold of the Grand Throne Room—not only because the fate of Earth hung on the skill of his powers of persuasion at this interview, but because the Morankimar Polisarch was one of the legendary figures of the galaxy and of the universe.

Rel Dominoor was his name, and he had held sway a hundred and eight years, having taken the Morankimar throne while Joroiran IV reigned in Jorus. During his years on Jorus, Navarre had learned to his sorrow the strength of this man Dominoor; nearly every attempt of his to plant a network of spies on Morank had been frustrated, and in the end he had simply abandoned hope of monitoring Morankimar activities the way he did those of Kariad and other worlds of the cluster. Old Dominoor was entirely too shrewd.

Navarre bowed deeply at the entrance to the throne room; a dry deep voice said, "You may rise," and the Earthman rose, looking about in some surprise for the Polisarch.

He found him, finally—eight feet above his head, a withered little figure clad in glistening querlon sheaths, sitting cross-legged on nothing in the air. The floor of the throne room, Navarre realized in astonishment, must be one gigantic graviton-repulsor plate, and the Polisarch's clothes equipped with the necessary resistile coils.

Navarre took three hesitant steps inward and the Polisarch drifted downward until his crossed feet were but three feet off the ground and his eyes level with Navarre's. "You're Navarre, Joroiran's man?" he said.

"I *was* Joroiran's man. It's two years since I left the Overlord's service."

One of the Polisarch's eyes swiveled disconcertingly upward. "You Earthmen exchange loyalties as other men exchange greetings. Have you come now to sell your services to me, Navarre? I stand in little need of new advisers at this late date . . . though I'm always willing to receive information."

The Polisarch's jewel-studded hand swept idly across his chest, gently touching a control stud; he began to rise, moving upward some eight feet. Navarre craned his neck, squinted up at the ruler, and said, "I bring you information, but there's a price for it."

Dominoor scowled expressively. "Earthmen haggle well. Let's hear the price, first; the information may come after, if I care to have it."

"Very well. The price is a fleet of Morankimar battleships—twelve of them, first-class, fully armed and manned, to be placed entirely under my command with no restrictions whatever as to their use."

Abruptly the Polisarch touched his controls again and dropped rapidly until he was Navarre's level. His expression was grave, almost fierce.

"I had heard Earthmen were bold, but boldness carried too far becomes insolence." There was no anger in his voice, merely a sort of didactic peevishness. "You'll sell your information for a mere twelve battleships, eh? I could flay you and get it for a less dear outlay."

Navarre met his gaze unflinchingly. "You *could* flay me, agreed. But then you'd be faced with solving the problem yourself. I offer a speedy and simple resolution. Your own spies will tell you what I have to tell you, soon enough—but that will hardly handle the situation adequately."

Dominoor smiled slowly. "I could like you, Earthman. Twelve battleships? All right. The terms are met. Now tell me what you came here to tell me, and see if you can save your skin from the hand of the flayer."

"Very well. Briefly, it's this: Jorus and Kariad plan to form an alliance. The balance of power in this cluster will be upset."

The Polisarch's pale, almost white skin began to deepen in color, passing through several subtle gradations of chartreuse and becoming finally an angry lemon-color that faded rapidly as the flood-tide of excitement receded.

Navarre waited patiently; he saw that his words had made their intended effect. Victory was almost in his grasp now.

Finally Dominoor said, "Do you have proof?"

"My word as an Earthman is all I can offer."

"Hmm. Let that matter pass, then. Tell me, why is this alliance coming about?"

Navarre took a deep breath. It was useless to lie to the old Polisarch; he was too wise, too keen-witted, to be easily fooled. Choosing his words with care,

Navarre said, "There is a settlement on Earth. Ten thousand Earthmen live there."

"I know."

Navarre smiled. "Morank has its spies too, then."

"We have sharp ears here," said the Polisarch gravely. "But continue."

"These ten thousand of Earth desire nothing but peaceful existence. But Kausirn the Lyrellan, the Overlord Joroiran's adviser, fears them. He thinks Earth is much stronger than it actually is. He is afraid to send a Joran fleet against Earth unaided. Hence his pact with Marhaill; together Jorus and Kariad will dispatch fleets to crush ten thousand unarmed Earthmen."

"I see the picture. Mutual deception, leading to an alliance of cowards. But go on."

"Naturally, Earth will be destroyed by the fleet—but the link between Jorus and Kariad will have been forged. This Kausirn is unscrupulous. And Marhaill is a weak man. Before too many months have passed, you'll see Jorus and Kariad under one rule."

"This would violate a treaty even older than I," Dominoor mused. "The three worlds are to remain separate and unallied, perpetually outstretched at the vertices of a triangle. This to ensure safety in our galaxy. An alliance of this sort would collapse the triangle. It would break the treaty."

"Treaties are scraps of paper, my Lord."

"So they are. But important scraps. We would have to go to war to protect our rights. It would be painful and costly for all of us. Our cities might be destroyed."

"War, between Morank and the allied worlds could be avoided," Navarre said.

"By giving you twelve of our ships?"

"Yes. My plan is this: your ships shall be unmarked, unidentified in every way. No one will know they originate on Morank. I'll undertake to repel the Jorus-Kariad fleet that is converging on Earth; driving them off in such a way that they think Earth is incalculably powerful. With luck, it'll smash the Jorus-Kariad axis. It'll incidentally save Earth. But also Morank will be untouched by war."

The Polisarch was smiling again.

"At worst, it would cost me twelve ships. Such a loss I could bear, if necessary. At best, I avoid a war in this cluster."

"You agree to the terms, then?"

"The twelve ships are yours. Take them, Navarre, and use them well. Keep Jorus and Kariad apart. Keep war from touching Morank. Save your Earthmen from destruction. And perhaps, thank an old man who has become a coward."

Navarre flushed. "Sire—"

"Don't try to contradict me. You see me humbled before you, Earthman. I give you the ships; play your little ruse. I want only to die in peace. Let those who follow after worry about checking the rising tide that will eventually pour forth from Earth. I worry only about today; at my age, tomorrow is too distant."

There was nothing Navarre could say. He had achieved his goal; at least, in doing it, he had not deceived old Dominoor.

Chapter Seventeen

There were fifty ships in the armada: fifty great golden-hulled vessels, sleek and powerful, advancing at a steady pace across the galaxies.

The flagship was a mighty gleaming ship that led the pack, a shark among sharks, a giant battleship of the realm of Jorus. The armada radiated confidence. They seemed to be saying, *Here we are, twenty-five ships of Jorus and twenty-five of Kariad, crossing the universe to wipe out once and for all the pestilence of the Earthmen.*

Hallam Navarre sat in his own flagship, a vessel that once had borne the name *Pride of Kariad*, but now carried no designation whatever. He watched the steady advance of the alien armada.

Fifty ships, he thought. Against eighteen.

But we know how many they have. They can't measure our numbers.

He sat poised behind his viewscreens, biding his time, thinking, waiting. They were fifty thousand light-years from Earth, now, and he had no intention of letting Kausirn's fleet come any closer than five thousand. If even one ship eluded the inner line of defense and got through to Earth . . .

Helna appeared and slipped into the seat next to his. She said, "It'll all be decided now, won't it? All the thousands of years of planning, ever since the Chalice was sealed and the sleepers put to rest."

Navarre nodded tightly. Thousands of years of planning, all dependent upon this one day, on these eighteen ships, ultimately on the mind of one man. He stared at his unquivering hands. He was steady, now; so much was at stake that his mind failed to encompass it, and apprehension was impossible.

He jacked in the main communication line and studied the deployment of his eighteen ships.

Four of them remained in close orbit around Earth, in constant radio contact with each other, ready to move rapidly when needed. He hoped they would *not* be needed; they were the last line of defense, the desperation blockaders, and it would be dark indeed if they had to be called into play.

The smaller colony on Procyon had two ships guarding it. Six more were deployed at the farthest edges of the sphere of conflict, forming a border for the coming battle. That was his second line of defense.

The remaining six ships formed a solid phalanx ten light-years across, turned outward toward the advancing combined armada. Navarre's flagship was among this group. These would make the initial attack.

The twelve ships given him by the Polisarch had been carefully recoated; their hulls no longer glowed in bright Morankimar colors, but now were an anonymous gray, all planetary designations concealed. Each of the ships had a small complement of Earthmen aboard, aiding the Morankimar captain. The aliens knew only that they were to take orders from the Earthmen; the Polisarch had made that amply clear in his instructions to the Grand Admiral.

It might work, Navarre thought. If not, well, it had been a game try—and perhaps there might be another Chalice on some other world. Earth was not that easily defeated, he told himself.

Time was drawing near. All the efforts, all the countless schemes, all Navarre's many identities and many journeys, all converged into one moment now.

He opened the all-fleet communicator and waited a moment until all the twenty-two bulbs at the side of the central monitor-board lit up.

Then, in a quiet voice, he said, "Attention, Unit A—low-intensity defense screens are to be replaced with full screens immediately.

"Unit B—stand by until called into action as previously instructed.

"Unit C—remain at your posts in orbit round the planets, and under no circumstances leave formation.

"Unit D—stand by for emergency use.

"The battle is about to begin."

There was a moment of silence. Quickly, Navarre reached up to shut off the all-fleet communicator; what he had to say now was directed at the armada. He signaled for a wide-beam subspace hookup.

"All right," he muttered. "Now it starts."

He drew the microphone toward him and said, in a ringing voice, "Attention invaders! Attention invaders! This is Hallam Navarre, Admiral of the Grand Fleet of Earth. Come in, invader flagship!"

He repeated the message three times in Joran and three times in Kariadi. Then he sat back, staring at the complex network of machinery that was the communicator panel, waiting for some reply.

Less than a thousand light-years separated the two fleets. The time-lag in communication should have been virtually nil. But a minute went by, and another, with no response. Navarre grew cold. Were they simply going to ignore him and move right on into their midst?

But after four minutes the speaker crackled into life.

"This is Flagship calling Admiral Navarre." The inflection was savagely sardonic. "Come in, Admiral Navarre. What do you want?"

Navarre's heart leaped. He hadn't expected *him* to be commanding the armada in person!

"Kausirn?"

"Indeed. What troubles you, Navarre?"

"You infringe on Terran domains, Kausirn. State the purpose of your invasion."

"I don't think we need to explain to you, Navarre. The Terran Empire passed out of existence thirty thousand years before; you have no claim to any domain as such. And we're here to see that no ghosts walk the starways."

"An invasion fleet?"

"Call it that, if you will."

"Very well," Navarre said sharply. "In that case I call on you to surrender or be destroyed. The full might of the Grand Fleet of Earth is waiting to hurl you back shattered to your own system."

Kausirn laughed harshly. "The full might! Six stolen ships! Six against fifty! You deceived me once, Ambassador Domell—you won't a second time!"

A moment later a bright energy flare licked out across space toward the Terran flagship. Navarre's screens easily deflected the thrust.

"I warn you, Kausirn. Your fleet is outnumbered six to one. Terra's resources are greater than you could have dreamed. Will you surrender?"

"Ridiculous!" But it seemed to Navarre there was false bravado in Kausirn's outburst; the Lyrellan appeared to be uncertain.

"We of Earth hate needless bloodshed," Navarre said. "I call upon the captains of the invading fleet to head their ships back to home. Kausirn is an alien; he hardly cares how many Joran or Kariadi lives he throws away."

"Don't listen!" came the Lyrellan's shout over the phones. "He's bluffing! He *has* to be bluffing!" It sounded a trifle panicky.

"All right," Navarre said. "Here we come."

He gave the prearranged signal, and the culminating battle that had been planned so long entered into existence. The six ships that comprised his fighting wedge moved forward, charging across hyperspace toward the evenly spaced invading fleet.

"You see!" Kausirn shouted triumphantly. "They have but six ships! We can crush them!"

Navarre's ship shook as the first heavy barrage crashed into it; the screens deflected the energy and a bright blue nimbus sprang into being around the ship as the overload was dissipated.

Six ships against fifty—but six rebuilt ships, six ships so laden with defense screens that they were no faster than snails. They moved steadily into the heart of the armada, shaking off the alien barrage and counterattacking with thrusts of their own.

They were unstoppable, those six ships—but difficult to maneuver, slow at returning fire. In time, the alien fleet could wear down their screens by continued assault, and that would end the battle.

"Six outmoded crawlers," Kausirn exulted. "And you ask us to surrender."

"The offer still goes," Navarre said curtly.

He gave the signal for the second third of the fleet to enter the fray.

They came down from six directions at once, their heavy-cycle guns spouting flame. They converged inward on the Joran-Kariadi fleet, six light Morankimar vessels equipped for massive offensive thrusts.

The invaders were caught unaware; four Joran ships crumbled and died in the first shock of the unsuspected attack.

Kausirn was silent. Navarre knew, or hoped he knew, what the Lyrellan was thinking: *I had expected only six defending ships. If the Earthmen have these additional six, how many more may they have?*

The radar screen was crisscrossed with light. Navarre's original six plowed steadily forward, drawing the heaviest fire of the aliens and controlling it easily, while the six new ships plunged and swerved in daring leaps, weaving in and out of the alien lines so fast they could not even be counted.

Navarre gave another signal. And suddenly three of his offensive platoon leaped from view, blanked out like extinguished candles, and reappeared at the far end of the battlefield. They drove downward from their new angle of attack, while the remaining trio likewise jumped out of warp and back in again. Navarre picked up bitter curses coming from the harassed aliens.

Three more ships had perished. The odds were narrowing—forty-three against eighteen, now. And the aliens were definitely bewildered.

The tactic was unheard of; it was suicide to leave and reenter hyperspace in a confined area barely a thousand light-years on a side. There was the ever-present consideration that one ship might re-materialize in an area already occupied; the detonation would be awesome.

There was always the chance. But Navarre had computed it, and in actuality the chance was infinitesimal that two ships would re-enter the same space in such an area. It was worth the risk. Like leaping silver-bellied fish, his ships flicked in and out of space-time. And now the alien vessels moved in confused circles.

Flick!

Two astonished Kariadi vessels thundered headlong into each other to avoid a Terran vessel that had appeared less than a light-minute away from them. The proximity strained the framework of hyperspace; the hapless ships were sucked downward, out of control, into a wild vortex.

Flick!

Flick!

Navarre's checkboard showed eleven invader losses already, and not one Terran ship touched. He grinned cheerfully as one of his six original attackers speared through the screens of a bedeviled Joran destroyer and sent it reeling apart.

"Kausirn? Are you convinced?"

No answer came this time.

Navarre frowned speculatively. So far the battle was going all Earth's way; but eventually the shattered and confused invader lines would re-group, and eventually they would realize that only twelve Earth ships opposed them, not hundreds.

Navarre gave one final signal. Suddenly, four more Terran ships warped into the area.

They were dummies, half-finished ships manned by skeleton crews. They carried no arms, only rudimentary defense-screens; Navarre had ordered them held in check for just this moment. And here they were.

At the same time the six warp-jumping ships stabilized themselves. Now sixteen Terran ships menaced the alien fleet at once, and there was no telling for the aliens how many more lurked in hidden reaches.

The armada milled hesitantly. Ships changed course almost at random.

Navarre's vessels formed into a tight wheel and spun round the confused aliens. He opened the communicator channels wide and said, "We have already destroyed thirteen of your number at no cost to ourselves. Will you surrender now, or do we have to pick you all off one by one? Speak up, Kausirn!"

Garbled noise came from the communicator—sure sign that more than one ship's captain was trying to speak at the same time. Navarre joyfully sensed indecision; he flashed one last-ditch signal along his communication channel, ordering the six defensive ships stationed round the planets to leave their base and join the fray. It was a rash move, but he knew the time had come to gamble all on the chance of success.

He heard Kausirn's cold steely voice saying insistently, "No! He's bluffing us! He *has* to be bluffing!"

The last six Terran ships winked into being, spitting death. The invader fleet rippled outward in disorganized retreat. Suddenly Navarre's subradio phones brought over the sound of a single agonized scream.

The sky was full of ships, now—twenty-two Terran ships, of which four were mere shells, and six more were so weighted with defense-screens that they were practically useless on offense.

"Well, Kausirn? Do we have to bring out the *real* fleet, now?"

No response.

Navarre wondered about the scream he had heard. "Kausirn?"

A new voice said suddenly, "The Lyrellan is dead. This is Admiral Garsignol of Kariad. By virtue of the authority vested in me by the Oligocrat Marhaill, I surrender to you the eighteen surviving Kariadi ships."

A moment later another voice broke into the channel, speaking in Joran. The nineteen Joran ships were likewise surrendering. They saw resistance was futile.

It was over at last, Navarre thought, as he stared from the window of his office in the city of Phoenix, on Earth, looking outward at the thirty-seven alien vessels the battle had yielded.

Victory was sweet.

Earth now had forty-three ships of first-class tonnage, plus four more half-finished ones, and twelve more belonging to the Polisarch of Morank. The Polisarch would never miss his ships, Navarre thought. And Earth needed them.

Fifty-nine ships. That comprised a major armada in itself; hardly a hundred worlds in the universe could muster fleets of such size. Earth would be safe during the time of rebuilding. There would be no Second Empire, merely the free world of Earth.

Earth numbered barely twelve thousand, now. But time would remedy that. The ancient legend had spoken truth: the Chalice indeed held the key to immortal life. Earth, reborn phoenix-like from its ashes of old, had once again won its place in the roll of worlds.

Navarre looked out the broad window at the brightening hillside. The sun was rising; the city was stirring busily with the coming of day. He opened the window and let the air of Earth wash through the room, bright, clean, fresh. It was a time for beginning, he thought. In the days to come, a thousand million worlds would have cause to remember the name of the planet they had once forgotten.

Earth.

Starhaven

Chapter One

It was a secluded part of the beach, and the corrugated metal shack was set some distance back from the shimmering tideless sea, close to a grove of green and purple trees. Inside the shack, the man who called himself Johnny Mantell lay on his thin cot. He groaned in his sleep, then abruptly awakened. With Mantell, there was no dim half-world of drowsy transition. At once he was awake and thoroughly alive.

Alive—but for how long?

He stepped to the washstand that he'd made and looked at his face in the fragment of mirror nailed over the basin.

The tired, thirtyish face of a man who had been on the toboggan slide to nowhere for too many years stared back at him. His eyes, alight with intelligence though they were, bore the timid, defeated look of an outcast. His face was deeply tanned from roaming the beaches in this part of the planet Mulciber, "Vacation Paradise of the Universe," as the advertisements proclaimed on the planets of the Galactic Federation, of which Earth was the capital.

Strange, he thought. He could see no change from the way he looked yesterday. Yet there had been a change, and a major one. Up to early this morning, he had been a beachcomber, managing to survive by selling brightly colored shells to tourists, as he had been doing for the past seven years.

But today, the day he had to leave Mulciber, he was a different man.

He was a fugitive from the law. He was a hunted killer.

In his own mental image, Mantell had always thought of himself as being a reasonably law-abiding man; one who held respect for the rights of others, not out of fear but through innate decency; it was, in fact, about the last thing he had—a small measure of his self-respect that a good many of the others seemed to lack. Just an average, decent sort of Joe who never went out of his way looking for trouble, but didn't let people push him around, either.

But this time he was really being pushed. And there was no way to push back.

Almost ever since he had arrived on Mulciber, Mantell had been putting off his departure, delaying because there was no special reason to go anywhere. Here, life was easy; by wading out a few yards into the quiet warm sea, all sorts of delicious fish and crustaceans could be caught by net or by hand. Nutritive fruits of many flavors grew on the trees all year round. There were no responsibilities here, except the basic one of keeping yourself alive. But it had come down to just that.

If Mantell wanted to stay alive any longer, he'd have to move fast. Right now. And to do it, he'd have to add one more criminal mark to his new record. He'd have to steal a spaceship. He knew where to go for sanctuary.

Starhaven.

Mike Bryson, one of the other beachcombers on Mulciber, had told Mantell about Starhaven. That had been years ago, back before the time the mudshark had sliced Bryson in half while he was wading for pearl oysters. Bryson had said, "Some day, when I get up the incentive, I'm going to steal a ship and light out for Starhaven, Johnny."

"Starhaven? What's that?"

Bryson smiled, screwing up his face and showing his yellowed teeth. "Starhaven's a planet of a red super-giant sun called Nestor. It's an artificial sort of planet, built twenty or twenty-five years ago by a fellow, name of Ben Thurdan." Bryson lowered his voice. "It's a sanctuary for people like us, Johnny. People who couldn't make the grade or fit in with organized society. Drifters and crooks and has-beens can go to Starhaven, and get decent jobs and live in peace. It's the place for me, and one day I'm going to get there."

But Mike Bryson never did make it, Mantell recalled. He tried to remember how long ago it had been that they had brought Bryson's bleeding body back from the beach. Three years? Four?

Mantell cradled his head in his hands and tried to think. It was hard to sort out the years. There were times when he could hardly remember the day before yesterday, and all his memories seemed like dreams. There were other times when it was all crystal-clear, when he could see all the way back across the years to the time when he had lived on Earth. He had been making the grade in society then.

As a twenty-four-year-old technician at Klingsan Defense Screens, for a while everything seemed to roll along well. Then he really got on the beam—or so he thought. Enthusiasm, energy seemed to exude from his pores. A latent inventive streak suddenly emerged in him. He knew his stuff all right; maybe too well.

Trouble was that his abounding faith in himself and in his innovations made him appear cocky, and his inventions, while basically sound, needed refinements to be practical. At the time the Klingsan plants were not geared to machine them. It would take special heavy presses of a new amalgam of metals; specially made dies as well as new electronic devices. All that represented an impressive outlay of capital. So, perhaps, if Johnny would work over his designs for a couple of years, then they could be presented to the board of directors, and . . .

Johnny, furious, told off his employers. He got another job in a similar plant, but became quarrelsome and edgy when they, too, decided not to produce his inventions. And then he thought he found the answer to his frustrations. If a drink or two would relax him in the evening, then four or six would do the job better. They did, all right. Soon he was working on a quart a day.

He drank himself right out of a job. Drank himself right off Earth, too, across the galaxy to Mulciber, where Mulciber's twin suns shone twenty hours a day and the temperature the year round was a flat seventy-seven, F. Yes, it was a tourists' paradise, right enough, and a fine place for a man like Johnny Mantell to lose what little backbone he had left, and live a dreamy, day-to-day existence, sustaining himself with neither effort nor responsibility.

And he'd been here for seven years. A blankness in time. . . .

It was early morning. The two lemon-yellow suns were up there in the chocolate sky, and little heat-devils danced over the roasting sand. Across the few yards of white sandy beach, the calm sea stretched out to the blank horizon. The tourists from Earth and the other rich worlds of the galaxy were splashing around in the wonderful water, down in the bathing area where the mud-sharks and bloater-toads and other native life forms had all been wiped out. They were diving and swimming and splashing each other with cascades of sparkling water. Some of them had nullgravs to help them float, and some paddled little boats.

Mantell had wandered into the casino bearing his stock in trade: sea shells, pearls, other little gewgaws and gimcracks that he peddled to the wealthy tourists who frequented Mulciber's fashionable North Coast. He hadn't been in the casino more than two minutes when someone pointed at him and bellowed, "There's the man! Come here, you! Right away!"

Mantell stared blankly. The rule on Mulciber was that you didn't raise your voice much if you were a beachcomber; you minded your business and peddled your wares, and you were tolerated. You couldn't hang around the tourists if you made a nuisance of yourself, and Mantell had tried not to do that.

So all he could do was say, in a soft voice, "You want me, mister?"

The tourist was half as tall as Mantell and twice as wide—a little potbellied walrus of a man, deeply tanned and blistering in a couple of places. He was wearing a costly yangskin wrap about his bulky middle, and he was clutching a flask of some local brew in one pudgy hand. The other one was pointing accusingly at Mantell, and the little man was shouting excitedly, "There's the man who stole my wife's brooch! Fifty thousand I paid for it on Turimon, and he stole it!"

Mantell could only shake his head and say, "You have the wrong man, mister. I didn't steal anybody's jewelry."

"Now you're lying, too, thief! Give me the brooch! Give it back!"

What followed after that was a confused muddle for Mantell. He remembered standing his ground and waiting for the angry approach of the little man, while a few curious tourists in the casino gathered round to see what was going on. He remembered the tourist standing in front of him, glaring up, pouring out a string of vile accusations, heedless of Mantell's protestations of innocence.

Then the tourist had drawn back his hand and slapped Mantell. Mantell had recoiled; he put up his hands to ward off another blow. Beachcombers didn't fight back when tourists played rough, but they weren't required to stand around and get pounded.

The fat little man had lunged for another blow. The stone floor was wet with some purple liquor that had been spilled. As he wound up for the roundhouse, the little man's sandaled foot caught in the puddle, twisted, and he went skidding backward, arms and legs flying, a wail of fear coming from his mouth.

He had fallen backward and cracked his head hard against a marble counter. People were bending over him, muttering and whispering to themselves. The little man's head was bent at a funny angle, and blood trickled from one ear.

"I didn't lay a finger on him," Mantell protested. "You all saw what happened. He swung and he missed and he fell down. I never touched him."

He turned to see Joe Harrell's face looking into his. Joe, one of the oldest beachcombers on Mulciber, a man who'd been on the beach so long he didn't remember what world he had come from. His face was stained from weed-chewing, his eyes dim and faded. But Joe had plenty of common sense.

And Joe was saying softly, "You better get going, boy. You better run fast."

"But you saw it, Joe. You saw I was minding my own business. I didn't touch him."

"Prove it."

"Prove it? I got witnesses!"

"Witnesses? Who? Me? What's the word of another bum on the beach?" Harrell laughed thickly. "You're cooked, son. That lad over there is out for good, and they're going to pin it on you if you don't get out of here. An Earthman's life is important."

"I'm an Earthman, too."

"You *were* an Earthman, maybe. Now you're just dirt, so far as they care. Dirt to be swept away. Go on! Scram! Get out of here!"

So Mantell had scrammed, slipping out of the casino in the confusion. He knew he had a little time, anyway. The only ones in the casino who knew who he was and where he could be found were other beachcombers, like Joe, and they weren't going to talk. So there would be a little time while the police were called, and while the police were en route. Eventually the police would reach the casino and find the dead man, and would start asking questions, and a half hour or an hour later, maybe, they would get around to identifying the man suspected of killing the tourist. They would send out an order, pick him up, try him on a charge of murder, or maybe manslaughter, if he was lucky. There would be a dozen tourists ready to swear he had provoked the attack, and nobody at all to stand up for him and substantiate his plea of innocence. So he would be duly tried and found guilty of homicide in whatever degree, and he would be punished.

Mantell knew what the punishment was. He would be given his choice: Rehabilitation or Hard Labor.

Of the two, Rehabilitation was by far the worse. It amounted to a death sentence. Using complicated encephalographic techniques, they could strip away a man's mind completely and build a new personality into his brain. A simple, robotlike personality in almost all cases, but at least one which was decent and law-abiding. Rehabilitation was demolition of the individual. So far as Johnny Mantell was concerned, it would be the end; six months or a year later his body would walk out of the hospital in perfect freedom, but the mind in the head of that body would be named Paul Smith or Sam Jones, and Paul or Sam would never know that his body had once belonged to an unjustly convicted murderer.

If the verdict were first degree murder, or some other equally serious crime, Rehabilitation was mandatory. On lesser counts, like manslaughter or larceny, you had your choice. You could submit voluntarily to the rehabilitators, or you could go off to the Penal Keep on Thannibar IX for a few months or a few years, and chop up rocks the way convicts had done for aeons.

Mantell didn't care for Rehabilitation much, nor for Hard Labor—not for a crime he hadn't committed, or even for one that he had. There was one way out. Starhaven.

It would take guts to steal a ship and pilot it halfway across the galaxy to Nestor, Starhaven's sun, but once, a long time ago, there had been a man inside the body that belonged to Johnny Mantell, and he wanted to think that the man was still there.

Actually, however, it wouldn't be too hard to swipe a ship. It had been done before by skylarking, half-tipsy tourists, but they had brought it back and declared themselves glad to pay the fine.

This time the ship would not come back. So Johnny Mantell fervently hoped.

Johnny planned to tuck in his shirttails and amble out to the spacefield and talk fast and smart to one of the boys on duty. He had kept up with technical developments and knew how to talk spaceship shop. Mulciber natives were soft-spoken, easygoing, and made it a point to be pleasant and obliging. It shouldn't be much of a trick to fast-talk himself right into a ship that had been fueled and was set to take off.

And then, so long, Mulciber!

So long to seven lousy years of beachcombing!

Legging it across the sand to the spacefield, his Mulciber memories became dreamlike again, almost as if his days here had never been, as if Mike Bryson and Joe Harrell and the little fat tourists, and all the rest were mere phantoms out of a dream.

He didn't want to be Rehabilitated. He didn't want to lose his past, even though there was nothing in it but disappointment and failure.

But as for the future—his future in the world that Ben Thurdan built—who knew what Starhaven held in store? Whatever it was, it was more promising than sticking around and waiting for the police to track him down. Starhaven was sanctuary. Sanctuary was the prime requirement for keeping alive right now, and so he would go to Starhaven.

Chapter Two

The three small ships came streaking across the dark backdrop of the skies. There was the vessel that Johnny Mantell had stolen on Mulciber, and there were the two squat little two-man Space Patrol ships that came whistling after him in eager pursuit. Across space they came, heading out of the Fifth Octant of the galaxy and into the darkness.

Mantell was not worrying too hard. The percentages lay with him—if he could somehow manage to keep ahead of his Patrol pursuers until he could reach Starhaven's orbit.

The chase had gone on for nearly two days, now—a dazzling pursuit in and out of hyperwarp, ever since Mantell had gotten away in the stolen ship. The SP men had been struggling to match velocities with Mantell's ship, clamp metamagnetic grapples around him, and haul him off to the Penal Keep on Thannibar IX.

Sweat dribbled down the sides of his face as be sat locked at his controls, feeling the frustration that all spacemen do: the curious disorientation that results when you cruise along at three point five times the speed of light and still seem utterly stationary, hung in an unbreakable motionless stasis.

That was the way it seemed to him in hyperwarp, with nothing but the grayness all around, and the two snub-nosed SP ships in formation behind him. He clung grimly to his course. They said anyone at all could operate a hyperwarp spaceship if he knew how to drive a car, and Mantell was discovering that that was true. He had guided the ship across hundreds of light-years without difficulty, without catastrophe.

Suddenly, his screen panel lit. The green blossom of light told him that he had reached the destination for which he had set the course-computer two days before. He nodded in satisfaction and jabbed down hard on the enameled red stud that wrenched him out of the grayness of hyperspace and back into the normal space-time continuum once again.

The ship's mass-detector buzzed once, twice, and he knew that his two pursuers had detected his action and had themselves made the shift-over maneuver only seconds after he had. But Mantell hardly cared about them now. The long chase was just about over. His goal was in sight.

Ahead of him, the massive bulk of Starhaven seemed to take up the entire sky.

He saw it as a giant coin floating in the dark sea of space, a burnished fiery copper coin studded with rivets the size of whales. He saw it full face, head-on, seeming to float with agonizing slowness toward him.

Behind him lay Nestor, the red super-giant sun whose faint rays barely managed to illuminate Starhaven's surface. Starhaven had no need of Nestor's radiation, though. It was shelled over entirely with metal, and it was completely self-sufficient powerwise.

He locked his ship into an automatic orbit around the metal world. Consulting his mass-detectors, he saw that his pursuers were doing the same thing. But for the first time since he had started his wild flight, hundreds of light-years away on Mulciber, he felt calm and confident. He couldn't be caught now. He had the same kind of ship as his pursuers rode, and it was operating now at full ion-drive velocity. They couldn't do any better than that. The gap between the ships would have to remain constant. All they could do was tag along behind him, staring at his red exhaust stream.

Mantell snapped on the communicator. After the first quick hum of contact the Space Patrol scramblers cut in, but Mantell speedily switched circuits on them, throwing his beam up into the Very High Frequencies where their scramblers could have no effect.

He said, "Come in, Starhaven. Come in!"

For half a minute, thirty ticking tense seconds, there was only silence. Swiveling in the pilot's bucket-seat, Mantell peered through the rear visis-creens and saw the two snub-nosed Patrol ships hanging in there grimly, waiting for him to make some kind of mistake, waiting for him to falter.

"Come on in, Starhaven," he said again.

A moment's pause. Then:

"This is Starhaven. Identify."

Mantell moistened his lips. His voice came out almost as a croak. "My name is Mantell, Johnny Mantell. I'm a fugitive from the Patrol. Two SP ships chased me down from Mulciber. They're still on my tail. Can you give me sanctuary?"

"We see the SP ships," came the calm reply. "But you're in an SP ship yourself, Mantell. Where did you get it?"

"Stole it." The ship went whipping around Starhaven for the fiftieth time since he had fixed it in its orbit, and behind came the hopeful pursuers. "I'm asking sanctuary. They want me on a murder rap."

A fake murder rap, he thought. But he didn't tell them that.

"Okay," the Starhaven operator replied. Then he turned offmike for a second and muttered something inaudible to Mantell. Then he said, "Keep in your orbit, Mantell. We'll handle your pals, and then pick you up."

Mantell grinned in relief and joy. "Thanks. Be seeing you soon."

"Yeah. Sure, Mantell."

He broke off contact and turned to keep his eye on the rear visiscreens. Now that he knew he was home free, he could afford to have a little fun for a moment. He jabbed buttons, cutting velocity ten per cent, just enough to seem to give the Patrolmen behind him one last fighting chance.

They were wide awake. A double blast of energy immediately raked his screens, but his defenses held. He chuckled. Then there was a sudden burst of light from the metal-skinned planet just ahead.

He knew what that light was. It meant that the legendary heavy-cycle guns of Starhaven were coming into play. He watched as the first of his pursuers drew a blast of energy. The Patrolman's ship shuddered as his defense screens labored to absorb the overload, the battery of energy guns below sent up an additional blast. The total megawattage must have been enough to sink a satellite. One moment the little Space Patrol ship was there; a second later, it wasn't.

As for the other Patrolman, he didn't seem minded to stay around and fight a one-man battle with the impregnable fortress that was Starhaven. He turned tail frantically and streaked for home at six gees.

The gunners below let him run for about six seconds, no more. Then a lazy spiral of energy came barrelling up from Starhaven to engulf the fleeing ship. Suddenly Mantell was alone in the sky.

Free. Safe.

He hung limply to his control rack, waiting for them to pick him up.

He didn't have to wait long. His ship completed another circuit in its orbit round Starhaven, and this time he noticed a hatch opening in the bright metal skin, fifty thousand feet below him.

On his next time around a spaceship had come forth from the hatch and was rising rapidly. On completion of one more circular swing, the Starhaven ship had matched orbit with him and was following him along quite nicely.

Only this was no tiny Space Patrol ship. It was a monster of a spacefaring vessel, and it overhauled him with ridiculous ease. He lowered his screens and let the other ship's metamagnetic grapples snare him without resistance; gently he was drawn "upward" into the belly of the big ship.

A hatch in the ship closed smoothly over him. His communicator crackled into life, and a heavy, deep voice said, "Stay right where you are, Mantell, and don't try anything. We'll come to get you out of your ship. Open your rear airlock."

He nudged the control panel and the lock slid open. There was silence outside, and darkness. He became conscious of a faint hissing sound that grew rapidly stronger, and he smelled a sickly sort of sweetness in the atmosphere.

Gas, he thought. In momentary panic he reached for the airlock control, but he debated shutting the lock for a fraction of a second and in that fraction of a second the gas robbed him of all volitional control over his muscles and nerves.

He rose uncertainly, tottered and fell. Darkness came, then nothingness.

Mantell awoke, feeling a cottony taste in his mouth. He was no longer wearing his space suit. He was in a cabin in the other ship, surrounded by four solemn-looking men in civilian clothes. One of them was holding a blaster pointed in the general vicinity of Mantell's midsection.

The one with the blaster said calmly, "Please don't move, Mantell. You're on your way to Starhaven now. We'll be entering the shell any minute."

Mantell shook his head, to help clear it of the effects of the gas. He felt soggy and angry. He said, "What's the idea of all this guff? Why the gun? How come you gave me the gas? A fine reception you guys hand out to friendly visitors!"

The man with the gun said, "We like Starhaven the way it is. We intend to keep it that way. And every stranger who wants to come here is suspect until he is qualified for residence."

"For all we know," said one of the others, "this is some kind of Space Patrol deal to slip a spy into Starhaven."

"An SP deal that costs them two ships and four lives?" Mantell snapped hotly. "That doesn't make sense. I'm—"

"You're nobody, until you've been psychprobed," the man with the blaster said.

"Psychprobed?"

"That's standard processing for everyone who enters Starhaven for the first time. It's a security measure."

Mantell knew his face was going pale. Psychprobing was no plaything for amateurs, even the usual psychologists. Its procedure was complex and took years to master. "How can you—I mean, do you have anyone here qualified to do the job? You can mess up a man's mind for good if your technique is off even the slightest bit."

The other grinned coolly. "Relax, Mantell. The head of our psychprobe is named Erik Harmon. Does that make you feel any better?"

Erik Harmon? Mantell blinked, digging back into old memories. Harmon, here? The famous scientist who had invented and then perfected principles and techniques of psychprobing, and who had mysteriously vanished from civilization nearly twenty years before?

"I guess he'll do," Mantell admitted wryly.

The ship glided to a feather-light landing. The steady whispering hum of the inertialess drive ceased abruptly and the landing stabilizers shot out on either side of the big ship. Mantell felt tense; a muscle throbbed in his cheek. He heard the hatch in Starhaven's metal surface clang resoundingly shut far above him.

The man with the blaster grinned amiably and broke the dead silence by saying, "Welcome to Starhaven, Mantell. Your first stop will be a visit with the boss. Come along and let's get your mind looked at."

Chapter Three

Five minutes later, after the landing and the skin of the ship decontaminated by the radion grids, Mantell found himself standing outside the big vessel, in the middle of an extremely well-equipped spaceport, on what seemed to him just like any sunny afternoon on any Earth-type planet of the galaxy. It was utterly impossible to tell that Starhaven was completely encased by a metal sheath.

Overhead the sky was blue, flecked with convincing puffy clouds, and a yellow sun glowed brightly. Even though he realized the sun was probably a deuterium-fusion synthetic of some kind, he was unable to keep from thinking of it as a real star.

As for the planet's metal skin, there was no sign of it. Most likely it was ten or twelve miles, perhaps as much as twenty, above ground level, and artfully disguised to look like an authentic sky. The engineers who had built this world, Mantell thought, had really known their stuff, regardless of which side of the law they had happened to operate on.

"You like the setup?" Mantell's guide asked. He seemed to take a personal pride in it.

"It's pretty convincing. You wouldn't know there was a roof overhead."

The other chuckled. "Oh, you know it all right, any time the Space Patrol decides to come after us. But they haven't made a dent in thirty years, ever since Ben Thurdan built Starhaven."

Just then a landcar came squirreling silently across the field to meet them. It drew up almost at Mantell's feet, a small tear-shaped bubble of a car whose driver waited patiently for Mantell and his cicerone to climb in. Mantell took one look back and saw that a gantry crane had been wheeled up alongside the big Starhaven ship; they were removing the tiny SP vessel from the hold of the monster that had picked him up in space.

He moistened his lips nervously. The idea of submitting to a psychprobe didn't amuse him very much, even with Dr. Erik Harmon himself doing the probing.

"Where are we heading?" he asked.

"To Ben Thurdan's headquarters. That's where all new arrivals get processed."

Mantell sat back silently as the car weaved its way through heavy traffic in a busy-looking city. He found himself wondering what kind of industries a world like Starhaven could have—a planet that was populated exclusively by criminals.

By criminals like me, he thought.

A sudden guilt-feeling racked him as he mentally retraced the trail that had brought him to Starhaven, to this dead-end, renegade planet, the outcast world among the other law-abiding worlds of the galaxy. He tried to tell himself that he was innocent, that they had kicked him around unjustly, that he had been handed a raw deal.

But he could hardly convince himself, any more. It had been so long since he had been a respected member of society that he had almost started believing the things they said about him.

Well, he had plenty of time to get used to the idea of being a criminal. Starhaven was a sanctuary, but nobody ever left it. Nobody with any sense, anyway. This was the one place in the galaxy where a wanted man could live in blissful safety.

The car pulled up outside an impressive-looking office building that loomed big over the other buildings in the vicinity. Mantell was escorted upstairs in a gravshaft, accompanied by men with drawn blasters. They were taking no chances.

"Do you go through this rigmarole with every new arrival?" Mantell asked.

"Every one, without exception."

A door rolled back smoothly on photon-impulse bearings, and Mantell saw a welcoming committee ready for him. Three people sat expectantly inside an office that was furnished as if for the use of the President of the Galactic Federation.

One of the three was a thin man in a white smock, old, tired-looking, his face a parchment of tiny crevices and canyons. That would have to be Erik Harmon, "The Father of the Psychprobe." To the right of the scientist stood a tall, fiercely glowering man in dramatic purple synthilk shirt and bright yellow tights; he was bald and looked about forty, but he was probably older. He seemed to radiate power. Obviously, Mantell thought, this must be Ben Thurdan, Starhaven's founder and guiding genius.

And next to him was a girl with hair the color of Thurdan's shirt and eyes the color of blue-white diamonds or blue-white suns. She was a highly decorative addition to the office furniture.

Thurdan said, "You're John Mantell, eh? You come here looking for sanctuary?" His voice, not unexpectedly, was a resounding booming basso.

Mantell nodded. "That's right."

Thurdan gestured to Dr. Harmon, who stood poised on the balls of his feet like a withered prune about to take flight. "Erik, suppose you take Mr. Mantell into the lab and give him the full probe treatment." He looked sharply at Mantell and said, "Of course you understand that this is a necessary precautionary measure. Part of our regular routine, Mr. Mantell."

Mister—to an ex-beachcomber who hadn't been called anything but "Hey, you," in seven years! Mantell nodded easily and said to Thurdan, "I understand."

"Good. Harmon, let's go, eh?"

Harmon beckoned to Mantell, and he followed the old man, accompanied by the gunmen. As Mantell passed through the golden actuator beam of the door, he heard Thurdan's low-pitched rumble, apparently replying to some unheard comment of the girl's: "Oh, sure . . . But it's exactly those who *look* 'all right' that we have to watch out for."

The girl said audibly, "I hope we don't have to kill this one, Ben. I think I like him."

Then the door scissored shut behind him, choking off the conversation.

Mantell entered a well-furnished laboratory. Sitting bulkily in the center of the room was the familiar spidery mass of a Harmon psychprobe, while flanking it was a standard-model electro-encephalograph and some other equipment that Mantell was unable to recognize, and which probably included some new gadgets of Harmon's.

Two assistants gently propelled Mantell to the couch and strapped him in. Harmon lowered the metal probedome to his scalp. Its skin was cold and hard. The knowledge that an incautious twist of a lever now could cook his brains or scramble his synapses did not tend to make Mantell much more cheerful.

Harmon's eyes were bright with enthusiasm. He touched his clawlike old hands to the enameled studs of the control panel. He smiled.

"Suppose you tell me a little about yourself, Mr. Mantell."

Mantell clenched his jaws a moment as he dug back into the old painful memories. In a tired voice he said, "I'm a former armaments technician who ran into a little trouble seven years back. I—lost my job. And then I went to Mulciber to live for a while, and it turned out I stayed there longer than I expected. I—"

As he spoke, Harmon went on busily making adjustments in the psychprobe, staring over Mantell's shoulder, at an image screen out of Mantell's line of sight, where the electric rhythms of his brain were being projected by an oscilloscope.

"I was out on the beach one morning combing for pearls when—"

Something seemed to crash down on his head like a ten-ton foundry stamp. He felt as if the hemispheres of his brain had been split apart, as if a giant cleaver were wedged deep in his scalp, to blast off fusion bombs back of each eye.

Slowly the tide of pain receded, leaving in its wake a numbing headache. Mantell thumbed his eyes and looked up at old Harmon, who was squinting gravely at his dials.

"What happened?" Mantell asked.

Harmon smiled apologetically. "A slight error in calibration, nothing more. My sincere apologies to you, young man."

Mantell shuddered. "I hope nothing like that happens when you psychprobe me, Doctor!"

Looking at him strangely, Harmon said, "But you've just *been* psychprobed. It's been over for fifteen minutes. You've been asleep all this time."

Fifteen minutes—and he had thought it had been perhaps half a second! Mantell rubbed his aching scalp. Something was throbbing fiercely in the area just behind his eyebrows, and he longed to be able to rip off the plate of cranial bone and press his hands soothingly against the ache.

From behind him the booming voice of Ben Thurdan said, "Is he conscious yet?"

"He's coming around. There was a stubborn stress-pattern I didn't foresee, and it knocked him out for a while."

"You'd better practice using your foresight, then, Erik," Thurdan warned. "You aren't any youngster. If you pull things like this, we'll have to let one of your technicians handle the probing. Mantell, are you steady on your feet yet?"

"I don't know," Mantell said uncertainly. "Let's see."

He clambered off the couch and wobbled around the laboratory for a moment or two. The shock of the psychprobing was beginning to diminish. "I guess I'm okay," Mantell said after a moment. "The pain's starting to fade. You know, I could have done quite well without this whole thing."

Thurdan grinned hollowly. "I'm sure you could. But *we* couldn't have."

"Did I pass?"

"For your information, you're clean and acceptable. Come on into my office and I'll fill you in on our general way of life here on Starhaven."

Still a little unsteady, Mantell followed the big man through the corridor that led from Harmon's laboratory into Thurdan's luxuriously appointed office. Thurdan sprawled out on a web-foam couch that had been specially designed to cradle his long powerful body, and casually gestured to Mantell to take a seat opposite.

"Drink?" Thurdan asked abruptly.

Mantell nodded, trying to hide his eagerness, and Thurdan nudged a sliding knob in the base of his couch. A sleek portable bar came rolling out of a corner of the room toward him. It stationed itself in front of Mantell.

After a little deliberation he dialed a sour choker, third strength. Almost before he was through punching out the signal, the robot bar was extending a crystal beaker three-quarters full of cloudy green liquid. Mantell took it. The bar swiveled away and went to Thurdan, who ordered a straight bourbon.

Mantell sipped and nodded in appreciation. "This is good stuff. From Muriak?"

"Synthetic—all synthetic. We don't bother smuggling liquor in any more, not when we have chemists good enough to whip up stuff like that." Thurdan leaned back and stared intently at Mantell. Slowly he said, "According to what you told Dr. Harmon, you used to be an armaments technician before you got into trouble. That automatically makes you a very valuable individual on Starhaven, Mantell."

He had quickly dropped the "mister." That must be only for newcomers who had not yet qualified, Mantell guessed.

"Valuable?" Mantell asked. "How so?"

"Starhaven lives and dies by its armaments. The moment our screens show any signs of weakening, we'll have a Space Patrol armada crashing down on us from every octant of the galaxy at once. I spent billions shielding Starhaven, Mantell. It's the first absolutely impregnable fortress in the history of the universe. But even so, it's no stronger than the technicians who maintain its screens and guns."

Mantell's hands began to quiver slightly. "It's a long time since I did anything like that," he told Thurdan. "Seven years. I hardly remember my stuff."

"You'll learn again," Thurdan said easily. "The psychprobe gave me your biography. Seven years of beach-combing and bumming after you lost your job. Then you killed a man, stole an SP ship, and headed for here."

"I didn't kill him. I was framed."

Thurdan smiled bleakly and shrugged. "The probe says you *did* kill him. The probe isn't prejudiced. It just reports what happened. Go argue with your own memories, Mantell."

Mantell sat very quietly, stunned, gripping his glass hard. He could remember every detail of that brawl in the beachside cafe, the fat, drunken tourist yelling that he had stolen his wife's jeweled brooch, then the tourist's flabby palm slamming into his cheek . . . And, the tourist slipping and cracking his skull open before Mantell laid a hand on him.

"I honestly thought I didn't do it," Mantell said quietly.

Thurdan shrugged again. "No use arguing with the probe. But that doesn't matter here. We don't believe in ex post facto laws." Thurdan rose and walked to the tri-di mural that swirled kaleidoscopically over the surface of one wall, a shifting pattern of reds and bright greens, a flowing series of contrasting textures and hues.

He stood with his back to Mantell, powerful hands locked: a big man who had done a big thing in his life, the man who had built Starhaven.

"We have laws here," he said after a while. "This place isn't just an anarchy. You break into a man's house and steal his money, and the law entitles him to go after you and make you give it back. If you cause too much trouble, we kill you. But nothing in between. No brain-burning, no jail sentence that lets a man rot away in a living death." He turned. "You, Mantell—you could still be happily working for Klingsan Defense Screens if you hadn't felt sorry for yourself, kept hitting the bottle, gotten yourself canned. But the forces of law and order threw you out, and ruined you as a man from there on."

Mantell took another drink and frowned questioningly at Thurdan. "Don't tell me I've run into some kind of reform school, now!"

Thurdan whirled, dark eyes hooded and angry. "Don't say that. There won't be any reforming here. Drink all you please, lie, cheat, gamble—Starhaven won't mind. We're not pious. A fast operator on Starhaven is a pillar of society, a good upstanding citizen. We won't preach to you here."

"You said you had laws. How does that square with what you just told me?"

Thurdan smiled. "We have laws, all right. Two of them. And only two."

"I'm listening."

"The first one is something generally known as the Golden Rule. I phrase it like this. *'Expect the same sort of treatment yourself that you hand out to others.'* That's simple enough, isn't it?"

"I suppose so. And the other?"

Thurdan grinned darkly and nipped at his drink before speaking. "The second law is even simpler: *'You'll do whatever Ben Thurdan tells you to do, without argument, question, or hesitation.'* Period. End of the Starhaven Constitution."

Mantell was silent for a moment, watching the big rawboned man in the glaring costume and thinking about the sort of world Starhaven was. Then he said, "That second law contradicts the first one, wouldn't you say? I mean, so far as you're concerned."

He nodded. "Oh, certainly."

"How come you rate, then? How come you can place yourself beyond the laws?"

His eyes flashed. "Because I built Starhaven," he said slowly. "I devoted my life and every penny I could steal to setting up a planet where guys like you could come and hide. In return, I get the right of absolute dominance. Believe me, I don't abuse my power. I'm no Nero. I set things up this way because Starhaven has to be run by a single forceful leader."

Mantell's brows knit. There was, he had to admit, even though reluctantly, plenty of truth in what he was saying. It was a weird, even devilish philosophy of government—but it seemed to work, at least here on Starhaven. It hung together consistently.

"Okay," Mantell said. "I'm with you."

Thurden smiled. "You never had any choice," he said. "Here. Take this."

He handed Mantell a small white capsule. Mantell studied it. "What is it?"

"It's the antidote to the poison that was in your drink," Thurdan said. "I suggest you take it within the next five minutes, if you're going to take it at all. Otherwise it may be unpleasant."

Mantell repressed a shiver and hastily popped the capsule into his mouth. It tasted faintly bitter, and dissolved against his tongue. He felt chilled. So this was what it was like to be in the absolute grasp of one man!

Well, he thought, I asked for it. I came to Starhaven of my own free will. Here I am, and here I'll stay.

Thurdan said, "You have a week to relax and learn the ropes here, Mantell. After that you'll have to begin earning your keep. There's plenty of work here for a skilled armaments man."

"I won't mind getting back to work."

Thurdan grinned at Mantell. "Have another drink?"

"Sure," Mantell said. He dialed and drank without hesitation. There was no better way to show that he trusted Thurdan.

Chapter Four

The two men drank, and finished their drinks. Mantell could distinguish no difference between the drink he had had before and this one—but he relied on the fact that Thurdan seemed to need him, and that the big man seemed too sane to poison a man for the sheer pleasure of it.

A few moments later Thurdan jabbed a button at his desk and the girl with star-blue eyes came in. She wore a large-sleeved synthilk blouse of electric blue, buttoned high on one shoulder, and a dark skirt of some soft clinging material that accentuated her graceful walk. If the outfit was calculated to make an effect on Mantell, it accomplished its purpose.

Thurdan said, "Mantell, this is Miss Myra Butler, my secretary." And Johnny Mantell was conscious of Thurdan's swift glance at the girl; a look that held both warmth and pride, and gave Mantell a sudden start. He thought: Lord! Thurdan's in love with her! He must be twenty years older, but I admire his taste.

"Hello," he said, smiling straight into the shining blue eyes that eclipsed even the crackling brilliant color of her blouse. Resolutely then he pulled his gaze away from hers. Watch your step, Johnny, he cautioned himself. If Thurdan is in love with her, you can land in a big bunch of trouble without half trying. Take it easy, boy, and live longer.

But on the other hand, he could never recall meeting a woman with the same magnetic appeal that Myra had for him. It was as if he were drawn to her by powerful invisible cables. To be sure, he had known beautiful women during his earliest days on Mulciber, before all his money and self-respect had gone. But in the dreary later years of combing the beaches and hawking shells to tourists, he knew that the only kind of woman who would have anything to do with Johnny Mantell was the kind of woman that Johnny Mantell didn't want to have anything to do with.

Thurdan said, "Mantell's going to be an armaments technician, Myra. He's going to be very useful to us, I think. I want you to show him around Starhaven.

Give him the number one guided tour. He has a week to get the feel of the place. You show him the sights."

"That sounds like a pretty pleasant week," Mantell said. It couldn't hurt to praise Thurdan's choice in women a little, he thought.

Thurdan ignored the remark. He took a crumpled handful of bills from his pocket and shoved them at Mantell.

"Here. Here's some walking-around money to see you through the week. You go on the regular payroll as soon as you start working."

Mantell looked at the bills. They were neatly printed, in various colors. They looked vaguely like the standard Terra-issued Galactic currency. But they weren't Galactic issues at all.

In the center, where the stylized star-cluster design is found on the high Galactic bills, and the atom-diagram symbol on the low ones, these notes had a portrait of Ben Thurdan, head and shoulders, in remarkable detail. The denominations were interesting too. Thurdan had given him two hundred-chip bills, a fifty, a twenty, and some single-chips.

"Chips?" Mantell said, puzzled.

Thurdan chuckled. "The local unit of currency. I've always thought it was appropriate on a world like Starhaven. Just so you can guide yourself, one chip equals one Galactic credit in purchasing power. A hundred cents equals one chip. Originally I was going to have blue chips, red chips, and so on, but that turned out to be too complicated. . . . Show him around, Myra."

They made their way through shining well-lighted halls, the girl slightly in the lead and Mantell behind, into a gravshaft that lowered them gracefully and smoothly to street level. They stepped outside into the fresh and pleasant air.

A car was waiting at the curb for them—a slinky dark teardrop style, in the latest model. Thurdan had obviously made his mind up that Starhaven would keep abreast of the current stream of galactic fashions, even though the planet was closed to normal trade and tourist travel.

Myra slid into the car and murmured something to the stony-faced man behind the wheel. By the time Mantell had both legs in the car, it had pulled away from the sidewalk and was under way.

Hardly any time later, it was pulling up again, outside a glittering chrome-trimmed building. Myra reached into her purse and handed Mantell a key.

"You see the building on the left?"

Mantell nodded.

The girl said, "The name of that place is Number Thirteen. It's a hotel that Ben runs. You're going to live here."

"Can I afford it?"

"Don't worry about that. Your room number is 1306. Any time you're anywhere in Starhaven and you want to get here, just ask a driver to take you to Number Thirteen. They'll know the place. Do you want to take a look at your room now?"

"Later will be fine," Johnny Mantell said, disliking the thought of being away from the girl.

Myra told the driver to get going again, and they drove on, down the wide, well-designed streets. Mantell kept one eye on the girl and one on the attractive scenery outside. He was deciding that Starhaven was quite a place.

As they passed each building of note, Myra pointed it out and named it. "That's the main hospital over there. See?"

"The double tower? Looks lovely. There's everything here, isn't there?"

"What did you expect to find on Starhaven? Three poolhalls and a barroom? Just because Starhaven is a sanctuary for—for criminals, that doesn't mean we aren't civilized here."

Mantell flinched and raised his hands as if to ward off her words. "Okay! Okay! I'm sorry!"

"Thurdan built this place himself, twenty years ago," she said. "It was an uninhabited world, too cold to be of any use to anyone. He had a lot of money—never mind where he got it. He got together a crew of men like him, and together they built the shell and the inner sun. That was the beginning of Starhaven. Then they built the armaments, and suddenly there was a fortress in space where before there had been just a cold empty world. And that was the beginning of Starhaven, Mantell. Twenty million people live here now, and no one hounds them with false piety."

Mantell looked at her. After a moment he asked the question that had been nagging at him ever since he had first seen her.

"How did *you* happen to come here?"

It was the wrong thing to ask. He saw the anger flare on her lovely face; she started to unsheathe her claws and let her fur rise like an insulted feline. Then her anger subsided.

"I almost forgot you were new, Mantell. We never ask anybody why he's here. Your past is your own secret. Ben Thurdan knows it, and you know it. But nobody else is entitled to know anything about you except what you want to tell them."

Mantell felt his face going red. "Sorry," he said.

"That's okay. It's an understandable mistake. But just remember not to ask it any more."

"Does Thurdan know every single person on the planet?"

"He tries to. It's impossible to know twenty million people, but he tries. Everyone who comes gets a personal welcome from him, same as you did. Only some days fifty or a hundred or five hundred show up, and they don't all get an individual drink and a handshake. Ben gives newcomers a job to do."

"You can't just do as you please?"

"Not at first. You put in a few years at an assigned job and if you're rich enough you can buy yourself off and loaf. You're in the armaments division, aren't you?"

Mantell nodded.

"The buying-off price is high there. But so is the pay. Anyone with a specialty like that is valuable property here. But someone has to drive the cabs and someone has to sell popcorn at the sensostims, and if Thurdan tells you that's your job, you do it, or else. It's the only way to make this world run."

"He seems to do a pretty fair job of making it run," Mantell said. "And he seems to know how to pick his secretaries, too."

"Keep me out of this," the girl said, but she was grinning. "We get off here."

The car whirred to a gentle halt. The gleaming doors telescoped open, and they got out. Mantell looked around and whistled.

They were in front of a vaulting domed building set back behind a smooth, almost unreal grassy lawn. The building seemed crowded. Sparkling lights radiated from the upper stories of the dome. It was immense, a hundred stories high or more.

"What is this place?"

"This," Myra said, "is the second most important building on Starhaven. It's second only to Thurdan's headquarters."

"What is it?"

"It's called the Pleasure Dome," she said. "Shall we go inside?"

They stepped onto a moving slidewalk and let themselves be carried up a gently sloping ramp that led into the front entrance of the vast building. Mantell found himself swept into a cavernous antechamber that was at least a hundred feet high and seemingly acres square. The enormous room was packed with people, though sound-absorbers damped their voices. The walls were decorated with highly suggestive murals fifty feet high. *Pleasure Dome*, Mantell thought. Of course. Starhaven was nothing but a private dream world for Ben Thurdan, a dream world to which outsiders could be admitted on request, and this was the factory from which most of the dreams flowed.

As Mantell stood there gaping, someone jostled against him, and he felt a hand slide gently but not altogether imperceptibly into his pocket. He clamped his fingers tightly around the wrist, whirled, and brought his other hand forth to grab the pickpocket by the throat.

He was a small ratty man half Mantell's size, with bright darting eyes and close-cropped black hair and a hooked corvine nose. Mantell tightened his grip on the pickpocket's throat and yanked his hand from his pocket. He glanced at Myra. She seemed to be laughing, as if this were all some tremendously amusing joke.

Mantell said, "Is this how they sell admission tickets to this place?"

The pickpocket looked very pale. In a whisper he said, "Let go of me, huh, fellow? I can't breathe."

"Let go of him, Johnny," Myra said. In the confusion he still managed to notice that this was the first time she had called him Johnny.

Mantell decided there was no point in strangling the little fellow. He shook the pickpocket once, just for good measure, and let him go.

Seconds later he had a blaster pointing in the vicinity of Mantell's navel.

"Okay, friend. Since subtlety didn't seem to work, I'll try a more direct approach. Hand over your cash, and be quick."

Mantell recoiled in astonishment and shock. People were milling around in the big lobby, and they were all ignoring the holdup going calmly on in their midst! Then he remembered where he was. This was Starhaven. Anything went. Coldly and reluctantly he drew his bills from his pocket.

Myra was still laughing. She put her hand over his, keeping it there for a second, and pushed the hand, money and all, back toward his pocket. With her other hand she deflected the pick-pocket's blaster.

"Put the gun away, Huel," she said. "He's new here. He just came from Thurdan. That's all the cash he has to his name."

The blaster was lowered. The runty little pickpocket grinned up at him amiably and said, "I didn't mean any harm by it, friend. It's just between pals, that's all." He winked at Myra. "Thurdan told me to do it. Just to show him the ropes."

"I thought so," she said. "You usually aren't that clumsy about getting caught."

Mantell understood the strange lesson he had been just taught. Thurdan had arranged this whole thing as a demonstration of the way the code of Starhaven worked; he wanted Mantell to see it in action.

It was perfectly all right for a pickpocket to practice his trade in public, if he wanted to—but he ran the risk of trouble if he happened to get himself caught by his intended victim. As for pulling the gun on Mantell, that was well within the Starhaven ethical code, too, You gave the same kind of treatment as you expected from others. In that sort of framework, a man could be as brave or as weak as he chose.

On Starhaven it was healthier to be brave and quick-triggered. They came out better on the percentages, in the long run.

It all made a crazy sort of sense, Mantell thought. A world run this way might be able to hang together—if it had someone like Thurdan backing up its code.

"This Pleasure Dome," Mantell said, after the little pickpocket had faded back into the crowd. "Just what kind of place is it?"

"Everything is here, every sort of entertainment a man might want. You can eat and drink and see shows, live and tri-dis and sensostims. There's gambling on the tenth level. There's a dance hall on the twentieth. They're very obliging here."

"And why did you bring me here?"

"For a meal, mostly," the girl said. "You've had a hard pull and you can stand some relaxation. We can dance a little, after the drinks and food, if you feel like it."

"And after the meal and the drinks and the dancing?" Mantell asked. "Won't it be too early to call it an evening?"

"Well—we'll see about that," she said.

Mantell looked at her strangely. For just a moment he wished he were a telepath—just for that moment. He wanted to know what was going on behind those radiant eyes. He wanted to know where he stood with her. And how deeply—if at all—she was involved with Thurdan.

But he wasn't a telepath, and wishing wouldn't make him one. However, maybe the meal and some wine would get him some information.

He extended his arm to her. She took it, laughing gaily, and suddenly all the long weary years of beach-combing on Mulciber dropped away from him. He was through scrabbling for meals and cadging drinks, through fishing around in the mud at low tide to find shells to peddle to over-bloated tourists. All those things were behind him now. He was on Starhaven, and there was a pretty girl clinging to his arm.

He could hold up his head again. After seven years, he was Somebody again.

Chapter Five

A gleaming slidewalk took them up twenty feet to a handsome mezzanine where a bank of liftshafts stood waiting. Mantell let the girl enter a shaft first, and followed her in. She dialed for Level Nine.

"The ninth-level dining hall is the best one," she explained. "Also the most expensive. Wait till you see it."

They zipped upward, passing the seven intermediate floors in one long dizzying swoop, and the lift tube came to a halt. A sheet of blank metal faced them—shining, highly polished, mirror-reflective. Myra reached out a hand and touched her ornate signet ring to the surface of the barrier. The door crumpled inward instantly. They went in.

A bland robot waited just inside, a sleek little machine with a single staring wide-perspective eye set in the middle of its otherwise blank face. It came rolling up as if greeting an old friend and said to the girl, "Good evening, Miss Butler. Your usual table?"

"Of course. This is John Mantell, by the way. My escort for the evening."

The robot's photonic register focused on Mantell for a moment. He heard an instant humming sound and knew that he had been photographed and permanently pigeonholed for future reference.

"Come this way, please," the robot invited.

The place was sheer luxury. Heavy red synthetic velvet draperies helped to muffle the sound. There were faint traces of aromatic scent in the air, and soft music from an invisible orchestra could be heard, all tingling violins and shimmering cellos. After his seven years on Mulciber, Mantell felt utterly out of place. But the robot glided along in front of them, leading them to their table, and Myra at his side moved with a gliding grace that seemed almost too perfect to be natural, yet had a life and a smoothness that no robot known could match.

They stopped at a freeform table set close against the curving silver wall. A little oval window, crystal-clear, looked out on the city below. It was a city of parks and greenish-blue lakes and soaring buildings. Ben Thurdan had built an incredible fairy garden of a world here on Starhaven, Mantell thought.

And dedicated it to crime. Mantell scowled at that, until he reminded himself that he himself was nothing but a criminal, a—a killer, no matter what he remembered of the incident. He had no right to pass judgment on Ben Thurdan. He was here and safe, and he had to be grateful for that fact.

The robot drew out Myra's chair, then his. He lowered himself to its plastic-covered seat. It clung to his body; sitting in the ingenious suspension-foam chair was like drifting in zero grav.

The violins in the background seemed to underscore the moment. Mantell sat quietly, looking at her. Those marvelous strange blue eyes held him—but that was far from all of her there was to see. It was impossible to fault Thurdan on his taste here. Myra was wide-shouldered, with flawless lips and a delicate thin-bridged nose. Her eyes flashed like gems when she spoke. Her voice was soft and well-modulated and just a little on the throaty side.

Mantell said, "Tell me something—does every newcomer to Starhaven get this sort of treatment? Violins and fancy meals, and all?"

"No."

The muscles around his jaws tightened. He sensed that he was being teased, and he didn't care for it.

"Why am I being singled out, then? I'm sure Thurdan doesn't send his—secretary out to dinner with every stray beachcomber who comes to Starhaven."

"He doesn't," she said sharply. Changing the subject clearly and emphatically she asked, "What would you like to drink?"

Mantell considered for a moment and finally ordered a double kiraj; she had vraffa, very dry. The wine steward was a robot, too, who murmured obsequiously and vanished to return with their drinks in a few seconds, bowed, and scuttled away.

Mantell sipped thoughtfully. After a moment he said. "You changed the subject on me pretty quickly. You're being mysterious, Miss Butler."

"My name is Myra."

"As you wish. But you changed the subject again. You're still being mysterious."

She laughed, reached across the table, took his hand. "Don't ask too many questions too soon, Johnny. It's a dangerous thing to do on Starhaven at any time—but don't ask questions so soon. You'll learn everything you want to know in time. Maybe."

"Okay," he said, shrugging.

He wasn't that anxious to pry, after all. Seven years of roaming the bleak shore line on Mulciber had left him detached, indifferent about many things. He had become experienced in the art of drifting along passively on the tide of events, letting things happen as they wanted to happen.

This girl had taken some special interest in him, it seemed. He decided to accept that on face value, for the moment, and let the explanations go till later.

"Starhaven's a little different from Mulciber, isn't it?" she asked suddenly, breaking into his reverie.

"Very different," he said.

"You spent seven years on Mulciber."

"You saw my psychprobe charts, didn't you? You don't need to get a verbal verification from me." He felt obscurely annoyed. They were fencing, dancing around a conversation rather than engaging in one. And it was very much like dancing at arm's length. He felt uncomfortable.

"I'm sorry," she said. "I didn't mean to rake up old wounds. Ben built this place so people like you could come here . . . and forget. Mulciber's nothing but a bad dream now, Johnny."

"I wish it were. But I spent seven years begging for nickels there. I killed a man there. You don't blot out a memory like that the way you do a bad dream." He spoke toughly, and she reacted as if he had slapped her across the face. The liquor was getting to him too fast, he thought.

"Let's forget it, shall we?" she said with forced lightheartedness. She lifted her glass. "Here's to Ben Thurdan and the world he built. Here's to Starhaven!"

"Here's to Starhaven," Mantell echoed.

They drank, draining their glasses, and then they ordered another from the wine steward. Mantell's head was beginning to swim a little, but it was a pleasant sensation. He was aware that somewhere during the third drink Myra ordered dinner, and not much later a couple of robots laden with trays came shuffling up and began to unload. Truffles, baked pheasant, white and red wines, Vengilani crabs on shell as a side dish. He stared at the array, aghast.

She said, "Is something the matter, Johnny? You don't look so well."

"This is a fifty-credit—fifty-*chip* dinner. That's a little out of my orbit."

She smiled. "Don't be silly, Johnny. This is Ben's treat. I have a pass that takes care of things like this. Dig in and don't worry about the check!"

He dug in. He hadn't eaten that well in his life—and certainly not since August 11, 2793, a day he remembered vividly. That was the day Klingsan Defense Screens of Terra, Incorporated, had decided it could do without his scientific services.

As he ate, he thought about the events of that day. He remembered, wincing involuntarily, reporting to work two hours late and a good three sheets to the wind, and finding the pink discharge slip on his desk. He had snorted angrily and gone storming down to the executive level to see Old Man Klingsan himself. He had burst into the office of the company head, demanding to know why he was being fired.

Klingsan had told him. Then Mantell had told Klingsan three or five things that had been on his mind for a while, and by the time he was through talking he had succeeded in getting himself blacklisted from Rim to Core; there wasn't a world in the galaxy that would give him employment now.

A well-meaning friend had lined up a cheap job for him on Mulciber, far from Earth. He had shot his last ninety credits getting there from Viltuun, just in time to learn that his reputation had preceded him and he wasn't wanted on Mulciber.

But he couldn't leave without fare money. And for seven solid years he had never managed to accumulate enough cash in one chunk to pay for his transportation off that lazy, enervating semi-tropical world. Not until the day the Space Patrol came after him on a murder charge, and he'd *had* to get off.

"You're brooding about something, Johnny," Myra said suddenly. "I told you not to think of Mulciber any more. Try to forget it."

"I wasn't thinking of Mulciber," he lied. "I was thinking—thinking that it's perfectly permissible for me to skip out of here without paying the check. I mean, the restaurant owners don't have any legal recourse. They can't. There's no specific law against it."

"That's true enough. But *you* won't have any recourse, either, if they catch you and slice you up for steak. Or—if you like this place and ever want to come back—they'll simply refuse you admittance. Or they could slip you some slow poison the next time you come in here to cadge a meal."

He thought that over for a moment or two. Then a new and startling conclusion struck him. "You know something? I almost think an upside-down free-flying setup like this works out better than one based on a complex system of laws based on high moral precepts and obsolete customs. Here, the crimes cancel each other out into zeros!"

She nodded. "That's Ben's big idea. If you take a group of people, none of whom are cluttered up by morals, and enforce this kind of code on them, their collective rascality will all even out into a pretty regular, practical kind of law-observance. It's only when you start throwing virtuous people into the system that it falls apart."

Mantell frowned. He had the feeling that there was an inconsistency somewhere in her glib argument, but at the moment he was not interested in finding it.

He grinned at her. "You know, I think I'm going to like this place," he said.

Chapter Six

There were a few stray threads of conversation after that, but they petered out quickly and they finished eating in silence. Against the backdrop of the singing violins (not violins really, he knew, but merely tones produced by an electronic musical synthesizer somewhere in the giant building) Mantell thought, This is quite a woman! He was trying to imagine—without success—what thing she could have done that would have forced her to take refuge here on Starhaven from the galactic police system.

It was hard to figure what crime lay in the girl's past. She seemed too clean, too pure. Mantell was well aware that she was no angel; but even so, she gave the appearance of innocence, making it seem as if she always acted out of the highest motives.

Mantell didn't regard himself as a hardened criminal, either. He kept telling himself he was just a victim of circumstances. The breaks of life could as easily have gone the other way for him, and instead of becoming a desperate wanderer on a tourist planet like Mulciber, he could have remained a skilled armaments technician back on Earth.

He scowled. He was *still* an armaments technician, he told himself. Only not on Earth but here on Starhaven, where nobody would plague him with cheap moralizing.

And where there was Myra.

He wondered, as he sat staring at her, how he was going to get away with it.

Obviously she was Thurdan's girl. That was an obstacle that would stop most men right away. On a planet like this, a man doesn't try to walk away with the absolute tyrant's girl if he intends to enjoy a long life. Of course, there was always the possibility that Thurdan might tire of her. . . .

Who are you kidding? he asked himself. Sure, Thurdan would tire of her. Any minute now, he thought bitterly. Who could ever tire of *her*?

Mantell's mood darkened. He told himself he would have to forget any intentions he might have in regard to Myra Butler. Otherwise he would be up to his ears in deep trouble, and he had been on Starhaven less than a day.

The robot servitors appeared and cleared away the remnants of the meal. There was still half a bottle of wine left, but Mantell had neither the desire nor the room for it now. He watched the robot clear the wine away with the rest of the things, and grinned.

"I never thought I'd last long enough to pass up a half-full bottle of wine," he said.

He leaned back. He felt warm and well-fed, with the taste of rare wine still on his lips.

"Where to now?" he asked.

She smiled. "Do you dance?"

"More or less. I'm a little out of practice."

"That doesn't matter. Come. The ballroom's three levels above."

Mantell felt little desire to dance just now. But she continued pleadingly, "I love to dance, Johnny. And Ben won't ever dance with me. He never will. He hates dancing of any kind."

Mantell shrugged agreeably. "Anything to oblige a lady, I always say. If you want to dance, let's go."

Together they drifted out of the dining hall and into the waiting lift tube, and up three levels to the ballroom. Mantell realized in astonishment that ninety per cent of the Pleasure Dome was still above them, even here on the twelfth level.

The ballroom was a huge arching room, magnificently decorated. Music throbbed out of a hundred concealed speakers. Glowing dabs of soft living light, red and blue and gentle violet, swung and bobbed mistily in the air just above the dancers. It was a stunning sight, a scene out of a picture book.

"For a man who doesn't like to dance, Thurdan built quite a dance hall," Mantell observed.

"That's one of Ben's specialties—catering to other people's likes. It keeps the people loyal to him."

"Ben's a shrewd man," Mantell said.

"The shrewdest there ever was," agreed Myra.

They stepped out onto the dance floor. Myra glided into his arms. They began to dance.

It had been years since the last time Mantell had been on a dance floor. On Mulciber he simply hadn't thought in terms of luxuries like dancing; the struggle for life was too intense. And on Earth, he had always been too busy with less frivolous things.

But here, on this pleasure planet, he could make up for lost time.

There was a modified antigravity shield mounted beneath the gleaming dark luciphrine plastic of the dance floor. The field was on lowest modulation, not strong enough to lift the dancers from the surface of the floor but mustering enough power to cut down their weight somewhere between thirty and forty per cent, Mantell estimated.

It was more like floating than dancing. Feet glided, skimming over the floor.

Mantell felt Myra lightly against him, clinging; the bobbing swirls of living light in the air circled playfully around them, giving Myra's face sharply accented multicolored highlights of curious effect. The music beat beneath them, swelling and surging deeply. Mantell found himself moving with a grace he had never known he possessed.

It was half due to the antigrav shield, he thought, and half to Myra, featherlight in his arms.

One thing struck him as incongruous. Around him in the crowded pavilion danced the people of Starhaven, each one carrying locked within his mind the burden of some crime, each a hunted man now safe forever from the hunters.

They laughed, joked, clung to each other, just like ordinary people. Just like those who lived everyday lives within the law. Men and women having a good time, but outlaws all.

Mantell and Myra danced on. An hour, two hours perhaps, slipped by. Under the low gravity, time seemed to speed imperceptibly. Mantell hardly cared. He let the hours move past.

Finally, as the music died for the hundredth time and the couples left the floor for a short breather between numbers, Myra said, "Had enough?"

Mantell grinned at her. "Hardly."

"But I think we'd better leave now, Johnny. It's getting late."

He looked at his watch. It was nearly midnight. He realized for the first time how tired he was. All in this same day he had run a race with the SP ships, undergone a painful psychprobing, and now spent hours with Myra. It had been a full schedule.

"Where do we go now?" he asked. "The gambling den? The bar?"

She shook her head lightly. "We go home," she said. "It's close to my bedtime."

The music began again, a lilting fast dance, and the crowds of pleasure-seekers coasted back onto the dance floor. Mantell made way through the throng, holding tightly to Myra's hand. He was able to get back to the liftshaft without too much trouble; they rode down and out into the brightly floodlit plaza outside the Pleasure Dome.

As if from nowhere the slinky teardrop car that had conveyed them to the Dome appeared. They got in.

"Take us to my place," Myra instructed the driver.

The trip was over almost before it had begun. They pulled up in front of a handsome apartment building. Myra got out; Mantell followed.

The doors of the building swung back at their approach. He escorted her up the liftshaft and as far as the door of her apartment.

She touched her thumb lightly to the doorplate and the door started to roll back. She said, "I won't ask you in, Johnny. It's late, and—well, I can't. Please understand, won't you?"

He smiled. "Okay. It's been a swell night, and I won't press my luck further. Good night, Myra. And thanks for everything."

"I'll be seeing you, Johnny. Don't worry about that."

He frowned and started to object, "But Ben—"

"Ben may not be with us too much longer," she whispered in a strange tone. "A lot depends on you. We're counting on you more than you can imagine."

"What? You—?"

"Remember what I said about asking too many questions too soon," she warned. "Good night, Johnny."

"Good night," he said, bewildered. She smiled enigmatically and then he found himself staring at the outside of her door, alone, well-fed and feeling warm inside.

The car was waiting downstairs when he emerged. It was after midnight, and the sky was dotted with convincing stars. Thurdan had not spared expense in making Starhaven a wonderland world come true.

He climbed into the car. The driver looked human, but from the rigid forward set of his head he might just as well have been a robot.

"She's a remarkable woman, isn't she?" Manfell said to the man. "Miss Butler, I mean."

"Yes, sir."

Mantell smiled. The driver wasn't much of a conversationalist, obviously. He said, "Take me home, to Number Thirteen."

"Yes, sir."

Relaxing, Mantell watched the buildings slip by on either side. He was tired now, and anxious to reach his room. He was more than tired: he was exhausted. It had been a fantastic day.

Chapter Seven

Mantell saw a man die, his second day on Starhaven. It taught him not to judge by first impressions. Starhaven wasn't entirely a pleasure-planet, a happy Utopia. There was violent death here, and evil.

He had slept late that day, ridding himself of his fatigue and weariness. At 1100 in the morning the room-phone buzzed loudly, waking him from a tortuously involved dream of Space Patrol men, fugitives, and ancient, fumbling scientists operating psychprobes.

He pulled himself out of bed, crossed the austere, simple room that had been assigned to him, and switched on the phone, rubbing sleep from his face. Slowly the pattern of colors that appeared on the visiscreen shaped itself into a meaningful configuration.

It was the face of Ben Thurdan.

Even on a visiscreen a foot square his face had a terrible brooding intensity, a dark-visaged strength. He smiled and said, "I hope I didn't wake you, Mantell. You must be pretty tired."

Mantell forced out a chuckle. "I guess I overslept. It's a bad habit of mine."

"What did you think of the Pleasure Dome?" Thurdan asked easily. Mantell's sleep-fogged mind started to frame an answer, but before he could speak Thurdan had added the words, ". . . and Myra."

That threw him off base. He said, "It's a fabulous place, Mr. Thurdan. I've never seen anything like it anywhere. And—and Miss Butler was very helpful in explaining Starhaven to me."

"Glad to hear that," Thurdan said slowly. There was a long, uncomfortable moment of silence. Mantell fidgeted before the screen, acutely conscious of the great reservoir of power that lay in the man. At length Thurdan said, "Mantell, I liked you the second I saw you. You've got *character*. I like a man with character."

Mantell wondered what the Starhaven boss was driving at. Keeping back his surprise, he said gravely, "Thank you, Mr. Thurdan."

"Call me Ben." The deep piercing eyes studied Mantell until his flesh began to crawl. "I trust you, Mantell. And let me tell you I don't trust very many people on Starhaven. Suppose you do me a little favor, Mantell. Yes. A little favor."

"If I can—Ben. What sort of favor do you mean?"

"I want you to keep your eyes open. Miss Butler—Myra—will be keeping company with you again today. Listen to things carefully, Mantell. And feel free to get in touch with me if you think there's anything I ought to know."

Mantell frowned and said, "I'm not sure I understand what you're getting at. But I think I grasp the general picture."

"Good. Stick with me, Mantell. Life can be very very good for a man on Starhaven, if Ben Thurdan is backing him."

Thurdan grimaced in what was probably supposed to be a friendly smile, and rang off. Mantell stared at the shining surface of the blank screen for a second, trying to figure things out.

The call from Thurdan, he thought, was linked in some manner with Myra's enigmatic words at her door just before he had left her last night. Obviously Ben Thurdan was afraid of something; an assassination plot, more likely than not—and had chosen Mantell to serve as an extra pair of eyes and ears for him.

Maybe—Mantell caught his breath—maybe he suspected that Myra herself was involved in some conspiracy against him, and had arranged for Mantell to keep company with her so he could gain her confidence and report back information.

Mantell shook his head. A tangled web was beginning to form. Too soon, he thought. He hadn't come here to Starhaven to play power politics and get enmeshed in palace intrigues. He had just wanted a place to hide; a place where he could rebuild his battered personality and forget the Mulciber years.

He gobbled a breakfast tab and looked at his hands. They were shaking. He was playing with big trouble, and he was afraid.

Calming himself, he dialed Myra's number. She appeared on the screen, looking awake and unafraid, and they exchanged light banter for a moment or two before Mantell explained that he had called to arrange a date for lunch with her at the Pleasure Dome.

"Meet you there in ninety minutes," she said. "Outside the ninth-level dining hall."

"Right."

He broke the contact and started to dress. He killed the better part of an hour pacing tensely around his room, then went downstairs and found a cab to take him to the Pleasure Dome.

Myra met him there on time, to the minute, and once again they took the table near the window, drawing much attention from the service-robots. They had a brief, nervous lunch: chlorella steak and fried diamante potatoes, with splits of golden Livresae beer. They had replaced the freeform table with a crystal-topped affair in which strange green-hued horned fish swam proudly and serenely. Neither Mantell nor the girl said very much. Both seemed to be under a sort of cloud.

Myra said finally, breaking a long silence, "Ben called you this morning, didn't he?"

Mantell nodded. "That man seems to have taken a liking to me. I guess something in my psychprobe chart must have impressed him."

She laughed softly and drained her beer, all but the foam. "Something in your psychprobe chart impressed everybody who saw it, Johnny. We can't figure out why you let yourself drift so long on Mulciber."

"I told you. Pressure of circumstances."

"According to your chart, you're the sort who pushes circumstances around to suit himself, not the other way."

Mantell laughed cynically. "Maybe Dr. Harmon *is* getting senile, then. I haven't been doing much pushing around. I've been getting pushed."

"It's puzzling, then. According to the chart there's a real and solid core of toughness in you. Ben spotted that in a flash, the second old Harmon brought your graphs in from the lab for him to look at. 'That guy Mantell's got something,' Ben said. 'I can use him.'"

I guess I hide my self-reliance well, then," Mantell said. He was remembering the shambling unshaven figure who was himself, weaving drunkenly over the shining sands of Port Mulciber, pleadingly cadging cheap drinks from sympathetic tourists. He wondered where that alleged core of toughness had been hiding all those lost years of beachcombing.

They fell silent for another few moments, while Mantell spun conflicting thoughts in his mind. Then he said, "Last night, just before you said good night, you made a strange remark. You—"

Terror suddenly appeared on her face, altering it for a flashing microsecond into a white mask of fear. She said, "That was just—a sort of a joke. Or a hope. I'll tell you more about it some day—maybe. I asked you not to be impatient."

"I can't help it. That's a lousy thing to do—I mean, dropping a lead that way and then not following through. But I won't try to push you. I'm starting to discover that you *can't* be pushed."

"There's a good boy," she said. She fingered the empty split of beer and said, "I want another of these beers. Then I'll take you up and give you the five-chip guided tour of the Dome's other amusement areas."

They had another beer apiece and left, Myra flashing her pass to take care of the check and the suave robot headwaiter nodding understandingly.

They moved past the barriers into the lift tube and rode upward one stop, to the tenth level. There they emerged in a hall lined with black onyx and gleaming chalcedony. Voices shrilled in noisy cacophony farther ahead down the corridor.

"There are eight casinos on this floor," Myra said. "They operate twenty-four hours a day."

Suddenly she turned down a narrower corridor; Mantell followed and the corridor opened out abruptly into a room the size of the ballroom they had visited the night before.

He was blinded by myriad pinwheeling lights. Spirals of circling radiance danced in the air. Noise, gaiety, color bombarded him. Richly dressed Starhavenites were everywhere.

"Most of these people are professional gamblers," Myra whispered to him. "Some of them practically live in here, around the clock. Last month Mark Chantal had a run of luck on the rotowheel table and played for eight days without stopping. Toward the end he had a couple of companions feeding him lurobrin tablets by the bushel to keep him awake and fed. But by the time he decided to quit he had won eleven million chips."

Mantell whistled appreciatively. "I'll bet the house must have hated that!"

"The house is Ben Thurdan," Myra said. "He didn't hate it. He was here cheering Chantal on for the last two days of the run. That's the way Ben is."

Mantell glanced dizzily around the crowded hall. Gaming devices of every sort were in profuse evidence, ringed round the gleaming concourse. Some of the tables were tended by robots, others by attractive young women with sweet voices and daring costumes. In the back of the big casino Mantell saw a row of card tables; sleek-faced house operators waited there, willing to take on all comers in any kind of game.

"What shall we play?" Myra asked.

Mantell shrugged. "How do I pick one game out of all this?"

"Go ahead. The rotowheel? Swirly? Or should we try our luck at radial dice?"

Mantell licked his lips and picked out a table almost at random. "Let's start over here," he said, indicating the green baize surface of a nearby radial dice table.

It did not seem overcrowded. Four or five smartly dressed gamblers clustered around it, studying the elaborate system of pitfalls and snares that inhibited the free fall of the dice, making alterations in the system and placing their bets.

The house man was a robot. He waited, his metal face frozen in a perpetual cynical smile, his complex circuitry computing the odds as they changed from one moment to the next.

Mantell frowned thoughtfully as he stared at the board. He drew a ten-chip bill from his wallet and started to put it down. Suddenly Myra touched his arm.

"Don't bet yet," she murmured tensely. "There's going to be trouble."

Slowly, he turned to follow her gaze. He was aware that the big room had become strangely quiet. Everyone was apparently staring with keen intensity at a newcomer who had just entered.

Mantell studied him. The stranger was remarkably tall—six feet eight, at a conservative estimate—and his face was chalk-pale. A livid scar ran jaggedly across his left cheek, standing out in odd contrast against his colorless skin. He was skeleton thin and wore black-and-white diamond-checked harlequin tights and a skin-tight gray-and-gold shirt.

A glittering blaster was strapped to his side just above his left hip. He was an arresting figure, standing quietly alone near the entrance.

"Who is he?" Mantell asked.

"Leroy Marchin. Everyone thought he left Starhaven more than a month ago. He shouldn't be here. Oh, the idiot! Stay here."

She started across the floor toward the other. Ignoring her order, Mantell followed her. The silence in the room shattered, finally, as a croupier began his droning chant once again. Myra seemed to have forgotten all about Mantell, now that Marchin, whoever he was, had arrived.

As Mantell drew near the pair he heard Marchin say, "Hello, Myra." His voice was deep but without resonance; it sounded hollow.

"What are you doing here?" Myra demanded. "Don't you know that Ben—?"

"Ben knows I'm here. The robots outside tipped him off ten minutes ago by remote wave."

"Get out of here, then!"

"No," Marchin said. "I'm hoping Ben will show up here in person. That way I have an even chance of getting in the first shot."

"Leroy—" Her tone rose in shrill urgency. "You can't—"

"Get away from me," Marchin interrupted brusquely. "I don't want you near me when the shooting starts."

He looked terribly pale and tired, but there was no fear on his face. With exaggerated casualness he stepped past Myra and Mantell, crossed the floor to the rotowheel table, and calmly put a hundred-chip bill down when the croupier called for bets.

Mantell turned to Myra and said, "What's this all about? Who is he?"

She was taut with nervousness. "He—tried to kill Ben, once. It was a conspiracy that didn't succeed. He and Ben built Starhaven together, in the early years, but Marchin was always pushed aside. Ben had to run this place as a one-man enterprise."

The suspense was becoming numbing. Mantell said, "Why did he come here?"

"He's been in hiding. I guess Ben flushed him out and Leroy decided to fight it out with him here in the casino. Oh—!"

Again the hall became silent. This time it was a silence markedly more profound than the last.

A robot entered the hall, moving on silent caterpillar treads—a square-built robot, stocky, at least eight feet tall. Mantell watched as Marchin turned round to face the robot. People who had been standing within ten or twenty feet of the pale man melted quietly away. Mantell was aware that Myra was trembling uncontrollably.

"Hello, Roy," the robot said. It was speaking in Ben Thurdan's own voice, thanks to the use of some kind of electronic remote-wave hookup.

Marchin's eyes blazed as he glared angrily at the robot.

"Damn you, Thurdan! Why didn't you come here yourself? Why did you have to send a robot here to do your filthy job for you?"

"Too busy to bother with such trivial things in person, Roy," was the calm reply. "And there's less doubt of the outcome this way."

Marchin drew his blaster. An instant later the house lights dimmed as though because of a sudden power drain, and a flickering transparent glow sprang up around the robot.

"Force screen," Myra muttered. "Marchin doesn't stand a chance."

Mantell nodded. A robot could wear a force screen, though a human being couldn't. A human being needed air to breathe, and a force screen blocked out everything—light and air as well as dangerous radiation. It was tremendously expensive to equip a robot with a force screen, but evidently Ben kept one around for jobs like this.

Marchin's finger tightened on the firing stud. A burst of flame leaped across the gap, bathing the robot in fire but actually merely splattering impotently against the impassable barrier that was the force screen.

The metal creature, unharmed by the deadly blast, waited impassively. Almost a minute slipped by while Marchin hopelessly continued to direct his fire at the barrier that shielded the robot's patient bulk. Then, seeing he was accomplishing nothing, Marchin cursed vividly and in a quick bitter gesture hurled the blaster across the room at the stiffly erect robot.

The weapon clanged off the creature's chest and fell to one side.

The robot laughed. The laugh was unmistakably the laugh of Ben Thurdan.

Marchin howled an imprecation, and began to run.

For a moment at first Mantell thought he was going to try to dash out the door, but that was not Marchin's intention, apparently. Instead he ran straight toward the robot in a mad suicidal dash.

He traveled ten feet. Then the robot lifted one ponderous arm and discharged a bolt of energy from grids in its fingers. The flare caught Marchin in the chest with such impact that it lifted him off the ground and hurled him backward the whole distance he had covered in his dash.

He tottered, clawed at his throat, and staggered into a swirly screen at a table behind him. He fell and didn't get up.

Its work complete, the robot about-faced and vanished without another word. From somewhere in the ceiling came the sound of light music, and the tension dissolved. The croupiers began to chatter again; the jingle of falling chips could be heard. It was as if everyone in the room was determined to pretend that nothing at all had taken place in the casino just now.

Two attendants appeared and removed the charred, blasted corpse. Mantell watched them until Myra tugged at his arm and pulled him back to the radial-dice table.

He felt a hard knot of fear in his stomach. He had just had another sample of the way Ben Thurdan governed Starhaven. Ben Thurdan was no man to cross.

Chapter Eight

The killing put finish to any pleasure he might have had from gambling that afternoon.

Myra, oddly, was outwardly unmoved, except for a certain paleness and tenseness of face. It puzzled him for a while. Evidently, at sometime in the past, she had known Marchin well. Yet she seemed callously unmindful of his fate.

After a while he realized the reason. She was used to the phenomenon of killing. Death—violent death—was nothing uncommon on Starhaven.

They gambled for perhaps an hour more; Mantell's mind was only faintly focused on what he was doing, and in a short time he had contrived to lose half his slim bank-roll on the rotowheel and at radial dice. Luckily Myra did well at swirly, and recouped most of their losses. But Mantell's heart was hardly in the sport now. He waited for Myra to collect her swirly winnings. Then, as she started across the room to the magneroulette board, he tugged on her sleeve and said, "No. No more games for now. Let's get out of here."

"Where?"

"Anywhere. I need a drink."

She smiled, understanding. Together they cut their way through the crowd, which was noisy now with a kind of desperate gaiety, heading for the entrance. A thick crowd of new arrivals was flocking into the casino as they left; evidently they had been attracted by reports of the excitement, no doubt filtering all through the Pleasure Dome now. Mantell and Myra had to fight their way out of the casino like fish swimming upstream in rapid current.

"Gambling is the number one industry of Starhaven," Myra said when they emerged at the liftshafts and stood wiping away some of the perspiration their exit had induced. "The working day starts around noon for most of the professionals. It gets heaviest at four or five in the afternoon, and continues all night."

Mantell mopped away perspiration without making any reply. He was not interested in small talk just now. He was thinking of a tall, gaunt, pale man named Leroy Marchin, who had been gunned down in full sight of five hundred people, without arousing more than polite comment here and there.

They rode upward and Myra led the way to a bar somewhere on the middle levels of the building. It was a dim place, smoky with alcohol vapors, lit only by faint and sputtering inert-gas light tubes.

Mantell found an empty table far to the rear, ornate and encrusted with possibly authentic gems. A vending robot came over and they dialed for their drinks.

He ordered straight rye, preferring not to drink anything fancy this time. Myra was drinking clear blue wine out of a crystal goblet. Mantell gulped his drink and had another.

Looking up, he spotted a tri-di video set mounted in the angle between the wall and the ceiling, back of the bar. He peered at it. He saw the drawn, weary face of Leroy Marchin depicted on the screen in bright harsh unreal colors.

"Look up there," he said.

Myra looked. The camera suddenly panned away from the figure of Marchin to show the entire casino as it had looked at the moment of the duel. There was the robot, massive, smugly supreme; there, facing it, Marchin. And he saw clearly in the vast screen his own lean face, staring at the scene uncomprehendingly. Myra was at his side. She was gripping his arm tensely in the shot; he didn't remember that, but he supposed it must have actually been that way. He had been too absorbed in the duel to notice.

An announcer's oily voice said, "This was the scene as Leroy Marchin got his in the Crystal Casino shortly after one-thirty today. Marchin, returning to Starhaven from self-imposed exile, after having made an unsuccessful attempt on the life of Ben Thurdan last year, entered the casino alone."

The audio pickup relayed the brief, bitter conversation between Marchin and the robot that spoke with Thurdan's voice. Then the drawing of blasters was shown, then the exchange of shots. . . .

And a final closeup of Marchin's seared body.

"Death Commissioner Brian Varnlee was on hand to certify that Marchin died of suicide," said the smooth-voiced announcer. "Meanwhile, on other news fronts, a report has reached Starhaven that . . ."

Mantell looked away, sickened. "That's all it is," he said darkly. "Just suicide. And no one seems to care. No one gives a damn that a man was shot down in public this afternoon."

Myra was staring at him anxiously. "Johnny, that's the way Starhaven works. It's our way of life and we—we don't question it. If you can't bring yourself to accept Ben's laws, you'd better get off Starhaven fast—because it'll kill you to stay here."

He moistened his lips. He wanted to reply to her, to make some kind of protest.

But something strange was happening to him; some as yet unidentifiable dark fear was welling up into his consciousness from the hidden depths of his brain. He weaved uncertainly and gripped the table with both hands, tight. He shuddered involuntarily as tides of pain swept up over him, racking him again and again.

He heard Myra's anxious exclamation—"Johnny! What's happening? What's wrong?"

It was a moment before the pain had subsided enough for him to speak. "Nothing's wrong," he murmured weakly. "Nothing."

But something *was* wrong. In one wild sweep the last seven years rose accusingly before him, from the day of his dismissal from Klingsan Defense to the day he had fled, a hunted murderer in a stolen ship, from the shores of Mulciber.

Those memories arrayed themselves in a solid column—and the column suddenly toppled and fell, shattering into a million pieces.

Starhaven spun around him. His palms ached as he squeezed the cold table top to keep from tumbling to the floor. Dimly he sensed Myra grasping his numbed hands, saying things to him, steadying him. Doggedly he fought to catch his breath.

It was all over in a second or two more. He sat back exhausted, bathed in sweat, his head quivering and his skin cold.

"What happened, Johnny?"

He shook his head. In a harsh voice he said, "I don't know what it was. It must have been some after-effect of the psychprobing. Harmon said he had miscalibrated and there might be after-effects. For a second—Myra, for a second I thought I was someone else!"

"Someone else?"

He shrugged, then laughed sharply. "Too many drinks, probably. Or else not enough. I guess I better have another one."

He ordered another rye and downed it hastily. The raw liquor soothed him a little. Nervously, he gathered up the fragments of the identity that had shattered a moment before and pasted them together. Once again he was Johnny Mantell, ex-beachcomber, late of Mulciber in the Fifth Octant of the galaxy, and now of Starhaven, home of galactic criminal outcasts.

Faint wooziness clung to him, but the spell, whatever it had been, was past. At least, for now.

"I feel a lot better," he said. "Let's get some fresh air."

Chapter Nine

The rest of Mantell's week of indoctrination passed pleasantly enough. He was finding out how Starhaven ran, and though it was hard for him to admire every aspect of the place, he had to admit without reservations that in building it Thurdan had achieved something astonishingly close to a miracle.

Mantell saw Myra often, though perhaps not as often as he would have liked to see her. Their meetings always seemed to be held at arms' length; invisible but tangible veils blocked any real communication between them, Mantell realized. Things were being kept back. There was something she was not telling Mantell because she would not tell him, and something he was not telling her because he did not know it himself.

The unsettling thing that had happened to him in the Pleasure Dome bar happened twice more during that week. Twice more he experienced the sudden cold sweat, the sudden swaying dizziness, the sudden feeling that he was someone else, that the life he had lived was not that of a beachcomber on Mulciber.

The first time it happened was in a river boat, a streamlined passenger vessel streaking upriver to the plantations to the north of Starhaven proper. Thurdan had set up vast food-producing dominions outside the rural area, and he and Myra were on their way to visit them when the attack struck. It passed quickly, though it left him shaken for the next hour.

The next attack happened two days later, at three in the morning. Mantell woke and sat upright in bed, staring into the darkness, shaking convulsively while the fit gripped him. When the most violent symptoms had exhausted themselves, he sank back, exhausted.

Then, on a wild impulse, he bolted to the phone and punched out Myra's number, hoping she would forgive him for waking her at this hour.

But he didn't wake her. She wasn't there.

The phone chimed eight, nine, ten, a dozen times in her apartment; then a robomonitor downstairs cut in, and the blank metal face told Mantell, "Miss Butler is not at home. Would you care to leave a message for her? Miss Butler is not at home. Would you care to leave a message for her? Miss Butler is—"

Mantell listened to the metallic chant for nearly a minute, held in a dreamy hypnotic grasp. Then he collected himself and said, "No thanks. I guess I don't have any messages for Miss Butler."

He broke the contact listlessly and returned to bed. But he remained awake until morning, tossing and rolling, restless and unable to return to sleep. He kept thinking that there was only one place where Myra could possibly be at such an hour.

She had to be with Ben Thurdan.

Mantell revolved that thought in his mind for five straight hours. He realized that he was being a fool, that he had no real claim on Myra Butler, that she—like everyone and everything else on this planet—belonged to Ben Thurdan. Ben Thurdan could do what he pleased, and people like Johnny Mantell ought to be grateful for whatever Ben cared to leave over for them.

But the picture of Myra in the big man's arms haunted him and tore him away from sleep. At eight in the morning he rose and stared at his face in the mirror. A ghost's face stared back at him, haggard and almost frightening in some ways.

He found a package of defatiguing tablets and gobbled down three of them. Three tablets were the equivalent of eight hours of deep sleep.

With a hearty if synthetic night's sleep now under his belt, Mantell headed alone for the Pleasure Dome to iron some of the tensions out of his system.

During that week, he drifted. It came naturally to him. His years as a beachcomber had taught him how to kill time gracefully and skillfully. Then, on the seventh day since his arrival on Starhaven, Ben Thurdan called him at his room in Number Thirteen.

He seemed to lean forward out of the screen as he said, "Johnny, it's time to put you to work. You've had a solid week to rest up. That's about enough."

"I'm ready any time you want to start me," Mantell said. "It's been seven years since I last had a job. That's more than enough vacation for any man."

Thurdan chuckled with surprising warmth. "Okay. Stay where you are and I'll pick you up right now."

Ten minutes later Thurdan met him in an aircab and they set off northward for a distant part of Starhaven. Mantell had already learned through Myra that though the metal shell extended around the entire planet, only part of one continent had actually been settled. Starhaven was really one gigantic city of some twenty million people, which sprawled ever outward, expanding at the margins with each influx of new inhabitants. Beyond the city borders lay, to the south and east, farmland, and everywhere else the barren and empty land that had been there before Thurdan had reshaped the planet.

The aircab came to rest lightly on a landing stage atop a square, dark windowless building far to the northwest of the last outskirt of the settled area.

Thurdan leaped easily from the aircab to the landing apron, with Mantell right behind.

"This is the guts and brain of Starhaven right here," Thurdan said with a sort of pride.

A door opened trapwise not far from them. Thurdan beckoned and they descended into the upper level of the building, while the trap swung closed above them.

Men in neat laboratory outfits moved busily to and fro inside. They greeted Thurdan with respect. Thurdan introduced Mantell as a newly arrived armaments technician. Hearing himself described as anything but a derelict was a pleasant experience.

The tour began.

"Starhaven's defenses operate on two principles," Thurdan said, as he and Mantell crawled through a narrow tunnel lined with electronic approach-perceptors. "One is that you need a protective barrier. That's why I built the metal shell. Second—and a lot more important—you need a good offense. An offensive power coupled with sturdy defense is impregnable. Starhaven has the best offensive battery in the universe—and when you measure that with our defensive screens, our energy-field, and the sheer strength of the outer shell itself, you'll understand why the Space Patrol is so helpless against us."

They entered a vast room walled completely about with chattering computers.

"Nothing is left to chance," Thurdan said proudly. "Every shot that's fired by one of our heavy-cycle guns is computed precisely before we release it. And we don't miss often."

Mantell was dazzled by the display. His eyes could hardly take in the full magnitude of the fortress Ben Thurdan had built.

A bright array of meters and dials met his eye on a higher level, and he pointed questioningly to them.

"Those are the energy flow controls," Thurdan said. "You ought to see what happens when we're under bombardment. Every watt of energy that's thrown at us is soaked up by our screens, fed through the power lines here, and converted neatly into energy that we can use for operating Starhaven."

"How often do these bombardments happen?"

"We haven't had a big one in years. The SP has gotten smart. For a long time we hardly needed to use our own generators at all, thanks to the free power the SP kept throwing at us. But they've wised up, and these days they only make token raids to let us know they haven't forgotten about us."

Mantell nodded. He was definitely impressed; his days as an armaments man were not that far behind him that he could not appreciate the splendor of the Starhaven defenses. It was awesome.

He said, "Tell me, Ben—what genius designed all this?"

"Genius is right," Thurdan said. "Lorne Faber built this for me. It took him three years to complete the designs, three years of day-and-night work. Ever hear of him?"

"Lorne Faber? I think I remember. . . . Ah, yes. Killed his wife, didn't he? I read about the case. Long time ago."

Thurdan nodded. "He was a brilliant electronics man. Too brilliant, nervous, jittery, brittle. I saw it coming. His brilliance killed him, eventually. I could tell he was half out of his mind when I first met him, years back."

"What happened to him?"

"One day he saw the ghost of his wife in a neutrino screen downstairs and took a hatchet to it," Thurdan said. "It took days to unscramble all the short circuits."

The tour of the building lasted nearly three hours. Mantell was dizzy by the end of it, partly from the immensity of the armament tower and partly from the forgotten knowledge that had come welling excitingly back into his mind. He remembered busy hours spent designing defense screens years before, calculating inputs, tabulating megawattage, compiling long intricate columns of resistances and amperages as he shaped his work. Had it been seven years ago? They seemed to fade into one, then lead right into the present.

They reached the topmost floor of the building. Thurdan led Mantell into a long room lined completely with vision screens. The room was similar in tone and in opulence of furnishings to Thurdan's other office back in the center of the city.

"This," Thurdan said, "is the sanctum sanctorum. The nerve center of the whole planet. From this room I can control the entire network of defensive screens, fire any gun from any of the emplacements, broadcast subradio messages to any world of the galaxy."

His deep voice was filled with pride. It was not difficult to see the transparent personality of the man. He gloried in this room, from which he could control an entire world of his own, and defy the universe.

He threw himself heavily into a relaxing cradle and rocked gently back and forth. "Well, Mantell. . . . Now you've seen it. What do you think?"

"It's incredible, Ben. Starhaven's absolutely impregnable. There's nothing like it in the galaxy."

Thurdan's face darkened. "I'm still worried," he said slowly, "about a serious flaw in our system. It's so serious, in fact, that so far neither I nor any of my best men have figured a way to repair it."

Mantell stared at him, puzzled. "Flaw? Where? I'm rusty, Lord knows, but I'd swear that this is the most unassailable fortification that could possibly be built."

A faint smile rippled across Thurdan's mouth, but his eyes were still clouded. "Your statement's true enough, as far as it goes. However, there is a weakness that, under certain conditions, could mean the end of Starhaven and of those who enjoy its sanctuary. This weakness is inside."

"Inside?"

"Starhaven is vulnerable from within. If someone got control of this room, for instance, he could knock down the screens and hand us over to the Patrol on a silver platter. Of course, he'd have to kill me first. The man whom you saw executed in the casino the other day tried to do that."

"Marchin, you mean?"

"Yes. He was one of my original colonists on Starhaven. But we never got along well, Marchin and I. I saw the conflict between us shaping for years, and yet I held my hand and let him strike first. I was stronger, as it turned out." He shook his big head sadly. "Well, enough of that. I've got a job for you, Mantell. A very special job."

"What kind of job?" Mantell asked.

Thurdan said, "According to your psychprobe charts, you were a damned good defense-screen man—once. Every indication was that you'd hit the top before you were through. You fouled up that chance, but unless either Harmon or his machine is way off the beam, you still have plenty of stuff in you. Johnny, you can have a second chance to be top dog in your job, and do me a big favor at the same time. Here we can fight together. For I've found out—never mind how—that there's a scheme under way to assassinate me."

"Assassinate—*you*?" Mantell gasped, incredulous. "B-But what—? Who could—?"

"Never mind the details, or who wants me murdered. That's for me to worry about, not you. But the fact remains that they have a chance to succeed before I can identify and stop them."

"But Marchin didn't succeed."

"Marchin was different. I had him tagged every minute. Right now, I tell you I'm in constant danger. Oh, I'm well protected, all right, but not well enough for this. So, my friend, I'm going to turn an entire laboratory over to you, with your pick of the whole scientific staff. The sky's the limit for you, Johnny"—and Thurdan's piercing eyes seemed to impale Mantell's as the absolute ruler of Starhaven paused impressively—"all I'm asking you to do for me is to accomplish the impossible. I want you to build me a personal defense screen. And get onto it at once!"

Chapter Ten

I want you to do the impossible for me," Thurdan had told him. And, Mantell reflected soberly, that was pretty close to the truth.

He stood silently looking down at the huge man in the relaxing cradle who had built Starhaven. The personal defense screen was the goal of every defense outfit and of every planet in the galaxy, but so far even the basic working principles had eluded everyone's grasp. The problem was a horribly complex one: there had to be an arrangement which would selectively block off blaster energy while still admitting air, and although this could be accomplished within the realm of technological possibility, there were all the additional fillips that made the thing impossible. The unit had to be made small enough for a man to carry it about with him; then there was the necessity of somehow grounding the diverted energy, as well as providing for a steady and unstoppable power flow.

And, Mantell thought, even if all these problems were to be solved, such a screen would be useless. Round and round, and no answer without new problems. If a screen could be devised that was portable and efficient, as a perfect defense against energy weapons, its only effect would be to make energy weapons obsolete. Then, perhaps, the old, crude weapons of the ancient past would be reborn. And if so, there would be the problem of how to devise a screen that would block off knives and bullets and acid and still not cut off air and food.

"Well?" Thurdan said.

"You hit the nail square," Mantell said. "A screen like that is damned close to being an impossibility."

"So was building Starhaven," Thurdan shot back immediately. "But I built it! I don't know a damned thing about electronics, but I found men who *did* know. I found the best men in their fields, and they laughed when I showed them my rough plans for Starhaven. But I didn't listen to them. I told them to go ahead and do what I was paying them to do. I never take 'impossibles' for answers, Mantell."

Mantell shrugged. "I didn't say I wouldn't try. I'm just not promising delivery until I know I can do it."

"Fair enough," Thurdan said. "Don't promise anything. Just deliver. I don't want to die, Johnny."

Mantell caught the undertone in Thurdan's voice as he spoke the last words, and it was a startling revelation of the big man's character. For behind the bold voice, the resounding tones of command, there lay fear of the unknown, of death, just as in every other human being. Ben Thurdan didn't want to die. He didn't want to lose the world and private empire that he had planned and brought into being.

Well, Mantell considered, you can't blame him for that.

"There's one other thing I want to talk about, Mantell." The fear was gone from Thurdan's voice. "It's the matter of Miss Butler."

Mantell tensed. "What does she—?"

"I asked her to accompany you around during your first few days on Starhaven, Johnny. To help you out until you got your footing here, you understand. But right now, let's avoid any future conflict by getting things clear at the beginning. *Myra isn't available.* I'm marrying her just as soon as I get this problem solved."

"I—I never—" Mantell stammered.

"You never—what?" Thurdan snapped. "You called her place at three o'clock the other morning. I don't know what you had to say to her at three o'clock in the morning, but I can pretty well guess. So keep your hands off. There are plenty of women on Starhaven, and if you're interested, I'll see that you have your pick. But you don't have Myra!"

Mantell met Thurdan's eyes, and flinched. There wasn't any arguing with the strength he saw there. If Thurban had kept tabs on him to the extent of monitoring his phone, then lying to him was pointless. Even possibly suicidal.

He said, "Thanks for warning me, Ben. I wouldn't want to cross you."

"No," Thurdan said quietly. "It wouldn't be wise even to consider it."

Mantell spent another hour listening to Thurdan daydream out loud about Starhaven. Thurdan showed him a small room not far from his which was to be Mantell's office, introduced him to three or four lab workers, technicians and scientists who would be responsible to him and who would supply him with any materials he might need in his research. As a last item, Thurdan handed him five hundred chips as pocket money, by way of a starting salary.

"From now on you'll draw your pay off the standard payroll here," Thurdan told him. "You'll be getting five hundred a week. That ought to keep you comfortable for a while."

"I imagine I can manage on five hundred. I scrounged for pennies for seven years."

Thurdan smiled grimly. "The penny-scrounging days are all done with now, Mantell. This is Starhaven. Things are different here."

They returned to the roof landing stage, boarded the waiting aircab, and Thurdan drove him back to the center of the city. Mantell watched the big broad-shouldered figure vanish into the doorway of his office. Then he turned and walked away.

He was thinking of Myra.

It was funny, Mantell reflected. From now on he would be getting five hundred a week, and for that he was supposed to figure out a way of preserving Ben Thurdan's life. But so long as Thurdan lived, Myra was his.

As Mantell stood there considering that, she came out of another office on the floor. They nearly collided. Backing off, they laughed.

"Hello, Johnny," she said—a little coolly, he felt. "I thought you were out in the control tower with Mr. Thurdan."

"I was. We just got back five minutes ago. He's in his office."

"Oh. I'll have to see him, then. Some urgent messages—"

She started away, but before she had taken three steps Mantell strode after her and caught her by the arm. Then he remembered that hidden photon-absorbers in the ceiling were probably soaking up every bit of this scene. Or perhaps Thurdan was watching it directly. He was as close to omniscient as a human being could be.

"What is it, Johnny?"

Mantell hesitated. "I—I just wanted to say so long, that's all. I suppose I won't be seeing much of you, now that—now that I'll be working at the tower. My week of loafing is all used up." His voice came haltingly; he was sure she knew what he was trying to say. Thurdan had probably warned her to keep away from him, too. Thurdan never missed his bets.

"Sure, Johnny. It was swell," she said.

She disengaged her hand from his grasp gently but emphatically, turned on a wholly mechanical and unconvincing smile, then clicked it off again like the closing of a camera shutter. She walked through the faintly glowing barrier-beam into Thurdan's office. Mantell stood looking after her. He shook his head and turned away.

He gravshafted downstairs, caught a passing cab and drove to his hotel room. As he entered the lobby of Number Thirteen, the robot attendant that guarded the place slid forward holding out a package.

"Mr. Mantell, this just came for you. It was delivered by special courier."

"Thanks," Mantell said abstractedly. He took the package and made his way to the lift tube. The package was bound in a plain plastic wrapper; it was about the size of a book. He frowned, wondering who might be sending him books.

Upstairs he threw the package on the bed, depolarized the window, stared out at Starhaven, stared up at the synthetic sky and at the synthetic sun, and at the synthetic clouds circling under the metal skin.

Starhaven, he thought. Property of Ben Thurdan, Esq., lord and master of a world of fugitives. And Mantell was the hope he had to avoid death.

Mantell tried to picture Starhaven without Thurdan. The entire planet revolved around his whims; he was an absolute monarch, even though an enlightened one. The social system he had evolved here *worked*—though whether or not it would work with any other man at its helm was a highly debatable point.

And what would happen if Thurdan died? Probably the whole delicate fabric of the Starhaven system would come tumbling in chaotically on itself, ending a unique experiment in political theory. It was easy to foresee a mad scramble for power; the man who grabbed possession of the control tower would rule unchallenged—until another assassin struck *him* down.

Suddenly Mantell went cold all over. If anybody were to gain control of that tower, it would be John Mantell! His research laboratory was close to the central control room, and it was safe to consider that he would become a close associate of Thurdan during the course of his work.

New, strange ideas occurred to him.

After a while he turned away from the window and glanced at the package lying forgotten on his bed. He snatched it up and held it to his ear. There was no sound of a mechanism within. Cautiously, he opened it

It had felt like a book, and it *was* a book—the old-fashioned bound kind, not a tape. Inscribed in dark letters on its jacket was its title: *A Study of Hydrogen—Breathing Life in the Spica System.*

Some kind of joke? he wondered. He opened the book to the title page.

A folded slip of paper lay nestling between the flyleaf and the title page. Mantell frowned and drew it out, unfolded it, read it.

A moment later the slip flared heatlessly in his hand became an ash, and was gone, drawn quickly into the circulating system of the room along with all other molecule-sized fragments of debris that happened to be in the air.

It had been a very interesting message, printed in square anonymous voco-type capitals, standard model. It said:

> TO JOHN MANTELL—
> IF YOU ARE INTERESTED IN DISCUSSING THURDAN, VISIT THE CASINO OF MASKS IN THE PLEASURE DOME DURING THE NEXT SEVEN DAYS, BETWEEN THE HOURS OF NINE AND TEN IN THE EVENING. NO DANGER TO YOU.

Chapter Eleven

Three days later, Mantell paid a visit to the Casino of Masks.

The decision cost him three days of agonizing inner conflict. His first reaction to the anonymous note had been one of immediate anger; he did not want any part of any conspiracy against the life of Thurdan, at least not yet.

But then he recalled Myra's strange words that first night, and started to think of the various possibilities Thurdan's death might hold for him. He began to consider the idea more seriously.

The book contained no further clues. He made a detailed examination of it and concluded it had simply been a dummy, a vehicle for the message, and he destroyed it rather than risk getting into a situation where he would be forced to explain what he was doing possessing so unlikely a volume. He had no hint of the sender. The wrapping had been utterly anonymous.

He had a week to make up his mind about going to the Casino of Masks.

During the first two days he spent most of his time in his newly outfitted lab, putting himself through an intensified refresher course in defense-screen logistics. It was astonishing how readily the old knowledge sprang brightly into the front of his mind again after so many years. He sketched out a few speculative preliminary functions toward the possible design of Thurdan's personal defense screen.

Mantell's sketches were simply trial hypotheses, wild shots in the dark, but it seemed to him that he saw a few stray glimmers of light ahead. It might take months or years of work before anything useful eventuated, but he could perceive a possible line of attack, and that was a big chunk of the battle already won.

During those first days in the laboratory Mantell had little contact with Thurdan and none at all with Myra Butler. When he thought of her it was only as a girl of a dead romance, of a moment's affair. There was a brief sad ache, nothing more. He hadn't known her long enough for anything more, and in any event, he had become well conditioned to disappointment in his life.

He buried himself in his work; it was an exciting experience to rediscover techniques and patterns of thought he believed he had forever lost. He met his fellow armament technicians; Harrell, Bryson, Voriloinen, and six or seven others. Most of them were brilliant and wayward eccentrics who had fallen afoul of the law in one fashion or another, and who had fled to Starhaven, where by Thurdan's wisdom, technicians of all kinds were given a warm and eager welcome.

The technician named Bryson gave Mantell an uneasy moment one day. Bryson was a small man with rounded shoulders and fingers stained permanent ochre by nicotine; he walked with a kind of shuffle. He was in Mantell's laboratory one morning observing and helping out, and it occurred to Mantell to ask, by way of conversation, where Bryson had acquired his impressive skill in electronics.

Bryson smiled and said, "Why, I used to work at Klingsan Defense Screens, on Earth. Before my trouble, that is, I mean."

Mantell was holding a packet of junction transistors.

He started violently, dropping them. They scattered everywhere. "*Klingsan,* you said?"

Bryson nodded. "You've heard of them?"

"I worked there once, too," Mantell said. "From '89 to '93. Then they sacked me."

"That's odd," Bryson said in a curious voice. "I was there from '91 to '96, and I thought I knew everyone in the armaments department. I should have known you, then. But I don't. I don't remember any Mantell there, not at all. And you don't look familiar, either. Did you go under the name of Mantell while you were there?"

"Yes." Puzzled, Mantell shrugged and said, "Hell, that was more than seven years ago. Nobody's memory is perfect. Anyway, maybe we worked in different departments."

"Maybe," Bryson agreed vaguely.

But Mantell felt troubled. He tried to remember a Bryson at Klingsan, and couldn't. Neither anyone of that name, nor anyone who resembled the little man with the stained fingers. That was odd, because if they *had* been there at overlapping times they would most certainly have worked in the same department, since they had the same skills.

Something, Mantell thought, is very wrong.

But he pushed it to the back of his mind, storing it back with his life on Mulciber and his brief few days with Myra and all the other things he wasn't particularly anxious to think about, and returned to his waiting workbench.

He lost himself once again in his work. Another problem had to be settled. He wrestled with it for a while, and by late afternoon his decision was made. He had to find out. . . .

That night he went to the Casino of Masks.

There were eight separate gambling casinos on the tenth level of the Pleasure Dome, each with its own individual name and its own circle of regular clientele. The casino Myra had taken him to was known as the Crystal Casino, largest and most popular of the group, the casino of widest appeal. Others, farther along the gleaming onyx hallway, were smaller; in some, the stakes ran dangerously high, highly dangerous.

The Casino of Masks was farthest from the liftshaft. Mantell identified it solely by the hooded statue mounted before its entrance.

The time was exactly nine. His throat felt dry; tension gripped him like a constricting fist. He stretched out a hand, poked it as far as the wrist through the barrier beam that operated the door. The door slid back and he entered.

He found himself in darkness so complete that he was unable to see his hand held before his face, or even the watch on his arm. In all probability, he thought, he was getting a black light scanning from above, just to make sure he was not on the Casino's proscribed list.

After a moment a gentle robot voice murmured, "Step to the left, into the booth, sir."

Obediently he stepped to the left.

"Welcome to the Casino of Masks, good sir," another robot voice said.

He wished he had had the chance to find out from Myra or someone else exactly what this Casino of Masks was like, but it was too late for that now.

His unseen mentor said, "You may now receive the mask. Please turn."

Turning, Mantell saw a dim red light begin to glow, and by its light he perceived a triangular slotted mask lying in a lucite case; above it, in a mirror, he saw his image.

"Lift the mask from its case and slip it over your head," he was instructed. "It will afford complete protection of privacy from any recognition."

With tense fingers he lifted the mask and donned it. The next instruction followed: "Activate the stud near your right ear."

He touched the stud. And suddenly the image in the mirror gave way to a blurred figure of the same height. Just a blur, a wavering blotch in the air, concealing him completely.

Mantell remembered now: he had heard of these masks. They scattered light in a field surrounding the wearer, allowing one-way vision only. They were ideal for those who desired anonymity, as in this casino.

"You are now ready to enter the Casino," the robot said blandly.

He extended his hand, or rather the blur that was his hand. Within the field, of course, he saw no blur, but looking over his shoulder he caught the mirror's view of himself and smiled.

The booth opened, and he stepped out into the Casino of Masks.

Mantell stood at the entrance, adjusting to the situation. It seemed to him that he wore nothing, and indeed he felt a faint chill. But as he looked across the long hall, seeing no people but only gray blurs here and there he knew he was utterly anonymous.

He wondered how the conspirators were going to achieve contact with him, cloaked as he was. Or whether there were any conspirators at all.

From the first he had considered the possibility that this was all some elaborate hoax of Thurdan's making. Well, for that eventuality he was prepared; he would simply tell Thurdan that he was conducting an unofficial investigation, answering the summons in the book because he hoped to unmask the conspirators.

He looked around.

The Casino was equipped with all the usual standard games of chance, but there were also a great many card tables in the back. It seemed logical, Mantell thought. He imagined that bluffing games, such as poker, would be the order of things here. No involuntary facial manifestations could give away strategy here.

But he did not want to get involved in a card game. Instead he drifted across to the rotowheel table. It was as good a place to begin as any.

The table was crowded. It was almost completely surrounded by gesticulating blurred figures, busily placing their bets for the next turn.

In the center of the huge round table was a metal wheel whose enameled surface was covered with numbers. The wheel would swing free and halt at random, and when it halted a beam of light from above would focus sharply on it, singling out a number.

The man who played the winning number was entitled to collect the numerical value of that number from every other player: if he won on number Twelve, everyone present at the table handed in twelve chips to go to him, and paid the house the amount of his own losing number as well, as a forfeit. It was possible to win or lose heavily on the rotowheel in a matter of minutes.

Mantell edged into the crowd. There were some sixty people at the wheel. When he was close enough to bet, he put his money on Twenty-Two.

"You don't want to do that, mister," advised a tall blur at his side. The stranger's voice was as metallic and anonymous as his face; the vocal distortion was a side-effect of the scattering-field, and was a further concealment of the mask.

"Why not?" Mantell asked.

"Because Twenty-Two just came up last time around."

"The wheel doesn't remember what number won last time," Mantell snapped.

"Go ahead, then. Throw your dough away."

Mantell left his chips where they were. A few minutes later the croupier called time and the wheel started to swing. Around. . . . around. . . .

. . . And came to rest on Forty-Nine. Shrugging, Mantell added forty-nine chips to the twenty-two out there already, and watched while the croupier swept them away. The lucky winner, face an impassive blur behind which was probably an unashamed grin of pleasure, moved forward to collect. His take, Mantell computed, would be nearly three thousand chips. Not bad at all.

Mantell stayed at the board about fifteen minutes, and in that time managed to lose two hundred and eighty chips without much difficulty. Then he cashed in on eleven—he was playing cautiously by then—and came away with winnings amounting to about five hundred chips.

There was, surprisingly, no clock in the Casino, and he had carelessly left his wristwatch back in his room. He had no way of knowing what time it was, but he estimated that it was still short of ten o'clock by some minutes.

While he stood to one side considering which game he should attempt next, a gong sounded suddenly, and the place became quiet. He saw a robot ascend a platform in the center of the hall.

"Attention, please! If the gentleman who recently lost a copy of the book entitled *A Study of Hydrogen—Breathing Life in the Spica System* will step forward, we will be able to return his book to him at this platform. Thank you."

The crowd buzzed in puzzled amusement, sensing some sort of joke, but not being sure just what it was. This, Mantell realized, was his message, and it had probably been read off every night during the past week, just in case he had decided to attend.

He paused for a moment, decided that since he had come this far he might as well go through with the rest of it, and made his way forward through the crowd of gaily laughing blurred figures to the dais.

He confronted the robot. "I own the missing book," he said. "I'm very anxious to have it returned."

"Of course. Will you come this way, sir?"

Mantell followed the robot back through the crowd to an alcove near the entrance. They paused there.

"To your left, sir," the robot said.

A door opened to his left and he stepped through. He entered a booth similar to the one in which he had donned his mask. Only there was a pink blur waiting for him in this one, holding out a copy of a yellow-bound book which looked very familiar.

The blur held the book up so he could see it and said in a mechanical distorted voice, "Is this the book you lost, sir?"

Mantell nodded stiffly. "It is. Thanks very much for returning it. I was very worried about it."

He stared at the blur, trying vainly to peer behind it and perceive the identity of the other. It was impossible. The waves of light danced mockingly before him, obscuring the face behind them.

He reached out to take the book, but it was gently drawn back out of his reach.

"Not yet, sir," the other said. "One question first. Have you read this book?"

"No—uh—I mean, yes, I have," he said, realizing the other was referring to the message between the pages, rather than to the text of the work itself. "Yes, I've read it."

"And are you interested in the subject with which it deals?"

He was silent for a moment, knowing that the "subject" she was talking about could only be the death of Ben Thurdan.

"Yes," he said finally, "I am. But—who are you?"

"You'll see. But I must have absolute assurance of secrecy in this matter."

He looked down at himself and felt sweat running down inside his shirt. "All right. I'll vow secrecy, if that's what you want."

The blur opposite moved slightly, lifting one hand to nudge the activating stud on the right side of the mask. Mantell heard a click—and then the unmasked face of a girl appeared before him. He gasped.

Almost immediately she clicked the studs again, and Mantell saw the delicate features, the star-blue eyes he knew so well, fade into a blurred veil of gray light—and Myra Butler became once more as distantly anonymous as any of the other Casino pleasure-seekers.

It took him a moment to recover from the double shock of seeing Myra revealed for that brief instant and of finding that she was part of the conspiracy against Ben Thurdan. Then pieces of a puzzle began slowly to form into a pattern. He stared steadily at the blur before him.

"Is this a joke?" he asked hoarsely.

"Hardly. It's been in the planning stage for a long time. Too long, maybe. But we have to gain strength first, before we can take over."

"Aren't you afraid to speak so openly in this booth?" Mantell asked, looking around nervously. "Ben seems to have spies everywhere. There might be a pipeline to—"

"No," she said. "This booth's all right. The manager of the Casino here is one of us. There isn't any danger."

He sat down limply on the bench in the booth. "Okay. Tell me about this thing, then, as long as I'm here. When do you plan to do it?"

Blurred pink lines that might have been soft shoulders lifted in a gentle shrug. "We haven't set the exact time yet. But we're certain of one thing: We must get rid of Thurdan."

Mantell didn't ask why. He said, "But you're taking a big chance, aren't you? How do you know I won't go running to Ben and tell him all about it? I'm sure he'd be highly interested."

"You won't do it," she said.

"How do you know?"

"Your psychprobe patterns. You won't betray us, Johnny. I saw your charts and I know the sort of a person you are, even if you don't know yourself. I picked you as one of us from the minute you were probed."

He sat looking at his fingers and thought about it. He realized that in this the probe had told the truth: it was almost as impossible for him to betray to Thurdan what Myra was telling him as it would be for him to grow wings. She was taking no risk with him.

"How about Marchin?" he asked. "Was he part of this thing, too?"

"No. Marchin knew about us, but he had his own plans. He stayed aloof. That was because he planned to rule the way Ben rules. Alone."

"And what does your group plan to do?"

"To set up a civilized form of government on Starhaven," was the steady reply. "To set up a democracy, instead of a tyranny."

"But tyranny sometimes works out. Ben is doing a good job of running his planet," Mantell said. "You can't deny that."

The blur that was Myra Butler moved from side to side, as if shaking her head in disagreement.

She said, "I won't try to argue with your statement. Certainly, Ben has Starhaven running on an even keel. But what would happen if he should die today?" She didn't wait for an answer. "I—we know very well what would happen. There would be a fierce scramble for power that would turn this planet into a raging mad-house of civil strife and death. And that's why we have to kill him and take over the planet ourselves. And nothing less than killing would work; he's too strong a man to be willing to take part in any other form of government than dictatorship. Ben can't just be deposed, he has to be put away permanently."

"I see the logic there. Ben himself is all right as a ruler, but the chances are that the next boss of Starhaven won't be so enlightened. So you get rid of the boss and the boss system now, and prevent the terrible destructive struggle for the throne before it can begin."

"You've got the idea. Well? Are you with us?"

Mantell hesitated. He was thinking of the giant named Ben Thurdan, who feared dying, and he was thinking also of Myra, and of many possibilities.

There was no longer any doubt in his mind.

"Of course I'm with you!" he said.

She sighed. "Thank God you said that, Johnny. I would have hated to kill you, Darling!"

Chapter Twelve

Knowing of the existence of a plot against Ben Thurdan's life didn't keep Mantell from working hard and long on his defense-screen project, even though he was conscious of the irony that success in his research would spell the end of all hopes for an assassination. He was definitely on the track of something, and he didn't necessarily have to turn it over to Thurdan when he had worked it out. And there would be some use for his personal defense screen, whether it was Thurdan or someone else—himself, perhaps—who benefited from it.

He withdrew almost completely into his laboratory. Myra had warned him not to see her again until everything was settled, and the promise of seeking her later took away most of the pain of not seeing her now.

They met briefly, twice more, in the Casino of Masks during the following week. They identified each other by a prearranged sign and spent a few hours at the tables. But it was a short and unsatisfying contact.

The second time he met her there, Mantell asked her again what was delaying them. His feeling was that they should strike at the first available opportunity. Ben had feed lines of data extending almost everywhere in Starhaven, and the longer they held back and polished their plans, the greater was Thurdan's chance of discovering their identities and killing both the conspiracy and themselves.

"It'll come soon, Johnny," she told him. "It's like a jigsaw puzzle. All the pieces have to be where they belong, to fit exactly and make the picture complete before the game is over."

Mantell slumped down in his seat, shoulders hunched. "I guess you know what you're doing," he said, frowning. "But I don't like this waiting. I'm getting impatient, and Ben's bound to find out before long."

She laughed, and the effect of the mask flattened the laugh into something strange. "*You're* impatient? Johnny, we've been living with this thing for years. You've only been on Starhaven a few *weeks*!"

After that, he stopped asking questions. Instead he plunged into his laboratory work with furious energy—the energy of seven years of idleness, dammed up and now rushing down the spillway.

He designed cumbersome defense screens that would be too massive for an elephant, and built them, and then refined and reduced them down, down— until, on one model that might be almost the proper size, the field winked out altogether, lacking sufficient strength. And he had to start all over again. He didn't mind that. Failure at this stage was only to be expected; success was not immediately to be hoped for. And he was working again, doing something, and that was enough.

Hardly a day went by without a call from Thurdan. Mantell learned that Starhaven was going through a period of peace, untroubled by the universe outside, and so Thurdan rarely visited the lab tower in person except when making routine checks.

Until the day of the Space Patrol raid. In a sudden instant, the peace and security of Starhaven was faced with abrupt destruction.

Yet the raid had been going on for almost a full hour before Mantell knew anything about it. His first hint that something was wrong came when the door of his laboratory opened as he bent low over his workbench squinting over microminiaturized positronic disperser and trying to coax them into their proper positions in the template he was building.

Startled, he glanced back over his shoulder and saw Ben Thurdan striding heavily into the room.

"Hello, Ben. Why the big rush?"

Thurdan's craggy face was tense. "Bombardment. A fleet of Patrol ships chased some fugitive here, and they're blasting us. Come with me and I'll show you something, Mantell. Come on!"

Mantell had to half-run after him down the hall to the central control room.

"What about the fugitive?" he asked, remembering his own arrival. "Did he get in okay?"

"He's here. An assassin."

Despite himself Mantell flinched. "What?"

"Killed the President of the Dryelleran Confederation then lit out for here."

"Did you take him in?"

"Of course. We take everyone in. Harmon's psychprobing him now. But he brought a Patrol armada behind him. They've got some new kind of heavy-cycle gun that I've never heard of before. If you listen you can pick up the sound."

Mantell listened. He heard a dull boom, and it seemed to him that the floor shook just a little. A moment later the boom was repeated.

"That's it," Thurdan said. "They're blasting at our screens."

He sat at the control console, in the big chair specially constructed to hold his weight, and switched on the visiscreens. Mantell saw the image take shape almost at once: a thick cloud of Patrol ships orbiting beyond Starhaven's metal skin, wheeling like stallions and discharging incredible bolts of radiant energy.

But now Thurdan was grinning. He emanated all the confidence and joy of an invincible warrior about to enter battle. His thick strong fingers rattled over the controls.

"Our defensive screens can soak all that stuff up, can't they?" Mantell asked uneasily.

"Most of it. Theoretically, they have unlimited capacity—but those boys up there are really pouring it on!" Thurdan pointed to a bank of meters whose quivering indicators swung dizzily up into the red area that meant overload and dropped back as Starhaven's enormous power piles drained away the dangerous excess. And again the Patrol ships slammed down their fierce bolts of force, and still the Starhaven defenses negated them.

"We've got to stay on the defensive for a few minutes, still," said Thurdan. "The load on our screens is too great to give us time to throw out a return blast. But we'll fix 'em! Watch this."

Mantell watched.

With strong staccato thrusts of his fingertips over the control boards, Thurdan brought the defense-screens of Starhaven out of synchronized equilibrium, establishing instead a shifting cycle-phase relationship.

"The screens are alternating now," he grunted. "Give me the differential."

Mantell squinted up at the dials, found the columns he wanted, and fed the figures rapidly to Thurdan. The big man made delicate adjustments, making mental computations that astonished Mantell.

Finally he sat back, grinning satanically. Sweat was pouring from every pore of his skin.

A chime sounded outside the room. Thurdan muttered, "See what they want, Johnny."

Mantell darted to the door and opened it. A handful of the defense-screen technicians stood there, pale, puzzled-looking.

Harrell said, "What's going on in here? The screens are phasing like crazy!"

"Close to overload," Bryson said.

Mantell smiled. "Ben's in charge," he said simply. "Come on in and watch."

He led them to where Thurdan sat staring broodingly into his vision plates, watching the cloud of orbiting Patrol Ships. There must have been hundreds of them out there, each one smashing every megawatt it could muster into the tough metal hide of Starhaven.

"They've been planning this attack for a year," Thurdan said half to himself, as he made compensating adjustments to absorb the ferocious onslaught. "Waiting for a chance to get this fleet out there and break Starhaven open, once and for all. And they're so sure they're going to do it, too—the poor fools!" Then he laughed. "Mantell, are you watching?"

Mantell nodded tensely, too absorbed to speak. He heard the other technicians murmur behind him.

"Here we go, then," Thurdan said grimly.

His right index finger jabbed sharply down on a projecting green stud of the control panel. The building shook. A violet flare of energy leaped into sight on the vision screen.

And where, a second ago, eleven Space Patrol ships had been arrayed in fighting formation, now there were none.

Thurdan chuckled. "They didn't expect that, I'd bet! They thought it was impossible to take this heavy an attack and still return fire! But I'm giving them their own juice back twice as hard!"

His finger came down again.

A flank of the Patrol attackers melted into nothingness.

Mantell saw what the strategy was: Thurdan was firing in the millionth-of-a-second pauses between each phase of the synchronized screens, squirting out a burst of energy in the micromoment when Starhaven was left unguarded. But the force of the beam coming up from the planet served as a screen itself, keeping the metal-shielded world from harm.

Again and again Thurdan's finger came down heavily on the firing stud, until the sky was cleared of ships. The angry cloud of buzzing, energy-spitting gnats that had been plaguing Starhaven was wiped out.

All except one, Mantell saw. One Space Patrol ship remained. He waited for Thurdan to spear it with a burst.

Instead he spoke into a microphone: "Get our ships up there, and grapple that one on. I want that ship. I want to study those guns."

He flicked away a stream of sweat from his forehead, rose, yawned and stretched. Again Starhaven had triumphed.

An hour later, Mantell was in Thurdan's office in central Starhaven when four of his private corpsmen brought in the crew of the captured SP ship.

At the moment Thurdan was expounding to him the virtues of his screen setup, with what Mantell considered was excusable pride. The big man had just given an awesome demonstration of skill, and Mantell had told him so. He felt sincerely impressed; and there was no reason why Thurdan shouldn't know it.

"A hundred and eighty-one ships they lost," Thurdan said. "Over five hundred Patrolmen dead, and at a cost of billions of credits to the Galactic Federation."

"And without a single Starhaven casualty," Mantell pointed out.

"That's only part of it!" Thurdan exclaimed. "We soaked up enough power in that raid to run Starhaven for a year. I've ordered the three auxiliary generators shut down indefinitely, until we're able to use up the trapped power surplus. We—"

The door chimed.

Myra appeared from the inner office and crossed to the door smoothly, saying, "I'll see who it is, Mr. Thurdan."

A moment later she reappeared.

"Well?" Thurdan growled.

"The captive SP men are here, under guard."

A scowl of surprise and annoyance darkened Thurdan's face. "Captive SP men?" he repeated. "*Captives?* Who said anything about prisoners? Myra, tell me—who brought in the SP ship?"

"Bentley and his crew."

"Get Bentley on the phone, fast."

Myra nodded and punched out the number. Mantell, at one side of Thurdan's desk, was trying to stare away from her, trying not to admire her liquid grace of movement. He knew Thurdan was still keeping close check on him.

The screen swirled colorfully and a face that Mantell recognized appeared. It belonged to the man who had brought him to Starhaven long ago.

Thurdan said, "Who issued orders authorizing you to take prisoners, Bentley?"

"Why, nobody, sir. I thought—"

"You *thought*! In the future, just don't attempt to think, Bentley. Leave that to me. It doesn't look good on you. Starhaven isn't a jail. We don't want prisoners here. You understand that?"

"Yes, sir."

"Good. Next time you happen to capture a ship, jettison any SP man you find aboard."

"Yes, sir."

Thurdan broke contact, whirled, and stared at Mantell. "Johnny, there's a bunch of SP men outside the office. Have them killed. Then report back to me."

He said it in a cool, even tone of voice. There was none of the anger in it that he had displayed when talking to the unfortunate Bentley.

"Have them killed." Just like that.

"What are you waiting for, Mantell?"

The room was very silent. "Killing's a little out of my line, Ben. I'm a research man. I can't murder a group of innocent SP men, just because you don't—"

Thurdan's fist came up faster than Mantell's eyes could flicker. Fireworks exploded in his head, then he crashed hard into the wall. He heard Myra gasp. He realized Thurdan had opened the fist at the last second and had merely slapped him. But even so, he felt as if he had been poleaxed.

His head rocked. He wobbled unsteadily away from the wall, making sure he was keeping well out of firing range of those fists.

Thurdan said, "I thought you were loyal, Johnny. I gave you an order. You stopped to argue. That doesn't go on Starhaven. I told you about that. See that you remember it from now on."

Mantell nodded. His jaw throbbed fiercely where Thurdan had slapped him.

"Yes, Ben."

"*Make sure you mean it!* Now get out of here and dispose of those SP men. Come back here when you've done the job. That's an order!"

His voice had regained the cool, level quality of his normal conversation by the time he finished speaking. There was nothing insane or paranoiac about Ben Thurdan, Mantell saw. Thurdan was simply the boss, and aimed to keep things that way.

Behind him, Myra was looking expressionlessly out the window.

"Okay, Ben," Mantell said hoarsely. "I'll take care of it right away."

Chapter Thirteen

Mantell stepped out into the anteroom where four pale SP men waited, standing stiffly at attention, guarded by Thurdan's private corpsmen. The corpsmen recognized him and nodded curtly.

"Thurdan wants these men put out of the way," Mantell said, in a dry, harsh voice.

The head corpsman said, "Locked up, you mean?"

"No. Killed. Destroyed."

"But Bentley said—"

"Those are orders!" Mantell scowled. "Thurdan just gave Bentley the devil because he brought in these prisoners," he said. He glanced at the SP men, who were registering as little emotion as possible. "Come on. Take them down the hall. We can shove them down the disposal unit there."

Mantell shuddered inwardly at his own calmness. But this was Ben Thurdan's way. This was Starhaven.

The corpsmen pushed the four SP captives roughly along, down the brightly lighted hall toward the empty room at the end of the corridor. They were herded inside.

"Okay, Mantell," the corpsman said. "You're in charge. Which one goes first?"

As Mantell hesitated, a tall SP man stared at him strangely and said to the corpsman, "Just a second. Did you say *Mantell*?"

"Yeah."

Mantell moistened his lips. Perhaps the fellow was from Mulciber, and knew about him.

"*Johnny* Mantell?" he went on.

"That's me," Mantell snapped. "What's the matter with you?"

"I *thought* I recognized you," said the SP man casually. "I'm Carter, Fourteenth Earth Platoon. What the hell are *you* doing in this outfit? And on Thurdan's side? When I knew you you were a lot different."

"I—" He stopped. "What do you mean, you *knew* me? Where?"

"In the Patrol, of course!"

"You're crazy!"

"It was five years ago, when we were serving in the Syrtis Insurrection." The way he said it, it sounded like self-evident truth. "You couldn't have forgotten *that* so soon, Johnny!"

"What are you trying to get away with?" Mantell asked roughly. "Five years ago I was a stumblebum on Mulciber. Seven years ago I was doing the same thing. Also one year ago. I don't know who you are or what you're trying to pull, but I never was in the Patrol. For the last seven years I've been running *away* from the SP—until I wound up on Starhaven."

The SP man was shaking his head incredulously. "They must have done something to you. Same name, same face—it *has* to be you!"

Mantell realized he was shaking with uneasiness. "You're just stalling for time," he said. He glanced at the corpsman leader. "Ledru, get going with this job."

"Sure, Mantell."

The Patrolman who had given his name as Carter was staring at him aghast, then looked at the disposal unit. "You're just going to shove us down that thing? *Alive?* But we're Patrolmen, Johnny! *Just like you!*"

Those last three words rocked Mantell. He knew the reputation of the Patrol well enough, knew they would pull any kind of trick at all to achieve their ends. That was why Thurdan didn't want them kept prisoners; SP men on Starhaven would be potentially dangerous, behind bars or not.

But there was something in the Patrolman's tone that rang of sincerity.

Impossible! Those seven stark years on Mulciber burned vividly in Mantell's memory—too vividly for them to have been only dreams.

"Is the disposal ready?" he asked in a stony voice.

Ledru nodded. He signaled to his men and they grabbed one of the SP boys.

The one named Carter said, "You must be out of your head, Mantell, to do this. They did something to you."

"Shut up," Mantell said. He looked at the cold-faced corpsman chief. He thought: They say I committed murder on Mulciber. I say I didn't, but they found it on my psychprobe charts. Even if I did, it was in a fight—it was manslaughter, nothing worse. This is cold-blooded murder!

But Thurdan must be watching, he thought.

"Ledru," he said, pointing at Carter, "put this one down the hole first."

"Sure."

At Ledru's gesture the corpsmen released the man they held and moved toward Carter.

Suddenly the strange thing that had happened to Mantell three times already on Starhaven happened again. He experienced that feeling of unreality, the conviction that all his past life was a mere hallucination. It came bursting up within him. He swayed.

Sweat poured down his body. The floor seemed to melt.

The corpsmen were dragging the struggling Carter toward the open disposal hatch, and Mantell knew he couldn't watch, that he had to get out of the room and get away from this thing that was happening.

He turned and ran to the door. He threw it open and lunged blindly out into the hall.

From behind him he heard a prolonged cry of sheer terror, as the last SP man hurtled through the disposal trap, out into endless space.

Then there was only silence that seemed deafeningly loud. . . .

Unreasoningly, Mantell started to run up the corridor, the hollow sounds of his own footsteps seeming to pursue him. At last out of breath, lungs gasping, he leaned against the cool, yielding wall to rest. Ahead of him, the bright, straight corridor stretched endlessly until walls, floor and ceiling seemed to meet together in the far distance.

The words of the SP man, Carter, kept drumming mechanically in his brain. "Five years ago when we were serving together in the Syrtis Insurrection. . . . Five years ago when we. . . ." He pressed his palms over his ears, trying to shut out their persistent echo.

"Lies! All lies!" Mantell heard himself shout. It had been only an SP trick, a last-minute attempt to escape the doom that Thurdan had decreed for the Earth prisoners.

Leaning there, still sucking air into his burning lungs, a strange hallucination came over him. For an instant he seemed transported, as in a dream, to another world, another time. He was crawling through the blood-red yambo forest floor on his stomach and elbows, the long nozzle of the blaster held before him, attached by a flexible tube to the magna-energy tank strapped to his back. Somewhere ahead, hidden by the twisted scarlet trunks, lay the secret spacefield they had to capture. Suddenly the entire forest came alive with scarlet-skinned Syrtians, their fanglike tusks glittering. He pressed the activator button of his blaster. Then abruptly the entire forest and himself along with it seemed to dissolve into nothingness. With recurrent flashes of consciousness, he remembered being dragged by his legs, and much later, a tall man grinning down at him, saying they'd secured the spacefield. . . .

He shook his head, shutting his eyes; his respiration steadying down. . . . And another vision rose before him, clearer and more real than the first one.

He was on the warm golden sands of Mulciber. On the broad raised walk before him, he looked up at the patronizing smug faces of the tourists. A fat man dressed in a loose chiton-like garment of red and yellow checks, laughed, pointed, and threw out some coins. Mantell knew what they were waiting to see; knew the show he was expected to put on.

So he raced, sand flying, on his hands and knees, scrabbling hungrily into the sand for the coins, while his ears burned with the laughter of the Earth tourists. . . .

"Five years ago when we were serving in the Syrtis Insurrection . . .

A hallucination! A lie! Mulciber was true; that was a direct recall. But that fight for the spacefield in the blood-red yambo forest? Only a dream, a fantasy that had no relation to actuality.

"Five years ago when we . . ."

The recurrent words and the deep voice kept up its measured, mechanical beat, like a pounding drum inside his head, interminably, torturingly.

And at last, as Mantell still stood there, doubt, like a hungry rodent, started gnawing at his mind. A hallucination? Yes. But whose? Carter's—or his own?

He shook uncontrollably and sobbed. Once again, compulsively, he started to run, hearing only the pound of his feet against the floor, seeing nothing, not knowing where he was heading.

He ran into something hard and rebounded, half stunned. He looked up, thinking he had collided with the wall or with a door.

He hadn't.

He stared up into the sculptured face of Ben Thurdan. It looked as bleak and as baleful as it had at the moment of the SP attack. He reached out and grasped Mantell's shoulder with an iron grip.

"Come on in my office a second, Mantell. I want to talk to you."

Numb inside, and chilled, Mantell faced Thurdan across the width of his office. The door was locked and sealed. Myra stood far off near the window, staring palely at him, then at the glowering Thurdan.

Thurdan said, "I didn't like the way you were talking when you went out of here, Mantell. I couldn't trust you. It was the first time I felt that way about you."

"Ben, I—"

"Keep quiet. I didn't trust you and I couldn't allow four SP men to run around Starhaven unchecked. So I used this"—he indicated a switch-studded control panel behind his desk—"and monitored your conversation all the way down into the room at the end of the hall."

Mantell tried to look cool. "What are you trying to say, Ben? The Space Patrol men are dead, aren't they?"

"They are. No thanks to you. Ledru and his men finished the job while you were dashing away at top speed up the hall. But listen to this."

Thurdan flipped a switch and a recorder unit came to life on playback. Mantell heard Carter's voice say, *"In the Patrol, of course! Five years ago, when we were serving in the Syrtis Insurrection! Don't tell me you've forgotten that so soon, Johnny!"*

Thurdan clicked the playback off and said, "What was that all about?"

"It's a trick," Mantell said calmly, blotting out his inner panic and confusion. "The Patrol is good at that, as you ought to know. He was trying to confuse us all and perhaps escape. And you—"

"I don't necessarily believe what an SP man says," Thurdan broke in. "You were psychprobed when you got here, and the probe said you had lived on Mulciber. It didn't say anything about your being in the Space Patrol." Thurdan's dark eyes narrowed and bored high-intensity holes through Mantell. "But just suppose maybe the psychprobe was wrong, though."

"How could that be?"

Thurdan shrugged. "Maybe the SP has discovered ways of planting fake memories good enough to fool a psychprobe. Or maybe my operator deliberately altered the readings for some reason of his own. Or he just bungled it out of sheer old age." Thurdan turned to Myra and said, "Send in Dr. Harmon."

A few moments passed, and then the spare figure of Harmon appeared at the door, withered-looking, mumbling to himself. He looked ancient.

He *was* ancient, Mantell thought—well over a hundred, certainly. Even modern techniques of gerontology weren't able to keep a man young and hale past eighty-five or so, and Harmon looked his age.

He said, "Something the matter, Ben?"

Thurdan glared at him. "Maybe or maybe not. I'm not sure. It seems one of the SP men Bentley captured today recognized Mantell here; claimed to have served with him five years ago!"

"Served with . . . but that's impossible, Ben. I probed Mantell myself. He hadn't been off Mulciber in seven years. That's what his chart says. And surely if I had seen anything about the Space Patrol there, don't you think I would have told you?"

"You're an old man, Erik. You were old when you ran into that vivisection scandal and had to come here, and you haven't been getting any younger since. Maybe you didn't do a very good job of probing Mantell. Maybe you overlooked some facts here and there."

Harmon went chalk-white and began to sputter incoherent angry phrases.

Annoyed, Mantell said, "Look here, Ben. Just because an SP man pulls a crazy desperate stunt to keep himself alive a few minutes more, that's no—"

"Shut up, Johnny. That SP man sounded convincing to me. I want to clear this business up to my own satisfaction right here and now."

Harmon said, "But how can you—?"

Thurdan snapped, "Harmon, set up your equipment. We're going to probe Mantell again."

There was an instant of dead silence in the room.

Myra and Mantell reached the same conclusion at the same split second, and looked at each other in that identical second, eyes wide with horror.

Mantell knew the consequences of his getting probed again. This time, they would discover the conspiracy against Thurdan. That hadn't been in his mind the last time Harmon had peered in it.

But now it was, and it would be curtains for Mantell and Myra the moment the delicate needles of the probe hit the surface of his cerebrum.

Myra reacted first. She came forward and gripped Thurdan's thick arm with her hand.

"Ben, you're not being fair. Johnny was just probed a few weeks ago. You're not supposed to probe a human being twice in the same month—if you do, you can damage his brain. Isn't that right, Dr. Harmon?"

"Indeed it is, and—"

"Quiet, both of you!" Thurdan paused a moment, listening to the obliging silence, then said, "Mantell's a valuable man to me. I don't want to lose him. But Starhaven's policy has always been to play the close ones, never to take unnecessary risk. If that SP man was telling the truth, Mantell's a spy—the first one ever to get past the gate! Erik, get your machine set up for the probe."

Harmon shrugged. "If you insist, Ben."

"I do."

Harmon started for the door. Thurdan called after him, "Get Dr. Polderson in to take the reading."

Polderson was Harmon's chief assistant. The old scientist turned and looked up, bitter-faced. "I'm still capable of handling the machine myself, Ben."

"Maybe you are—or maybe you aren't. But I want somebody else to take the reading on Mantell. Is that understood?"

"Very well," Harmon said with obvious reluctance, after a brief pause.

Mantell could see what the old man had at stake—his professional pride. Well, he would be vindicated, of course, Mantell thought. Polderson's reading would coincide with the one Harmon had taken on his arrival, in all but one trifling detail—that detail being the conspiracy.

Mantell's hands were shaking as he walked through the passageway from Thurdan's office to the psychprobe laboratory.

It would be over soon. Everything.

The laboratory looked very much the same as it had the other time. There was the couch, the psychprobing paraphernalia, the rows of books and the mysterious gadgetry. Only one thing was new: Polderson.

Dr. Harmon's right-hand man was a cadaverous youngster with deep-set, dark brooding eyes and the outgoing gaiety of a decomposing corpse. He peered at Mantell with some curiosity.

"Are you the subject?" he asked in a grave voice.

"I am," Mantell said hesitantly. Behind him, walking in the shuffle of the extremely old, came Harmon. Thurdan and Myra had remained behind, in the other office.

Polderson intoned, "Would you kindly lie down on this couch for the psychprobe reading? Dr. Harmon, is the machine ready?"

"I want to make a few minor checks," the old man muttered. "Have to see that everything's functioning as it ought to be. This must be a perfect reading. Absolutely perfect."

He was puttering around in back of the machine, doing something near a cabinet of drugs. Mantell watched nervously.

Harmon looked up, finally, and, crossing the room, smiled a withered smile, clapped Polderson affectionately on the back and said, "Do a good job, Polderson. I know you're capable of it."

Polderson nodded mechanically. But when he turned his attention back to fastening Mantell into the machine, his eyes seemed to have lost their former intense glitter, and now were vague and dream-veiled.

Dr. Harmon was grinning. He held up one hand for Mantell to see.

Strapped to the inside of his middle finger was the tiny bulb of a pressure-injection syringe. And Polderson, shambling amiably about the machine, had been neatly and thoroughly drugged.

Chapter Fourteen

Mantell climbed obediently onto the couch and permitted Polderson to strap him in. He placed the cold probe-dome on Mantell's head. Harmon hovered nearby, smiling to himself, watching.

Suddenly the old doctor leaned over and whispered something in Polderson's ear. The first few words were inaudible to Mantell, but he caught the conclusion: "—see to it that his probe-chart is identical to the earlier one in all respects. You understand that? Identical!'

Polderson nodded dimly. He crossed the room, opened a pressure-sealed file drawer, and thoughtfully examined a folio that probably contained the record of Mantell's last probing, while Mantell watched curiously and wondered exactly what was going on.

Polderson seemed satisfied after a few moments' scrutiny. He nodded his head in content, closed the file, and turned back to the machine.

Mantell, waiting for the probing to begin, suddenly heard the sound of voices.

Myra was saying, "Ben, I tell you it's cruel to probe him a second time! He might lose his mind, for all you know! He might—"

Mantell heard the sound of a slap, and winced. Then Thurdan threw open the lab door and bellowed, "*Harmon!* I thought I told you to have an assistant conduct the psychprobe!"

"I'm so doing," Harmon said mildly. "Dr. Polderson here is performing the actual probe. I'm merely supervising the mechanics of the work."

"I don't want you anywhere near Polderson or near Mantell or near the machine while this is going on," Thurdan snapped. "I want an absolutely untinkered response."

Sighing, Harmon nodded and moved away. He said, "Then let's all wait in your office. It's bad to have so many people in here while a probe is going on."

And he moved slowly and with considerable display of wounded dignity past Thurdan into the passageway. Thurdan turned and followed him, closing the door. Mantell was alone with Polderson—and the machine.

Polderson's lean fingers caressed the keyboard of the psychprobe as if he were fondling a loved one. In a drug-shrouded voice he murmured, "Relax, now, relax. You're much too tense. You have to ease up a little. Ease up, I tell you."

"I'm eased," Mantell lied. He was stiff with tension. "I'm as eased as I'm going to get."

"Loosen up, please. You're much too tense, Mr. Mantell. *Much* too tense. There's really no danger. None at all. The probe is a scientific instrument, totally harmless, that merely—"

Wham!

For the second time since he had come to Starhaven Mantell felt as if his skull had been cleft in two. He rocked under the impact of the probe, clung feebly to consciousness for an instant, and let go.

When he woke he found himself staring up into the face of Ben Thurdan. The *smiling* face of Ben Thurdan.

Thurdan said in surprisingly gentle tones, "Are you up, Johnny?"

Mantell nodded groggily.

"I guess I owe you an apology, Mantell," Thurdan said. "Polderson just showed me your new psychprobe chart. The reading's the same as it was when Harmon took it. That SP man was talking nonsense."

"You could have saved me a headache," Mantell said. His skull was spinning on a dizzy orbit. "I told you all along I wasn't an SP man."

"I couldn't accept that, Johnny. I have to make sure—*have to!* Do you see that, Johnny?"

"Sort of. But I hope you're not going to probe me any time somebody says some crazy thing about me."

Thurdan chuckled warmly. "I think I can trust you now, Johnny."

"I hope so, Ben."

Mantell looked around and saw other figures in the room: Polderson, Dr. Harmon, Myra. His head began to stop whirling just a little. The effects of the psychprobe were diminishing.

"And I owe you an apology, too, Erik," Thurdan was saying to Harmon. "Don't ever say Ben Thurdan can't back down when he's wrong. It takes a big man to admit he's made a mistake. Eh, there?"

Harmon smiled, showing yellowed teeth. "Right you are, Ben. Right you are!"

Thurdan turned and left. Myra followed him.

Harmon said, "All right, Polderson. Thanks for your help. I'll take care of the lab now, and you can go."

"Certainly, Dr. Harmon."

Polderson left also. Mantell was alone with the old scientist.

We had a close escape that time," Harmon said, leaning close to him and whispering confidentially. "Would you care for a drink, Mr. Mantell?"

"Please. Yes."

A closet in the far corner of the laboratory divulged a small portable bar. Harmon dialed two sour chokers, took them from the bar as they came filtering out, and brought them across the room. He handed one to Mantell, who took it and sipped thirstily.

After a moment Mantell said, "What did you mean, *we* had a narrow escape?"

"Those of us who stood to risk exposure if Thurdan ever saw a true psychprobe chart of your mind."

Mantell blinked in surprise. "You mean—*you're* one of us?"

Harmon nodded smilingly. "I was the first. Then came Myra and the others. It would have been all over for us if Thurdan had seen your true psychprobe, knowing what you now know."

"How did you keep him from seeing it?"

"I slipped Polderson a hypnodrug while he was beginning to set up the machine. The rest of it was simple; I merely ordered him to see only those things I wanted him to see. He took your probe. There was no mention of—ah—*us*—on it."

Suddenly Mantell sat bolt upright. "What about that Space Patrolman's story, though? Was it just a wild hoax, or was there any truth in it? I mean, about his knowing me back when—"

Harmon shook his head vigorously. "No. Your first psychprobing and this one said the same thing: you spent the last seven years on Mulciber. Unless new techniques for misleading the psychprobe have been invented, that's the truth, Mantell."

He nodded. That was one bit of reality he had salvaged from all this, then.

He climbed off the couch, feeling his feet rocking beneath him. "And—was there anything in what Myra said to Ben—about a second psychprobing being likely to damage my mind?"

"Such a thing has been known to happen," Harmon admitted. "But it didn't, in this particular case. Let's be thankful for that."

Relieved, Mantell straightened out his rumpled clothing and followed Harmon down the corridor back toward Thurdan's office. Ben was sitting behind his desk. He looked every bit as massive seated as he did when standing. Mantell wondered how big Thurdan really was. Six feet six, probably, and two hundred seventy pounds. Probably Ben would be a rough man to tangle with in a fight, even figuring his age at sixty or so.

"Feeling better?" Thurdan rumbled.

"A little. Not much."

Mantell flopped into a beckoning foam cradle and tried to scrub the throbbing out of his forehead with his fingertips. Every beat of his pulse, every contraction of his heart seemed to echo noisily through the caverns of his skull.

"May I leave?" Harmon asked. "I'm very tired myself. I'd like to—"

"Stay here," Thurdan said, in that smooth, level voice that was so terribly unanswerable. "You're a scientist, Erik. I want you to hear what Mantell's going to tell us. You may be interested. Johnny, suppose you tell Myra and Dr. Harmon what you've been working on in the lab for the past few weeks."

Mantell moistened his lips and looked straight at Harmon. "I've been developing a personal defense screen," he said. "Invisible field and body-size. The kind of shield a man could wear and be absolutely invulnerable while he had it on."

Myra tossed an interested glance his way. He saw that Thurdan was knuckling the portfolio he had sent him on the previous day, outlining the progress of his work so far.

Harmon looked more than a little impressed. In his feather-light voice he asked, "Is such a thing possible—this personal screen?"

"Tell them, Johnny."

"I didn't think it was possible, either," Mantell said. "Until I built one."

"What? You have succeeded?"

"It's not finished yet," Mantell added hastily. "It won't be for a week or more, at least. But when I'm done with it, it will—"

"It's going to keep me safe," Thurdan broke in. "At last." He peered intensely at the three figures ringing his desk. "You see? You see what Johnny is doing for me—and yet I was willing to run the risk of damaging his brain rather than let a possible threat to Starhaven's security go unchecked."

There was no reply to that. Thurdan was sweating. He seemed to be under some tremendous strain. His powerful fingers toyed with the crystal knick-knacks on his desk.

"All right," he said finally, his voice knifing through the tense silence. "You can go. All of you. Leave me alone."

In the face of a dismissal like that, there was nothing to do but leave. Mantell and Myra and Harmon filed silently out of Thurdan's office without looking back, and without a word once they reached the outer corridor. Mantell had already had one experience with Thurdan's concealed audio pickups in the hall.

Myra and Harmon vanished in opposite directions down the corridor, heading toward their respective offices. Mantell caught the lift tube down and left the building. A cab lurked outside, and he engaged it and took it back to Number Thirteen.

He wanted to rest. The probing had left him thoroughly exhausted.

He reached the room a few minutes later, feeling soggy and bedraggled. He showered; the brisk play of ions on his skin refreshed him and left him clean. He swallowed a fatigue tab and sprawled out on the bed, utterly worn out from the strain and from the probing.

It had been a close thing, he thought.

Only Harmon's fast work had saved them this time—and there was no way of telling how soon it would be before some accident would put information of the conspiracy into Thurdan's hands.

That would be the end. Ben was quick and ruthless, and he would spare no one in order to keep Starhaven under his domination.

And—Thurdan had to die. Mantell felt an ungrudging admiration for the colossal old tyrant, but Myra and her group had logic on their side. Thurdan had to be put away now, before a number of contenders to the throne arose and made the task of continuing the peace of Starhaven impossible.

Mantell half-dozed. Some time passed, and he was barely conscious of its passing. Then the door chime rang twice before he climbed wearily off the pad and answered it.

One of the house robots stood outside in the hallway, smiling mechanically at him. It held a package in its rubberized grips.

"Mr. Mantell? Package for you."

"Thanks very much," Mantell said limply. He took the package from the robot and shut the door.

The package was the size and shape of a book. He knew by now that it must contain another message; this seemed to be the approved way of contacting people on a world where one man held access into all electronic means of communication.

He unwrapped it. The book, bound in attractive quarter-morocco, was called *Etiology and Empiricism*, by one Dr. F. G. Sze. Opening it, Mantel found a folded note inserted between pages 86 and 87.

Withdrawing the note, Mantell unfolded it. It said:

> J.M.—
>   AFFAIRS REACHING A CRISIS. WE CAN'T RUN MORE
> RISKS. MEET ME CASINO OF MASKS TONIGHT TO DISCUSS
> B.T. IMMEDIATE ACTION. I'LL BE THERE AT 9 SHARP.
>   DON'T BE LATE, DARLING.
>
> M.B.

Mantell stared at the note, reading it again and again, his eyes coming to rest each time on the "darling" at the end, looking so impersonal and yet so meaningful in the capitalized vocotype.

Then the note began to wither. In an instant it was but a pinch of brown dust in his hand, and then not even that.

Chapter Fifteen

The Casino of Masks was thronged that night as Mantell threaded his way into the main hall. He found himself confronted with hundreds of shadowy faceless figures, people of uncertain line and undeterminable identity.

One of them was Myra. But which?

He wandered to the swirly board, where the croupier was pleading for new players. He watched the interplay of bright colors a while, placed and lost ten chips on a combination of blue-green-red-black. Red-violet-orange-green came in instead, and Mantell turned away in mild disappointment.

Looking through the crowd he saw several pink blurs who might have been Myra, or might not have been; there was no way of telling. He was patient. He and Myra had prearranged a signal, but first he had to waste some time in planting false leads for possible pursuers.

He lost five more chips in a quick interchange of Flicker, then picked up a hundred and fifty with a lucky cast on the Rotowheel. He decided enough time had gone by. He operated the prearranged signal by going to the card tables at the back of the casino and taking a seat at an unoccupied one.

Almost immediately a house girl, identifiable by the crimson ribbon she wore tied to her mask, appeared. "Looking for a partner, sir?"

"No, thanks. I'm waiting for someone."

Mantell turned down four more offers of a game, three from men, one from another house girl. Finally a pink blur approached, and said, in the flat unmodulated voice produced by the mask effect, "I'll play with you if the stakes are in my league, stranger."

Mantell smiled. It was Myra.

"I don't play penny ante, Miss."

She sat down. "Put your cards out where I can see them, and start dealing."

He dealt. He sorted out the cards and dealt a hand of pseudo-rummy, and as he dealt he murmured lightly under his breath, "Your message reached me. I think you're right. It's time to act."

"So do we. It's inevitable that Ben will psychprobe someone and find out all about it before long. We have to strike at once."

"When?"

She tossed three cards to the table. They were aces. "Tonight," she said. "At midnight."

The words seemed to reverberate through the noisy casino. Mantell's hand shook as he produced the useless fourth ace, drawing it from the cards he held in his hand and dropping it atop the ones she had laid out.

"Tonight? How will it be done?"

"I'm going to do it," Myra said. The distortion of the scattering field robbed her voice of any emotional overtone. "Thurdan has asked me to come to his apartment tonight. We have dinner, then do some work—minor details that he doesn't have time to handle during the day. I'll come tonight—with a knife. He'll be surprised."

Mantell dragged in the cards that lay scattered on the table and shuffled them mechanically, paying little attention to his actions.

He was staring at the electronically induced blur sitting across the table from him. He was realizing that he hardly knew the girl concealed behind it. She of the ice-blue eyes, Ben Thurdan's secretary and fiancee, who casually proposed to assassinate Starhaven's overlord tonight in his own home!

And yet Mantell knew he loved her.

"We're all prepared for the attack," she said. "Key men are ready to take over the moment he's dead. There won't be any lapse in the possession of power. Dr. Harmon will issue the public proclamation. The head of Ben's private bodyguard corps, McDermott, is one of us too, and he'll see to it that there's no public disturbance. There'll be a force on hand to capture the control tower. By morning the provisional government will be in complete control of Starhaven—we hope without a shot being fired."

"Very neat," Mantell said. "And who's going to head this provisional government that's taking over? You? Harmon? McDermott?"

"No," said Myra tranquilly. "You are."

Mantell sat very quietly, absorbing the implications of that, filtering out the noise of the casino and letting Myra's calm words fill his mind.

"You are."

Provisional Ruler of Starhaven. Johnny-on-the-spot. *You are.*

"Why me?" he asked finally. "There must be others around more—"

"No. There aren't. You're new here, Johnny. You haven't involved yourself in any feuds or made any enemies. People who would object to one leader or another will settle on you as being least objectionable, since you've had no contact with them, and so haven't aroused any anger. You—"

"How do you know I want the job?"

"You said you'd do whatever you could to help us. This will help us."

"I'm not cut out to be a dictator."

"You won't be. You'll simply be acting head of the provisional government, until constitutional law can be established on Starhaven."

He considered that. The time was nine forty-five. In two hours and fifteen minutes, Ben Thurdan would be dead. And Johnny Martell, late of Mulciber, former defense-screen technician, general drifter and man-about-the-beach, would rule the iron world of Starhaven.

It was a fast rise, he thought.

The revolution would be quick too. By morning it would be over.

"Let's get out of here," he said. He started to rise from the table. She caught his arm and tugged him back into his seat.

"Not yet," she said. "We haven't finished our game." She dealt out the cards.

Some twenty minutes later they decided it was safe to leave the Casino, and they repaired to the entrance, shed their masks. They met outside the Casino in the onyx corridor. Myra was wearing a clinging blue spray-on tunic that outlined her soft figure revealingly.

Tonight, Mantell thought, she would see Ben Thurdan for the last time. Tomorrow she'll be mine.

They stepped out into the cool Starhaven night, strolling the broad plaza that fronted the Pleasure Dome. Overhead the sky was black, except for the mirror-bright moon and the sharp-focused stars. Ben Thurdan had put the moon and the stars up there deliberately, to cloak the artificiality of Starhaven. Mantell knew that they were simply a lens projection that crossed the metal sky each night on a carefully computed schedule, and vanished by "morning." It was like a giant planetarium—a planetarium the size of a world.

A faintly chill rain-laden wind was blowing down on them out of the east as they stood together in the darkness, thinking of tomorrow and the tomorrows yet to come. Thurdan's weather engineers were shrewd planners. There was nothing synthetic seeming about Starhaven's weather. When it rained, it rained wet.

"Ben's a great man," Myra said softly, apropos of nothing, after a while. "That's why we have to kill him. He's big—too big for Starhaven. As Caesar was too big for Rome."

"You loved him, didn't you?"

"I loved Ben, yes. For all his cruelty and his ruthlessness, he was something special, something unique. Something a little more than a man."

"Do we have to talk about him?" Mantell asked.

"If it hurts you, I won't. But I'm trying to square things with my own conscience, Johnny. Ben *has* to die—now. Or else there'll be hell on Starhaven when he dies naturally, and that day will have to come someday too. But still—"

It was strange, hearing her talk of conscience on this planet where conscience seemed to be a forgotten myth. Mantell turned to face her.

"Can I pry, Myra?"

"Into what?"

"You never told me why you came to Starhaven. Is it going to be a secret from me forever?"

She glanced sharply up at him. "Do you really want to know?" she asked.

He was silent for a moment, thinking. How terrible could her secret be, he wondered? Would it be some crime so ghastly it would drive a wedge between them forever, something that was better left untold?

He made up his mind. Nothing should be left untold. "Yes," he said. "I want to know."

"It wasn't because I committed any crime, Johnny. I'm one of the few people on Starhaven who isn't a fugitive from the law in some way."

His eyes widened. "You're not—"

"No. I'm no fugitive."

"Then how did you come here?" he asked, bewildered. "And why?"

She was silent a moment. "Eight years ago," she said finally, speaking as if from a great distance away. "Ben Thurdan left Starhaven for the first time since he had built it. He took a vacation. He travelled incognito to the planet of Luribar IX, and he spent a week at a hotel there. He met me there."

"You're from Luribar?"

She nodded. "My family helped to colonize it a century and a half ago. Ben took me dancing—once. He was so terribly clumsy I laughed at him. Then I saw I had hurt him. Imagine, hurting a powerful giant of a man like that! He was next to tears. I felt I had to apologize. He's never gone on a dance floor again, with me or with anybody else. But he left Luribar the next night, to return to Starhaven. He told me who he was and what he was, and asked me to come with him to Starhaven."

"And you did."

"Yes."

"Oh," Mantell said, after a while.

He glanced up at the star-speckled bowl of the night, thinking of Ben Thurdan who had put those stars up there and who had built an iron shell around this planet, and who was soon going to be dead.

Then he turned to Myra.

She seemed to flow into his arms.

Chapter Sixteen

At 10:45 he left her. Thurdan was expecting her to arrive at his place in less than an hour, and she had to pick up her briefcase and then go to central headquarters for the papers he wanted. In seventy-five minutes Thurdan would be dead, Mantell thought. The seconds dragged by interminably.

Myra had asked him to arrive at Thurdan's apartment at about ten minutes past midnight, to help her with the body. Until then, he was simply to stay out of trouble. He passed half an hour in a bar not far from the Pleasure Dome, a small place with poor lighting and worse liquor. A girl was dancing in the back, accompanying herself by singing in a nasal drone. When she finished her song a thin pockmarked man circulated and passed the hat among the patrons of the bar.

Mantell tossed in a single-chip note. The pockmarked man thanked him effusively and moved on. Mantell ordered a beer and sipped it reflectively. The minutes were crawling.

After a while he got tired of the bar, and left. He paced the Starhaven streets for nearly another half hour. He had already consumed the greater part of the seventy-five minutes he had to waste.

Now it was eleven thirty-five.

He found another bar, stopped in long enough to buy himself a second beer, drank half of it and left. He was feeling less calm with each passing minute. She was so slim and small, he thought, and Thurdan so powerful—

Eleven forty.

Eleven forty-five. She would be just about arriving at his apartment by now. Mantell flagged down an aircab and in a tension-tightened voice gave the robodriver a street not far from the address of Thurdan's private dwelling.

Eleven fifty.

He stood alone beneath a flickering street lamp, waiting for the minutes to pass.

Eleven fifty-two.

Eight minutes to go. Then seven. Mantell started to walk toward the building. He was thinking: A month ago I was just a bum, wandering around the beaches, and now I'm on my way to help out in the assassination of the ruler of a world! It was almost like moving in a dream, except that this was real.

He reached the building at eleven fifty-seven. Three minutes. Of course, there was no positive assurance that Myra would act precisely on the dot of twelve. They had not bothered to synchronize watches too precisely, and in any event there might be unforeseen delays of a moment or two before she would strike. He prayed the blade would be sharp, her aim true.

A robot sat behind a desk in the lobby of Thurdan's building and surveyed him owlishly as he passed through the main doors.

"Yes, please?"

"I'm visiting Mr. Thurdan," Mantell said.

"Sorry, please. Mr. Thurdan is very busy on important government matters, and cannot be interrupted."

Mantell glanced at his watch. Eleven fifty-nine.

The tension was mounting. "This is most urgent," he said.

At this very moment Myra might be unsheathing the weapon. The robot grinned obstinately, blocking his path.

"Mr. Thurdan is not to be disturbed," the robot said.

Mantell shrugged and drew the blaster he carried inside his jacket. He fired once, aiming for the robot's neural channel. The smile remained fixed idiotically on the metal face and the voice continued, locked now in an endless monotone.

"Mr. Thurdan is not to be disturbed Mr. Thurdan is not to be disturbed Mr. Thurdan is not to be disturbed Mr. Thurdan is not to be—"

Mantell fired again. The robot sagged and toppled to the deep wine-red carpet, quivered once, subsided, and lay there in a useless chrome-plated heap. It was just scrap, now, its delicate cryotronic brain hopelessly shorted out.

Midnight.

The elevator seemed to take little short of forever to climb the forty-eight stories to Thurdan's penthouse. Mantell counted seconds, waiting, watching the clock hands moving.

Twelve-of-one. He had plenty of time. Myra had told him to be there at ten past twelve.

He stepped through the lift tube door on the forty-eighth level and found himself in an endless brightly lighted corridor. Unsurprisingly, there was a robot patrolling the area; Thurdan was not a man to take many chances. His apartment, like Starhaven itself, was well guarded—but always subject to attack from within.

The robot turned and shouted a quick *"Halt"* at him.

Mantell knew that this one had its response channels set for guard duty; it wouldn't be as slow on the draw as the defunct lobby attendant had been.

He slid into an alcove, hoping the robot wasn't equipped with range perceptors keen enough to smell him out where he crouched. Or with a portable force screen, as the one who killed Marchin had been.

Metal feet clattered down the hallway.

"Halt! You are ordered to appear from hiding! Mr. Thurdan does not wish to be disturbed!"

The robot steamed on past Mantell without seeing him. He emerged from the alcove and fired once, blasting through its spinal column, paralyzing it and blocking its motor responses. Then, ducking in front of it, he shorted out its brain and put a stop to its impotent whirrings.

The time was twelve-oh-five. Mantell sprinted down the corridor toward Thurdan's suite.

And stopped outside. And listened.

And heard the sound of sobbing. It was Myra. In an agony of remorse, he wondered?

Twelve-oh-six.

Thurdan lay six minutes dead now. Mantell knew what his job was now: to go inside, to snap Myra out of the state of shock she probably had gone into after the killing. He pushed against the door, and to his surprise it gave readily. She had left it open for him.

He flung the door open and burst into Thurdan's apartment. The suite seemed to stretch in every direction. Rare and costly draperies cloaked the oval windows; rich thick rugs brocaded the floor. This was the suite of a czar, of a possession-hungry potentate. Paintings filled the wall space.

The sound of sobbing grew louder. Mantell ran toward it.

He heard Myra shouting to him—"Johnny! Johnny! *No!*"

But by then it was too late.

He blundered into the room and in virtually the same instant two hundred forty pounds of irresistible force crashed into him. The drawn blaster he had been clutching went clattering across the room; he reeled back, struggling for balance.

Ben Thurdan was still alive.

The living room was brightly lighted. With terrible clarity Mantell saw the huge disordered desk, the crumpled papers on its top stained with blood. Myra entered.

Her face was tear-streaked and blotchy; her upper lip was split, and a dab of blood oozed from it. One whole side of her face was livid and swollen where she had received a ferocious blow. She was sobbing hysterically, her whole body quaking with each outcry.

A jagged red line ran some six inches across the front of his shirt at the chest, beginning below the left clavicle and ending just above his left breast. Mantell saw it was only a flesh wound.

He understood what had happened. Somehow Myra had failed in her attempt, scratching Thurdan where she should have torn.

"Are you in this thing too, Mantell?" Thurdan bellowed in monumental rage. Even coatless, and in his ripped shirt, he was a figure of terrifying authority. Sweat poured down his hairless scalp. "You're all against me, then? Harmon and Polderson and Ledru and McDermott and Myra—and even you, Mantell. Even you."

He advanced slowly toward Mantell. They were both unarmed. Myra's knife, that was to have finished Thurdan, was nowhere in sight, and the blaster Mantell had carried now lay out of reach. Mantell knew that Thurdan needed no weapon. He could tear him to pieces barehanded.

He backed up, moving warily to keep from stumbling. As he stared at Thurdan's grim face he was astonished to see tears starting to form in the fierce eyes—tears of rage, probably. Learning that your closest associates had banded together to betray you is something that even the strongest of men cannot take without a sharp emotional pang.

"All of you wanted to kill me, didn't you?" Thurdan said slowly. "I didn't do enough for you. I didn't build Starhaven practically with my own two hands, and take you all in when you came running. That wasn't enough, so you decided to try to kill me. But you won't kill Ben Thurdan! *You won't!*"

Mantell tried desperately to signal to Myra to scramble across the room and seize the blaster where it lay. But she was too dumb and dazed with shock to understand the meaning of his gestures. She lay on a sofa, arms wrapped over her eyes, shaking violently, a pale huddled figure.

Thurdan reached out for him. He ducked, swept it under his mighty fumbling paws, and landed a solid punch on the jutting jaw. It was like hitting a boulder. Thurdan didn't seem to feel the blow, though Mantell's arm rippled with pain at the contact.

Thurdan's hands clutched at his shoulder; he twisted and slipped away.

"The blaster, Myra—*get the blaster!*" he called harshly. "Pick it up!"

That was a mistake.

Thurdan flicked a hasty glance over his shoulder, saw the blaster where it lay not more than three feet behind him, and scooped it up in one huge paw. In the same motion he hurled it through the open window, far out into the night.

Now it was bare hands against bare hands, and that sort of conflict could have only one conceivable finish.

Mantell edged back as far from Thurdan's reach as he possibly could. His breath was coming hard and thick.

"Kill me, will you?" he demanded. "I'll show you! I'll show all of you!"

Thurdan charged forward, caught Mantell around the middle with one great hand, and hurled him like a toy across the room. He crashed numbingly into a table laden with fine pottery. Mantell rolled over, trying to get up and failing, and waited for Thurdan to pounce and finish him off.

But he didn't pounce. He stood over him, rocking unsteadily, face contorted by some deep inner stress. He made no attempt to touch the fallen Mantell, who lay looking up.

Finally Thurdan said, "I built Starhaven and I can destroy it too!"

Wildly he laughed and swung away, running down the hall and out into the darkness.

Chapter Seventeen

Mantell slowly pulled himself to his feet and stood frozen a moment, shaking away the pain. His back felt numb. Thurdan's sudden flight left him utterly bewildered. He turned to Myra.

"Did you see that? He just ran out!"

She nodded faintly. Her left eye was nearly puffed closed, he saw. She drew a tattered robe around herself. She was making a visible effort to regain control over her nerves.

"Come on," she said. "There's a private landing port out on the balcony. That's probably where he went."

"What—?"

She didn't wait to explain. She headed off in the direction Thurdan had gone, and Mantell had no choice but to follow.

They passed through a darkened hallway into a large sitting room whose balcony doors hung open, swaying back and forth in the night breeze. Myra pointed to something just beyond the balcony.

"There he goes!"

An aircar had just taken off, using the balcony as a landing stage; a fiery streak against the blackness indicated its direction. Two more cars were parked on the balcony landing strip. Evidently Thurdan kept them there for emergency use.

"He's heading for the control tower," Mantell said. "Like Samson bringing down the temple—he's going to lift the screens and bring all Starhaven down to ruin around him!"

Hastily they leaped into one of the waiting aircars and Mantell flipped on the engine. The car sprang away from the balcony. He managed to prod the engine into highest gear within moments after take-off, and they soared out over Starhaven.

The city, far below them, looked tiny and almost insignificant.

Myra huddled against him for warmth. She was still quivering, and not entirely from the cold of the night.

Mantell kept his eyes on the course. "What happened before I got there?" he asked.

She said, "Everything went as scheduled . . . until I drew the knife. I . . . hesitated. Just a fraction of a second too long. Ben saw what I was doing. I managed to strike anyway, but he dodged just in time and I only scratched his skin. And then—then he knocked the knife out of my hand and hit me. I thought he was going to kill me. Then you came."

"And what about Harmon and all the others? Are they still waiting?"

"I guess so. We allowed for something like this to happen. They were waiting to hear from me. I was supposed to give the signal before we made the announcement of Ben's death. And now—"

"Now everything's changed," Mantell said.

The dark windowless bulk of the control tower loomed up in the blackness ahead; he saw the smoking exhaust of Thurdan's aircar, and brought the vessel down on the landing stage nearby.

They sprang from the car and plunged through the entrance into the control tower itself, Mantell half-dragging Myra behind him. His hand encircled her wrist tightly; there was no time to waste now.

"He must be in his little control center room," Mantell guessed. "Lord knows what he's doing in there!"

"How do we get there? I don't know my way around this building."

"Come this way," he snapped. "The lift tubes are over here."

But the first lift tube they tried did not respond; it had been shut down for the night. So had the second, and so had the third.

"I don't have any idea how to get them started again," he told her.

They raced around the level, circling it completely in search of a functioning lift. The thought of running wildly upstairs through the darkened tower was hardly appealing. At last they found a single lift tube that was in operation. They took it.

They emerged in the corridor, just outside Mantell's defense-screen laboratory; not far down the hall was Ben Thurdan's private control room, the nerve center of Starhaven.

And the light was on in there.

Mantell released his grip on Myra's wrist and dashed down the hall, leaving her behind. Thurdan was in there, and he had the door locked and the small room screen barrier turned on, so it was impossible to enter. He had barricaded himself.

But it was possible to hear what he was saying. The visiscreen was on, and through the plexilite door-window Mantell could see that Thurdan was talking to a gray-faced man in the uniform of the Space Patrol.

"I'm Ben Thurdan, Commander. You heard me, *Thurdan*. You know who I am. I'm calling direct from Starhaven." Thurdan looked wild, half-mad almost. The iron reserve of poise had crumbled away completely.

The SP man looked skeptical. "Is this some kind of joke, Thurdan? Your foolishness doesn't interest me. One of the days you'll find we've broken through your defenses, and—"

"Shut up and let me talk!" Thurdan roared like some wounded animal in anguish. "I'm offering you Starhaven on a plutonium platter, Commander Whitestone! You say you have a fleet? All right, *send* your damned fleet—*I'm dropping the screens!* I'm surrendering. Can you understand that, Whitestone?"

The figure in the screen raised eyebrows curiously and peered out at the wild-looking, sweating, half-naked Thurdan. "Surrendering, Thurdan? I find it hard to believe that—"

"Damn you, I mean it! Send a fleet!"

As he stood with his face pressed against the panel, listening and watching, Mantell heard Myra approaching behind him.

"What's going on in there?" she asked.

"Thurdan has cracked up completely. Right now he's busy surrendering Starhaven to Commander Whitestone of the Space Patrol. He's inviting them to send out a fleet, and he's promising to drop the screens when the fleet gets here."

"No! He can't be serious!"

"I think he is," Mantell said. "He would never be able to understand the reasons why you tried to kill him tonight. He thinks the conspiracy was the ultimate betrayal of everything he's worked for in Starhaven—and it threw him off his trolley!"

"We have to stop him!" Myra said determinedly. "If the Patrol ever gets in here they'll carry everyone in Starhaven off to the prison keeps for brainwashing. People who have been law-abiding citizens for twenty years are going to suffer. The place will be destroyed—"

"If we could only get in there and stop him—but he's got a barrier-screen around the room."

"Screens can be turned off. You're supposed to be barrier-screen expert, Johnny. Can't you think of something?"

"No," he said. "Yes. Yes. I can. Wait here, will you! And scream good and loud if Thurdan comes out of that room before I get back."

"What are you—"

"Never mind. Just wait here. And sing out if he opens that door!"

Mantell raced hurriedly down the hall to his laboratory, punched his thumb savagely into the doorplate, and kicked the door open when his print released the lock. The light switched on automatically.

He began to rummage through his cluttered workbench for that unfinished pilot model, for which he had once had such high hopes, and which he had never dreamed would be put to a use such as this. . . .

Ah! There it was.

He snatched it up, out of the tangle of punch-coils and transistors in which it lay. Glancing around the room he found a pocket welding torch, the only instrument within sight that could serve as an effective weapon. He gathered these things up, turned, ran out and back up the corridor to the place where Myra stood waiting for him.

"Did anything happen while I was gone?"

"He's still talking to that SP man," she told him. "I've been trying to listen. I think Whitestone finally believes Ben's serious."

"Okay. Watch out."

Mantell hammered loudly on the plexiplate door with his fists, while the conversation within came to an end and the screen went dead.

"Ben!" he yelled. "Ben Thurdan!"

Thurdan turned and blinked through the panel at him. Mantell called his name again, and yet again.

"What do you want?" Thurdan growled. "Liar! Betrayer! You'll die with all the rest of them!"

"You don't understand, Ben! I'm with you! I'm on your side! It's all a big mistake. You have to trust me. Look! I've brought you the personal defense screen, Ben."

He held up the model—the useless, unfinished, unworkable model. "I finished it tonight," he said desperately. "I was working on it all evening. Then I ran the final tests. It's a success! You can strap it around your waist and no weapon can touch you."

"Eh?" Thurdan grunted suspiciously. "I thought you said it would take a week to finish it."

"I thought so, too. But I worked at nights. It's finished now."

Thurdan was staring intently through the thick plastic of the door, shielded both by that and by the bubble of force that cloaked his entire room. There was no way Mantell could possibly get inside. But if he could induce Thurdan to come out. . . .

He seized Myra roughly and thrust her forward. She stood there, arms outstretched to Thurdan.

"I brought her, too," Mantell said. "She's yours. She wants to explain. There never was anything serious between her and me, Ben. Come on out of there. Don't give up Starhaven now. Don't give up everything you've built, all you've planned, just for *this*!"

Mantell saw he was getting through to him now, communicating. Thurdan's lips were fumbling for words; his deep hard eyes flicked back and forth, bewildered, confused.

Poor Ben! Mantell thought with real compassion. It was a saddening thing to watch a man like that crack open like a moldy melon.

Thurdan's hand wavered on the switch, and he grimaced to show his inner conflict. Then in a quick convulsive gesture he yanked downward sharply, cutting off the screen-field that was a barrier around the room. A long moment passed. Mantell heard him jiggling with the lock; then the door swung slowly open.

Thurdan came out.

He was walking unsteadily, swaying and faltering like a mighty oak about to fall. In a surprisingly quiet voice, in a voice that was being held in tight rein to keep it from turning into a hysterical babble, he said, "All right, Johnny. Give me the screen."

Mantell tossed the worthless model to him. Thurdan caught it with one great hand.

"There," Mantell said. "Go ahead. Strap it to your waist."

Myra was sobbing gently behind him, a low steady sound. For once Mantell felt no sensation of fear, only a cold, icy calmness inside him that seemed to fill his entire body. He watched as Thurdan carefully strapped the rig around himself.

Then Thurdan said crooningly, "Come here, Myra. Here to me."

"Just a second, Ben." Mantell interposed himself between Thurdan and the girl. "We have to test the thing first. Don't you want to test it?"

Thurdan's eyes flashed. "What the hell is this?"

Mantell pulled out the pocket welding torch. "You can trust me, Ben. Can't you?"

"Sure, Johnny. I trust you. About as far as I can throw you!"

Suddenly sane, realizing he had been tricked into coming out of the impregnable safety of his room, Thurdan came lumbering toward the two of them, murder blazing in his eyes.

Mantell waited just a moment and then turned on the welding torch.

There was a momentary sputtering hiss as the arc formed; then the globe of light spurted out and cascaded down over him. Thurdan howled and flailed out with his arms, hitting nothing. He took one difficult last step, like a man slogging grimly forward through a sea of molasses. He was dead then, but he didn't know it.

Mantell heard a whimper. Then Thurdan fell.

He clicked off the torch. Ben Thurdan was dead at last, dead by a trick, lured and baited to his death like a great mountain bear.

Mantell looked away from the charred thing on the floor. It wasn't pretty.

"Sorry, Ben," he said softly. "And you'll never understand why we had to do it. You never would have understood."

Inside the room, a quick glance at the meters told Mantell that the defense screens were down all over Starhaven. Thurdan had lowered them before he finished talking to the SP Commander. For the first time in decades, the sanctuary planet lay utterly open to Space Patrol attack.

Mantell jabbed down on the communicator stud and when the operator responded with the semi-automatic "Yes, Mr. Thurdan," Mantell said, "This isn't Thurdan. It's John Mantell. Get me back the call that was on this line a minute ago—SP headquarters on Earth. Thurdan was talking to Commander Whitestone."

The ten-second delay of subradio communication followed, while arcs leaped across the grayness of hyper-space, meshed, locked, returned.

The vision screen brightened. The face of Whitestone reappeared on the screen.

"The fleet's on its way, Thurdan," the SP man began immediately. "Don't tell me you've changed your mind, or—"

He stopped. Mantell said quickly, "Thurdan's dead. There's been a sort of a revolution on Starhaven, and I'm in charge. My name is—"

"Mantell?" The SP Commander burst in suddenly, interrupting. "You're still alive, Mantell? Then why didn't you report to us? What's been going on all this time, man?"

Stunned, Mantell looked up at the image in the vision screen. When he spoke, his voice came out as a harsh croaking whisper:

"What did you say? How do you know me?"

"Know you? I picked you for this job myself, Mantell! We probed every member of the Patrol until we found one who could adapt well enough."

The floor seemed to quake under Mantell. He took a hesitant step backward, groped for what had been Thurdan's chair, and sank numbly into it.

"You say I'm in the Patrol?"

"A member of the Fourteenth Earth Patrol, Mantell," was the calm and utterly believable reply. "And we chose you to enter Starhaven bearing a false set of memories. It was a brand-new technique our espionage system had developed in order to get you past Thurdan's psychprobing."

"This can't be true."

"We invented a wholly fictitious background for you and instilled it subhypnotically, with a posthypnotic command implanted that would enable you to revert to your true identity twenty-four hours after you had been subjected to Thurdan's psychprobe."

"Johnny, what's he talking about?" Myra asked in a wondering voice.

"I wish I knew," Mantell said hollowly.

"What's that, Mantell? You're in complete charge of Starhaven now, you say? Fine work, boy! The fleet will arrive in less than an hour to take care of the job of mopping up."

"You don't seem to understand," Mantell said in a flat, dead voice. "Something went wrong. I never recovered my—my true identity, as you say. I don't know anything about this business of my being an SP man. So far as I know I was a beachcomber on the planet Mulciber for seven years, and before that I was a defense-screen technician on Earth."

"Yes, yes, of course that's so—that's the identity pattern we established— though you were a trained defense-screen man originally, of course. But—"

"But I don't remember anything about the SP!" Mantell protested. "Only my own memories are real!"

T he SP man was silent a long moment.

Finally he said, "They assured me the treatment would be a success—that you would recover your original identity once you were past Thurdan's psychprobes."

"I didn't."

"That's easily fixed. We'll have our psychosurgeons restore your original identity just as soon as you're back on Earth."

Mantell shook his head dizzily, trying to comprehend the magnitude of this thing Whitestone seemed to be telling him.

The room, Myra, the image of Whitestone, Starhaven itself, finally the universe—all took on a strange semblance of utter unreality, like the purplish glow objects get when one stares at them just the right way through a prism. Mantell seemed to be moving in a world of dreams—of nightmares.

Myra was very close to him, almost touching him.

"Is this true?" she asked. "Or is it just some SP trick?"

"I don't know," Mantell murmured. "Right now I don't know anything at all."

Whitestone said, "It appears that the project was a success, at any rate. Whether you're in full possession of your self-awareness or not, the fact remains that your mission has been fulfilled, Mantell. Starhaven's screens are down. Within an hour an SP squadron will be there, cleaning out the universe's sorriest hell-hole. Thanks to you, Mantell."

"I'm not so sure of that," Mantell said heavily, weighing each word and releasing it individually, syllable by syllable.

"What did you say?"

Without answering, Mantell sank back tiredly in the chair, and a torrent of images flooded through his mind.

The days at Klingsan Defense on Earth; the long weary years on Mulciber, years of scrabbling for crusts of bread and cadging drinks.

Now this faded little man in a Space Patrol uniform was trying to tell him that all this was unreal, that the memories in his mind were artificially implanted memories, placed there by skilled psychosurgeons solely for the purpose of getting an SP man through the defenses of Ben Thurdan's fortress, Starhaven.

Well, perhaps they were.

Perhaps.

But to Mantell, they were real. To him, this was the life he had lived. That suffering he remembered was real. It had actually happened to him.

And Starhaven was real.

The SP—that, he thought, was a vague dream, a shining bubble of unreality, a hated enemy.

Where had it begun? Had he actually killed a man on Mulciber and fled to Starhaven in a stolen SP ship? Or had he been released from some point in space after they had fixed up his mind, and had two dummy remote-operated ships been rigged to "pursue" him to Starhaven?

A moment of choice faced him. He knew he could go back to Earth, and there have Mulciber and all its attendant bitterness peeled from his mind like the outer skin of an onion, and emerge fresh, clean, once again an honored member of the Space Patrol.

Or he could stay here. With Myra.

"Mantell, are you all right?" Whitestone's image demanded loudly from the screen. "Your face has turned utterly white."

"I'm thinking," Mantell said.

He was thinking of Ben Thurdan's dream, and of what the Patrol would do to Starhaven once they had finally penetrated its defenses. Twenty million fugitives would be carted off to justice at last; honor and decency would be restored to the galaxy.

But was that the only way?

What, he thought, if Starhaven were to be allowed to continue as it was, as a sanctuary for criminals—but run by Myra and himself, neither of whom was a law-breaker. Suppose—suppose they were gradually to transform Ben Thurdan's metal fortress into a planet for rehabilitation—without the knowledge of those subtly being rehabilitated.

That seemed like a better idea to Mantell than opening the planet up to the SP. Much better.

Very quietly he said, "You'd better tell that fleet of yours to turn right around and head for home, Whitestone."

"Eh? What's that?"

"I'm suggesting that you might as well save the government a lot of lost time. Because when that fleet gets here, they'll discover that Starhaven is just as impregnable as ever. I've decided to stay here, Whitestone. I'm putting the screens back up again. And Starhaven doesn't want anything further to do with the galaxy."

"Mantell, this is madness! You're an SP man, a native of Earth! Where's your loyalty! Where's your sense of honor, Mantell?"

Mantell smiled broadly. "Honor? Loyalty? I'm Johnny Mantell of Starhaven, late of the planet Mulciber, before that a drunk and disorderly employee of Klingsan Defense Screens. That's what my memory tells me, and that's who I am. And I'm not letting Starhaven fall into the hands of the SP."

He moistened his dry lips and managed a grin. Whitestone stared incredulously at him and started to say something. Mantell reached up and broke the contact; the face dissolved into an electronic whirl of colors, and was gone.

Mantell felt very tired, suddenly.

Am I right? he thought. *Should I do this?*

Yes, he answered himself.

It had been a busy day. Thunder boomed in the sky outside. That meant it was nearly two in the morning—for, at two, thunder sounded over Starhaven, and then the nightly rains came, refreshing the planet, sweeping away the staleness of the day and leaving everything clean and bright and new.

Myra was smiling at him.

He reached forward and tugged down the master switch; instantly, meters and dials leaped into jiggling life. Once again, Starhaven was surrounded by an impassable network of force-shields; once again, they were protected from the outside.

And within the shield, Mantell thought, the greatest experiment in criminal reform in the history of the universe was about to begin. On a planet without law the galaxy's most hardened criminals would be converted into useful citizens—segregated from the rest of the galaxy. Starhaven would become a giant prison barred in both directions, Mantell thought.

The rain started to fall, pattering lightly down. Mantell pulled Myra close against him for a moment.

Then he released her. There was time for that later. "You'd better get in touch with the rest of the Provisional Government of the Republic of Starhaven and let them know that Ben's dead," he told her. "We have plenty of work to do."

Shadow on the Stars

To Randall Garrett

Chapter One

Ewing woke slowly, sensing the coldness all about him. It was slowly withdrawing down the length of his body; his head and shoulders were out of the freeze now, the rest of his body gradually emerging. He stirred as well as he could, and the delicately spun web of foam that had cradled him in the journey across space shivered as he moved.

He extended a hand and heaved downward on the lever six inches from his wrist. A burst of fluid shot forward from the spinnerettes above him, dissolving the web that bound him. The coldness drained from his legs. Stiffly he rose, moving as if he were very old, and stretched gingerly.

He had slept eleven months, fourteen days, and some six hours, according to the panel above his sleeping area. The panel registered time in Galactic Absolute Units. And the second, the Galactic Absolute Unit of temporal measure, was an arbitrary figure, accepted by the galaxy only because it had been devised by the mother world.

Ewing touched an enameled stud and a segment of the inner surface of the ship's wall swung away, revealing a soft glowing vision-plate. A planet hung centered in the green depths of the plate—a planet green itself, with vast seas bordering its continents.

Earth.

Ewing knew what his next task was. Moving quickly, now that circulation was returning to his thawed limbs, he strode to the compact bulk of the subetheric generator on the opposite wall and spun the contact dial. A blue light glowed.

"Baird Ewing speaking," he said to the pickup grid. "I wish to report that I've taken up a position in orbit around Earth after a successful flight. All's well so far. I'll be descending to Earth shortly. Further reports will follow."

He broke contact. This very moment, he knew, his words were leaping across the galaxy toward his home world, via subetheric carrier wave. Fifteen days would elapse before his message arrived on Corwin.

Ewing had wanted to stay awake, all the long months of his solitary trip. There was reading he wanted to do, and music disks to play. The idea of spending nearly a year asleep was appalling to him; all that time wasted!

But they had been adamant. "You're crossing sixteen parsecs of space in a one-man ship," they told him. "Nobody can stay awake all that time and come out of it sane, Ewing. And we need you sane."

He tried to protest. It was no good. The people of Corwin were sending him to Earth at great expense to do a job of vital importance; unless they could be absolutely certain that he would arrive in good condition, they would do better sending someone else. Reluctantly, Ewing yielded. They lowered him into the nutrient bath and showed him how to trip the foot levers that brought about suspension and the hand levers that would release him when his time was up. They sealed off his ship and shot it into the dark, a lonely raft on the broad sea, a coffin-sized spaceship built for one. . . .

At least ten minutes went by before he was fully restored to normal physiological functioning. He stared in the mirror at the strange silken stubble that had sprouted on his face. He looked oddly emaciated; he had never been a fleshy man, but now he looked skeletonic, his cheeks shrunken, his skin tight—drawn over the jutting bones of his face. His hair seemed to have faded too; it had been a rich auburn on that day in 3805 when he left Corwin on his emergency mission to Earth, but now it was a dark, nondescript mud-brown. Ewing was a big man, long-muscled rather than stocky, with a fierce expression contradicted by mild, questioning eyes.

His stomach felt hollow. His shanks were spindly. He felt drained of vigor. But there was a job to do.

Adjoining the subetheric generator was an in-system communicator. He switched it on, staring at the pale ball that was Earth in the screen on the far wall. A crackle of static rewarded him. He held his breath, waiting, waiting for the first words he would have heard in pure Terrestrial. He wondered if they would understand his Anglo-Corwin.

After all, it was nearly a thousand years since the colony had been planted, and almost five hundred since the people of Corwin had last had intercourse of any kind with Earth. Languages diverge, in five hundred years.

A voice said, "Earth station Double Prime. Who calls, please? Speak up. Speak, please."

Ewing smiled. It was intelligible!

He said, "One-man ship out of the Free World of Corwin calling. I'm a stabilized orbit fifty thousand kilometers above Earth ground level. Request permission to land at coordinates of your designation."

There was a long silence, too long to be attributed sheerly to transmission lag. Ewing wondered if he had spoken too quickly, or if his words had lost their Terrestrial meanings.

Finally came a response: "Free World of *which*, did you say?"

"Corwin. Epsilon Ursae Majoris XII. It's a former Terrestrial colony."

Again there was an uncomfortable pause. "Corwin . . . Corwin. Oh. I guess it's okay for you to land. You have a warp-drive ship?"

"Yes," Ewing said. "With photonic modifiers, of course. And ion-beam for atmospheric passage."

His Earthside respondent said, "Are photonic modifiers radioactive?"

Ewing was taken aback for a moment. Frowning at the speaker grid, he said, "If you mean radioactive in the normal sense of emitting hard particles, no. The photonic modifier merely converts—" He stopped. "Do I have to explain the whole thing to you?"

"Not unless you want to stay up there all day, Corwin. If your ship's not hot, come on down. Coordinates for landing will follow."

Ewing carefully jotted the figures down as they came in, read them back for confirmation, thanked the Earthman, and signed off. He integrated the figures and programmed them for the ship's calculators.

His throat felt dry. Something about the Earthman's tone of voice troubled him. The man had been too flip, careless of mind, impatient.

Perhaps I was expecting too much, Ewing thought. *After all, he was just doing a routine job.*

It was a jarring beginning, nonetheless. Ewing realized he, like the Corwinites, had a highly idealized mental image of an Earthman as a being compassionately wise, physically superb, a superman in all respects. It would be disappointing to learn that the fabled inhabitants of the legendary mother world were mere human beings themselves, like their remote descendants on the colony worlds.

Ewing strapped himself in for the downward jaunt through the atmospheric blanket of Earth and nudged the lever that controlled the autopilot. The ultimate leg of his journey had begun. Within an hour, he would actually stand on the soil of Earth herself.

I hope they'll be able to help us, he thought. Bright in his mind was a vivid mental image: faceless hordes of barbaric Klodni sweeping down on the galaxy out of Andromeda, devouring world after world in their relentless drive inward toward civilization's heart.

Already four worlds had fallen to the Klodni since the aliens had begun their campaign of conquest. The timetable said they would reach Corwin within the next decade.

Cities destroyed, women and children carried into slavery, the glittering spire of the World Building a charred ruin, the University destroyed, the fertile fields blackened by the Klodni scorched-earth tactics—

Ewing shuddered as his tiny ship spiraled Earthward, bobbing in the thickening layers of atmosphere. *Earth will help us,* he told himself comfortingly, *Earth will save her colonies from conquest.*

Ewing felt capillaries bursting under the increasing drag of deceleration. He gripped the handrests and shouted to relieve the tension on his eardrums, but there was no way of relieving the tension within. The thunder of his jets boomed through the framework of the ship, and the green planet grew frighteningly huge in the clear plastic of the view-screen. . . .

Minutes later, the ship came to rest on a broad ferroconcrete landing apron; it hung poised a moment on its own jet-wash, then settled gently to earth. With gravity-heavy fingers Ewing unfastened himself. Through the vision-screen he saw small beetle-like autotrucks come rumbling over the field toward his ship. The decontamination squad, no doubt; robot-manned of course.

He waited until they had done their job, then sprung the hatch on his ship and climbed out. The air smelled good—strange, since his home had a twenty-three percent oxygen content, two parts in a hundred richer than Earth's—and the day was warm. Ewing spied the vaulting sweep of a terminal building, and headed toward it.

A robot, blocky and faceless, scanned him with photo-beams as he passed through the swinging doors. Within, the terminal was a maze of blinking lights, red-green, on-off, up-down. Momentarily, Ewing was dazed.

Beings of all kinds thronged the building. Ewing saw four semi-humanoid forms with bulbous heads engaged in a busy discussion near where he stood. Further in the distance swarms of more Terrestrial beings moved about. Ewing was startled by their appearance.

Some were "normal"—oddly muscular and rugged-looking, but not so much that they would cause any surprised comment on Corwin. But the others!

Dressed flamboyantly in shimmering robes of turquoise and black, gray and gold, they presented a weird sight. One had no ears; his skull was bare, decorated only by jeweled pendants that seemed to be riveted to the flesh of his scalp. Another had one leg and supported himself by a luminous crutch. A third wore gleaming emeralds on a golden nose ring.

No two of them seemed to look alike. As a trained student of cultural patterns, Ewing was aware of the cause of the phenomenon; overelaboration of decoration was a common evolution for highly advanced societies, such as Earth's. But it made him feel terribly provincial to see the gaudy display. Corwin was a new world, even after a thousand years of colonization; such fancies were yet to take root there.

Hesitantly, he approached the group of dandified Terrestrials nearest him. They were chattering in artificial-sounding, high-pitched voices.

"Pardon," Ewing said. "I've just arrived from the Free World of Corwin. Is there some place where I can register with the authorities?"

The conversation ceased as if cut off with an ax. The trio whirled, facing Ewing. "You be from a colony world?" asked the uniped, in barely intelligible accents.

Ewing nodded. "Corwin. Sixteen parsecs away. We were settled by Earth a thousand years ago."

They exchanged words at a speed that made comprehension impossible; it seemed like a private language, some made-up doubletalk. Ewing watched the rouged faces, feeling distaste.

"Where can I register with the authorities?" he asked again, a little stiffly.

The earless one giggled shrilly. "What authorities? This is Earth, friend! We come and go as we please."

A sense of uneasiness grew in Ewing. He disliked these Terrestrials almost upon sight, after just a moment's contact.

A new voice, strange, harshly accented, said, "Did I hear you say you were from a colony?"

Ewing turned. One of the "normal" Terrestrials was speaking to him—a man about five-feet-eight with a thick, squarish face, beetling brows looming over dark smoldering eyes, and a cropped, bullet shaped head. His voice was dull and ugly sounding.

"I'm from Corwin," Ewing said.

The other frowned, screwing up his massive brows. He said, "Where's that?"

"Sixteen parsecs. Epsilon Ursae Majoris XII. Earth colony."

"And what are you doing on Earth?"

The belligerent tone annoyed Ewing. The Corwinite said, in a bleak voice, "I'm an officially accredited ambassador from my world to the government of Earth. I'm looking for the customs authority."

"There are none," the squat man said. "The Earthers did away with them about a century back. Couldn't be bothered with them, they said." He grinned in cheerful contempt at the three dandies, who had moved further away and were murmuring busily to each other in their private language. "The Earthers can't hardly be bothered with anything."

Ewing was puzzled. "Aren't you from Earth yourself? I mean—"

"Me?" The deep chest emitted a rumbling, sardonic chuckle. "You folk really *are* isolated, aren't you? I'm a Sirian. Sirius IV—oldest Terrestrial colony there is. Suppose we get a drink. I want to talk to you."

Chapter Two

Somewhat unwillingly, Ewing followed the burly Sirian through the thronged terminal toward a refreshment room at the far side of the arcade. As soon as they were seated at a gleaming translucent table, the Sirian stared levelly at Ewing and said, "First things come first. What's your name?"

"Baird Ewing. You?"

"Rollun Firnik. What brings you to Earth, Ewing?"

Firnik's manner was offensively blunt. Ewing toyed with the golden-amber drink the Sirian had bought for him, sipped it idly, put it down. "I told you," he said quietly. "I'm an ambassador from the government of Corwin to the government of Earth. It's as simple as that."

"It is? When did you people last have any contact with the rest of the galaxy?"

"Five hundred years ago. But—"

"Five hundred years," Firnik repeated speculatively. "And now you decide to reopen contact with Earth." He squinted at Ewing, chin resting on balled fist. "Just like that. Poof! Enter one ambassador. It isn't just out of sociability, is it, Ewing? What's the reason behind your visit?"

"I'm not familiar with the latest news in this sector of the galaxy," Ewing said. "Have you heard any mention of the Klodni?"

"Klodni?" the Sirian repeated. "No. The name doesn't mean a thing to me. Should it?"

"News travels slowly through the galaxy," Ewing said. "The Klodni are a humanoid race that evolved somewhere in the Andromeda star cluster. I've seen solidographs of them. They're little greasy creatures, about five feet high, with a sort of ant-like civilization. A war-fleet of Klodni is on the move."

Firnik rolled an eyebrow upward. He said nothing.

"A couple thousand Klodni ships entered our galaxy about four years ago. They landed on Barnholt—that's a colony world about a hundred fifty light-years deeper in space than we are—and wiped the place clean. After about a year they picked up and moved on. They've been to four planets so far, and no one's been able to stop them yet. They swarm over a planet and destroy everything they see, then go on to the next world."

"What of it?"

"We've plotted their probable course. They're going to attack Corwin in ten years or so, give or take one year either way. We know we can't fight them back, either. We just aren't a militarized people. And we can't militarize in less than ten years and hope to win." Ewing paused, sipped at his drink. It was surprisingly mild, he thought.

He went on: "As soon as the nature of the Klodni menace became known, we radioed a message to Earth explaining the situation and asking for help. We got no answer, even figuring in the subetheric lag. We radioed again. Still no reply from Earth."

"So you decided to send an ambassador," Firnik said. "Figuring your messages must have gone astray, no doubt. You wanted to negotiate for help at first hand."

"Yes."

The Sirian chuckled. "You know something? It's three hundred years since anybody on Earth last fired anything deadlier than a popgun. They're total pacifists."

"That can't be true!"

Suddenly the sardonic amiability left Firnik. His voice was almost toneless as he said, "I'll forgive you this time, because you're a stranger and don't know the customs. But the next time you call me a liar I'll kill you."

Ewing's jaw stiffened. *Barbarian,* he thought. Out loud he said, "In other words, I've wasted my time by coming here, then?"

The Sirian shrugged unconcernedly. "Better fight your own battles. The Earthers can't help you."

"But they're in danger too," Ewing protested. "Do you think the Klodni are going to stop before they've reached Earth?"

"How long do you think it'll take them to get as far as Earth?" Firnik asked.

"A century at least."

"A century. All right. They have to pass through Sirius IV on their way to Earth. We'll take care of them when the time comes."

And I came sixteen parsecs across the galaxy to ask for help, Ewing thought.

He stood up. "It's been very interesting talking to you. And thanks for the drink."

"Good luck to you," the Sirian said in parting. It was not meant in a spirit of cheer. It sounded openly derisive, Ewing thought.

He made his way through the crowded room to the long shining-walled corridor of the spaceport arcade. A ship was blasting off outside on the ferroconcrete apron; Ewing watched it a moment as it thundered out of sight. He realized that if any truth lay in the Sirian's words, he might just as well return to Corwin now and report failure.

But it was hard to accept the concept of a decadent, spineless Earth. True, they had had no contact with the mother world for five centuries; but the legend still gleamed on Corwin and the other colony worlds of its immediate galactic area—the legend of the mother planet where human life first began, hundreds of centuries before.

He remembered the stories of the pioneers of space, the first bold venturers to the other planets, then the brave colonists who had extended Earth's sway to half a thousand worlds. Through a natural process, contact with the homeland had withered in the span of years; there was little reason for self-sufficient worlds a sky apart to maintain anything as fantastically expensive as interstellar communication systems simply for reasons of sentiment. A colony world has economic problems as it is.

There had always been the legend of Earth, though, to guide the Corwinites. When trouble arose, Earth would be there to help.

Now there was trouble on the horizon. And Earth, Ewing thought? Can we count on her help?

He watched the throngs of bejeweled dandies glumly, and wondered.

He paused by a railing that looked out over the wide sweep of the spacefield. A plaque, copper-hued, proclaimed the fact that this particular section of the arcade had been erected A.D. 2716. Ewing, a newcomer in an ancient world, felt a tingle of awe. The building in which he stood had been constructed more than a century before the first ships from Earth blasted down on Corwin, which then had been only a nameless world on the star charts. And the men who had built this building, eleven hundred years ago, were as remote in space-time from the present-day Terrans as were the people of Corwin at this moment.

It was a bitter thought, that he had wasted his trip. There was his wife, and his son—for more than two years Laira would have no husband, Blade no father. And for what? All for a wasted trip to a planet whose glories lay far in its past?

Somewhere on Earth, he thought, *there will be someone who can help. This planet produced us all. A shred of vitality must remain in it somewhere. I won't leave without trying to find it.*

Some painstaking questioning of one of the stationary robot guards finally got him the information he wanted: there *was* a place where incoming outworlders could register if they chose. He made provisions for the care and storage of his ship until his departure, and signed himself in at the Hall of Records as Baird Ewing, Ambassador from the Free World of Corwin. There was a hotel affiliated with the spaceport terminal; Ewing requested and was assigned a room in it. He signed a slip granting the robot spaceport attendants permission to enter his ship and transfer his personal belongings to his hotel room.

The room was attractive, if a little cramped. Ewing was accustomed to the spaciousness of his home on Corwin, a planet on which only eighteen million people lived in an area greater than the habitable landmass of Earth. He had helped to build the home himself, twelve years ago when he married Laira. It sprawled over nearly eleven acres of land. To be confined to a room only about fifteen feet on a side was a novel experience for him.

The lighting was subdued and indirect; he searched for the source unsuccessfully. His fingers probed the walls, but no electroluminescent panels were in evidence. The Earthers had evidently developed some new technique for diffused multi-source lighting.

An outlet covered with a speaking grid served as his connection with the office downstairs. He switched the communicator panel on, after some inward deliberation. A robot voice said immediately, "How may we serve you, Mr. Ewing?"

"Is there such a thing as a library on the premises?"

"Yes, sir."

"Good. Would you have someone select a volume of Terran history covering the last thousand years, and have it sent up to me. Also any recent newspapers, magazines, or things like that."

"Of course, sir."

It seemed that hardly five minutes passed before the chime on his room door bleeped discreetly.

"Come in," he said.

The door had been attuned to the sound of his voice; as he spoke, there was the whispering sound of relays closing, and the door whistled open. A robot stood just outside. His flat metal arms were stacked high with microreels.

"You ordered reading matter, sir."

"Thanks. Would you leave them over there, near the viewer?"

When the robot had gone, he lifted the most massive reel from the stack and scanned its title. *Earth and the Galaxy* was the title. In smaller letters it said, *A Study in Colonial Relationships.*

Ewing nodded approvingly. This was the way to begin, he told himself: fill in the background before embarking on any specific course of action. The mocking Sirian had perhaps underestimated Earth's strength deliberately, for obscure reasons of his own. He did not seem like a trustworthy sort.

He opened the reel and slid it into the viewer, twisting it until he heard the familiar *click!* The viewer was of the same model in use on Corwin, and he had no difficulties with it. He switched on the screen; the title page appeared, and a moment's work with the focusing switches rendered the image brightly sharp.

Chapter One, he read. *The earliest period of expansion.*

The Age of Interstellar Colonization may rightly be said to have opened in the year 2560, when the development of the Haley Subwarp Drive made possible—

The door chimed again. Irritated, Ewing looked up from his book. He was not expecting visitors, nor had he asked the hotel service staff for anything.

"Who is it?"

"Mr. Ewing?" said a familiar voice. "Might I come in? I'd like to talk to you again. We met briefly at the terminal this afternoon."

Ewing recognized the voice. It belonged to the earless Earther in turquoise robes who had been so little help to him earlier. *What can he want with me?* Ewing wondered.

"All right," he said. "Come in."

The door responded to the command. It slid back obediently. The slim Terrestrial smiled apologetically at Ewing, murmured a soft greeting, and entered.

Chapter Three

He was slim, delicate, fragile-looking. It seemed to Ewing that a good gust of wind would smash him to splinters. He was no more than five feet tall, pale, waxy skinned, with large serious eyes and thin, indecisive lips. His domed skull was naked and faintly glossy. At regular intervals on its skin, jeweled pendants had been surgically attached; they jiggled as he moved.

With prim fastidiousness he made his way across the room toward Ewing.

"I hope I'm not intruding on your privacy," he said in a hesitant half-whisper.

"No. Not at all. Won't you be seated?"

"I would prefer to stand," the Earther replied. "It is our custom."

"Very well."

Ewing felt a curious inner revulsion as he stared at the grotesque little Earther. On Corwin, anyone dressed in such clownish garb would meet with derision.

The Earther smiled timidly. "I am called Scholar Myreck," he said finally. "And you are Baird Ewing, of the colony-world Corwin."

"That's right."

"It was my great fortune to meet you at the spaceport terminal building earlier today. Apparently I created a bad first impression—one of frivolity, perhaps, or even of oppressive irresponsibility. For this I wish to beg your pardon, Colonist Ewing. I would have had the opportunity then, but for that Sirian ape who seized your attention before I could speak."

Somewhat to his surprise Ewing noticed that the little Earther was speaking with barely a trace of what he had come to regard as the Earther accent. He frowned; what did the foppish little man want?

"On the contrary, Scholar Myreck, no apologies should be needed. I don't judge a man by my first impression of him—especially on a world where I'm a stranger to the customs and way of life."

"An excellent philosophy!" Sadness crossed Myreck's mild face for a moment. "But you look tense, Colonist Ewing. Might I have the privilege of relaxing you?"

"Relaxing me?"

"Minor neural adjustments; a technique we practice with some skill here. May I?"

Doubtfully Ewing said, "Just what does it involve, actually?"

"A moment's physical contact, nothing more." Myreck smiled imploringly. "It pains me to see a man so tense. It causes me actual physical pain."

"You've aroused my curiosity," Ewing said. "Go ahead—relax me."

Myreck glided forward and put his hands gently round Ewing's neck. The Corwinite stiffened in immediate alarm. "Gently," Myreck sang. "Let the muscles relax. Don't fight me. Relax."

His thin, childlike fingers dug in without warning, pinching sharply at the base of Ewing's skull. Ewing felt a quick, fierce burst of light, a jarring disruption of sense-perception, for no more than a fifteenth of a second. Then, suddenly, he felt the tension drain away from him. His deltoids and trapezoids eased so abruptly that he thought his back and shoulders had been removed. His neck, chronically stiff, loosened. The stress patterns developed during a year in stasis-sleep were shaken off.

"That's quite a trick," he said finally.

"We manipulate the neural nexus at the point where the medulla and the spinal column become one. In the hands of an amateur it can be fatal." Myreck smiled. "In the hands of a professional such as myself it can also be fatal—but only when the operator so intends."

Ewing moistened his lips. He said, "May I ask a personal question, Scholar Myreck?"

"Of course."

"The clothes you wear—the ornamentation—are these things widespread on Earth, or is it just some fad that you're following?"

Myreck knotted his waxy fingers together thoughtfully. "They are, shall we say, cultural manifestations. I find it hard to explain. People of my personality type and inclinations dress this way; others dress differently, as the mood strikes them. My appearance indicates that I am a Collegiate Fellow."

"Scholar is your title, then?"

"Yes. And also my given name. I am a member of the College of Abstract Science of the City of Valloin."

"I'll have to plead ignorance," Ewing said. "I don't know anything about your College."

"Understandable. We do not seek publicity." Myreck's eyes fastened doggedly on Ewing's for a moment. "That Sirian who took you away from us—may I ask his name?"

"Rollun Firnik," Ewing said.

"A particularly dangerous one; I know him by reputation. Well, to the point at last, Colonist Ewing. Would you care to address a convocation of the College of Abstract Science some time early next week?"

"I? I'm no academician, Scholar. I wouldn't know what to talk about."

"You come from a colony, one that none of us knows anything about. You offer an invaluable fund of experience and information."

"But I'm a stranger in the city," Ewing objected. "I wouldn't know how to get to you."

"We will arrange for your transportation. The meeting is Fournight of next week. Will you come?"

Ewing considered it for a moment. It was as good an opportunity as any to begin studying the Terrestrial culture at close range. He would need as broad and as deep a fund of knowledge as possible in order to apply the leverage that would ultimately preserve his home world from destruction by the alien marauders.

He looked up. "All right. Fournight of next week it is, then."

"We will be very grateful, Colonist Ewing."

Myreck bowed. He backed toward the door, smiling and nodding, and paused just before pushing the opener stud. "Stay well," he said. "You have our extreme gratitude. We will see you on Fournight."

The door slid closed behind him.

E wing shrugged; then, remembering the reels he had requested from the hotel library, he returned his attention to the viewer.

He read for nearly an hour, skimming; his reading pace was an accelerated one, thanks to his mnemonic training at the great University of Corwin. His mind efficiently organized the material as fast as his eyes scanned it, marshaling the facts into near, well-drilled columns. By the end of the hour, he had more than a fair idea of the shape of Terrestrial history in the thirteen hundred years since the first successful interstellar flight.

There had been an immediate explosive outward push to the stars. Sirius had been the first to be colonized, in 2573: sixty-two brave men and women. The other colonies had followed fast, frantically. The overcrowded Earth was shipping her sons and daughters to the stars in wholesale batches.

All through the second half of the Third Millennium the prevailing historical tone was one of frenzied excitement. The annals listed colony after colony.

The sky was full of worlds. The seventeen-planet system of Aldebaran yielded eight Earth-type planets suitable for Colonization. The double system of Albireo had four. Ewing passed hastily over the name-weighted pages, seeing with a little quiver of recognition the name of Blade Corwin, who seeded a colony on Epsilon Ursae Majoris XII in the year 2856.

Outward. *By the opening of the thirtieth century,* said the book, *human life had been planted on more than a thousand worlds of the universe.*

The great outward push was over. On Earth, the long-over-due establishment of population controls had ended forever the threat of overexpansion, and with it some of the impetus for colonization died. Earth's population stabilized itself at an unvarying five and a half billion; three centuries before, nearly eleven billion had jostled for room on the crowded little planet.

With population stabilization came cultural stabilization, the end of the flamboyant pioneer personality, the development of a new kind of Earthman who lacked the drive and intense ambition of his ancestors. The colonies had skimmed off the men with outward drive; the ones who remained on Earth gave rise to a culture of esthetes, of debaters and musicians and mathematicians. A subclass of menials at first sprang up to insure the continued maintenance of the machinery of civilization, but even these became unnecessary with the development of ambulatory robots.

The history of the Fourth Millennium was a predictable one; Ewing had already extrapolated it from the data given him, and it was little surprise to come across confirmation. There had been retrenchment. The robot-served culture of Earth became self-sufficient, a closed system. Births and deaths were carefully equalized.

With stability came isolation. The wild men on the colony worlds no longer had need for the mother world, nor Earth for them. Contacts withered.

In the year 3800, said the text, *only Sirius IV of all Earth's colonies still retained regular communication with the parent planet. Representatives of the thousand other colonies were so rare on Earth as to be virtually nonexistent there.*

Only Sirius IV. It was odd, thought Ewing, that of all the colonies the harsh people of Sirius IV should alone be solicitous of the mother world. There was little in common between Rollun Firnik and the Scholar.

The more Ewing read, the less confident he became that he would find any aid for Corwin here. Earth had become a planet of gentle scholiasts, it seemed; was there anything here that could serve in the struggle against the advancing Klodni?

Possibly not. But Ewing did not intend to abandon his quest at its very beginning.

He read on, well into the afternoon, until he felt hunger. Rising, he disconnected the viewer and rewound the reels, slipping them back into their containers. His eyes were tired. Some of the physical fatigue Myreck had taken from him had begun to steal back into his body.

There was a restaurant on the sixty-third level of the hotel, according to the printed information sheet enameled on the inside of his door. He showered and dressed formally, in his second-best doublet and lace. He checked the chambers of his ceremonial blaster, found them all functioning, and strapped the weapon to his hip. Satisfied at last, he reached for the housephone, and when the subservient roboperator answered said, "I'm going to eat dinner now. Will you notify the hotel dining room to reserve a table for one for me?"

"Of course, Mr. Ewing."

He broke the contact and glanced once again in the mirror above his dresser to make sure his lace was in order. He felt in his pocket for his wallet; it bulged with Terrestrial paper money, enough to last him the length of his stay.

He opened the door. Just outside the door was an opaque plastic receptacle which was used for depositing messages and to Ewing's surprise the red light atop it was glowing, indicating the presence of a message within.

Pressing his thumb to the identiplate, he lifted the top of the box and drew out the note. It was neatly typed in blue capital letters. It said:

COLONIST EWING: IF YOU WANT TO STAY IN GOOD
HEALTH, KEEP AWAY FROM MYRECK AND HIS FRIENDS.

It was unsigned. Ewing smiled coldly; the intrigue was beginning already, the jockeying back and forth. He had expected it. The arrival of a strange colonial on Earth was a novel enough event; it was sure to have its consequences and repercussions as his presence became more widely known.

"Open," he said shortly to his door.

The door slid back. He reentered his room and snatched up the house phone.

The desk robot said, "How may we serve you, Mr. Ewing?"

"There seems to be a spy vent in my room some place," Ewing said. "Send someone up to check the room over, will you?"

"I assure you, sir that no such thing could—"

"I tell you there's a concealed camera or microphone someplace in my room. Either find it or I'll check into some other hotel."

"Yes, Mr. Ewing. We'll send an investigator up immediately."

"Good. I'm going to the dining room, now. If anything turns up, contact me there."

Chapter Four

The hotel dining room was gaudily, even garishly decorated. Glowing spheres of imprisoned radiant energy drifted at random near the vaulted ceiling, occasionally bobbing down to eye level. The tables themselves were banked steeply toward the outside edge, and in the very center of the room, where the floor level was lowest, a panchromaticon swiveled slowly, casting multicolored light over the diners.

A burnished, bullet-headed robot waited at the door.

"I have a reservation," Ewing said. "Baird Ewing. Room 4113."

"Of course, sir. Come this way, please."

Ewing followed the robot into the main concourse of the dining room, up a sort of ramp that led to the outermost rim of the great hall, where a few empty tables were visible. The robot came to a halt in front of a table at which someone was already sitting: a Sirian girl, Ewing guessed, from her brawny appearance.

The robot pulled out the chair facing her. Ewing shook his head. "There's been some mistake made. I don't know this lady at all. I requested a table for one."

"We ask indulgence, sir. There are no tables for one available at this hour. We consulted with the person occupying this table and were told that there was no objection to your sharing it, if you were willing to do so."

Ewing frowned and glanced at the girl. She met his glance evenly, and smiled. She seemed to be inviting him to sit down.

He shrugged. "All right. I'll sit here."

"Very good, sir."

Ewing slipped into the seat and let the robot nudge it toward the table for him. He looked at the girl. She had bright red hair, trimmed in what on Corwin would be considered an extremely mannish style. She was dressed in a tailored suit of some clinging purple material; it flared sharply at the shoulders and neck. Her eyes were dark black. Her face was broad and muscular looking, with upjutting cheekbones that gave her features an oddly slant-eyed cast.

"I'm sorry if I caused you any inconvenience," Ewing said. "I had no idea they'd place me at your table—or at any occupied table."

"I requested it," she said. Her voice was dark of timbre and resonant. "You're the Corwinite Ewing, I understand. I'm Byra Clork. We have something in common. We were both born on colonies of Earth."

Ewing found himself liking her blunt, forthright approach, even though in her countryman Firnik it had been offensive. He said, "So I understand. You're a Sirian, aren't you?"

"That's right. How did you know?"

"I guessed," Ewing said evasively. He directed his attention to the liquor panel set against the wall. "Drink?" he asked her.

"I've had one. But I don't mind if you do."

Ewing inserted a coin and punched out a cocktail. The drink emerged from a revolving slot in the wall. The Corwinite picked it up and tasted it. It was sweet, with a disturbing undertaste of acridity.

"You said you requested my presence at your table," Ewing remarked. "And you knew me by name. How come?"

"It isn't every day that a stranger comes to Earth," she said, in that impossibly deep, husky, almost-masculine voice. "I was curious."

"Many people seem to be curious about me," Ewing said.

A robowaiter hovered at his shoulder. Ewing frowned; he said, "I don't have any idea what the speciality of the house is. Miss Clork, would you care to recommend something for my dinner?"

She said to the robot, "Give him the same thing I ordered. Venison, creamed potatoes, green beans."

"Certainly," murmured the robot. As it scuttled away Ewing said, "Is that the tastiest dish they have?"

"Probably. I know it's the most expensive."

Ewing grinned. "You don't spare my pocketbook, do you?"

"You gave me free reign. Besides, you must have some money in your pocket. I saw you converting a stack of bills at the desk this morning."

"You saw me, then?" An idea struck him. "You didn't send me a note this afternoon, did you?"

"Note?" Her broad face showed seemingly, genuine confusion. "No, I didn't send you any note. Why?"

"Someone did," Ewing said. "I just wondered who it might have been."

He sipped his drink thoughtfully. A few minutes later a robot arrived with their dinners. The meat smelled pungent and good. Obviously it was no synthetic; that explained its high cost.

They ate in silence for a while. When Ewing had made substantial inroads on his plate, he paused, looking up, and said, "What do you do on Earth, Miss Clork?"

She smiled. "I'm with the Sirian Consulate. I look out for the interests of any of my people who happen to visit Earth. It's a very dull job."

"There seem to be quite a few Sirians on Earth," Ewing remarked casually. "It must be very popular among your people as a tourist attraction."

She seemed momentarily disconcerted by Ewing's remark. Her voice hesitated slightly as she said, "Y-yes, it's very popular. Many Sirians like to vacation on Earth."

"How many Sirians would you say there were on Earth right now?"

This time she stiffened visibly; Ewing realized he had accidently asked a question which touched on very delicate grounds. "Just why are you interested, Colonist Ewing?"

He smiled disarmingly. "A matter of curiosity, that's all. No ulterior motives."

She pretended the question had never been asked. Music welled up about them, blending with the vague general hum of conversation. She finished her dinner quietly, and while starting on the dessert said, "I suppose you didn't think much of Firnik."

"Of who?"

"You met him this morning," she said. "The Sirian. He tends to be rather clumsy at times. He's my boss, actually. Sirian Vice-Consul in Valloin."

"Did he tell you to wangle dinner with me?" Ewing asked suddenly.

A blaze flamed in the Sirian girl's eyes, but it died down quickly enough, though with reluctance. "You put things crudely."

"But accurately?"

"Yes."

Ewing smiled and reached into his doublet pocket; he drew forth the anonymous note he had received earlier, unfolded it, and shoved it across the table toward her. She read it without displaying any apparent reaction, and nudged it back toward him.

"Is this the note you suspected me of having sent you?" she asked.

Ewing nodded. "I had a visit from Scholar Myreck this afternoon. Several hours later I found this note outside my door. Perhaps Vice-Consul Firnik sent it, eh?"

She stared at him as if trying to read his mind. Ewing sensed that a chess game of sorts was going on, that he was rapidly becoming the center of a web of complications. While they stared silently at each other a robot glided up to them and said, "Mr. Ewing?"

"That's right."

"I bear a message from the manager of the hotel."

"Let's have it," Ewing said.

"The message is: a spyvent outlet has been discovered in your room at the intersection of the wall and the ceiling. The outlet has been removed and a protective device planted in the room to prevent any future re-insertion of spying equipment. The manager extends his deep regrets and requests you to accept a week's rent as partial compensation for any inconvenience this may have caused you."

Ewing grinned. "Tell him I accept the offer, and that he'd better be more careful about his rooms the next time."

When the robot was gone, Ewing stared sharply at Byra Clork and said, "Somebody was listening and watching today when I had my visitor. Was it Firnik?"

"Do you think so?"

"I do."

"Then so be it," the girl said lightly. She rose from the table and said, "Do you mind putting my meal on your account? I'm a little short of cash just now."

She started to leave. Ewing caught a robot's eye and quickly instructed, "Bill me for both dinners. Ewing, room 4113."

He slid past the metal creature and caught up with the Sirian girl as she approached the exit to the dining room. The sphincter-door widened; she stepped through, and he followed her. They emerged in a luxurious salon hung with abstract paintings of startling texture and hue. Fierce atonal music came pulsing out of speakers concealed near the paintings.

She was ignoring him, pointedly. She moved at a rapid pace down the main corridor of the salon, and stopped just before an inlaid blue-and-gold door. As she started to enter, Ewing grasped her by the arm. Her biceps were remarkably sturdy.

She wriggled loose and said, "Surely you don't intend to follow me in *here*, Mr. Ewing!"

He glanced at the inscription on the door. "I'm a rude, untutored, primitive colonial," he said grimly. "If it serves my purpose to go in there after you, I'll go in there after you. You might just as well stay here and answer my questions as try to run away."

"Is there any reason why I should?"

"Yes," he said. "Because I ask you to. Did you or Firnik spy on me this afternoon?"

"How should I know what Firnik does in his free time?"

Ewing applied pressure to her arm, and at the same time silently recited verses designed to keep his own inward metabolism on a level keel during a time of stress. His pulse was pounding; methodically, he forced it to return to its normal rate.

"You're hurting me," she said in a harsh whisper.

"I want to know who planted that spy ray in my room, and why I should be warned against dealing with Myreck."

She twisted suddenly and broke loose from his grasp. Her face was flushed, and her breathing was rapid and irregular. In a low voice she said, "Let me give you some free advice, Mr. Corwinite Ewing. Pack up and go back to Corwin. There's only trouble for you on Earth."

"What sort of trouble?" he demanded relentlessly.

"I'm not saying anything else. Listen to me, and get as far from Earth as you can. Tomorrow. Today, if you can." She looked wildly around, then turned and ran lithely down the corridor. Ewing debated following her, but decided against it. She had seemed genuinely frightened, as if trouble loomed for her.

He stood for a moment before a mounted light-sculpture, pretending to be staring at the intertwining spirals of black and pearl-gray, but actually merely using the statuary as pretext for a moment's thought. His mind was racing; rigidly, he forced his adrenalin count down. When he was calm again, he tried to evaluate the situation.

Someone had gimmicked his room. He had been visited by an Earther, and a Sirian girl had maneuvered him into eating dinner with her. The incidents were beginning to mount up, and they grew more puzzling as he attempted to fit them into some coherent pattern. He had been on Earth less than fifteen hours. Events moved rapidly here.

He had been trained in theories of synthesis; he was a gifted extrapolator. Sweat beaded his forehead as he labored to extract connectivity from the isolated and confusing incidents of the day.

Minutes passed. Earthers in dazzling costumes drifted past him in twos and sometimes threes, commenting in subdued tones on the displays in the salon. Painstakingly, Ewing manipulated the facts. Finally a picture took shape; a picture formed on guesswork, but nonetheless a useful guide to future action.

The Sirians were up to no good on Earth. Quite possibly they intended to make the mother world a Sirian dominion. Assuming that, then the unexpected arrival of a colonist from deep space might represent a potential threat to their plans.

New shadows darkened the horizon, Ewing saw. Perhaps Firnik suspected him of intending to conspire with the Scholars against the Sirians. Doubtless that had been Myreck's intention in proffering the invitation.

In that case—

"Mr. Ewing?" a gentle voice said.

He turned. A robot stood there, man-high, armless, its face a sleek sheet of viewing plastic.

"That's right, I'm Ewing. What is it?"

"I speak for Governor-General Mellis, director of Earth's governing body. Governor-General Mellis requests your presence at the Capital City as soon as is convenient for you."

"How do I get there?"

"If you wish I will convey you there," the robot purred.

"I so wish," Ewing said. "Take me there at once."

Chapter Five

A jetcar waited outside the hotel for them—sleek, stylishly toned, and yet to Ewing's eyes old-fashioned in appearance. The robot opened the rear door and Ewing climbed in.

To his surprise the robot did not join him inside the car; he simply closed the door and glided away into the gathering dusk. Ewing frowned and peered through the door window at the retreating robot. He rattled the doorknob experimentally and discovered that he was locked in.

A bland robot voice said, "Your destination, please?"

Ewing hesitated. "Ah—take me to Governor-General Mellis."

A rumble of turbogenerators was the only response; the car quivered gently and slid forward, moving as if it ran on a track of oil. Ewing felt no perceptible sensation of motion, but the spaceport and the towering bulk of the hotel grew small behind him, and soon they emerged on a broad twelve-level superhighway a hundred feet above the ground level.

Ewing stared nervously out the window. "Exactly where is the Governor-General located?" he asked, turning to peer at the dashboard. The jetcar did not even have room for a driver, he noted, nor a set of manual controls. It was operated totally by remote control.

"Governor-General Mellis' residence is in Capital City," came the precise, measured reply. "It is located one hundred ninety-three miles to the north of the City of Valloin. We will be there in forty-one minutes."

The jetcar was strict in its schedule. Exactly forty-one minutes after it had pulled away from the plaza facing the Grand Valloin Hotel, it shot off the highway and onto a smaller trunk road that plunged downward at a steep angle. Ewing saw a city before him—a city of spacious buildings spaced far apart, radiating spirally out from one towering, silver-hued palace.

A few minutes later the car came to a sudden halt, giving Ewing a mild jolt.

The robot voice said, "This is the palace of the Governor-General. The door at your left is open. Please leave the car now and you will be taken to the Governor-General."

Ewing nudged the door-panel and it swung open. He stepped out. The night air was fresh and cool, and the street about him gave off a soft gentle glow. Accumulator batteries beneath the pavement were discharging the illumination the sun had shed on them during the day.

"You will come this way, please," a new robot said.

He was ushered speedily and efficiently through the swinging door of the palace, into a lift, and upward. The lift opened out onto a velvet-hung corridor that extended through a series of accordion-like pleats into a large and austerely furnished room.

A small man stood alone in the center of the room. He was gray haired but unwrinkled, and his body bore no visual sign of the surgical distortions that were so common among the Earthers. He smiled courteously.

"I am Governor-General Mellis," he said. His voice was light and flexible, a good vehicle for public speaking. "Will you come in?"

"Thanks," Ewing said. He stepped inside. The doors immediately closed behind him.

Mellis came forward—he stood no higher than the middle of Ewing's chest—and proffered a drink. Ewing took it. It was a sparkling purplish liquid, with a mildly carbonated texture. He settled himself comfortably in the chair Mellis drew up for him, and looked up at the Governor-General, who remained standing.

"You wasted no time in sending for me," Ewing remarked.

The Governor-General shrugged gracefully. "I learned of your arrival this morning. It is not often that an ambassador from an outworld colony arrives on Earth. In truth"—he seemed to sigh—"you are the first in more than three hundred years. You have aroused considerable curiosity, you know."

"I'm aware of that." Casually he sipped at his drink, letting the warmth trickle down his throat. "I intended to contact you tomorrow, or perhaps the next day. But you've saved me that trouble."

"My curiosity got the better of me," Mellis admitted with a smile. "There is so little for me to do, you see, in the way of official duties."

"I'll make my visit brief by starting at the beginning," Ewing said. "I'm here to ask for Earth's help, on behalf of my planet, the Free World of Corwin."

"Help?" The Governor-General looked alarmed.

"We face invasion by extra-galactic foes," Ewing said. Quickly he sketched out an account of the Klodni depredations thus far, adding, "And we sent several messages to Earth to let you know what the situation was. We assume those messages have gone astray en route. And so I've come in person to ask for Earth's aid."

Mellis moved about the room in impatient birdlike strutting motions before replying. He whirled suddenly, then calmed himself, and said, "The messages did not go astray, Mr. Ewing."

"No?"

"They were duly received and forwarded to my office. I read them!"

"You didn't answer," Ewing interrupted accusingly. "You deliberately ignored them. Why?"

Mellis spread his fingers on his thighs and seemed to come stiffly to attention. In a quiet, carefully modulated voice he said, "Because there is no possible way we can help you or anyone else, Mr. Ewing. Will you believe that?"

"I don't understand."

"We have no weapons, no military forces, no ability or desire to fight. We have no spaceships."

Ewing's eyes widened. He had found it impossible to believe it when the Sirian Firnik had told him Earth was defenseless; but to hear it from the lips of the Governor-General himself!

"There must be some assistance Earth can give. There are only eighteen million of us on Corwin," Ewing said. "We have a defense corps, of course, but it's hardly adequate. Our stockpile of nuclear weapons is low—"

"Ours is nonexistent," Mellis interrupted. "Such fissionable material as we have is allocated to operation of the municipal atom piles."

Ewing stared at the tips of his fingers. Chill crept over him, reminding him of the year spent locked in the grip of frost as he slept through a crossing of fifty light-years. For nothing.

Mellis smiled sadly. "There is one additional aspect to your request for help. You say the Klodni will not attack your world for a decade, nor ours for a century."

Ewing nodded.

"In that case," Mellis said, "the situation becomes academic from our viewpoint. Before a decade's time has gone by, Earth will be a Sirian protectorate anyway. We will be in no position to help anybody."

The Corwinite looked up at the melancholy face of Earth's Governor-General. There were depths to Mellis' eyes that told Ewing much; Mellis was deeply conscious of his position as ruler in the declining days of Terrestrial power.

Ewing said, "How sure can you be of that?"

"Certain as I am of my name," Mellis replied. "The Sirians are infiltrating Earth steadily. There are more than a million of them here now. Any day I expect to be notified that I am no longer even to be Earth's figurehead. "

"Can't you prevent them from coming to Earth?"

Mellis shook his head. "We're powerless. The events to come are inevitable. And so your Klodni worry us very little, friend Corwinite. I'll be long since dead before they arrive—and with me Earth's glories."

"And you don't care about the colony worlds?" Ewing snapped angrily. "You'll just sit back and let us be gobbled up by the aliens? Earth's name still means something among the colony worlds; if you issued a general declaration of war, all the colonies would send forces to defend us. As it is, the scattered worlds can't think of the common good; they only worry about themselves. They don't see that if they band together against the Klodni they can destroy them, while singly they will be overwhelmed. A declaration from Earth—"

"—would be meaningless, hollow, invalid, null, void, and empty," Mellis said. "Believe that, Mr. Ewing. You face an unfortunate fate. Officially, I weep for you. But as an old man soon to be pushed from his throne, I can't help you."

Ewing felt the muscles of his jaw tighten. He said nothing. He realized there was nothing at all for him to say.

He stood up. "I guess we've reached the end of our interview, then. I'm sorry to have taken up your time, Governor-General Mellis. If I had known the situation as it stood on Earth, perhaps I might not have made this trip across space."

"I had hoped—" Mellis began. He broke off, then shook his head. "No. It was foolish."

"Sir?"

The older man smiled palely. "There had been a silly thought in my mind today, ever since I learned that an ambassador from Corwin had landed in Valloin. I see clearly now how wild a thought it was."

"Might I ask—"

Mellis shrugged. "The thought I had was that perhaps you had come in the name of Terrestrial independence—to offer us a pledge of your world's aid against the encroachments of the Sirians. But you need aid yourself. It was foolish of me to expect to find a defender in the stars."

"I'm sorry," Ewing said quietly.

"For what? For being unable to help? We owe each other apologies, in that case." Mellis shook his head. "We have known brightness too long. Now the shadows start to lengthen. Aliens steal forth out of Andromeda to destroy, and children of Earth turn on their mother."

He peered through the increasing gloom of the room at Ewing. "But I must be boring you with my ramblings Mr. Ewing. You had better leave, now. Leave Earth, I mean. Go to defend your homeworld against its enemies. We are beyond help."

He pulled a wall switch and a robot servitor appeared, gliding noiselessly through the opening doors. The Governor-General turned to it.

"Conduct Mr. Ewing back to the car, and see that he is transported to his residence in Valloin as comfortably as possible."

Ewing felt a flood of pity for the old man whose misfortune it was to hold the supreme office of Earth at this dark time. He clenched his fists; he said nothing. Corwin now seemed strangely remote. His wife, his son, living under the menace of alien hordes, hardly mattered now compared with Earth and the fate, less violent but more painful, that was befalling it.

In silence he left the old man and followed the robot through the corridors to the lift. He descended on a shaft of magnetic radiance to the street level.

The car was waiting for him. He got in; the turbos thrummed briefly and the homeward journey began.

He amused himself on the way home by drafting the text of the message he would send via subradio to Corwin in the morning. In the afternoon he would leave Earth forever, setting out on the year-long return trip to Corwin, bringing with him sad confirmation of the fact that there was no help for them against the Klodni horde.

Chapter Six

It was past midnight when Ewing stepped out of the liftshaft on the forty-first floor of the Grand Valloin Hotel. He reached his room and examined the message box. Empty. He had half expected to find another threatening note in it.

He pressed his thumb to the identity-attuned plate of the door and said in a low voice, pitched so it would not awaken any of his neighbors, "Open."

The door rolled back. Unexpectedly, the light was on in his room.

"Hello," said Byra Clork.

Ewing froze in the doorway and stared bewilderedly at the broad-shouldered Sirian girl. She was sitting quite calmly in the relaxochair by the window. A bottle of some kind rested on the night table, and next to it two glasses, one of them half filled with amber liquid. She had made herself quite comfortable, it seemed.

He stepped inside.

"How did you get into my room?" he asked.

"I asked the management to give me a pass key to your room. They obliged."

"Just like that?" Ewing snapped. "I guess I don't understand the way Terrestrial hotels operated. I was under the innocent impression that a man's room was his own so long as he paid the rent, and that no strangers would be permitted to enter."

"That's the usual custom," she said lightly. "But I found it necessary to talk to you about urgent matters. Matters of great importance to the Sirian Consulate in Valloin, whom I represent."

Ewing became aware of the fact that he was holding the door open. He released it, and it closed automatically. "It's a little late in the evening for conducting Consulate business, isn't it?" he asked.

She smiled. "It's never too late for some things. Would you like a drink?"

He ignored the glass she held out to him. He wanted her to leave his room.

"How did you get in my room?" he repeated.

She pointed behind him, to the enameled sheet of regulations behind the door. "It's up there plainly enough on your door. I'll quote, in case you haven't read the regulations yet: *'The management of this Hotel reserves the right to enter and inspect any of the rooms at any time.'* I'm carrying out an inspection."

"You're not the management!"

"I'm employed by the management," she said sweetly. She dug into the reticule suspended from her left wrist and produced a glossy yellow card which she handed over to the puzzled Ewing.

He read it.

ROLLUN FIRNIK
Manager, Grand Valloin Hotel

"What does this mean?"

"It means that the robots at the desk are directly responsible to Firnik. He runs this hotel. Sirian investors bought it eight years ago, and delegated him to act as their on-the-spot representative. And in turn he delegated me to visit you in your room tonight. Now that everything's nice and legal, Ewing, sit down and let's talk. Relax."

Uncertainly Ewing slipped off his coat and sat down on the edge of the bed, facing her.

"We've had one conversation already today, haven't we? A highly inconclusive and fragmentary one, which ended when—"

"Forget about that!"

The sudden whiteness of her face told him one thing he had been anxious to know: they were being watched. He had nearly revealed something she had not wanted the watchers to find out.

"I—have different instructions now," she said hesitantly. "Won't you have a drink?"

He shook his head. "I've already had more than my share today, thanks. And I'm tired. Now that you've gotten in here, suppose you tell me what you want."

"You visited Governor-General Mellis tonight, didn't you?" she asked abruptly.

"Did I?"

"You don't have to be mysterious about it," she said sharply. "You were seen leaving and returning in an official car. Don't waste your breath by denying you had an interview with the Governor-General."

Ewing shrugged. "How would it concern you, assuming that I did?"

"To be perfectly frank with you, Mr. Ewing, your presence on Earth worries us. By us I mean the interests of the Sirian government, whom I represent. We have a definite financial interest in Earth. We don't want to see that investment jeopardized."

Ewing frowned in curiosity. "You haven't made things much clearer," he said.

"Briefly, we wondered whether or not you—representing Corwin or possibly a league of the outworld colonies—have territorial designs on Earth," she said slowly. "I've been utterly blunt, now. Too blunt, perhaps. We Sirians are poor at diplomacy; we have a racial characteristic of always coming directly to the point."

"Corwinites share that characteristic," Ewing said. "Maybe it's a concomitant of colonial life. I'll answer you with equal bluntness: there's no outworld colony league, and I'm not on Earth with the remotest intention of establishing a dominion here."

"Then why *are* you here?"

He scowled impatiently. "I explained all that to our friend Firnik this morning, only a few minutes after I had entered the spaceport terminal. I told him that Corwin's in danger of an alien invasion, and that I had come to Earth seeking help."

"Yes, you told him that. And you expected him to *believe* that story?"

Exasperated, Ewing howled, "Dammit, why not? It's the *truth!*"

"That any intelligent person would cross fifty light-years simply to ask military aid from the weakest and most helpless planet in the universe? You can think up better lies than that one," she said mockingly.

He stared at her. "We're an isolated planet," he said in a quiet but intense voice. "We didn't know anything at all about the current state of Earth's culture. We *thought* Earth could help us. I came on a fool's errand, and I'm going home again tomorrow, a sadder and wiser man. Right now I'm tired and I want to get some sleep. Will you please leave?"

She rose without warning and took a seat next to him on the bed. "All right," she said in a husky but surprisingly soft voice. "I'll tell Firnik you're here for the reasons you say you are."

Her words might have startled him, but he was expecting them. It was a gambit designed to keep him off guard. The Sirian methods were crude ones.

"Thanks," he said sarcastically. "Your faith in me is heart-warming."

She moved closer to him. "Why don't you have a drink with me? I'm not *all* Sirian Consulate, you know. I do have an after-hours personality too, much as you may find it hard to believe."

He sensed her warmth against his body. She reached out, poured him a drink, and forced the glass into his reluctant hand. Ewing wondered whether Firnik were watching this at the other end of the spy beam.

Her hands caressed his shoulders, massaging gently. Ewing looked down at her pityingly. Her eyes were closed, her lips moist, slightly parted. Her breathing was irregular. *Maybe she isn't faking,* he thought. But even so, he wasn't interested.

He moved suddenly away from her, and she nearly lost her balance. Her eyes opened wide; for an instant naked hatred blazed in them, but she recovered quickly and assumed a pose of hurt innocence.

"Why did you do that? Don't you like me?"

Ewing smiled coldly. "I find you amusing. But I don't like to make love in front of a spy beam."

Her eyes narrowed; her lips curled downward in a momentary scowl, and then she laughed—derisive, silver laughter. "You think that was an *act*? That I was doing all that for the greater glory of the Fatherland?"

He nodded. "Yes."

She slapped him. It was utterly predictable; he had been waiting for it from the moment the affirmative word left his lips. The blow had an astonishing amount of force behind it; Byra Clork packed quite a wallop, Ewing decided ruefully. He wondered if he had misjudged her intentions; it made no difference, really.

"Will you leave now?" he asked.

"I might as well," she muttered bitterly. She glowered at him. "If you're a sample of Corwinite manhood, I'm glad they don't come here more often than once every five hundred years. Machine! Robot!"

"Are you quite through?"

She picked up a light wrap that had been on the back of the chair, and arranged it around her shoulders. Ewing made no move to help her. He waited impassively, arms folded.

"You're incredible," she said, half scornfully, half otherwise. She paused; then a light entered her eyes. "Will you have a drink with me, at least, before I go?"

She was being crafty, he thought, but clumsily so. She had offered him the drink so many times in the past half hour that he would be a fool not to suspect it of being drugged. He could be crafty too.

"All right," he said. "I'll have a drink."

He picked up the glass she had poured for him, and handed her the half-full glass that she had held—untasted—throughout the time. He looked expectantly at her.

"What are you waiting for?" she asked.

"Waiting for you to take a drink first," he told her.

"Still full of strange suspicions, eh?" She lifted her glass and plainly took a deep draft. Then she handed her glass to Ewing, took his, and sipped it also.

"There," she said, exhaling briefly. "I'm still alive. No deadly poison lurks in either glass. Believe me?"

He smiled. "This time, if no other."

Still smiling, he lifted the glass. The liquor was warm and potent; he felt it course down his throat. A moment later, his legs wobbled.

He struggled to stay up. The room swirled around him; he saw her triumphant, grinning face above him, circling madly as if in orbit. He dropped to his knees and clung to the carpeting for support.

"It *was* drugged," he said.

"Of course. It was a drug that doesn't happen to react on Sirian metabolisms. We weren't sure whether it worked on Corwinites; now we know."

He gripped the carpet. The room rocked wildy. He felt sick, and bitterly angry at himself for having let her trick him into taking the drink. He fought for consciousness. He was unable to rise.

Still conscious, he heard the door of his room open. He did not look up. He heard Byra say, "Did you watch it the whole time?"

"We did." The voice was Firnik's. "You still think he's holding back?"

"I'm sure of it," Byra said. Her tone was vindictive. "He'll need some interrogation before he starts talking."

"We'll take care of that," Firnik said. He barked an order in a language incomprehensible to Ewing. The Corwinite tried to cry for help, but all that escaped his quivering lips was a thin, whining moan.

"He's still fighting the drug," he heard Byra say. "It ought to knock him out any minute."

Shimmering waves of pain beat at him. He lost his grip on the carpet and went toppling over to one side. He felt strong hands gripping him under the arms and lifting him to his feet, but his eyes would not focus any longer. He writhed feebly and was still. Darkness closed in about him.

Chapter Seven

Coldness clung to him. He lay perfectly still, feeling the sharp cold all about him. His hands were pinned to his sides. His legs were likewise pinioned. And all about him was the cold, chilling his skin, numbing his brain, freezing his body.

He made no attempt to move and scarcely any even to think. He was content to lie back here in the darkness and wait. He believed he was on the ship heading homeward to Corwin.

He was wrong. The sound of voices far above him penetrated his consciousness, and he stirred uncertainly, knowing there could be no voices aboard the ship. It was a one-man ship. There was no room for anyone else.

The voices continued—rumbling low murmurs that tickled his auditory nerves without resolving themselves into sequences of intelligible words. Ewing moved about restlessly. Where could he be? Who could be making these blurred, fuzzy sounds?

He strained toward consciousness now; he fought to open his eyes. A cloud of haze obscured his vision. He sat up, feeling stiff muscles protest as he pushed his way up. His eyes opened, closed again immediately as a glare of light exploded in them, and gradually opened again. His head cleared. He adjusted to the light.

His mouth tasted sour; his tongue seemed to be covered with a thick fuzz. His eyes stung. His head hurt, and there was a leaden emptiness in his stomach.

"We've been waiting more than two days for you to wake up, Ewing," said a familiar voice. "That stuff Byra gave you must have really been potent."

He broke through the fog that hazed his mind and looked around. He was in a large room with triangular, opaqued windows. Around him, where he lay on some sort of makeshift cot, were four figures: Rollun Firnik, Byra Clork, and two swarthy Sirians whom he did not know.

"Where am I?" he demanded.

Firnik said, "You're in the lowest level of the Consulate building. We brought you here early Sixday morning. This is Oneday. You've been asleep."

"Drugged is a better word," Ewing said bleakly. He sat up and swung his legs over the side of the cot. Immediately, one of the unknown Sirians stepped forward, put one hand on his chest, grabbed his ankles in his other hand, and heaved him back to the cot, Ewing started to rise again; this time he drew a stinging backhand slap that split his lower lip and sent a dribble of blood down his chin.

Ewing rubbed the moist spot tenderly. Then he came halfway to a sitting position. "What right do you have to keep me here? I'm a citizen of Corwin. I have my rights."

Firnik chuckled. "Corwin's fifty light-years away. Right now you're on Earth. The only rights you have are the ones I say you have."

Angrily, Ewing attempted to spring to his feet. "I demand that you release me! I—"

"Hit him," Firnik said tonelessly.

Again the barrel-bodied Sirian moved forward silently and slapped him—in the same place. Ewing felt the cut on his lip widen, and this time one of his lower teeth abraded the delicate inner surface of his lip as well. He did not make any further attempts to rise.

"Now, then," Firnik said in a conversational voice. "If you're quite sure you'll refrain from causing any more trouble, we can begin. You know Miss Clork, I think."

Ewing nodded.

"And these gentlemen here"—Firnik indicated the two silent Sirians—"are Sergeant Drayl and Lieutenant Thirsk of the City of Valloin Police. I want you to realize that there'll be no need for you to try to call the police, since we have two of their finest men with us today."

"Police? Aren't they from Sirius IV?"

"Naturally." Firnik's eyes narrowed. "Sirians make the best policemen. More than half of the local police are natives of my planet."

Ewing considered that silently. The hotels, the police—what else? The Sirians would not need a bloody coup to establish their power officially; they had already taken control of Earth by default, with the full consent, if not approval, of the Terrestrials. When the time came, all the Sirians needed to do was to give Governor-General Mellis formal notice that he was relieved of his duties, and Earth would pass officially into Sirian possession.

The Corwinite let his gaze roam uneasily around the room. Unfamiliar-looking machines stood in the corners of the room. *The latest in torture devices*, he thought. He looked at Firnik.

"What do you want with me?"

The Sirian folded his thick arms and said, "Information. You've been very stubborn, Ewing."

"I've been telling the truth. What do you want me to do—make something up to please you?"

"You're aware that the government of Sirius IV is soon to extend a protector-ate to Earth," Firnik said. "You fail to realize that this step is being done for the mother world's own good, to protect it in its declining days against possible depredations from hostile worlds in this system. I'm not talking about hypothetical invaders from other galaxies."

"Hypothetical? But—"

"Quiet. Let me finish. You, representing Corwin and possibly some of the other distant colonies, have come to Earth to verify the rumor that such a protectorate is about to be created. The worlds you represent have arrived at the totally false conclusion that there is something malevolent about our attitude toward Earth—that we have so-called imperialistic 'designs' on Earth. You fail to understand the altruistic motives behind our decision to relieve the Terrestrials of the tiresome burden of governing themselves. And so your planet has sent you here as a sort of spy, to determine in actuality what the relationship between Sirius IV and Earth is, and to make the necessary arrangements with the Terrestrials to defend Earth against us. To this end you've already conferred with Governor-General Mellis, and you have an appointment to visit one Myreck, a dangerous radical and potential revolutionary. Why do you insist on denying this?"

"Because you're talking idiotic gibberish! I'm no spy! I'm—"

The side of Sergeant Drayl's stiffened hand descended on Ewing at the point where his neck joined his shoulder. He gagged but retained control over himself. His clavicle began to throb.

"You've told both Miss Clork and myself," Firnik said, "that your purpose in coming to Earth was to seek Terrestrial aid against an alleged invasion of non-human beings from beyond the borders of this galaxy. It's such a transparently false story that it makes you and your planet look utterly pitiful."

"It happens to be true," Ewing said doggedly.

Firnik snorted. "True? There is no such invasion!"

"I've seen photos of Barnholt—"

The barrage of punches that resulted nearly collapsed him. He compelled himself to cling to consciousness, but he was dizzy with pain. A red haze swirled around his head, it seemed.

"You pose a grave threat to joint Sirian-Terrestrial security," Firnik said sonorously. "We must have the truth from you, so we can guide our actions accordingly. "

You've had the truth, Ewing said silently. He did not speak it aloud; that would only be inviting a blow.

"We have means of interrogation," Firnik went on. "Most of them, unfortunately, involve serious demolition of the personality. We are not anxious to damage you; you would be more useful to us with your mind intact."

Ewing stared blankly at him—and at Byra, standing wordlessly at his side.

"What do you want me to tell you?" he asked.

"Details of the Corwinite plans. Full information on the essence of your interview with Governor-General Mellis. Information on possible belligerent intentions on the part of other colony worlds."

"I've told you all I can tell you," Ewing said wearily. "Anything else will be lies."

Firnik shrugged. "We have time. The present mode of interrogation will continue until either some response is forthcoming or we see that your defenses are too strong. After that"—he indicated the hooded machines in the corners of the room—"other means will be necessary."

Ewing smiled faintly despite the pain and the growing stiffness of his lips. He thought for a flickering moment of his wife Laira, his son Blade, and all the others on Corwin, waiting hopefully for him to return with good news. And instead of a triumphant return bearing tidings of aid, he faced torture, maiming, possible death at the hands of Sirians who refused to believe the truth.

Well, they would find out the truth soon enough, he thought blackly. After the normal means of interrogation were shown to be useless, when they had put into use the mind-pick and the brain-burner and the other cheerful devices waiting in the shadowy corners for him. They would turn his mind inside out and reveal its inmost depths, and then they would find he had been telling the truth.

Perhaps then they would begin to worry about the Klodni. Ewing did not care. Corwin was lost to the aliens whether he returned or not, and possibly it was better to die now than to live to see his planet's doom.

He looked up at the Sirian's cold, heavy features with something like pity. "Go ahead," he said gently. "Start interrogating. You're in for a surprise."

Chapter Eight

A timeless stretch of blurred minutes, hours, perhaps even days slipped by. They had taken away Ewing's watch, along with his wallet and other personal belongings, and so he had no way of perceiving the passage of time. After the first few hours, he hardly cared.

The questioning went on round-the-clock. Usually it was Firnik who stood above him and urged him to confess, while Drayl or Thirsk hovered at one side, punching him from time to time. Sometimes it was Byra who interrogated him, in a flat metallic voice that might have issued from the throat of a robot.

He felt his resources weakening. His answers became mere hazy mumbles, and when they became too incoherent they dashed cold water in his face to revive him.

His tormentors were showing signs of weakening too. Firnik looked red-eyed from the strain; occasionally his voice took on a ragged, rasping quality. He pleaded with Ewing, cajoled him to end his stubbornness and yield the information.

Once, when Ewing had muttered for the millionth time, "I told you the truth the first time," Byra looked sharply at Firnik and said, "Maybe he's sincere. Maybe we're making a mistake. How long can we keep this up?"

"Shut up!" Firnik blazed. He wheeled on the girl and sent her spinning to the floor with a solid slap. A moment later, ignoring Ewing, he picked her up and muttered an apology. "We'll have to use the mind-pick," he said. "We are getting nowhere this way."

Vaguely, Ewing heard something being rolled over the stone floor toward his cot. He did not look up. He heard Byra saying, "There'll be nothing left of him when the pick's through digging through his mind."

"I can't help that, Byra. We have to know. Drayl, have you accounted for the power drain?"

"Yes."

"Then lower the helmet and attach the electrodes."

Ewing opened his eyes and saw a complex instrument by the side of his cot; its myriad dials and meters looked like fierce eyes to him. A gleaming copper helmet hung from a jointed neck. Sergeant Drayl was moving the helmet toward him, lowering it over his head. Clamps within the helmet gripped his skull gently.

He felt metal things being attached to his wrists. He remained perfectly still. He felt no fear, only a dull sensation of relief that the interrogation was at last approaching its conclusion.

"It's ready to function, sir," came Drayl's voice.

"Very well." Firnik sounded a little tense. "Ewing, can you hear me?"

"Yes," he said after some moment's silence.

"Good. You have your last chance. Why did the Free World of Corwin decide to send you to Earth?"

"Because of the Klodni," Ewing began wearily. "They came out of Andromeda and—"

Firnik cut him off: "Enough! I'm turning on the pick."

Under the helmet, Ewing relaxed, waiting for the numbing thrust. A second passed, and another. *Is this what it's like?* he wondered dully.

He heard Firnik's voice, in sudden alarm: "Who are you? How did you get in here?"

"Never mind that." It was a strange voice, firm and commanding. "Get away from that machine, Firnik. I've got a stunner here, and I'm itching to use it on you. Over there, against the wall. You too, Byra. Drayl, unclamp his wrists and get that helmet off him."

Ewing felt the machinery lifting away from him. He blinked, looked around the room without comprehending. A tall figure stood near the door, holding a glittering little gun firmly fixed on the Sirians. He wore a face mask, a golden sheath that effectively concealed his features.

The newcomer crossed the room, coming to the side of Ewing's cot, and lifted him with one hand while keeping the stunner trained on the baffled Sirians. Ewing was too weak to stand on his own power; he wobbled uncertainly, but the stranger held him up.

"Get on the phone, Firnik, and make sure you keep that vision off. Call the Consulate guard and tell him that the prisoner is being remanded to custody and will leave the building. The stunner's on full intensity now. One phony word and I'll freeze your brains for good."

Ewing felt like a figure in a dream. Cradled against his rescuer's side, he watched uncomprehendingly as a bitterly angry Firnik phoned upstairs and relayed the stranger's message.

"All right, now," the stranger said. "I'm leaving the building and I'm taking Ewing with me. But first"—he made an adjustment on the gun he was carrying—"I think it's wise to take precautions. This ought to keep you out of circulation for a couple of hours, at least."

Firnik made a strangled sound deep in his throat and leaped forward, arms clawing for the masked stranger. The stranger fired once; a blue stream of radiance came noiselessly from the muzzle of the gun, and Firnik froze in his tracks, his face locked in an expression of rage. Calmly the stranger directed his fire around the room until Byra, Drayl, and Thirsk were just three more statues.

Ewing felt the stranger tighten his hold on him. He tried to share the burden by moving himself, but his feet refused to support him.

Half-dragged, half-stumbling, he let himself be carried from the room and into a lift. He sensed upward motion. The lift stopped; he was moving forward. Gray waves of pain shuddered through him. He longed to stop where he was and go to sleep, but the inexorable pressure of the stranger's arm carried him along.

Fresh air reached his nostrils. He coughed. He had become accustomed to the foul staleness of the room that had been his prison.

Through half-open eyes he watched the companion hail a cab; he was pushed inside, and heard the voice say, "Take us to the Grand Valloin Hotel, please."

"Looks like your friend's really been on a binge," the driver said. "Don't remember the last time I saw a man looking so used up."

Why is he taking me back to the hotel? Ewing wondered. *Firnik has spy beams planted there.*

The gentle motion of the cab was soothing; after a few moments he dropped off to sleep. He woke later, once again being supported by the stranger. Upward. Into a corridor. Standing in front of a door.

The door opened. They went in.

It was his room at the hotel.

He staggered forward and fell face-first on the bed. He was aware of the stranger's motions as he undressed him, washed his face, applied depilatory to his beard.

"I want to go to sleep," he said.

"Soon. Soon."

He was carried into the adjoining room and held under the shower until the ion-beam had peeled away the grime. Then, at last, he was allowed to sleep. The bedsheets were warm and womblike; he nestled in them gratefully, letting his tortured body relax, letting sleep sweep up over him and engulf him.

Vaguely he heard the door close behind him. He slept.

He woke some time later, his body stiff and sore in a hundred places. He rolled over in the bed, clamping a hand to his forehead to stop the throbbing back of his eyes.

What happened to me?

Memory came flooding back. He recalled finding Byra in his room, taking the drugged liquor, being carried off to the Sirian Consulate. Blurred days of endless torment, interrogation, a mind-pick machine lowered over his unresisting head—

Sudden rescue from an unknown source. Sleep. His memories ended there.

Achingly, he crawled from the bed and switched on the room telestat, dialed the news channel. The autotyper rattled, and a news report began to unwind from the machine:

Fourday, 13th Fifthmonth, 3806. The office of Governor-General Mellis announced today that plans are continuing for construction of the Gerd River Dam, despite Sirian objections that the proposed power plant project would interfere with the power rights granted them under the Treaty of 3804. The Governor-General declared—

Ewing did not care what the Governor-General had declared. His sole purpose in turning on the telestat had been to find out the date.

Fourday, the thirteenth of Fifthmonth. He calculated backward. He had had his interview with Mellis the previous Fiveday evening; that had been the seventh of Fifthmonth. On Fiveday night—Sixday morning, actually—he had been kidnapped by Firnik.

Two days later, on Oneday, he had awakened and the torture began. Oneday, Twoday, Threeday—and this was Fourday. The torture had lasted no more than two days, then. The stranger had rescued him either on Twoday or Threeday, and he had slept through until today.

He remembered something else: he had made his appointment with Myreck for Fournight. Tonight.

The house phone chimed.

Ewing debated answering it for a moment; it chimed again more insistently, and he switched it on. The robotic voice said, "There is a call for you, Mr. Ewing. Shall we put it through?"

"Who's it from?" he asked cautiously.

"The party did not say."

He considered. "Okay," he said finally. "Put whoever it is on."

Moments later the screen brightened and Ewing saw the hairless image of Scholar Myreck staring solicitously at him. "Have I disturbed you?" Myreck asked.

"Not at all," Ewing said. "I was just thinking about you. We had an appointment for tonight, didn't we?"

"Ah—yes. But I have just received an anonymous call telling me you have had a rather unfortunate experience. I was just wondering if I could be of any service to you in alleviating your pain."

Ewing remembered the miraculous massage Myreck had given him earlier. He also considered the fact that the hotel he was in belonged to Firnik, and no doubt the Sirian would be fully recuperated from his stunning soon and out looking for him. It was unwise to remain in the hotel any longer.

He smiled. "I'd be very grateful if you would be. You said you'd arrange to pick me up, didn't you?"

"Yes. We will be there in a few minutes."

Chapter Nine

It took only eleven minutes from the time Ewing broke contact to the moment when Myreck rang up from the hotel lobby to announce that he had arrived. Ewing took the rear liftshaft down, and moved cautiously through the vast lobby toward the energitron concession, which was where the Scholar had arranged to meet him.

A group of Earthers waited there for him. He recognized Myreck, and also the uniped he had seen the first morning at the terminal. The other two were equally grotesque in appearance. In a pitiful quest for individuality, they had given themselves up to the surgeon's knife. One had a row of emerald-cut diamonds mounted crest-fashion in a bare swath cut down the center of his scalp; the inset jewels extended past his forehead, ending with one small gem at the bridge of his nose. The fourth had no lips, and a series of blue cicatrices incised in parallel lines on his jaws. For the first time Ewing felt no distaste at the sight of these altered Earthmen, partly because he was so exhausted physically and partly because he was growing accustomed to the sight of them.

Myreck said, "The car is outside."

It was a stubby three-color model which seemed not to have any windows whatever. Ewing wondered whether it was robocontrolled, or whether the driver drove by guesswork. He found out quickly enough when he got in, and discovered that the dome of green plastic that roofed the car was actually a sheet of some one-way viewing material; far from having no access to the outside world, the driver and passengers had a totally unobstructed view in all directions, and unlimited privacy as well.

Myreck drove; or rather, he put the car in motion, and then guided it by deft occasional wrist-flicks on the directional control. They turned south, away from the spaceport, and glided along a broad highway for nearly eight miles, turning eastward sharply into what seemed like a surburban district. Ewing slumped tiredly in his corner of the car, now and then peering out at the neat, even rows of houses, each one surmounted by its own glittering privacy shield.

At last they pulled up at the side of the road. Ewing was startled to see nothing before them but an empty lot. There were some houses further down the street, and plenty of parking space in front of them; why had Myreck chosen to park here?

Puzzled, he got out. Myreck stared cautiously in all directions, then took a key made of some luminous yellow metal from his pocket and advanced toward the empty lot, saying, "Welcome to the home of the College of Abstract Science."

"Where?"

Myreck pointed to the lot. "Here, of course."

Ewing squinted; something was wrong about the air above the lot. It had a curious pinkish tinge, and seemed to be shimmering, as if heat-waves were rising from the neatly tended grass.

Myreck held his key in front of him, stepped into the lot and groped briefly in mid-air, as if searching for an invisible keyhole. And indeed he seemed to find it; the key vanished for three-quarters of its length.

A building appeared.

It was a glistening pink dome, much like the other houses in the neighborhood; but it had a curious impermanence about it. It seemed to be fashioned of dream-stuff. The lipless Earther grasped him firmly by the arm and pushed him forward, into the house. The street outside disappeared.

"That's a neat trick," Ewing said. "How do you work it?"

Myreck smiled. "The house is three microseconds out of phase with the rest of the street. It always exists just a fraction of an instant in Absolute Past, not enough to cause serious temporal disturbance but enough to conceal it from our many enemies."

Goggle-eyed, Ewing said, "You have temporal control?"

The Earther nodded. "The least abstract of our sciences. A necessary defense."

Ewing felt stunned. Gazing at the diminutive Earther with new-found respect, he thought, *This is incredible!* Temporal control had long been deemed theoretically possible, ever since the publication of Blackmuir's equations more than a thousand years before. But Corwin had had little opportunity for temporal research, and such that had been done had seemed to imply that Blackmuir's figures were either incorrect or else technologically un-implementable. And for these overdecorated Earthers to have developed them! Unbelievable!

He stared through a window at the quiet street outside. In Absolute Time, he knew, the scene he was observing was three microseconds in the future, but the interval was so minute that for all practical purposes it made no difference to the occupants of the house. It made a great difference to anyone outside who wanted to enter illegally, though; there was no way to enter a house that did not exist in present time.

"This must involve an enormous power-drain," Ewing said.

"On the contrary. The entire operation needs no more than a thousand watts to sustain itself. Our generator supplies fifteen-amp current. It's astonishingly inexpensive, though we never could have met the power demands had we tried to project the house an equivalent distance into the *future*. But there's time to talk of all this later. You must be exhausted. Come."

Ewing was led into a comfortably-furnished salon lined with microreels and music disks. Plans were pinwheeling in his head, nearly enough to make him forget the fatigue that overwhelmed his body. *If these Earthers have temporal control,* he thought, *and if I can induce them to part with their device or its plans* . . .

It's pretty far-fetched. But we need something far-fetched to save us now. It might work.

Myreck said, "Will you sit here?"

Ewing climbed into a relaxing lounger. The Earther dialed him a drink and slipped a music disk into the player. Vigorous music filled the room: four-square harmonics, simple and yet ruggedly powerful. He liked the sort of sound it made—a direct emotional appeal.

"What music is that?"

"Beethoven," Myreck said. "One of our ancients. Would you like me to relax you?"

"Please."

Ewing felt Myreck's hands at the base of his skull once again. He waited. Myreck's hands probed the sides of his neck, lifted, jabbed down sharply. For one brief moment Ewing felt all sensation leave his body; then physical awareness returned, but without consciousness of the pain.

"That feels wonderful," he said. "It's as if Firnik never worked me over at all, except for these bruises I have as souvenirs."

"They'll vanish shortly. Somatic manifestations usually do once the pain-source is removed."

He leaned back, exulting in the sensation of feeling no pain as if he had spent all his life, and not merely the past three of four days, in a state of hellish physical discomfort. The music was fascinating, and the drink he held warmed him. It was comforting to know that somewhere in the city of Valloin was a sanctuary where he was free from Firnik for as long as he chose.

The Earthers were filing in now—eleven or twelve of them, shy little men with curious artificial deformities of diverse sorts. Myreck said, "There are the members of the College currently in residence. Others are doing research elsewhere. I don't know what sort of colleges you have on Corwin, but ours is one only in the most ancient sense of the word. We draw no distinctions between master and pupil here. We all learn equally, from one another.

"I see. And which of you developed the temporal control system?"

"Oh, none of us did that. Powlis was responsible, a hundred years ago. We've simply maintained the apparatus and modified it."

"*A hundred years?*" Ewing was appalled. "It's a hundred years since the art was discovered and you're still lurking in holes and corners, letting the Sirians push you out of control of your own planet?"

Ewing realized he had spoken too strongly. The Earthers looked abashed; some of them were almost at the verge of tears. *They're like children,* he thought wonderingly.

"I'm sorry," he said.

A slim Earther with surgically-augmented shoulders said, "Is it true that your world is under attack by alien beings from a far galaxy?"

"Yes. We expect attack in ten years."

"And will you be able to defeat them?"

Ewing shrugged. "We'll try. They've conquered the first four worlds they've attacked, including two that were considerably stronger than we are. We don't have much hope of winning. But we'll try."

Sadly Myreck said, "We had been wondering if it would be possible for us to leave Earth and emigrate to your world soon. But if you face destruction . . ." He let his voice trail off.

"Emigrate to Corwin? Why would you do that?"

"The Sirians soon will rule here. They will put us to work for them, or else kill us. We're safe as long as we remain in this building—but we must go out from time to time."

"You have temporal control. You could duck back into yesterday to avoid pursuit."

Myreck shook his head. "Paradoxes are caused. Multiplication of personality. We fear these things, and we would hesitate to bring them about."

Shrugging, Ewing said, "You have to take chances. Caution is healthy only when not carried to excess."

"We had hoped," said a dreamy-eyed Earther sitting in the corner, "that we could arrange with you for a passage to Corwin. On the ship you came on, possibly."

"It was a one-man ship."

Disappointment was evident. "In that case, perhaps you could send a larger ship for us. We have none, you see. Earth stopped building ships two centuries ago, and gradually most of the ones we had were either sold or fell into disuse. The Sirians now control such industries on Earth, and refuse to let us have ships. So the galaxy we once roamed is closed to us."

Ewing wished there were some way he could help these futile, likable little dreamers. But no solutions presented themselves. "Corwin has very few ships itself," he said. "Less than a dozen capable of making an interstellar journey with any reasonable number of passengers. And any ships we might have would certainly be requisitioned by the military for use in the coming war against the Klodni. I don't see any way we could manage it. Besides," he added, "even if I left Earth tomorrow, I wouldn't be back on Corwin for nearly a year. And it would take another year for me to return to Earth with a ship for you. Do you think you could hold out against the Sirians that long?"

"Possibly," Myreck said, but he sounded doubtful. There was silence a moment. Then the Scholar said, "Please understand that we would be prepared to pay for our passage. Not in money, perhaps, but in service. Possibly we are in command of certain scientific techniques not yet developed on your world. In that case you might find our emigration quite valuable."

Ewing considered that. Certainly the Earthers had plenty to offer—the temporal-control device, foremost among them. But he could easily picture the scene upon his return to Corwin, as he tried to get the Council to approve use of a major interstellar freighter to bring refugee scientists from the Earth that had failed to help them. It would never work. If they only had some super-weapon—

But, of course, if they had a super-weapon they would have no need of fleeing the Sirians. Round and round, with no solution.

He moistened his lips. "Perhaps I can think of something," he said. "The cause isn't quite hopeless yet. But meanwhile—"

Myreck's eyes brightened. "Yes?"

"I'm quite curious about your temporal-displacement equipment. Would it be possible for me to examine it?"

Myreck exchanged what seemed like a dubious glance with several of his comrades. After a moment's hesitation he returned his attention to Ewing and said, in a slightly shaky voice, "I don't see why not."

They don't fully trust me, Ewing thought. *They're half afraid of the bold, vigorous man from the stars. Well, I don't blame them.*

Myreck rose and beckoned to Ewing. "Come this way. The laboratory is downstairs."

Ewing followed, and the other Earthers tagged along behind. They proceeded down a winding staircase into a room below, brightly lit with radiance streaming from every molecule of the walls and floor. In the center of the room stood a massive block of machinery, vaguely helical in structure, with an enormous pendulum held in suspension in its center. A platform stood at one side. Elsewhere in the room were metering devices and less identifiable types of scientific equipment.

"This is not the main machine," Myreck said. "In the deepest level of the building we keep the big generator that holds us out of time-phase with relation to the outside world. I could show it to you, but this machine is considerably more interesting."

"What does this one do?"

"It effects direct temporal transfer on a small-scale level. The theory behind it is complex, but the basic notion is extraordinarily simple. You see—"

"Just a moment," Ewing said, interrupting. An idea had struck him which was almost physically staggering in its impact. "Tell me: this machine could send a person into the immediate Absolute Past, couldn't it?"

Myreck frowned. "Why, yes. Yes. But we could never run the risk of—"

Again Ewing did not let the Earther finish his statement. "This I find very interesting," he broke in. He moistened his suddenly dry lips. "Would you say it was theoretically possible to send—say, me—back in time to—oh, about Twoday evening of this week?"

"It could be done, yes," Myreck admitted.

A pulse pounded thunderously in Ewing's skull. His limbs felt cold and his fingers seemed to be quivering. But he fought down the feeling of fear. Obviously, the journey had been taken once, and successfully. He would take it again.

"Very well, then. I request a demonstration of the machine. Send me back to Twoday evening."

"But—"

"I insist," Ewing said determinedly. He knew now who his strange masked rescuer had been.

Chapter Ten

A look of blank horror appeared on Myreck's pale face. His thin lips moved a moment without producing sound. Finally he managed to say, in a hoarse rasp. "You can't be serious. There would be a continuum doubling if you did that. Two Baird Ewings existing conterminously, you see. And—"

"Is there any danger in it?" Ewing asked.

Myreck looked baffled. "We don't know. It's never been done. We've never dared to try it. The consequences might be uncontrollable. A sudden explosion of galactic scope, for all we know."

"I'll risk it," Ewing said. He knew there had been no danger that *first* time. He was certain now that his rescuer had been an earlier Ewing, one who had preceded him through the time-track, reached this point in time, and doubled back to become his rescuer, precisely as he was about to do. His head swam. He refused to let himself dwell on the confusing, paradoxical aspects of the situation.

"I don't see how we could permit such a dangerous thing to take place," Myreck said mildly. "You put us in a most unpleasant position. The risks are too great. We don't dare."

A spanner lay within Ewing's reach. He snatched it up, hefting it ominously, and said, "I'm sorry to have to threaten you, but you'd never be able to follow me if I tried to explain why I have to do this. Either put me back to Twonight or I'll begin smashing things."

Myreck's hands moved in a little dance of fear and frustration. "I'm sure you wouldn't consider such a violent act, Mr. Ewing. We know you're a reasonable man. Surely you wouldn't—"

"Surely I would!" His hands gripped the shaft tightly; sweat rolled down his forehead. He knew that his bluff would not be called, that ultimately they would yield, since they *had* yielded, once—when? When this scene had become played out for the first time. First? Ewing felt cold uneasiness within.

Limply Myreck shook his head up and down. "Very well," the little man said. "We will do as you ask. We have no choice." His face expressed an emotion as close to contempt as was possible for him—a sort of mild, apologetic disdain. "If you will mount this platform, please . . ."

Ewing put the spanner down and suspiciously stepped forward onto the platform. He sensed the oppressive bulk of the machine around and above him. Myreck made painstaking adjustments on a control panel beyond his range of vision, while the other Earthers gathered in a frightened knot to watch the proceedings.

"How do I make the return trip to Fourday?" Ewing asked suddenly.

Myreck shrugged. "By progressing through forward time at a rate of one second per second. We have no way of returning you to this time or place at any accelerated rate." He looked imploringly at Ewing. " I beg you not to force me to do this. We have not fully worked out the logic of time travel yet; we don't understand—"

"Don't worry. I'll be back. Somehow. Sometime."

He smiled with a confidence he did not feel. He was setting foot into the darkest of realms—*yesterday*. He was armed with one comforting thought: that by venturing all, he might possibly save Corwin. By risking nothing, he would lose all.

He waited. He realized he was expecting a crackle of energy, an upwelling flare of some supernatural force that would sweep him backward across the matrix of time, but none of these phenomena materialized. There was merely the gentle murmur of Myreck's voice as he called off equations and made compensations on his control panel; then came a final "Ready," and the Earther's hand reached for the ultimate switch.

"There'll probably be a certain amount of spacial dislocation," Myreck was saying. "I hope for our sakes that you emerge in the open, and not—"

The sentence was never finished. Ewing felt no sensation whatever, but the laboratory and the tense group of Earthers vanished as if blotted out by the hand of the cosmos, and he found himself hovering a foot in the air in the midst of a broad greensward, on a warm, bright afternoon.

The hovering lasted only an instant; he tumbled heavily to the ground, sprawling forward on his hands and knees. He rose hurriedly to his feet. His knee stung for an instant as he straightened up; he glanced down and saw that he had scraped it, on a stone in the field, causing a slight abrasion.

From nearby came a childish giggle. A high voice said, "Look at the funny man doing handsprings!"

"Such a remark is impolite," came a stuffy, mechanical-sounding response. "One does not loudly call attention to eccentric behavior of any kind."

Ewing turned and saw a boy of about eight being admonished by a tall robot governess. "But where did the man come from?" the boy persisted. "He just dropped out of the sky, didn't he? Didn't you see?"

"My attention was elsewhere. But people do not drop out of the sky. Not in this day and age in the City of Valloin."

Chuckling to himself, Ewing walked away. It was good to know he was still in the City of Valloin, at any rate; he wondered if the boy was going to continue asking about the man who had dropped from the sky. That governess didn't seem to have any humor circuits. He pitied the boy.

He was in a park; that much was obvious. In the distance he saw a children's playground and something that might have been a zoological garden. Concessions sold refreshments nearby. He walked toward the closest of these booths, where a bright-haired young man was purchasing a balloon for a boy at his side from a robot vender.

"Excuse me," he said. "I'm a stranger in Valloin, and I'm afraid I've got myself lost."

The Earther—his hair, a flaming red, had apparently been chemically treated to look even brighter—handed the robot a coin, took the balloon, gave it to the child, and smiled courteously at Ewing.

"Can I help you?"

Ewing returned the smile. "I was out for a walk, and I'm afraid I lost my way. I'd like to get back to the Sirian Consulate. That's where I'm staying."

The Earther gaped at him a moment before recovering control. "You *walked* all the way from the Sirian Consulate to Valloin Municipal Park?"

Ewing realized he had made a major blunder. He reddened and tried to cover up for himself: "No—no, not exactly. I know I took a cab part of the way. But I don't remember which way I came, and—well—"

"You could take a cab back, couldn't you?" the young man suggested. "Of course, it's pretty expensive from here. If you want, take the Number Sixty bus as far as Grand Circle, and transfer there for the downtown undertube line. The Oval Line tube will get you to the Consulate if you change at the Three Hundred Seventy-eighth Street station."

Ewing waited patiently for the flow of directions to cease. Finally he said, "I guess I'll take the bus, then. Would it be troubling you too much to show me where I could get it?"

"At the other side of the park, near the big square entrance."

Ewing squinted. "I'm afraid I don't see it. Could we walk over there a little way? I wouldn't want to inconvenience you in any way . . ."

"Perfectly all right."

They left the vendor's booth and started to cross the park. Halfway toward the big entrance, the Earther stopped. Pointing, he said, "It's right over there. See? You can't miss it."

Ewing nodded. "There's one final thing—"

"Of course."

"I seem to have lost all my money in an unfortunate accident this morning. I lost my wallet, you see. Could you lend me about a hundred credits?"

"A hundred credits! Now, see here, fellow. I don't mind giving travel directions, but a hundred credits is a little out of line! Why it won't cost you more than one credit eighty to get to the Consulate from here."

"I know," Ewing said tightly. "But I need the hundred." He pointed a finger through the fabric of his trouser pocket and said, "There's a stun-gun in this pocket, and my finger's on the stud. Suppose you very quietly hand me a hundred credits in small notes, or I'll be compelled to use the stunner on you. I wouldn't want to do that."

The Earther seemed on the verge of tears. He glanced quickly at the boy with the balloon, playing unconcernedly fifteen feet away, and then jerked his head back to face Ewing. Without speaking, he drew out his billfold and counted out the bills. Ewing took them in equal silence and stored them in the pocket where he had kept his wallet, before Firnik had confiscated it.

"I'm really sorry about having to do this," he told the young Earther. "But I can't stop to explain, and I need the money. Now I'd like you to take the child by the hand and walk slowly toward that big lake over there, without looking back and without calling for help. The stunner is effective at distances of almost five hundred feet, you know."

"Help a stranger and this is what you get," the Earther muttered. "Robbery in broad daylight, in Municipal Park!"

"Go on—move!"

The Earther moved. Ewing watched him long enough to make sure he would keep good faith, then turned and trotted rapidly toward the park entrance. He reached it just as the rounded snout of a Number Sixty bus drew up at the corner. Grinning, Ewing leaped aboard. An immobile robot at the entrance said, "Destination, please?"

"Grand Circle."

"Nothing and sixty, please."

Ewing drew a one-credit note from his pocket, placed it in the receiving slot, and waited. A bell rang; a ticket popped forth, and four copper coins jounced into the change slot. He scooped them up and entered the bus. From the window he glanced at the park and caught sight of the little boy's red balloon; the flame-haired man was next to him, back to the street, staring at the lake. Probably scared stiff, Ewing thought. He felt only momentary regret for what he had done. He needed the money. Firnik had taken all of *his* money, and his rescuer had unaccountably neglected to furnish him with any.

Grand Circle turned out to be just that—a vast circular wheel of a street, with more than fifteen street-spokes radiating outward from it. A monument of some sort stood in a grass plot at the very center of the wheel.

Ewing dismounted from the bus. Spying a robot directing traffic, he said, "Where can I get the downtown undertube line?"

The robot directed him to the undertube station. He transferred at the Three Hundred Seventy-eighth Street station, as his unfortunate acquaintance had advised, and shortly afterward found himself in the midst of a busy shopping district.

He stood thoughtfully in the middle of the arcade for a moment, nudging his memory for the equipment he would need. A privacy mask and a stun-gun; that seemed to be about all.

A weapons shop sign beckoned to him from the distance. He hurried to it, found it open, and stepped through the curtain of energy that served as its door. The proprietor was a wizened little Earther who smiled humbly at him as he entered.

"May I serve you, sir?"

"You may. I'm interested in buying a stun-gun, if you have one for a good price."

The shopkeeper frowned. "I don't know if we have any stun-guns in stock. Now let me see . . . ah, yes!" He reached below the counter and drew forth a dark-blue plastite box. He touched the seal; the box flew open. "Here you are, sir. A lovely model. Only eight credits."

Ewing took the gun from the little man and examined it. It felt curiously light; he split it open and was surprised to find it was hollow and empty within. He looked up angrily. "Is this a joke? Where's the force chamber?"

"You mean you want a *real* gun, sir? I thought you simply were looking for an ornament to complement that fine suit you wear. But—"

"Never mind that. Do you have one of these that actually functions?"

The shopkeeper looked pale, almost sick. But he vanished into the back room and reappeared a moment later with a small gun in his hand. "I happen to have one, sir. A Sirian customer of mine ordered it last month and then unfortunately died. I was about to return it, but if you're interested it's yours for ninety credits."

Ninety credits was almost all the money he had. And he wanted to save some to hand over to the rescued man.

"Too much. I'll give you sixty."

"Sir! I—"

"Take sixty," Ewing said. "I'm a personal friend of Vice-Consul Firnik's. See him and he'll make up the difference."

The Earther eyed him meekly and sighed. "Sixty it is," he said. "Shall I wrap it?"

"Never mind about that," Ewing said, pocketing the tiny weapon, case and all, and counting out sixty credits from his slim roll. One item remained. "Do you have privacy masks?"

"Yes, sir. A large assortment."

"Good. Give me a golden one."

With trembling hands the shopkeeper produced one. It fit the memory he had of the other reasonably well. "How much?"

"T-ten credits, sir. For you, eight."

"Take the ten," Ewing said. He folded the mask, smiled grimly at the terrified shopkeeper, and left. Once he was out on the street, he looked up at a big building-clock and saw the time: 1552.

Suddenly he clapped his hand to his forehead in annoyance: he had forgotten to check the most important fact of all! Hastily he darted back into the weapons shop. The proprietor came to attention, lips quivering. "Y-yes."

"All I want is some information," Ewing said. "What day is today?"

"What *day*? Why—why, Twoday, of course. Twoday, the eleventh."

Ewing crowed triumphantly. Twoday on the nose! He burst from the store a second time. Catching the arm of a passerby, he said, "Pardon. Can you direct me to the Sirian Consulate?"

"Two blocks north, turn left. Big building. You can't miss it."

"Thanks," Ewing said.

Two blocks north, turn left. A current of excitement bubbled in his heart.

He began to walk briskly toward the Sirian Consulate, hands in his pockets. One clasped the coolness of the stun-gun, the other rested against the privacy mask.

Chapter Eleven

Ewing had to push his way through a good-sized crowd at the Consulate—Sirians all, each of them bound on some private business of his own. Ewing was surprised that there were so many Sirians in Valloin.

The Consulate was a building of imposing dimensions; evidently one of the newest of Valloin's edifices, its architecture was out of key with that of the surrounding buildings. Clashing planes and tangential faces made the Consulate a startling sight.

Ewing passed through the enormous lobby and turned left to a downramp. He gave only passing thought to the question of how he was going to reach the subterranean dungeon, where at this moment another version of himself was undergoing interrogation. He knew that he had been rescued once, and so it could be repeated.

He made his way down, until a sergeant stationed at the foot of the last landing said, "Where are you going?"

"To the lowest level. I have to see Vice-Consul Firnik on urgent business."

"Firnik's in conference. He left orders that he wasn't to be disturbed."

"Quite all right. I have special permission. I happen to know he's interrogating a prisoner down below, along with Byra Clork, Sergeant Drayl, and Lieutenant Thirsk. I have vital information for him, and I'll see to it you roast unless I get in there to talk to him."

The sergeant looked doubtful. "Well . . ."

Ewing said, "Look—why don't you go down the hall and check with your immediate superior, if you don't want to take the responsibility yourself? I'll wait here."

The sergeant grinned, pleased to have the burden of decision lifted from his thick shoulders. "Don't go away," he said. "I'll be right back."

"Don't worry," Ewing said.

He watched as the man turned and trudged away. After he had gone three paces, Ewing drew the stunner from his pocket and set it to low intensity. The weapon was palm-size, fashioned from a bit of translucent blue plastic in whose glittering depths could dimly be seen the reaction chamber. Ewing aimed and fired. The sergeant froze.

Quickly, Ewing ran after him, dragged him back his original position, and swung him around so he seemed to be guarding the approach. Then he ducked around him and headed down toward the lower level. Another guard, this one in a lieutenant's uniform, waited there. Ewing said quickly, "The sergeant sent me down this way. Said I could find the Vice-Consul down here. I have an urgent message for him."

"Straight down the passageway, second door on your left," the lieutenant said.

Ewing thanked him and moved on. He paused for a moment outside the indicated door, while donning the privacy mask, and heard sounds from within:

"Good. You have your last chance. Why did the Free World of Corwin decide to send you to Earth?"

"Because of the Klodni," said a weary voice. The accent was a familiar one, a Corwinite one, but the voice was higher in pitch than Ewing would have expected. It was his own voice. A blur of shock swept through him at the sound. "They came out of Andromeda and—"

"Enough!" came the harsh crop of Firnik's voice. "Byra, get ready to record. I'm turning on the pick."

Ewing felt a second ripple of confusion, outside the door. Turning on the pick? Why, then this was the very moment when he had been rescued, two days earlier in his own time-track! In that case, he was now his own predecessor along the time-line, and—he shook his head. Consideration of paradoxes was irrelevant now. Action was called for, not philosophizing.

He put his hand to the door and thrust it open. It gave before his push; he stepped inside, stun-gun gripped tightly in his hand.

The scene was a weird tableau. Firnik, Byra, Drayl, and Thirsk were clustered around a fifth figure who sat limp and unresisting beneath a metal cone. And that fifth figure—

Me!

Firnik looked up in surprise. "Who are you? How did you get in here?"

"Never mind that," Ewing snapped. The scene was unrolling with dreamlike clarity, every phase utterly familiar to him. *I have been here before,* he thought, looking at the limp, tortured body of his earlier self slumped under the mind-pick helmet. "Get away from that machine, Firnik," he snapped. "I've got a stunner here, and I'm itching to use it on you. Over there, against the wall. You, too, Byra. Drayl, unclamp his wrists and get that helmet off him."

The machinery was pulled back, revealing the unshaven, bleary-eyed face of the other Ewing. The man stared in utter lack of comprehension at the masked figure near the door. The masked Ewing felt a tingle of awe at the sight of himself of Twoday, but he forced himself to remain calm. He crossed the room, keeping the gun trained on the Sirians, and lifted the other Ewing to his feet.

Crisply he ordered Firnik to call the Consulate guard upstairs and arrange for his escape. He listened while the Sirian spoke; then, saying, "This ought to keep you out of circulation for a couple of hours, at least," he stunned the four Sirians and dragged his other self from the room, out into the corridor, and into a lift.

It was not until Ewing had reached the street level that he allowed any emotional reaction to manifest itself. Sudden trembling swept over him for an instant as he stepped out of the crowded Sirian Consulate lobby, still wearing the privacy mask, and dragged the semi-conscious other Ewing into the street. The muscles in his legs felt rubbery; his throat was dry. But he had succeeded. He had rescued himself from the interrogators, and the script had followed in every detail that one which seemed "earlier" to him but which was, in reality, not earlier at all.

The script was due to diverge from its "earlier" pattern soon, Ewing realized grimly. But he preferred not to think of the dark necessity that awaited him until the proper time came.

He spied a cab, one of those rare ones not robot-operated, and hailed it. Pushing his companion inside he said, "Take us to the Grand Valloin Hotel, please."

"Looks like your friend's really been on a binge," the driver said. "Don't remember the last time I saw a man looking so used up."

"He's had a rough time of it," Ewing said, watching his other self lapse off into unconsciousness.

It cost five of his remaining eighteen credits to make the trip from the Consulate to the hotel. Quickly, Ewing got his man through the hotel lobby and upstairs into Room 4113. The other—Ewing-sub-two, Ewing was calling him now—immediately toppled face-down onto the bed. Ewing stared curiously at Ewing-sub-two, studying the battered, puffy-eyed face of the man who was himself two days earlier. He set about the job of undressing him, depilating him, cleaning him up. He dragged him into the shower and thrust him under the ion-beam; then, satisfied, he put the exhausted man to bed. Within seconds, he had lost his consciousness.

Ewing took a deep breath. So far the script had been followed; but here, it had to change.

He realized he had several choices. He could walk out of the hotel room and leave Ewing-sub-two to his own devices, in which case, in the normal flow of events, Ewing-sub-two would awaken, be taken to Myreck's, request to see the time machine, and in due course travel back to this day to become Ewing-sub-one, rescuing a new Ewing-sub-two. But that path left too many unanswered and unanswerable questions. What became of the surplus Ewing-sub-ones? In every swing of the time-cycle, another would be created—to meet what fate? It was hopelessly paradoxical.

But there was a way paradox could be avoided. Ewing thought. A way of breaking the chain of cycles that threated to keep infinite Ewings moving on a treadmill forever. But it took a brave man to make that change.

He stared in the mirror. *Do I dare?* he wondered.

He thought of his wife and child, and of all he had struggled for since coming to Earth. *I'm superfluous,* he thought. The man on the bed was the man in whose hands destiny lay. Ewing-sub-one, the rescuer, was merely a supernumerary, an extra man, a displaced spoke in the wheel of time.

I have no right to remain alive, Ewing-sub-one admitted to himself. His face, in the mirror, was unquivering, unafraid. He nodded; then, he smiled.

His way was clear. He would have to step aside. But he would merely be stepping aside for himself, and perhaps there would be no sense of discontinuity after all. He nodded in the firm decision.

There was a voicewrite at the room desk; Ewing switched it on, waited a moment as he arranged his thought, and then began to dictate:

"Twoday afternoon. To my self of an earlier time—to the man I call Ewing-sub-two, from Ewing-sub-one. Read this with great care, indeed memorize it, and then destroy it utterly.

"You have just been snatched from the hands of the interrogators by what seemed to you miraculous intervention. You must believe that your rescuer was none other than yourself, doubling back along his time-track from two days hence. Since I have already lived through the time that will now unfold for you, let me tell you what is scheduled to take place for you, and let me implore you to save our mutual existence by following my instructions exactly.

"It is now Twoday. Your tired body will sleep around the clock, and you will awaken on Fourday. Shortly after awakening, you will be contacted by Scholar Myreck, who will remind you of your appointment with him and will make arrangements with you to take you to his College in the suburbs. You will go. While you are there, they will reveal to you the fact that they are capable of shifting objects in time—indeed, their building itself is displaced by three microseconds to avoid investigation.

"At this point in my own time-track, I compelled them to send me back in time from Fourday to Twoday, and upon arriving here proceeded to carry out your rescue. My purpose in making this trip was to provide you with this information, which *my* rescuer neglected to give me. *Under no conditions are you to make a backward trip in time!* The cycle must end with you.

"When Myreck shows you the machine you are to express interest, but you are not to request a demonstration. This will automatically create a new past in which Ewing-sub-three actually did die under Firnik's interrogation, while you, Ewing sub-two, remain in existence, a free agent ready to continue your current operations. If this phase is not clear to you read it very carefully.

"As for me, I am no longer needed in the plan of events, and so intend to remove myself from the time-stream upon finishing this note. For your information, I intend to do this by short-circuiting the energitron booth in the lobby while I am inside it, a fact which you can verify upon awakening by checking the telestat records for Twoday, the Eleventh. This action, coupled with your refusal to use Myreck's machine, will put an end to the multiplicity of existing Ewings and leave you as the sole occupant of the stage. Make the most of your opportunities. I know you are capable of handling the task well.

"I wish you luck. You'll need it.

"Yours in—believe me—deepest friendship,

"Ewing-sub-one."

When he had finished the note, Ewing drew it from the machine and read it through three times, slowly. There was no rush now. He folded it, drew from his pocket ten credits—something else his predecessor along the time-track had neglected—and sealed the message and the money in an envelope which he placed on the chair next to the sleeping man's head

Satisfied, he tiptoed from the room, locking the door behind him, and rode down to the hotel lobby. There was no longer any need for the mask, so he discarded it; he had left the stun-gun upstairs, in case Ewing-sub-two might have need for it.

He picked up a phone in the lobby, dialed Central Communications, and said, "I'd like to send a message to Scholar Myreck, care of College of Abstract Science, General Delivery, City of Valloin Branch Office 86." It was the dummy address Myreck had given him. "The message is, quote: Baird Ewing has been interrogated and severely beaten by your enemies. At present he is asleep in his hotel room. Call him this afternoon and arrange to help him. Unquote. Now, that message is not to be delivered before Fourday, no later than noon. Is that clear?"

The robot operator read the message back, including instructions for delivery, and finished with, "One credit, please."

Ewing dropped coins into the slot until the operator signaled acknowledgement. He nodded in satisfaction; the wheels were fully in motion, now, and he could retire from the scene.

He crossed the lobby to a loitering Earther and said, "Excuse me. Could I trouble you for change of a one-credit bill? I'd like to use the energitron booth and I don't have any coins."

The Earther changed the bill for him; they exchanged a few pleasant words, and then Ewing headed for the booth, satisfied that he had planted his identity. When the explosion came, there would be a witness to say that a tall man had just entered the booth.

He slipped a half-credit coin into the booth's admission slot; the energy curtain that was its entrance went light pink long enough for Ewing to step through, and immediately returned to its glossy black opacity afterward. He found himself facing a beam of warm red light.

The energitron booth was simply a commercial adaptation of the ordinary ion-beam shower; it was a molecular spray that invigorated the body and refreshed the soul, according to the sign outside. Ewing knew it was also a particularly efficient suicide device. A bright enamel strip said.

CAUTION!

The operator is warned not to approach the limit-lines inscribed in the booth or to tamper with the mechanism of the energitron. It is highly delicate and may be dangerous in unskilled hands.

Ewing smiled coldly. His time had come to quit the scene—but the body and the personality of Baird Ewing of Corwin would not be obliterated, merely one superfluous extension of it. With steady hands he reached for the sealed control-box; he smashed it open and twisted the rheostat within sharply upward. The quality of the molecular beam changed; it became fuzzier, and crackled.

At the limit-lines of the booth, he knew an area existed where planes of force existed in delicate imbalance; interposing an arm or a leg in such a place could result in a violent explosion. He moved toward the limit-lines and probed with his hands for the danger area.

A sudden thought struck him: *What about my rescuer?* He had left him out of the calculations completely. But yet another Ewing-one had existed, one who had not left any notes nor stun-guns nor money, and who perhaps had not committed suicide, either. Ewing wondered briefly about him; but then he had no further time for wondering, because a blinding light flashed, and a thunderous wave of force rose from the booth and crushed him in its mighty grip.

Chapter Twelve

Ewing woke.

He felt groggy, stiff and sore in a hundred places, his forehead throbbing. He rolled over in bed, clamped a hand to his forehead, and hung on.

What happened to me?

Memories drifted back to him a thread at a time. He remembered discovering Byra in his room, drinking the drugged liquor she gave him, being hustled away to the Sirian Consulate. Blurred days of endless torment, interrogation, a mind-pick machine lowered over his unresisting head—

Sudden rescue from an unknown source. Sleep. His memories ended there.

Achingly he crawled from the bed and stared at himself in the mirror. He looked frighteningly haggard. Dark circles ringed his eyes like crayon marks, and the skin of his face hung loose under his chin, stretched tight elsewhere. He looked worse than he had at the moment of awakening, some days before, aboard the ship.

An envelope lay on a chair by the side of the bed. He frowned, picked it up, fingered it. It was sealed and addressed to him. He opened it. Five two-credit notes came fluttering out, and along with them a note. He stacked the banknotes neatly on the bed, unfolded the note, and sat down to read.

Twoday afternoon. To myself of an earlier time—to the man I call Ewing-sub-two, from Ewing-sub-one . . .

Bleary-eyed as he was, he came awake while reading the note. His first reaction was one of anger and incredulity; then he rubbed his chin thoughtfully as he considered certain turns of phrase, certain mannerisms of punctuation. He had a fairly distinctive style of voicewrite dictation. And this was a pretty good copy, or else the real thing.

In which case . . .

He switched on the house phone and said, "What's today's date, please?" There was no fear of ridicule from a robot operator.

"Fourday, the thirteenth of Fifthmonth," came the calm answer.

"Thanks. How can I get access to the telestat reports for Twoday the eleventh?"

"We could connect you with Records," the robot suggested.

"Do that," Ewing said, thinking to himself, *This is foolishness. The note's a hoax.*

He heard the *click-click-click* of shifting relays, and then a new robotic voice said, "Records. How may we serve you?"

"I'm interested in the text of a news item that covers an event which took place Twoday afternoon. The short-circuiting of an energitron machine in the lobby of the Grand Valloin Hotel."

Almost instantly the robot said, "We have your item for you. Shall we read it?"

"Go ahead," Ewing said in a rasping voice. "Read it."

"Twoday, 11th Fifthmonth, 3806. Explosion of an energitron booth in the lobby of the Grand Valloin Hotel this afternoon took one life, caused an estimated two thousand credits' worth of damage, injured three, and disrupted normal hotel service for nearly two hours. The cause of the explosion is believed to have been a successful suicide attempt.

"No body was recovered from the demolished booth, but witnesses recalled having seen a tall man in street clothes entering the booth moments before the explosion. A check of the hotel registry revealed that no residents were missing. Valloin police indicate they will investigate."

The robot voice paused and said, "That's all there is. Do you wish a permanent copy? Should we search the files for subsequent information pertinent to the matter?"

"No," Ewing said. "No, no thanks." He severed the contact and sat down heavily on the edge of the bed.

It could still be a prank, of course. He had been asleep several days, long enough for the prankster to hear about the explosion and incorporate the incident retroactively in the note. But Occam's Razor made hash of the hoax theory; there were too many inexplicable circumstances and unmotivated actions involved. Assuming that a prior Ewing had doubled in time to carry out the rescue and leave the note was a vastly simpler hypothesis, granting the one major improbability of time-travel.

There would be one fairly definite proof, though. Ewing found a small blue stun-gun lying on his dresser, and studied it thoughtfully.

According to the note, Scholar Myreck would call him soon after he had awakened.

Very well, Ewing thought, *I'll wait for Myreck to call.*

An hour later he was sitting in a relaxing lounger in a salon in the College of Abstract Science, feeling the pain of Firnik's torture leaving him under the ministrations of Myreck's expert fingers. Music welled around him, fascinating ancient music—Beethoven, Myreck had said. He sipped at his drink.

It was all quite incredible to him: the call from Myreck, the trip across Valloin in the domed car, the miraculous building three microseconds out of phase with the rest of the city, and above all the fact that the note in his room was indubitably true. These Earthers had the secret of time travel, and, though none of them were aware of the fact, they had already sent Baird Ewing back through time at least once from a point along the time-stream that still lay ahead, this afternoon of Fourday.

He realized his responsibility, tremendous already, was even greater now. A man had given up his life for him, and though no actual life had ended; it seemed to Ewing that a part of him he had never known had died. Once again he was sole master of his fate.

The conversation moved smoothly along. The Earthers, alert, curious little men, wanted to know about the Klodni menace, and whether the people of Corwin would be able to defeat them when the attack came. Ewing told them the truth: that they would try, but there was not much hope of success.

And then Myreck introduced a new theme: the possibility of arranging transportation for the members of the College to Corwin, where at least they would be safer than on an Earth dominated by Sirius IV

It seemed a doubtful proposition to Ewing. He explained to the visibly disappointed Earthers what a vast enterprise it would be to transport them, and how few ships Corwin had available for the purpose. He touched on the necessary delays the negotiations would involve.

He saw the hurt looks on their faces; there was no help for it, he thought. Corwin faced destruction; Earth, mere occupation. Corwin needed help more urgently. From which direction, he wondered? From whom?

"I'm sorry," he said. "I just don't see how we can offer you asylum. But it seems to me that you would be in an even worse position on Corwin than you will be here under Sirian rule. The Klodni onslaught will be fierce and destructive; the Sirians will probably keep things much as they are, except you'll pay your taxes to them instead of to Mellis' government."

He felt a depressing cloud of futility settle around him. He had accomplished nothing on Earth, found no possible solution for Corwin's problem, not even succeeded in helping these Earthers. They were caught under the heel of Sirius IV, while Corwin now would have to wait for the coming of the Klodni and the inevitable accompanying murderous conquest.

He had failed. Whatever bold plan had been in the mind of the dead Ewing who had left him the note did not hold a corresponding position in his own mind. Clearly, that Ewing had seen some solution for Corwin, some way in which the planet could be defended against the Klodni. But he had said nothing about it in his note.

Perhaps he had had some experience while traveling back in time, something that might have given him a clue to the resolution of the dilemma . . .

Ewing felt a tempting thought: *Perhaps I should make the trip back in time once again, rescue the Ewing I find there, dictate the note to him once again, and add to it whatever information was missing—*

No. He squelched the idea firmly and totally. Another trip through time was out of the question. He had a chance to end the cycle now, and cut himself loose from Earth. It was the sensible thing to do. Return to Corwin, prepare for the attack, defend his home and country when the time came to do so— that was the only intelligent course of action now. It was futile to continue to search Earth for a nonexistent super-weapon.

Better leave Earth to her sad fate, he thought, *and go back to Corwin.*

The conversation straggled to a dull stop. He and the Earthers had little left to say to each other. Each had appealed to the other for help, and neither was in a position to offer aid.

Myreck said, "Let us change the subject, shall we? This talk of fleeing and destruction depresses me."

"I agree," Ewing said.

The music disk ended. Myreck rose, removed it from the player and popped it back into the file. He said, "We have a fine collection of other Earth ancients. Mozart, Bach, Vurris—"

"I'm afraid I've never heard of any of them," Ewing said. "We only have a few surviving disks of the early Terrestrial composers on Corwin. I've heard them all in the museum." He frowned, trying to remember their names. "Schoenberg . . . and Stravinsky, I think. And Bartok. They belonged to one of the original colonists."

Myreck played Bach—a piece called the Goldberg Variations, for a twangy, not unpleasant-sounding instrument called the harpischord. As he explained it, it operated as a sort of primitive sonomar, the tones being produced by the mechanical plucking of strings.

Several of the Scholars were particularly interested in music old and new, and insisted on expounding their special theories. Ewing, at another time, might have been an eager participant in their discussion; now, he listened out of politeness only, paying little attention to what was said. He was trying to recall the text of the note he had read and destroyed earlier in the day. They would show him their time machine. He was to refuse the demonstration. That would cause the necessary alterations in time past, to fit the design intended by Ewing-sub-one.

Whatever *that* had been, Ewing thought.

The afternoon slipped by. At length Myreck said, "We also have done much work in temporal theory, you know. Our machines are in the lower levels of the building. If you are interested—"

"No!" Ewing said, so suddenly and so harshly it was almost a shout. In a more modulated tone he went on, "I mean—no, thanks. I'll have to beg off on that. It's getting quite late, and I'm sure I'd find the time machines so fascinating I'd overstay my visit."

"But we are anxious to have you spend as much time with us as you can," Myreck protested. "If you want to see the machines—"

"No," Ewing repeated forcefully. "I'm afraid I must leave."

"In that case, we will drive you to your hotel."

This must be the point of divergence, Ewing thought as the Earthers showed him to the door and performed the operations that made it possible to pass back into phase with the world of Fournight the Thirteenth outside. *My predecessor never got back out of this building. He doubled into Twonight instead. The cycle is broken.*

He entered the car, and it pulled away from the street. He looked back, at the empty lot that was not empty.

"Some day you must examine our machines," Myreck said.

"Yes . . . yes, of course," Ewing replied vaguely. "As soon as I've taken care of a few pressing matters."

But tomorrow I'll be on my way back to Corwin, he thought. *I guess I never will see your machines.*

He realized that by his actions this afternoon he had brought a new chain of events into existence; he had reached back into Twoday and, by *not* rescuing Firnik's prisoner, had created a Ewing-sub-three who had been mind-picked by the Sirian and who presumably had died two days before. Thus Firnik believed Ewing was dead, no doubt. He would be surprised tomorrow when a ghost requisitioned the ship in storage at Valloin Spaceport and blasted off for Corwin.

Ewing frowned, trying to work out the intricacies of the problem. Well, it didn't matter, he thought. The step had been taken.

For better or for worse, the time-track had been altered.

Chapter Thirteen

E wing checked out of the Grand Valloin Hotel that next afternoon. It was a lucky thing, he thought, that the management had awarded him that week's free rent; otherwise, thanks to the kidnaping, he would never have been able to settle up. He had only ten credits, and those were gifts from his phantom rescuer, now dead. The bill came to more than a hundred.

The desk-robot was distantly polite as Ewing signed the forms severing him from relationship with the hotel, waiving right to sue for neglected property, and announcing notification of departure from Valloin. "I hope you have enjoyed your stay in this hotel," the robot said in blurred mechanical tones as Ewing finished.

Ewing eyed the metal creature jaundicedly and said, "Oh, yes. Very much. Very much indeed." He shoved the stack of papers across the marbled desktop and accepted his receipted bill. "You'll have my baggage delivered to the spaceport?" he asked.

"Of course, sir. The voucher guarantees it."

"Thanks," Ewing said.

He strolled through the sumptuous lobby, past the light-fountain, past the relaxing-chairs, past the somewhat battered area of the energitron booth, where robots were busily replastering and repainting the damage. It was nearly as good as new. By the end of the day, there would scarcely be an indication that a man had died violently there only three days before.

He passed several Sirians on his way through the lobby to the front street, but he felt oddly calm all the same. So far as Rollun Firnik and the others were concerned, the Corwinite Baird Ewing had died under torture last Twoday. Anyone resembling him resembled him strictly by coincidence. He walked boldly through the cluster of Sirians and out onto the street level.

It was late afternoon. The street-glow was beginning to come up. A bulletin transmitted via telestat had informed the hotel patrons that eighteen minutes of light rain was scheduled for 1400 that Fiveday, and Ewing had delayed his departure accordingly. Now the streets were fresh and sweet-smelling.

Ewing boarded the limousine that the hotel used for transporting its patrons to and from the nearby spaceport, and looked around for his final glance at the Grand Valloin Hotel. He felt tired and a little sad at leaving Earth; there were so many reminders of past glories here, so many signs of present decay. It had been an eventful day for him, but yet curiously eventless; he was returning to Corwin with nothing concrete gained, nothing learned but the fact that there was no help to be had.

He pondered the time-travel question for a moment. Obviously the Earther machine—along with other paradoxical qualities—was able to create matter where none had existed before. It had drawn from *somewhere* the various Ewing bodies, of which at least two and possibly more had existed simultaneously. And it seemed that once a new body was drawn from the fabric of time, it remained in existence, conterminous with his fellows. Otherwise, Ewing thought, my refusal to go back and carry out the rescue would have snuffed me out. It didn't. It merely ended the life of that "Ewing" in the torture-chamber on Twoday.

"Spaceport," a robot voice announced.

Ewing followed the line into the Departures shed. He noticed there were few Earthers in Departures; only some Sirians and a few non-humanoid aliens were leaving Earth. He joined a line that inched up slowly to a robot clerk.

When it was Ewing's turn, he presented his papers. The robot scanned them quickly.

"You are Baird Ewing of the Free World of Corwin?"

"That's right."

"You arrived on Earth on Fiveday, seventh of Fifthmonth of this year?"

Ewing nodded.

"Your papers are in order. Your ship has been stored in Hangar 107-B. Sign this, please."

It was a permission-grant allowing the spaceport attendants to get his ship from drydock, service it for departure, store his belongings on board, and place the vessel on the blasting field. Ewing read the form through quickly, signed it, and handed it back.

"Please go to Waiting Room Y and remain there until your name is called. Your ship should be ready for you in less than an hour."

Ewing moistened his lips. "Does that mean you'll page me over the public address system?"

"Yes."

The idea of having his name called out, with so many Sirians in the spaceport, did not appeal to him. He said, "I'd prefer not to be paged by name. Can some sort of code word be used?"

The robot hesitated. "Is there some reason—"

"Yes." Ewing's tone was flat. "Suppose you have me paged under the name of . . . ah . . . Blade. That's it. Mr. Blade. All right?"

Doubtfully the robot said, "It's irregular."

"Is there anything in the regulations specifically prohibiting such a pseudonym?"

"No, but—"

"If regulations say nothing about it, how can it be irregular? Blade it is, then."

It was easy to baffle robots. The sleek metal face would probably be contorted in bewilderment, if that were possible. At length the robot assented; Ewing grinned cheerfully at it and made his way to Waiting Room Y.

Waiting Room Y was a majestic vault of a room, with a glittering spangled ceiling a hundred feet above his head, veined with glowing rafters of structural beryllium. Freeform blobs of light, hovering suspended at about the eight-foot level, provided most of the illumination. At one end of the room a vast loud-speaker had been erected; at the other, a screen thirty feet high provided changing kaleidoscopic patterns of light for bored waiters.

Ewing stared without interest at the whirling light-patterns for a while. He had found a seat in the corner of the waiting room, where he was not likely to be noticed. There was hardly an Earther in the place. Earthers stayed put, on Earth. And this great spaceport, this monument to an era a thousand years dead, was in use solely for the benefit of tourists from Sirius IV and the alien worlds.

A bubble-headed creature with scaly purple skin passed by, each of its claw-like arms clutching a smaller version of itself. *Mr. XXX from Xfiz V,* Ewing thought bitterly. *Returning from a family outing. He's taken the kiddies to Earth to give them an instructive view of dying civilization.*

The three aliens paused not far from where Ewing sat and exchanged foamy, sibilant sentences. *Now he's telling them to take a good look round,* Ewing thought. *None of this may be here the next time they come.*

For a moment despair overwhelmed him, as he realized once again that both Earth and Corwin were doomed, and there seemed no way of holding back the inexorable jaws of the pincer. His head drooped forward; he cradled it tiredly with his fingertips.

"Mr. Blade to the departure desk, please. Mr. Blade, please report to the departure desk. Mr. Blade . . ."

Dimly, Ewing remembered that they were paging *him.* He elbowed himself from the seat.

"Mr. Blade to the departure desk, please . . ."

"All right," he murmured. "I'm coming."

He followed a stream of bright violet lights down the center of the waiting room, turned left, and headed for the departure desk. Just as he reached it, the loud-speaker barked once more, *"Mr. Blade to the departure desk . . ."*

"I'm Blade," he said to the robot he had spoken with an hour before. He presented his identity card. The robot scanned it.

"According to this your name is Baird Ewing," the robot announced after some study.

Ewing sighed in exasperation. "Check your memory banks! Sure, my name is Ewing—but I arranged to have you page me under the name of Blade. Remember?"

The robot's optic lenses swiveled agitatedly as the mechanical filtered back through its memory bank. Ewing waited impatiently, fidgeting and shifting his weight from foot to foot. After what seemed to be a fifteen-minute wait the robot brightened again and declared, "The statement is correct. You are Baird Ewing, pseudonym Blade. Your ship is waiting in Blast Area Eleven."

Gratefully, Ewing accepted the glowing identity planchet and made his way through the areaway into the departure track. There he surrendered the planchet to a waiting robot attendant who ferried him across the broad field to his ship.

It stood alone, isolated by the required hundred-meter clearance, a slim, graceful needle, golden-green, still bright in the late-afternoon sunlight. He climbed up the catwalk, sprang the hatch, and entered.

The ship smelled faintly musty after its week in storage. Ewing looked around. Everything seemed in order: the somnotank in which he would sleep during the eleven-month journey back to Corwin, the radio equipment along the opposite wall, the vision-plate. He spun the dial on the storage compartment and opened it. His few belongings were aboard. He was ready to leave.

But first, a message.

He set up the contacts on the subetheric generator, preparatory to beaming a message via subspace toward Corwin. He knew that his earlier message, announcing arrival, had not yet arrived; it would ride the subetheric carrier wave for another week yet, before reaching the receptors on his home world.

And, he thought unhappily, the second message, announcing departure, would follow it by only a few days. He twisted the contact dial. The *go-ahead* light came on.

He faced the pickup grid. "Baird Ewing speaking, and I'll be brief. This is my second and final message. I'm returning to Corwin. The mission was an absolute failure—repeat, *absolute failure*. Earth is unable to help us. It faces immediate domination by Terrestrial-descended inhabitants of Sirius IV, and culturally they're in worse shape than we are. Sorry to be delivering bad news. I hope you're all still there when I get back. No reports will follow. I'm signing off right now."

He stared reflectively at the dying lights of the generator a moment, then shook his head and rose. Activating the in-system communicator, he requested and got the central coordination tower of the spaceport.

"This is Baird Ewing, in the one-man ship on Blasting Area Eleven. I plan to depart under automatic control in fifteen minutes. Can I have a time check?"

The inevitable robotic voice replied, "The time now is sixteen fifty-eight and thirteen seconds."

"Good. Can I have clearance for departure at seventeen thirteen and thirteen?"

"Clearance granted," the robot said, after a brief pause.

Grunting acknowledgment, Ewing fed the data to his autopilot and threw the master switch. In fourteen-plus minutes, the ship would blast off from Earth, whether or not he happened to be in the protective tank at the time. But there was no rush; it would take only a moment or two to enter the freeze.

He stripped off his clothes, stored them away, and activated the tap that drew the nutrient bath. The autopilot ticked away; eleven minutes to departure.

So long, Earth.

He climbed into the tank. Now his subliminal instructions took over; he knew the procedure thoroughly. All he had to do was nudge those levers with his feet to enter the state of suspension; needles would jab upward into him and the thermostat would begin to function. At the end of the journey, with the ship in orbit around Corwin, he would automatically be awakened to make the landing manually.

The communicator chimed just as he was about to trip the footlevers. Irritated, Ewing glanced up. What could be the trouble?

"Calling Baird Ewing . . . Calling Baird Ewing . . ."

It was central control. Ewing glanced at the clock. Eight minutes to blast off. And there'd be nothing left of him but a pool of jelly if blasting time caught him still wandering around the ship.

Sourly he climbed from the tank and acknowledged the call. "Ewing here. What is it?"

"An urgent call from the terminal, Mr. Ewing. The party says he must reach you before you blast off."

Ewing considered that. Firnik, pursuing him? Or Byra Clork? No. They had seen him die on Twoday. Myreck? Maybe. Who else could it be? He said, "Very well. Switch over the call."

A new voice said, "Ewing?"

"That's right. Who are you?"

"It doesn't matter just now. Listen—can you come to the spaceport terminal right away?"

The voice sounded tantalizing familiar. Ewing scowled angrily. "No. I can't! My autopilot's on and I'm due for blasting in seven minutes. If you can't tell me who you are, I'm afraid I can't bother to alter flight plans."

Ewing heard a sigh. *"I could tell you who I am. You wouldn't believe me, that's all. But you mustn't depart yet. Come to the terminal."*

"No."

"I warn you," the voice said. "I can take steps to prevent you from blasting off—but it'll be damaging to both of us if I do so. Can't you trust me?"

"I'm not leaving this ship on account of any anonymous warnings," Ewing said hotly. "Tell me who you are. Otherwise I'm going to break contact and enter suspension."

Six minutes to blast.

"All right," came the reluctant reply. "I'll tell you. My name is Baird Ewing, of Corwin. I'm *you*. Now will you get out of that ship?"

Chapter Fourteen

With tense fingers Ewing disconnected the autopilot and reversed the suspension unit. He called the control tower and in an unsteady voice told them he was temporarily canceling his blasting plans and was returning to the terminal. He dressed again, and was ready when the robocar came shuttling out across the field to pick him up.

He had arranged to meet the other Ewing in the refreshment room where he had had his first meeting with Rollun Firnik after landing on Earth. A soft conversational hum droned in the background as Ewing entered. His eyes, as if magnetically drawn, fastened on the tall, conservatively-dressed figure at the table near the rear.

He walked over and sat down, without being asked. The man at the table favored him with a smile—cold, precise, the very sort of smile Ewing himself would have used in this situation. Ewing moistened his lips. He felt dizzy.

He said, "I don't know quite where to begin. Who are you?"

"I told you. Yourself. I'm Baird Ewing."

The accent, the tone, the sardonic smile—they all fitted. Ewing felt the room swirl crazily around him. He stared levelly at the mirror image on the other side of the table.

"I thought you were dead," Ewing said. "The note you left me—"

"I didn't leave any notes," the other interrupted immediately.

"Hold on there." It was a conversation taking place in a world of nightmare. Ewing felt as if he were stifling. "You rescued me from Firnik, didn't you?"

The other nodded.

"And you took me to the hotel, put me to bed, and wrote me a note explaining things; you finished off by saying you were going downstairs to blow yourself up in an energitron booth—"

Eyes wide in surprise, the other said, "No, not at all! I took you to the hotel and left. I didn't write any notes, or threaten to commit suicide."

"You didn't leave me money? Or a blaster?"

The man across the table shook his head vehemently. Ewing closed his eyes for a moment. "If you didn't leave me that note, *who did*?"

"Tell me about this note," the other said.

Briefly Ewing summarized the contents of the note as well as he could from memory. The other listened, tapping his finger against the table as each point was made. When Ewing was through, the other remained deep in thought, brow furrowed. Finally he said:

"I see it. There were four of us."

"What?"

"I'll put it slowly: I'm the first one of us to go through all this. It begins with a closed-circle paradox, the way any time distortion would have to: me, in the torture chamber, and a future me coming back to rescue me. There were four separate splits in the continuum—creating a Ewing who died in Firnik's torture chamber, a Ewing who rescued the tortured Ewing and left a note and committed suicide, a Ewing who rescued the tortured Ewing and did *not* commit suicide, and a Ewing who was rescued and did not himself go back to become the rescuer, thereby breaking the chain. Two of these are still alive— the third and the fourth. You and me."

Very quietly Ewing said, "I guess that makes sense, in an impossible sort of way. But that leaves an extra Baird Ewing, doesn't it? After you carried out the rescue, why did you decide to stay alive?"

The other shrugged. "I couldn't risk killing myself. I didn't know what would happen."

"You did," Ewing said accusingly. "You knew that the next man in sequence would stay alive. You could have left him a note, but you didn't. So he went through the chain, left *me* a note, and removed himself."

The other scowled unhappily. "Perhaps he represented a braver facet of us than I do."

"How could that be? We're all the same?"

"True." The other smiled sadly. "But a human being is made of complex stuff. Life isn't a procession of clear-cut events; it's a progression from one tough decision to the next. The seeds of my decision were in the proto-Ewing; so were the bases for the suicide. I picked things one way; *he* picked them the other. And I'm here."

Ewing realized it was impossible to be angry. The man he faced was himself, and he knew only too well the bundle of inner contradictions, of strengths and weaknesses, that was Baird Ewing—or any human being. This was no time to condemn. But he foresaw grave problems arising.

He said, "What do we do now—*both of us*?"

"There was a reason why I called you off the ship. And it wasn't simply that I didn't want to be left behind on Earth."

"What was it, then?"

"The time machine Myreck has can save Corwin from the Klodni," the other Ewing said flatly.

Ewing sat back and let that soak in. "How?"

"I went to see Myreck this morning and he greeted me with open arms. Said he was so glad I had come back for a look at the time machine. That was when I realized you'd been there yesterday and hadn't gone back on the merry-go-round." He shook his head. "I was counting on that, you see—on being the only Ewing that actually went forward on the time-track, while all the others went round and round between Fourday and Twoday, chasing themselves. But you broke the sequence and fouled things up."

"*You* fouled things up," Ewing snapped. "You aren't supposed to be alive."

"And you aren't supposed to be existing in Fiveday.

"This isn't helping things," Ewing said more calmly. "You say the Earther time machine can save Corwin. How?"

"I was getting to that. This morning Myreck showed me all the applications of the machine. It can be converted into an exterior-operating scanner—a beam that can be used to hurl objects of any size backward into time."

"The Klodni fleet," Ewing said instantly.

"Exactly! We set up the projector on Corwin and wait for the Klodni to arrive—and shoot them back five billion years or so, with no return-trip ticket!"

Ewing smiled. "And I was running away. I was on my way home, while you were finding all this out."

The other shrugged. "You had no reason to suspect it. You never had a first-hand demonstration of the way the time machine functioned. I did—and I guessed this might be possible. You guessed so, too."

"Me?"

"Right after Myreck told you he had temporal control, the thought came to you that something like this might be worked out. But you forgot about it. I didn't."

It was eerie, Ewing thought, to sit across a table from a man who knew every thought of his, every secret deed, from childhood up to a point three days ago in Absolute Time. After that, of course, their lives diverged as if they were different people.

"What do you suggest we do now?" Ewing asked.

"Go back to Myreck. Team up to get the plans for the device away from him. Then high-tail it back here, get aboard . . ."

His voice trailed off. Ewing stared blankly at his alter ego and said, "Yes? What then? I'm waiting."

"It's—it's a one-man ship isn't it?" the other asked in a thin voice.

"Yes," Ewing said. "Damned right it is. After we've taken the plans, how do we decide who goes back to Corwin and who stays here?"

He knew the other's anguished frown was mirrored by his own. He felt sick, and knew the other sensed the same unease. He felt the frustration of a man staring into a mirror, trying desperately to make some maneuver that would not be imitated by the imprisoned image.

"We'll worry about that later," said the other Ewing uncertainly. "First let's get the plans from Myreck. Time to settle other problems later."

They took a robot-operated cab to the surburban district where the College of Abstract Science was located. On the way, Ewing turned to the other and said, "How did you know I was on my way home?"

"I didn't. As soon as I found out from Myreck both that you existed and that his machine could help Corwin, I got back to the Grand Valloin. I went straight up to your room, but the identity plate didn't work—and that door was geared to my identity just as much as yours. So I went downstairs, phoned the desk from the lobby, and asked for you. They told me you had checked out and were on your way to the spaceport. So I followed—and got there just in time."

"And suppose I had refused to come out of the ship and meet you?" Ewing asked.

"There would have been a mess. I would have insisted I was Ewing and you were stealing my ship—which would be true, in a way—and would have demanded they check me against their records of Ewing. They would have found out *I* was Ewing, of course, and they would have wondered who the deuce *you* were. There would have been an investigation, and you would have been grounded, But either way it would have been risky—either if they had discovered there actually was an extra Ewing, or if you had ignored the grounding orders and blasted off. They'd have sent an interceptor after you and we'd really be in trouble."

The cab pulled up near the empty lot that was the College of Abstract Science. Ewing let his alternate pay the bill. They got out.

"You wait here," the other said. "I'll put myself within their receptor field and wait for them to let me in. You wait ten minutes and follow me through."

"I don't have a watch," Ewing said. "Firnik took it.

"Here—take mine," said the other impatiently. He unstrapped it and handed it over. It looked costly.

"Where'd you get this?" Ewing said.

"I borrowed it from some Earther, along with about five hundred credits, early Threeday morning. You—no, not you, but the Ewing who became your rescuer later—was asleep in our hotel room, so I had to find another place to stay. And all I had was about ten credits left over after buying the mask and the gun."

The ten credits someone left for me, Ewing thought. The paradoxes multiplied. The best he could do was ignore them.

He donned the watch—the time was 1850, Fivenight—and watched his companion stroll down the street toward the empty lot, wander with seeming aimlessness over the vacant area, and suddenly vanish. The College of Abstract Sciences had swallowed him up.

Ewing waited for the minutes to pass. They crept by. Five . . . six . . . seven.

At eight, he began to stroll with what he hoped looked like complete casualness toward the empty lot. At nine he was only a few yards away from the borders of the lot. He forced himself to remain quite still, letting the final minute pass. The stun-gun was at his hip. He had noticed that the other Ewing also wore a stun-gun—the twin of his own.

At nine minutes and forty-five seconds he resumed his stroll toward the lot, reaching it exactly at the ten-minute mark. He looked around the way the other Ewing had—and felt the transition from *now-minus-three-microseconds* sweep over him once again. He was inside the College of Abstract Science, having vanished abruptly from the tardy world outside.

He was facing an odd tableau. The other Ewing stood with his back to one wall, the stun-gun drawn and in activated position. Facing him were seven or eight members of the College, their faces pale, their eyes reflecting fright. They stood as if at bay.

Ewing found himself looking down at the accusing eyes of Scholar Myreck, who had admitted him.

"Thank you for letting my—ah—brother in," the other Ewing said. For a moment the two Ewings stared at each other. Ewing saw in his alter ego's eyes deep guilt, and knew that the other man was more than a twin to him than any brother could have been. The kinship was soul-deep.

"We're sorry for this," he said to Myreck. "Believe us, it pains us to do this to you."

"I've already explained what we came for," the other Ewing said. "There's a scale model and a full set of schematics downstairs, plus a few notebooks of theoretical work. It's more than one man can carry."

"The notebooks are irreplaceable," Myreck said in a softly bitter voice.

"We'll take good care of them," Ewing promised. "But we need them more than you. Believe us."

The other Ewing said, "You stay here, and keep your gun on them. I'm going below with Myreck to fetch the things we're taking."

Ewing nodded. Drawing his gun, he replaced the other against the wall, holding the unfortunate Earthers at bay. It was nearly five minutes before Ewing's alternate and Myreck returned, bearing papers, notebooks, and a model that looked to weigh about fifty pounds.

"It's all here," the other said. "Myreck, you're going to let me through your time-phase field and out of the building. My brother here will keep his gun on you all the time. Please don't try to trick us."

Ten minutes later, both Ewings stood outside the College of Abstract Science, with a nearly man-high stack of plunder between them.

"I hated to do that," Ewing said.

The other nodded. "It hurt me, too. They're so gentle—and it's a miserable way to repay hospitality. But we need that generator, if we want to save everything we hold dear."

"Yes," Ewing said in a strained voice. "Everything *we* hold dear." He shook his head. Trouble was approaching. "Come on," he said, looking back at the vacant lot. "Let's get out of here. We have to load all this stuff on the ship."

Chapter Fifteen

They made the trip back to the spaceport in tight silence. Each man had kept a hand atop the teetering stack on the floor of the cab; occasionally, Ewing's eyes met those of his double, and glanced guiltily away.

Which one of us goes back? he wondered.

Which one is really Baird Ewing? And what becomes of the other?

At the spaceport, Ewing requisitioned a porter-robot and turned the stolen schematics, notes, and model over to it, to be placed aboard the ship. That done, the two men looked strangely at each other. The time had come for departure. Who left?

Ewing scratched his chin uneasily and said, "One of us has to go up to the departure desk and reconfirm his blastoff plans. The other—"

"Yes. I know."

"How do we decide? Do we flip a coin?" Ewing wanted to know.

"One of us goes back to Laira and Blade. And it looks as if the other—"

There was no need to say it. The dilemma was insoluble. Each Ewing had firmly believed he was the only one still in the time-track, and each still partially believed that it was the other's duty to yield.

The spaceport lights flickered dizzily. Ewing felt dryness grow in his throat. The time for decision was now. But how to decide?

"Let's go get a drink," he suggested.

The entrance to the refreshment booth was congested with a mob of evening travelers hoping to get a last drink down before blasting off. Ewing ordered drinks for both of them and they toasted grimly: "To Baird Ewing—whichever he may be."

Ewing drank, but the drink did not soothe him. It seemed at that moment, that the impasse might last forever, that they would remain on Earth eternally while determining which one of them was to return with Corwin's salvation and which to remain behind. But an instant later, all that was changed.

The public address system blared: *"Attention, please! Your attention! Will everyone kindly remain precisely where he is right at this moment!"*

Ewing exchanged a troubled glance with his counterpart. The loud-speaker voice continued. *"There is no cause for alarm. It is believed that a dangerous criminal is at large somewhere in the spaceport area. He may be armed. He is six feet two inches in height, with reddish-brown hair, dark eyes, and out-of-fashion clothing. Please remain precisely where you are at this moment while peace officers circulate among you. Have your identification papers ready to be examined on request. That is all."*

A burst of conversation greeted the announcement. The two Ewings huddled each into the corner of the room and stared in anguish at each other.

"Someone turned us in," Ewing said. "Myreck, perhaps. Or the man you burgled. Probably Myreck. "

"It doesn't matter who turned us, in," the other snapped. "All that matters is the fact that they'll be coming around to investigate soon. And when they find *two* men answering to the description—"

"Myreck must have warned them there were two of us."

"No. He'd never do that. He doesn't want to give away the method that brought both of us into existence, does he?"

Ewing nodded. "I guess you're right. But if they find two of us with the same identity papers—with the same identity—they'll pull us both in. And neither of us will ever get back to Corwin."

"Suppose they only found one of us?" the other asked.

"How? We can't circulate around the spaceport. And there's no place to hide in here."

"I don't mean that. Suppose one of us voluntarily gave himself up—destroyed his identity papers first, of course, and then made an attempt to escape? In the confusion, the other of us could safely blast off for Corwin."

Ewing's eyes narrowed. He had been formulating just such a plan, too. "But which one of us gives himself up? We're back to the same old problem."

"No, we're not," the other said. "I'll volunteer!

"No," Ewing said instantly. "You can't just volunteer! How could I agree? It's suicide." He shook his head. "We don't have time to argue about it now. There's only one way to decide."

He fumbled in his pocket and pulled forth a shining half-credit piece. He studied it. On one side was engraved a representation of Earth's sun, with the nine planets orbiting it; on the other, an ornamental 50.

"I'm going to flip it," he said. "Solar system, you go; denomination, I go. Agreed?"

"Agreed," said the other tensely.

Ewing mounted the coin on his thumbnail and flicked it upward. He snapped it out of the air with a rapid gesture and slapped it down against the back of his left hand. He lifted the covering hand.

It was denomination. The stylized 50 stared up at him.

He smiled humorlessly. "I guess it's me," he said. He pulled his identity papers from his pocket and—ripped them into shreds. Then he stared across the table at the white, drawn face of the man who was to become Baird Ewing. "So long. Good luck. And kiss Laira for me when you get back . . ."

Four Sirian policemen entered the bar and began to filter through the group. One remained stationed near the door; the other three circulated. Ewing rose from his seat; he felt calm now. It was not as if he were really going to die. *Which is the real me, anyway? The man who died in the torture chamber, or the one who blew himself up in the energitron booth, or the man sitting back there in the corner of the bar? They're all Baird Ewing. There's a continuity of personality. Baird Ewing won't die—just one of his superfluous Doppelgangers. And it has to be this way.*

Icily, Ewing made his way through the startled group sitting at the tables. He was the only figure moving in the bar except for the three circulating police officers who did not appear to have noticed him yet. He did not look back.

The stun-gun at his hip was only inches from his hand. He jerked it up suddenly and fired at the policeman mounted by the door; the man froze and toppled. The other three policemen whirled.

Ewing heard one of them, "Who are you? What are you doing there? Stand still!"

"I'm the man you're looking for," Ewing shouted, in a voice that could have been heard for hundreds of yards. "If you want me, come get me!"

He turned and sprinted out of the refreshment room into the long arcade.

He heard the sound of pursuers almost immediately. He clutched the stun-gun tightly, but did not fire. An energy flare splashed above his head, crumbling a section of the wall. He heard a yell from behind him: "Stop him! There's the man! Stop him!"

As if summoned magically, five policemen appeared at the upper end of the corridor. Ewing thumbed his stunner and froze two of them; then he cut briskly to the left, passing through an automatic door and entering onto the restricted area of the spacefield itself.

A robot came gliding up to him. "May I see your pass, sir? Humans are not allowed on this portion of the field without a pass."

In answer, Ewing tilted the stun-gun up and calcified the robot's neural channels. It crashed heavily as its gyrocontrol destablized. He turned. The police were converging on him; there were dozens of them.

"You there! Give yourself up! You can't hope to escape!"

I know that, Ewing said silently. *But I don't want to be taken alive, either.*

He wedged himself flat against a parked fueler and peppered the advancing police with stun-gun beams. They fired cautiously; there was expensive equipment on the field, and they preferred to take their man alive in any event. Ewing waited until the nearest of them was within fifty yards.

"Come get me," he called. Turning, he began to run across the broad spacefield.

The landing apron extended for two or three miles; he ran easily, lightly, sweeping in broad circles and pausing to fire at his pursuers. He wanted to keep them at reasonable distance until—

Yes. Now.

Darkness covered the field. Ewing glanced up to see the cause of this sudden eclipse.

A vast ship hung high overhead, descending as if operated by a pulley and string. Its jets were thundering, pouring forth flaming gas as it came down for a landing. Ewing smiled at the sight.

It'll be quick, he thought.

He heard the yells of astonishment from the police. They were backing off as the great ship dropped toward the landing area. Ewing ran in a wider circle, trying to compute the orbit of the descending liner.

Like falling into the sun. Hot. Quick.

He saw the place where the ship would land. He felt the sudden warmth; he was in the danger zone now. He ran inward, where the air was frying. *For Corwin,* he thought. *For Laira. And Blade.*

"The idiot! He'll get killed!" someone screamed as if from a great distance. Eddies of flaming gas seemed to wash down over him; he heard the booming roar of the ship. Then brightness exploded all about him, and consciousness and pain departed in a microsecond.

The ship touched down.

I n the terminal, the public address system blared: *"Attention, please. We thank you very much for your cooperation. The criminal has been discovered and is no longer menacing society. You may resume normal activity. We thank you again for your cooperation during this investigation, and hope you have undergone no inconvenience."*

In the terminal refreshment room, Ewing stared bleakly at the two half-finished drinks on the table—his, and the dead man's. With a sudden, brusque gesture he poured the other drink into his glass, stirred the two together, and drank the glassful down in eager gulps. He felt the stinging liquor jolt into his stomach.

What are you supposed to say and think and do, he wondered, *when a man gives up his life so you can get away? Nothing. You can't even say "Thanks. " It wouldn't be in good taste, would it?*

He had watched the whole thing from the observation window of the bar. The desperate pursuit, the fox-and-hounds chase, the exchange of shots. He had become sickly aware that a liner was overhead, fixed in its landing orbit, unable to check its fall whether there was one man or a regiment drilling on the field.

Even through the window's protective glass, the sudden glare had stung his retinas. And throughout his life he would carry with him the image of a tiny man-shaped dot standing unafraid in the bright path of the liner, vanishing suddenly in a torrent of flame.

He rose. He felt very tired, very weary, not at all like a man free at last to return to his home, his wife, his child. His mission was approaching to a successful conclusion, but he felt no sense of satisfaction. Too many had given up life or dreams to make his success possible.

He found the departure desk somehow, and pulled forth the papers that the dead man who was himself had filled out earlier in the day. "My ship's on

Blasting Area Eleven," he told the robot. "I was originally scheduled to leave about 1700 this evening, but I requested cancellation and rescheduling."

He waited numbly while the robot went through the proper procedures, gave him new papers to fill out, and finally sent him on through the areaway to the departure track. Another robot met him there and conducted him to the ship.

His ship. Which might have left for Corwin five hours before, with a different pilot.

Ewing shrugged and tried to brush away the cloud of gloom. Had the ship left earlier, with the other Ewing aboard, it would have been to conclude an unsuccessful mission; the delay of five hours made an infinite difference in the general effect.

And it was foolishness to talk of a man dead. Who had died? Baird Ewing? I'm still alive, he thought. So who died?

He entered the ship and glanced around. Everything was ready for departure. He frowned; the other Ewing had said something about having sent a message back to Corwin presumably telling them he was on his way back empty-handed. He activated the subetheric communicator and beamed a new message, advising them to disregard the one immediately preceding it, saying that a new development had come up and he was on his way back to Corwin with possible salvation.

He called the central control tower and requested blast-off permission twelve minutes hence. That gave him ample time. He switched on the autopilot, stripped, and lowered himself into the nutrient bath.

With quick foot-motions he set in motion the suspension mechanism. Needles jabbed at his flesh; the temperature began its downward climb. A thin stream of web came from the spinnerettes above him, wrapping him in unbreakable foam that would protect him from the hazards of high-acceleration blast-off.

The drugs dulled his mind. He felt a faint chill as the temperature about him dropped below sixty. It would drop much lower than that, later, when he was asleep. He waited drowsily for sleep to overtake him.

He was only fractionally conscious when blast-off came. He barely realized that the ship had left Earth. Before acceleration ended, he was totally asleep.

Chapter Sixteen

Hours ticked by, and Ewing slept. Hours lengthened into days, into weeks, into months. Eleven months, twelve days, seven and one half hours, and Ewing slept while the tiny ship speared along on its return journey.

The time came. The ship pirouetted out of warp when the pre-set detectors indicated the journey had ended. Automatic computer units hurled the ship into fixed orbit round the planet below. The suspension unit deactivated itself; temperature gradually returned to normal, and a needle plunged into Ewing's side, awakening him.

He was home.

After the immediate effects of the long sleep had worn off, Ewing made contact with the authorities below. He waited, hunched over the in-system communicator, staring through the vision-plate at the blue loveliness of his home planet.

After a moment, a response came:

"World Building, Corwin. We have your call. Please identify."

Ewing replied with the series of code symbols that had been selected as identification. He repeated them three times, reeling them off from memory.

The acknowledging symbols came back instantly, after which the same voice said, "Ewing? At last!"

"It's only been a couple of years, hasn't it?" Ewing said. "Nothing's changed too much."

"No. Not too much."

There was a curious, strained tone in the voice that made Ewing feel uneasy, but he did not prolong the conversation. He jotted down the landing coordinates as they came in, integrated and fed them to his computer, and proceeded to carry out the landing.

He came down at Broughton Spacefield, fifteen miles outside Corwin's capital city, Broughton. The air was bright and fresh, with the extra tang that he had missed during his stay on Earth. After descending from his ship he waited for the pickup truck. He stared at the blue arch of the sky, dotted with clouds, and at the magnificent row of 800-foot-high Imperator trees that bordered the spacefield. Earth had no trees to compare with those, he thought.

The truck picked him up; a grinning field hand said, "Welcome back, Mr. Ewing!"

"Thanks," Ewing said, climbing aboard. "It's good to be back."

A hastily-assembled delegation was on hand at the terminal building when the truck arrived. Ewing recognized Premier Davidson, three or four members of the Council, a few people from the University. He looked around, wondering just why it was that Laira and his son had not come to welcome him home.

Then he saw them, standing with some of his friends in the back of the group. They came forward, Laira with an odd little smile on her face, young Blade with a blank stare for a man he had probably almost forgotten.

"Hello, Baird," Laira said. Her voice was higher than he had remembered it as being, and she looked older than the mental image he carried. Her eyes had deepened, her face grown thin. "It's so good to have you back. Blade, say hello to your father."

Ewing looked at the boy. He had grown tall and gangling; the chubby eight-year-old he had left behind had turned into a coltish boy of nearly eleven. He eyed his father uncertainly. "Hello—Dad."

"Hello there, Blade!"

He scooped the boy off the ground, tossed him easily into the air, caught him, set him down. He turned to Laira, then, and kissed her. But there was no warmth in his greeting. A strange thought interposed:

Am I really Baird Ewing?

Am I the man who was born on Corwin, married this woman, built my home, fathered this child? Or did he die back on Earth, and am I just a replica indistinguishable from the original?

It was a soul-numbing thought. He realized it was foolish of him to worry over the point; he wore Baird Ewing's body, he carried Baird Ewing's memory and personality. What else was there to a man, besides his physical existence and the tenuous Gestalt of memories and thoughts that might be called his soul?

I am Baird Ewing, he insisted inwardly, trying to quell the doubt rising within him.

They were all looking earnestly at him. He hoped none of his inner distress was visible. Turning to Premier Davidson, he said, "Did you get my messages?"

"All three of them—there *were* only three, weren't there?"

"Yes," Ewing said. "I'm sorry about those last two—"

"It really stirred us up, when we got that message saying you were coming home without anything gained. We were really counting on you, Baird. And then, about four hours later, came the second message—"

Ewing chuckled with a warmth he did not feel. "Something came up at the very last minute. Something that can save us from the Klodni." He glanced around uncertainly. "What's the news there? How about the Klodni?"

"They've conquered Borgman," Davidson said. "We're next. Within a year, they say. They changed their direction after Lundquist—"

"They got Lundquist too?" Ewing interrupted.

"Lundquist and Borgman both. Six planets, now. And we're next on the list."

Ewing shook his head slowly. "No; we're not. They're on *our* list. I've brought something back from Earth with me, and the Klodni won't like it."

He went before the Council that evening, after having been allowed to spend the afternoon at home, renewing his acquaintance with his family, repairing the breach two years of absence had created.

He took with him the plans and drawings and model he had wrung from Myreck and the College. He explained precisely how he planned to defeat the Klodni. The storm burst the moment he had finished.

Jospers, the delegate from Northwest Corwin, immediately broke out with; "Time travel? Impossible!"

Four of the other delegates echoed the thought. Premier Davidson pounded for order. Ewing shouted them down and said, "Gentlemen, I'm not asking you to believe what I tell you. You sent me to Earth to bring back help, and I've brought it."

"But it's fantastic to tell us—"

"Please, Mr. Jospers. This thing *works*."

How do you know?"

Ewing took a deep breath. He had not wanted to reveal this. "I've tried it," he said. "I've gone back in time. I've talked face-to-face with myself. You don't have to believe that, either. You can squat here like a bunch of sitting ducks and let the Klodni blast us the way they've blasted Barnholt and Borgman and Lundquist, and all the other colony worlds in this segment of space. But I tell you I have a workable defense here."

Quietly Davidson said, "Tell us this, Baird: how much will it cost us to build this—ah—weapon of yours, and how long will it take?"

Ewing considered the questions a moment. He said, "I would estimate at least six to eight months of full-time work by a skilled group of engineers to make the thing work in the scale I intend. As for the cost, I don't see how it could be done for less than three million stellors."

Jospers was on his feet in an instant. "Three million stellors! I ask you, gentlemen—"

His question never was asked. In a voice that tolerated no interruptions, Ewing said, "I ask *you*, gentlemen—how much is life worth to you, and expensive nonsense as well. But what of the cost? In a year the Klodni will be here, and your economies won't matter a damn. Unless you plan to beat them your own way, of course."

"Three million stellors represents twenty percent of our annual budget," Davidson remarked. "Should your device prove to be of no help—"

"Don't you see?" Ewing shouted. "It doesn't *matter*! If my device doesn't work, there won't be any more budgets for you to worry about!"

It was an unanswerable point. Grudgingly, Jospers conceded, and with his concession the opposition collapsed. It was agreed that the weapon brought back from Earth by Ewing would be built. There was no choice. The shadow of the advancing Klodni grew longer and longer on the stars, and no other weapon existed. Nothing known to man could stop the advancing hordes.

Possibly, something unknown could.

Ewing had been a man who enjoyed privacy, but now there was no privacy for him. His home became a perpetual open house; the ministers of state were forever conferring with him, discussing the new project. People from the University wanted to know about Earth. Publishers prodded Ewing to write books for them; magazines and telestat firms

He refused them all. He was not interested in capitalizing on his trip to Earth.

He spent most of his time at the laboratory that had been given him in North Broughton, supervising the development of the time projector. He had no formal scientific training himself; the actual work was under the control of a staff of engineers from the University. But he aided them with suggestions and theoretical contributions, based on his conversations with Myreck and his own experiences with the phenomenon of time transfer.

The weeks passed. At home, Ewing found family life strained and tense. Laira was almost a stranger to him; he told her what he could of his brief stay on Earth, but he had earlier determined to keep the account of his time-shift to himself forever, and his story was sketchy and inconsistent.

As for Blade, he grew used to his father again. But Ewing did not feel comfortable with either of them. They were, perhaps, not really his; and, preposterous though the thought was, he could not fully accept the reality of his existence.

There had been other Ewings. He was firmly convinced he had been the first of the four, that the others had merely been duplicates of him, but there was no certainty in that. And two of those duplicates had given up their lives so that he might be home on Corwin.

He brooded over that, and also about Myreck and about Earth. Earth, which by now was merely a Sirian protectorate. Earth, which had sent her boldest sons forth to the stars, and had withered her own substance at home.

He saw pictures of the devastation on Lundquist and Borgman. Lundquist had been a pleasure world, attracting visitors from a dozen worlds to its games parlors and lovely gardens, luminous and radiant. The pictures showed the lacy towers of Lundquist's dreamlike cities crumbling under the merciless Klodni guns. Senselessly, brutally, the Klodni were moving forward.

Scouts checked their approach. The fleet was massed on Borgman, now. If they held to their regular pattern, it would be nearly a year before they rumbled out of the Borgman system to make their attack on nearby Corwin. And a year would be enough time.

Ewing counted the passing days. The conical structure of the time-projector took shape slowly, as the technicians, working from Myreck's model, carried out their painstaking tasks. No one asked exactly how the weapon would be put in use. Ewing had specified that it be installed in a space ship, and it had been designed accordingly.

At night he was haunted by the recurring image of the Ewing who had willingly thrown himself under the jets of a descending spaceliner. *It could have been me,* he thought. *I volunteered. But he wanted to toss for it.*

And there had been another Ewing, equally brave, whom he had never known. The man who had taken the steps that would render him superfluous, and then had calmly and simply removed himself from existence.

I didn't do that. I figured the others would be caught in the wheel forever, and that I'd be the only one who would get loose. But it didn't happen that way.

He was haunted too, by the accusing stare in Myreck's eyes as the twin Corwinites plundered the College of its secrets and abandoned Earth to its fate. Here, again, Ewing had his rationalizations: there was nothing he could have done to help. Earth was the prisoner of its own woes.

Laira told him finally that he had changed, that he had become bitter, almost irascible, since making the journey to Earth.

"I don't understand it, Baird. You used to be so warm, so—so *human.* And you're different now. Cold, turned inward, brooding all the time." She touched his arm lightly. "Can't you talk things out with me? Something's troubling you. Something that happened on Earth, maybe?"

He whirled away. *"No!* Nothing." He realized his tone was harsh; he saw the pain on her face. In a softer voice he said, "I can't help myself, Laira. There's nothing I can say. I've been under a strain, that's all."

The strain of seeing myself die, and of seeing a culture die. Of journeying through time and across space. I've been through a lot. Too much, maybe.

He felt very tired. He looked up at the night sky as it glittered over the viewing-porch of their home. The stars were gems mounted on black velvet. There were the familiar constellations, the Turtle and the Dove, the Great Wheel, the Spear. He had missed those configurations of stars while he was on Earth. They had seemed to him friendly aspects of home.

But there was nothing friendly about the cold stars tonight. Ewing held his wife close and stared up at them, and it seemed to him that they held a savage menace. As if the Klodni hordes hovered there like moisture particles in a rain cloud, waiting for their moment to descend.

Chapter Seventeen

The alarm came early on a spring morning, a year after Ewing had returned to Corwin. It was a warm, muggy morning. A soft rain was falling, automatically energizing the deflectors on the roof of Ewing's home; their polarizing cells kept the rain from tattooing on the flat roof. Ewing lay in uneasy sleep.

The phone rang. He stirred, turned over, buried his face in the pillow. He was dreaming of a figure limned briefly in a white flare of jet exhaust on Valloin Spacefield. The phone continued to ring.

Groggily, Ewing felt a hand shaking him. A voice—Laira's voice—was saying, "Wake up, Baird! There's a call for you! Wake up!"

Reluctantly, he came awake. The wall clock said 0430. He rubbed his eyes, crawled out of the bed, groped his way across the room to the phone extension. He choked back a yawn.

"Ewing here. What is it?"

The sharp, high-pitched tones of Premier Davidson cut into his sleep-drugged mind. "Baird, the Klodni are on their way!"

He was fully awake now. "What?"

"We just got word from the scout network," Davidson said. "The main Klodni attacking fleet left Borgman about four hours ago, and there are at least five hundred ships in the first wave."

"When are they expected to reach this area?"

"We have conflicting estimates on that. It isn't easy to compute super-light velocities. But on the basis of what we know, I'd say they'll be within firing range of Corwin in not less than ten nor more than eighteen hours, Baird."

Ewing nodded. "All right. Have the special ship serviced for immediate blast-off. I'll drive right out to the spaceport and pick it up there."

"Baird—"

"What is it?" Ewing asked impatiently.

"Don't you think—well, that some younger man should handle this job? I don't mean that you're *old*, but you have a wife, a son—and it's risky. One man against five hundred ships? It's suicide, Baird."

The word triggered dormant associations in Ewing, and he winced. Doggedly he said, "The Council has approved what I'm doing. This is no time to train someone else. We've been over this ground before."

He dressed rapidly, wearing, for sentiment's sake, the blue-and-gold uniform of the Corwin Space Force, in which he had served the mandatory two-year term a dozen years before. The uniform was tight, but still fitted.

While Laira fixed a meal he stood by a window, looking outward at the gray, swirling, pre-dawn mists. He had lived so long in the shadow of the Klodni advance that he found it hard to believe the day had actually come.

He ate moodily, scarcely tasting the food as he swallowed it, saying nothing.

Laira said, "I'm frightened, Baird."

"Frightened?" He chuckled. "Of what?"

She did not seem amused. "Of the Klodni. Of this crazy thing you're going to do." After a moment she added, "But you don't seem afraid, Baird. And I guess that's all that matters."

"I'm not," he said truthfully. "There's nothing to be afraid of. The Klodni won't even be able to see me. There isn't a mass-detector in the universe sensitive enough to spot a one-man ship a couple of light-years away. The mass is insignificant; and there'll be too much background noise coming out of the fleet itself."

Besides, he added silently, *how can I be afraid of these Klodni?*

They were not even human. They were faceless, mindless brutes, a murdering ant-horde marching through the worlds out of some fierce inner compulsion to slay. They were dangerous, but not frightening.

Fright had to be reserved for the real enemies—the human beings who turned against other humans, who played a double game of trust and betrayal. There was cause to respect the strength of the Klodni, but not to dread them for it. Dread was more appropriate applied to Rollun Firnik and his kind, Ewing thought.

When he had eaten, he stopped off briefly in Blade's bedroom to take a last look at the sleeping boy. He did not wake him. He merely looked in, smiled, and closed the door.

"Maybe you should wake him up and say goodbye," Laira suggested hesitantly.

Ewing shook his head. "It's too early. He needs his sleep at his age. Anyway, when I get back I guess I'll be a hero. He'll like that."

He caught the expression on her face, and added, "I *am* coming back. You could gamble our savings on it."

Dawn streaked the sky by the time he reached Broughton Spacefield. He left his car with an attendant and went to the main administration building, where a grim-faced group of Corwin officials waited for him.

This is it. Ewing thought. *If I don't make it, Corwin is finished.*

A world's destiny rode on the wild scheme of one man. It was a burden he did not relish carrying.

He greeted Davidson and the others a little stiffly; the tension was beginning to grip him now. Davidson handed him a portfolio.

"This is the flight chart of the Klodni armada," the Premier explained. "We had the big computer extrapolate it. They'll be overhead in nine hours and fifty minutes."

Ewing shook his head. "You're wrong. They won't be overhead at all. I'm going to meet them at least a light-year from here, maybe further out if I can manage it. They won't get any closer."

He scanned the charts. Graphs of the Klodni force had been inked in.

"The computer says there are seven hundred seventy-five ships in the fleet," Davidson said.

Ewing pointed to the formation. "It's a pure wedge, isn't it? A single flagship, followed by two ships, followed by a file of four, followed by eight. And right on out to here. That's very interesting."

"It's a standard Klodni fighting formation," said gravel-voiced Dr. Harmess of the Department of Military Science. "The flagship always leads and none of the others dares to break formation without order. Complete totalitarian discipline."

Ewing smiled. "I'm glad to hear it."

He checked his watch. Approximately ten hours from now, Klodni guns would be thundering down on a virtually defenseless Corwin. A fleet of seven hundred seventy-five dreadnoughts was an unstoppable armada. Corwin had perhaps a dozen ships, and not all of them in fighting trim despite vigorous last-minute work. No planet in the civilized galaxy could stand the burden of supporting a military force of nearly eight hundred first-line ships.

"All right," he said after a moment's silence. "I'm ready to leave."

They led him across the damp, rain-soaked field to the well-guarded special hangar where Project X had been installed. Security guards smiled obligingly and stood to one side when they recognized Ewing and the Premier. Field attendants swung open the doors of the hangar, revealing the ship.

It was a thin black spear, hardly bigger than the vessel that had taken him to Earth and back. Inside, though, there was no complex equipment for suspending animation. In its place, there now rested a tubular helical coil, whose tip projected micromillimeters from the skin of the ship. At the base of the coil was a complex control panel.

Ewing nodded in approval. The field attendants wheeled the ship out; gantry cranes tilted it to blasting angle and carried it to the blast-field.

A black ship against the blackness of space. The Klodni would never notice it, Ewing thought. He sensed the joy of battle springing up in him.

"I'll leave immediately," he said.

The actual blast-off was to be handled automatically. Ewing clambored aboard, settled himself in the cradle area, and let the spinnerettes weave him an unshatterable cradle of spidery foamweb. He switched on the vision-plate and saw the little group waiting tensely at the edge of the clear part of the field.

He did not envy them. Of necessity, he would have to maintain total radio silence until after the encounter. For half a day or more, they would wait, not knowing whether death would come to their world or not. It would be an uncomfortable day for them.

With an almost impulsive gesture Ewing tripped the blasting lever, and lay back as the ship raced upward. For the second time in his life he was leaving Corwin's soil.

The ship arced upward in a wide hyperbolic orbit, while Ewing shuddered in his cradle and waited. Seconds later, the jets cut out. The rest of the journey would be carried out on warp-drive. That was less strenuous, at least.

The pre-plotted course carried him far from Corwin during the first two hours. A quick triangulation showed that he was almost one and a half light-years from the home world—a safe enough distance, he thought. He ceased forward thrust and put the ship in a closed million-mile orbit perpendicular to the expected line of attack of the Klodni. He waited.

Three hours slipped by before the first quiver of green appeared on his ship's mass-detector. The line wavered uncertainly. Ewing resolved the fine focus and waited.

The line broadened. And broadened. And broadened again.

The Klodni wedge was drawing near.

Ewing felt utterly calm, now that the waiting was over. Moving smoothly and unhurriedly, he proceeded to activate the time-transfer equipment. He yanked down on the main lever, and the control panel came to life; the snout of the helical core advanced nearly an inch from the skin of the ship, enough to insure a clear trajectory.

Working with one eye on the mass-detector and one on the transfer device's control panel, Ewing computed the necessary strength of the field. The Klodni formation opened out geometrically: one ship leading, followed by two, with four in the third rank, eight in the fourth, sixteen in the fifth. Two massive ranks of about two hundred fifty ships each served as rearguard for the wedge, providing a double finishing-thrust for any attack. It was the width of these last two files that mattered most.

No doubt they were traveling in a three-dimensional array, but Ewing took no chances, and assumed that all two hundred and fifty were moving in a single parallel bar. He computed the maximum width of such a formation. He added twenty percent at each side. If only a dozen Klodni ships slipped through. Corwin still would face a siege of havoc.

Compiling his data, he fed it to the transfer machine and established the necessary coordinates. He punched out the activator signals. He studied the mass-detector; the Klodni fleet was less than an hour away, now.

He nodded in satisfaction as the last of his computations checked and canceled out. Here goes, he thought.

He tripped the actuator.

There was no apparent effect, no response except for a phase-shift on one of the meters aboard the ship. But Ewing knew there had been an effect. A gulf had opened in the heavens, an invisible gulf that radiated outward from his ship and sprawled across space.

A gulf he could control as a fisherman might, a net—a net wide enough to hold seven hundred seventy-five alien vessels of war.

Ewing waited.

His tiny ship swung in its rigid orbit, round and round, carrying the deadly nothingness round with it. The Klodni fleet drew near. Ewing scratched out further computations. At no time, he thought, would he be closer to a Klodni ship than forty-light minutes. They would never pick him up at such a distance.

A minnow huddled in the dark, waiting to trap the whales.

The green line on the mass-detector broadened and became intense. Ewing shifted out of his locked orbit, placing the vessel on manual response. He readied his trap as the Klodni flagship moved serenely on through the void.

Now! he thought.

He cast his net.

The Klodni flagship moved on—and vanished! From Ewing's vantage point it seemed as if the great vessel had simply been blotted out; the green wedge on the scope of his mass-detector was blunt-snouted now that the flagship was gone.

But to the ships behind it, nothing seemed amiss. Without breaking formation they followed on, and Ewing waited. The second rank vanished through the gulf, and the third, and the fourth.

Eighteen ships gone. Thirty-two. Sixty-four.

He held his breath as the hundred-twenty-eight-ship rank entered the *cul-de-sac*. Now for the test. He stared at the mass-detector intently as the two biggest Klodni formations moved toward him. Two hundred fifty ships each, the hammers of the Klodni forces—

Gone.

The mass-detector was utterly blank. There was not a Klodni ship anywhere within detectable range. Ewing felt limp with relief. He disconnected the transfer mechanism, clamping down knife-switches with frenzied zeal. The gulf was sealed, now. There was no possible way back for the trapped Klodni ships.

He could break radio silence now. He sent a brief, laconic message: "Kiodni fleet destroyed. Am returning to home base."

One man had wiped out an armada. He chuckled in relief of the crushing tension.

He wondered briefly how the puzzled Klodni would react when they found themselves in the midst of a trackless void, without stars, without planets. No doubt they would proceed on across space in search of some place to land, until their provisions became exhausted, their fuel disappeared, and death finally claimed them. Eventually, even their ships would crumble and disappear.

According to the best scientific theory, the stars of the galaxy were between five and six billion years old. The range of the Earther time-projector was nearly infinite.

Ewing had hurled the Klodni fleet five billion years into the past. He shuddered at the thought, and turned his tiny ship homeward, to Corwin.

Chapter Eighteen

The return voyage seemed to take days. Ewing lay awake in the protecting cradle, staring through the open vision-plate at the blurred splendor of the heavens as the ship shot through notspace at super-light velocities. At these speeds, the stars appeared as blotchy pastel things; the constellations did not exist.

Curiously, he felt no sense of triumph. He had saved Corwin, true—and in that sense, he had achieved the goal in whose name he had set out on his journey across space to Earth. But he felt as if his work were incomplete.

He thought, not of Corwin now, but of Earth. Two years had gone by on the mother world since his departure; certainly, time enough for the Sirians to make their move. Firnik, no doubt, was high in command of the Sirian Governor-General instead of holding a mere vice-consul's job. Byra Clork was probably a noblewoman of the new aristocracy.

And Myreck and the others—well, perhaps they had survived, hidden three microseconds out of phase. But more likely they had been caught and put to death, like the potential dangers they were.

Dangers. There were no true dangers to the Sirians. Earth was self-weakened; it had no capacity to resist tyranny.

Guiltily, Ewing told himself that there was nothing he could have done. Earth's doom was foreordained, self-inflicted. He had saved his own world; there was no helping Earth.

There was a way, something in his mind said reproachfully. *There still is a way.*

Leave Corwin. Cross space once again, return to Earth, lead the hapless little Earthers in a struggle for freedom. All they needed was a man with the bold vigor of the outworld colonies. Leadership was what they lacked. They outnumbered the Sirians a thousand to one. In any kind of determined rising, they could win their freedom easily. But they needed a focal point; they needed a leader.

You could be that leader, something within him insisted. *Go back to Earth.*

Savagely, he forced the idea to die. His place was on Corwin, where he was a hero, where his wife and child awaited him. Earth had to work out its own pitiful destiny.

He tried to relax. The ship plummeted onward through the night, toward Corwin.

It seemed that the whole populace turned out to welcome him. He could see them from above, as he maneuvered the ship through the last of its series of inward spirals and let it come gently to rest on the ferroconcrete landing surface of Broughton Spacefield.

He let the decontaminating squad do its work, while he watched the massed crowd assembled beyond the barriers. Finally, when the ship and the area around it were both safely cool, he stepped out.

The roar was deafening.

There were thousands of them. In the front he saw Laira and Blade, and the Premier, and the Council. University people. Newsmen. People, people, people. Ewing's first impulse was to shrink back into the lonely comfort of his ship. Instead, he compelled himself to walk forward toward the crowd. He wished they would stop shouting; he held up a hand, hoping to get silence, but the gesture was interpreted as a greeting and called forth an even noisier demonstration.

Somehow, he reached Laira and got his arms around her. He smiled; she said something, but her voice was crushed by the uproar. He read her lips instead. She was saying, "I was counting the seconds till you got back, darling."

He kissed her. He hugged Blade to him. He smiled to Davidson and to all of them, and wondered quietly why he had been born with the particular conglomeration of personality traits that had brought him to this destiny, on this world, on this day.

He was a hero. He had ended a threat that had destroyed six worlds.

Corwin was safe.

He was swept inside, carried off to the World Building, smuggled into Premier Davidson's private chambers. There, while officers of the peace kept the curiosity seekers away, Ewing dictated for the air-waves a full account of what he had done, while smiling friends looked on.

There were parades outside. He could hear the noise where he sat, seventy-one floors above the street level. It was hardly surprising; a world that had lived under sentence of death for five years found itself miraculously reprieved. It was small wonder the emotional top was blowing off.

Sometime toward evening, they let him go home. He had not slept for more than thirty hours, and it was beginning to show.

A cavalcade of official cars convoyed him out of the capital city and toward the surburban area where he lived. They told him a guard would be placed round his house, to assure him continued privacy. He thanked them all, and wished them good night, and entered his house. The door shut behind him, shutting out the noise, the celebration, the acclaim. He was just Baird Ewing of Corwin again, in his own home. He felt very tired. He felt hollow within, as if he were a villain rather than a hero. And it showed.

Laira said, "That trip didn't change you, did it?"

He blinked at her. "What do you mean?"

"I thought that the cloud would lift from you. That you were worried about the invasion and everything. But I guess I was wrong. We're safe, now—and something's still eating you."

He tried to laugh it off. "Laira, you're overtired. You've been worrying too much yourself. Why don't you get some sleep?"

She shook her head. "No, Baird. I'm serious. I know you too well; I see something in your eyes. Trouble, of some kind." She put her hands round his wrists and stared up into his eyes. "Baird, something happened to you on Earth that you haven't told me about. I'm your wife. I ought to know about it, if there's anything—"

"There's *nothing!* Nothing." He looked away. "Let's go to sleep, Laira. I'm exhausted."

But he lay in bed turning restlessly, and despite his exhaustion sleep did not come.

How can I go back to Earth? he asked himself bitterly. *My loyalties lie here. Earth will have to take care of itself—and if it can't, more's the pity.*

It was a hollow rationalization, and he knew it. He lay awake half the night, brooding, twisting, drowning in his own agonized perspiration.

He thought:

Three men died so I could return to Corwin safely. Two of them were deliberate, voluntary suicides. I owe them a debt. I owe Earth a debt, for making possible Corwin's salvation.

Three men died for me. Do I have any right to be selfish?

Then he thought:

When Laira married me, she thought she was getting Citizen Baird Ewing, period. She wasn't marrying any hero, any world saver. She didn't ask the Council to pick me for its trip to Earth. But she went through two years of widowhood because they did pick me.

How could I tell her I was leaving, going to Earth for good? Leaving her without a husband, and Blade without a father? It simply isn't fair to them. I can't do it.

And then he thought:

There must be a compromise. A way I can serve the memory of the dead Baird Ewings and be fair to my family as well. There has to be some kind of compromise.

There was. The answer came to him shortly before morning, crystal sharp, bearing with it no doubts, no further anxiety. He saw what his path must be. With the answer came a welling tide of peace, and he drifted into sound sleep, confident he had found the right way at last.

Premier Davidson, on behalf of the grateful people of the world of Corwin, called on him the next morning. Davidson told him he might pick anything, anything at all as his reward.

Ewing chuckled. "I've got everything I want already," he said. "Fame, fortune, family—what else is there in life?"

Shrugging, the rotund little Premier said, "But surely there must be some fitting—"

"There is," Ewing said. "Suppose you grant me the freedom of poking around with those notebooks I brought back with me from Earth. All right?"

"Certainly, if that's what you want. But can that be all that—"

"There's just one other thing I want. No, two. The first one may be tough. I want to be left alone. I want to get out of the limelight and stay there. No medals, no public receptions, no more parades. I did the job the Council sent me to do, and now I want to return to private life.

"As for the second thing—well, I won't mention it yet. Let's just put it this way: when the time comes, I'm going to want a favor from the Government. It'll be an expensive favor, but not terribly so. I'll let you know what it is I want, when and if I want it."

Slowly, the notoriety ebbed away, and Ewing returned to private life as he had wished. His life would never be the same again, but there was no help for that. The Council voted him a pension of 10,000 stellors a year, transferable to his heirs in perpetuity, and he was so stunned by their magnanimity that he had no choice but to accept.

A month passed. The tenseness seemed to have left him. He discovered that his son was turning into a miniature replica of his father, tall, taciturn, with the same inner traits of courage, dependability, conscience. It was a startling thing to watch the boy unfolding, becoming a personality.

It was too bad, Ewing thought, as he wrestled with his son or touched his wife's arm, that he would have to be leaving them soon. He would regret parting with them. But at least they would be spared any grief.

A second month passed. The apparatus he was building in his basement, in the sacrosanct den that neither Blade nor Laira ever dared to enter, was nearing completion. The time was drawing near.

He ran the final tests on a warm midsummer day. The machine responded perfectly. The time had come.

He called upstairs via the intercom. Laira was reading in the study; Blade was watching the video. "Blade? Laira?"

"We're here, Baird. What do you want?" Laira asked.

Ewing said, "I'll be running some very delicate experiments during the next twenty minutes or so. Any shift in the room balance might foul things up. Would you both be kind enough to stay put, in whatever room you're in now, until I give the signal from downstairs?"

"Of course, darling."

Ewing smiled and hung up. Quite carefully he took a massive crowbar from his tool-chest and propped it up at the side of the wall, near the outer door of the den. He glanced at his watch. The time was 1403:30.

He recrossed the room and made some final adjustments on the apparatus. He stared at his watch, letting the minutes go by. Six . . . seven . . . eight . . .

At 1411:30 he reached up and snapped a switch. The machinery hummed briefly and threw him back ten minutes in time.

Chapter Nineteen

He was hovering inches in the air above his own front lawn. He dropped, landing gently, and looked at his watch. The dial said: 1401:30.

At this very moment, he knew, his earlier self was on the house phone, calling upstairs to Laira. Ewing moistened his lips. This would take careful coordination. *Very* careful.

On tiptoe he ran round the house, entering at the side door that led to his basement workshop. He moved stealthily down the inner corridor until he was only a few feet from the workshop door. There, he waited.

There was an intercom outlet mounted in the hall. Gently he lifted the receiver from the hook and put it to his ear.

He heard himself say, "Any shift in the room balance might foul things up. Would you both be kind enough to stay put, in whatever room you're in now, until I give the signal from downstairs?"

"Of course, darling," Laira's voice responded.

Outside, in the hall, Ewing looked at his watch. It read 1403:10. He waited a moment. At 1403:30 he heard the faint *clink* as the crowbar was propped up against the wall near the door.

So far, everything was right on schedule. But here was where he intended to cause a split in the time-track once again.

He edged forward and peered through the partly open door into the workshop. A familiar-looking figure sat with his back to the door, hunched over the time-projector on the table, making fine adjustments preparatory to jumping back in time ten minutes.

His watch said 1405:15.

He stepped quickly into the room and snatched up the crowbar he had so carefully provided for himself. He crossed the room in four quick bounds; his double, absorbed in his work, did not notice until Ewing put his hand on the shoulder of the other and lifted him away from the work bench. In the same motion he swung the crowbar; it smashed into the main section of the time-projector, sending it tumbling to the floor in a tingling crash of breaking tubes and crumbling circuits.

"I hated to do that," he remarked casually. "It represented a lot of work. But you know why I did it."

"Y-yes," the other said uncertainly. The two men faced each other over the wreckage of the projector, Baird Ewing facing Baird Ewing, the only difference between them being that one held a crowbar ready for further use. Ewing prayed Laira had not heard the crash. Everything would be ruined if she chose this moment to violate the sanctity of his workroom.

Slowly, he said to his double, "You know who I am and why I'm here, don't you? And where I came from?"

The other ruefully stared down at the wreckage. "I guess so. You got there ahead of me, didn't you? You're one notch up on me in the Absolute time-track."

Ewing nodded. "Exactly. And keep your voice down. I don't want any trouble from you."

"You're determined to do it?"

Ewing nodded again. "Listen to me very carefully, now. I'm going to take my—our—car and drive into Broughton. I'm going to make a call to Premier Davidson. Then I'm going to drive out to the spaceport; get into a ship, and leave. That's the last you'll ever hear from me.

"In the meantime, you're to stay down here until at least 1420 or so. Then call upstairs to Laira and tell her you've finished the experiment. Sweep up the wreckage, and if you're a wise man you won't build any more of these gadgets in the future. From now on, no extra Baird Ewings. You'll be the only one. And take good care of Laira and Blade. I love them, too."

"Wait a minute," the other Ewing said. You're not being fair."

"To whom?"

"To yourself. Look, I'm as much Baird Ewing as you are. And it's as much my responsibility to—to leave Corwin as it is yours. You don't have any right to take it upon yourself to give up everything you love. Let's at least flip a coin to see who goes."

Ewing shook his head. In a quiet, flat voice he said, "No. *I* go. I've watched too many of my alter egos sacrifice themselves to keep me safe and sound."

"So have I, remember?"

Ewing shrugged. "That's tough for you, then: But this is my ride through the time-track, and *I'm* going. You stay here and nurse your guilty conscience, if you like. But you shouldn't moan too much. You'll have Laira and Blade. And Baird Ewing will be doing what he ought to be doing, as well."

"But—"

Ewing lifted the crowbar menacingly. "I don't want to skull you, brother. Accept defeat gracefully."

He looked at his watch. It was 1410. He walked to the door and said, "The car will be parked at the spaceport. You figure out some explanation for how it got there."

He turned and walked out.

The car was waiting in its garage; he touched his finger to the burglar-proof identiplate that controlled the garage door, and the car came out. He got in, switched on the directional guide, and left via the back route, so no one in the house could see him.

As soon as he was comfortably distant from the house, he snapped on the phone circuit and gave the operator Premier Davidson's number.

After a short pause, Davidson acknowledged.

"Hello, Baird. What's on your mind?"

"A favor. You owe me one, remember? I asked for *carte blanche* the day after the Klodni thing."

Davidson chuckled. "I haven't forgotten about it, Baird. Well?"

"I want to borrow a spaceship," Ewing said quietly. "A one-man ship. The same sort of ship I used to get to Earth in, a few years ago."

"A *spaceship*?" The Premier sounded incredulous. "What would you be wanting a spaceship for?"

"That doesn't matter. An experiment of mine, let's say. I asked for a favor, and you said you'd grant it. Are you backing down, now?"

"No, no, of course not. But—"

"Yes. I want a spaceship. I'm on my way to Broughton Spacefield now. Will you phone ahead and tell them to release a military-owned one-man job for me, or won't you?"

I t was nearly 1500 when he reached the spacefield. He left his car in the special parking lot and made it on foot across to the trim little building used by the military wing of Corwin's government.

He asked for and was taken to the commanding officer on duty. The officer turned out to be a wry-faced colonel who looked up questioningly as Ewing entered his office.

"You're Ewing, of course."

"That's right. Did Premier Davidson phone?"

The colonel nodded. "He authorized me to give you one of our one-man ships. I guess I don't have to ask if you can operate it, do l?"

Ewing grinned and said, "I guess not."

"The ship's on Field B right now, being serviced for you. It'll be fully fueled, of course. How long are you planning to stay aloft?"

Shrugging, Ewing said, "I really haven't decided that yet, colonel. But I'll advise for clearance before I come down."

"Good."

"Oh—one more thing. Is the ship I'm getting equipped for suspension?"

The colonel frowned. "All our ships are. Why do you ask? Not planning *that* long a trip, are you?"

"Hardly," Ewing lied. "I just wanted to examine the suspension equipment once again. Sentimental reasons, you know."

The colonel signaled and one of the cadets led him across the field to the waiting ship. It was a twin of the one that had borne him across to Earth; for all he knew, it might have been the very same one. He clambered aboard, switched on the controls, and advised he would be leaving Corwin in eleven minutes.

From memory, he punched out the coordinates for his journey on the auto-pilot. He activated the unit, stripped, and lowered himself once again into the suspension tank.

He thought:

Firnik thinks I'm dead. He'll be surprised when a ghost turns up on Earth, leading the underground revolt against the Sirians. And I'll have to explain everything very carefully to Myreck as soon as I get back—if I can find Myreck.

And he thought:

My double back home is going to have some fancy explaining to do, too. About what happened to the ship he took up with him, and how his car got to the space-port while he was in the workship. He'll have plenty of fast talking to do. But he'll manage. He's a pretty shrewd sort. He'll get along.

He paused for a moment to wish a silent good-bye to the wife and son who would never know he had left them. Then he stretched out his feet and switched on the suspension unit. The temperature began to drop.

Darkness swirled up around him.

Chapter Twenty

The time was 1421, of a warm midsummer afternoon on Corwin. Baird Ewing finished sweeping the shattered fragments of his painstakingly constructed projector into the disposal unit, looked around, put the crowbar back in the tool shelf.

Then he snapped on the housephone and said, "Okay, Laira. The experiment's over. Thanks for helping out."

He hung up and trotted up the stairs to the study. Laira was bent over her book; Blade stared entranced at the video screen. He crept up behind the boy, caught him suddenly with one big hand at the back of his neck, and squeezed affectionately. Then, leaving him, he lifted Laira's head from her viewing screen, smiled warmly at her, and turned away without speaking.

Later in the afternoon he was on his way to Broughton Spacefield via public transport to reclaim his car. He was still some miles distant when the sudden overhead roar of a departing spaceship sounded.

"One of those little military jobs taking off," someone in the bus said.

Ewing looked up through the translucent roof of the bus at the clear sky. No ship was visible, of course. It was well on its way Earthward now.

Good luck, he thought. And Godspeed.

The car was in the special parking field. He smiled to the attendant, unlocked it, climbed in.

He drove home.

Home—to Laira and Blade.

Chapter Twenty

Baird Ewing woke slowly, sensing the coldness all about him. It was slowly withdrawing down the length of his body; his head and shoulders had come out of the freeze, and the rest of him was gradually emerging.

He looked at the time-panel. Eleven months, fourteen days, six hours had elapsed since he had left Corwin. He hoped they hadn't held their breaths while waiting for him to return their ship.

He performed the de-suspending routine and emerged from the tank. He touched the stud and the vision-plate lit up. A planet hung centered in the green depths of the plate—a green planet, with vast seas bordering its continents.

Earth.

Ewing smiled. They would be surprised to see him, all right. But he could help them, and so he had come back. He could serve as coordinator for the resistance movement. He could spearhead the drive that would end the domination of the Sirians.

Here I come, he thought.

His fingers moved rapidly over the manual-control bank of the ship's instrument panel. He began setting up the orbit for landing. Already, plans and counterplans were forming in his active mind.

The ship descended to Earth in a wide-sweeping arc. Ewing waited, impatient for the landing, as his ship swung closer and closer to the lovely green world below.

About the Author

ROBERT SILVERBERG (1935–) began writing in the mid-1950s for science fiction magazines such as *Amazing Stories*, *Science Fiction Adventures*, and *Super-Science Fiction*. He has gone on to author more than one hundred science fiction and fantasy novels, including *A Time of Changes*, *Roma Eterna*, *The Last Song of Orpheus*, and the bestselling Majipoor cycle, and is widely regarded today as one of the all-time greatest science fiction and fantasy writers. He is also the author of more than sixty nonfiction works, in addition to editing or co-editing sixty-plus anthologies, including *The Science Fiction Hall of Fame, Volume One (1929–1964)*, *Legends I & II*, and *Far Horizons*. He has won five Nebula Awards, four Hugo Awards, and the Prix Tour-Apollo Award. In 1999, he was inducted into the Science Fiction Hall of Fame, and in 2004, the Science Fiction and Fantasy Writers of America presented him with the prestigious Damon Knight Memorial Grand Master Award.

Collect all of these exciting Planet Stories adventures!

THE WALRUS AND THE WARWOLF
BY HUGH COOK
INTRODUCTION BY CHINA MIÉVILLE

Sixteen-year-old Drake Duoay loves nothing more than wine, women, and getting into trouble. But when he's abducted by pirates and pursued by a new religion bent solely on his destruction, only the love of a red-skinned priestess will see him through the insectile terror of the Swarms.

ISBN: 978-1-60125-214-2

WHO FEARS THE DEVIL?
BY MANLY WADE WELLMAN
INTRODUCTION BY MIKE RESNICK

In the back woods of Appalachia, folk-singer and monster-hunter Silver John comes face to face with the ghosts and demons of rural Americana in this classic collection of eerie stories from Pulitzer Prize-nominee Manly Wade Wellman.

ISBN: 978-1-60125-188-6

THE SECRET OF SINHARAT
BY LEIGH BRACKETT
INTRODUCTION BY MICHAEL MOORCOCK

In the Martian Drylands, a criminal conspiracy leads wild man Eric John Stark to a secret that could shake the Red Planet to its core. In a bonus novel, *People of the Talisman*, Stark ventures to the polar ice cap of Mars to return a stolen talisman to an oppressed people.

ISBN: 978-1-60125-047-6

THE GINGER STAR
BY LEIGH BRACKETT
INTRODUCTION BY BEN BOVA

Eric John Stark journeys to the dying world of Skaith in search of his kidnapped foster father, only to find himself the subject of a revolutionary prophecy. In completing his mission, will he be forced to fulfill the prophecy as well?

ISBN: 978-1-60125-084-1

THE HOUNDS OF SKAITH
BY LEIGH BRACKETT
INTRODUCTION BY F. PAUL WILSON

Eric John Stark has destroyed the Citadel of the Lords Protector, but the war for Skaith's freedom is just beginning. Together with his foster father Simon Ashton, Stark will have to unite some of the strangest and most bloodthirsty peoples the galaxy has ever seen if he ever wants to return home.

ISBN: 978-1-60125-135-0

THE REAVERS OF SKAITH
BY LEIGH BRACKETT
INTRODUCTION BY GEORGE LUCAS

Betrayed and left to die on a savage planet, Eric John Stark and his foster-father Simon Ashton must ally with cannibals and feral warriors to topple an empire and bring an enslaved civilization to the stars. But in fulfilling the prophecy, will Stark sacrifice that which he values most?

ISBN: 978-1-60125-084-1

CITY OF THE BEAST
BY MICHAEL MOORCOCK
INTRODUCTION BY KIM MOHAN

Moorcock's Eternal Champion returns as Michael Kane, an American physicist and expert duelist whose strange experiments catapult him through space and time to a Mars of the distant past—and into the arms of the gorgeous princess Shizala. But can he defeat the Blue Giants of the Argzoon in time to win her hand?

ISBN: 978-1-60125-044-5

LORD OF THE SPIDERS
BY MICHAEL MOORCOCK
INTRODUCTION BY ROY THOMAS

Michael Kane returns to the Red Planet, only to find himself far from his destination and caught in the midst of a civil war between giants! Will his wits and sword keep him alive long enough to find his true love once more?

ISBN: 978-1-60125-082-7

MASTERS OF THE PIT
BY MICHAEL MOORCOCK
INTRODUCTION BY SAMUEL R. DELANY

A new peril threatens physicist Michael Kane's adopted Martian homeland—a plague spread by zealots more machine than human. Now Kane will need to cross oceans, battle hideous mutants and barbarians, and perhaps even sacrifice his adopted kingdom in his attempt to prevail against an enemy that cannot be killed!

ISBN: 978-1-60125-104-6

NORTHWEST OF EARTH
BY C. L. MOORE
INTRODUCTION BY C. J. CHERRYH

Ray-gun-blasting, Earth-born mercenary and adventurer Northwest Smith dodges and weaves his way through the solar system, cutting shady deals with aliens and magicians alike, always one step ahead of the law.

ISBN: 978-1-60125-081-0

BLACK GOD'S KISS
BY C. L. MOORE
INTRODUCTION BY SUZY MCKEE CHARNAS

The first female sword and sorcery protagonist takes up her greatsword and challenges gods and monsters in the groundbreaking stories that inspired a generation of female authors. Of particular interest to fans of Robert E. Howard and H. P. Lovecraft.

ISBN: 978-1-60125-045-2

THE ANUBIS MURDERS
BY GARY GYGAX
INTRODUCTION BY ERIK MONA

Someone is murdering the world's most powerful sorcerers, and the trail of blood leads straight to Anubis, the solemn god known as the Master of Jackals. Can Magister Setne Inhetep, personal philosopher-wizard to the Pharaoh, reach the distant kingdom of Avillonia and put an end to the Anubis Murders, or will he be claimed as the latest victim?

ISBN: 978-1-60125-042-1

Collect all of these exciting Planet Stories adventures!

THE SWORDSMAN OF MARS
BY OTIS ADELBERT KLINE
INTRODUCTION BY MICHAEL MOORCOCK

Harry Thorne, outcast scion of a wealthy East Coast family, swaps bodies with a Martian in order to hunt down another Earthman before he corrupts an empire. Trapped between two beautiful women, will Harry end up a slave, or claim his destiny as a swordsman of Mars?

ISBN: 978-1-60125-105-3

THE OUTLAWS OF MARS
BY OTIS ADELBERT KLINE
INTRODUCTION BY JOE R. LANSDALE

Transported through space by powers beyond his understanding, Earthman Jerry Morgan lands on the Red Planet only to find himself sentenced to death for a crime he didn't commit. Hunted by both sides of a vicious civil war and spurned by the beautiful princess he loves, Jerry soon finds he must lead a revolution to dethrone his Martian overlords—or die trying!

ISBN: 978-1-60125-151-0

ROBOTS HAVE NO TAILS
BY HENRY KUTTNER
INTRODUCTION BY F. PAUL WILSON

Heckled by an uncooperative robot, a binge-drinking inventor must solve the mystery of his own machines before his dodgy financing and reckless lifestyle get the better of him.

ISBN: 978-1-60125-153-4

ELAK OF ATLANTIS
BY HENRY KUTTNER
INTRODUCTION BY JOE R. LANSDALE

A dashing swordsman with a mysterious past battles his way across ancient Atlantis in the stories that helped found the sword and sorcery genre. Also includes two rare tales featuring Prince Raynor of Imperial Gobi!

ISBN: 978-1-60125-046-9

THE DARK WORLD
BY HENRY KUTTNER
INTRODUCTION BY PIERS ANTHONY

Sucked through a portal into an alternate dimension, Edward Bond finds himself trapped in the body of the evil wizard Ganelon. Will Bond-as-Ganelon free the Dark World from its oppressors—or take on the mantle of its greatest villain?

ISBN: 978-1-60125-136-7

THE SHIP OF ISHTAR
BY A. MERRITT
INTRODUCTION BY TIM POWERS

When amateur archaeologist John Kenton breaks open a strange stone block from ancient Babylon, he finds himself hurled through time and space onto the deck of a golden ship sailing the seas of another dimension—caught between the goddess Ishtar and the pale warriors of the Black God.

ISBN: 978-1-60125-177-0

THE SWORD OF RHIANNON
BY LEIGH BRACKETT
INTRODUCTION BY NICOLA GRIFFITH

Captured by the cruel and beautiful princess of a degenerate empire, Martian archaeologist-turned-looter Matthew Carse must ally with the Red Planet's rebellious Sea Kings and their strange psychic allies to defeat the tyrannical people of the Serpent.

ISBN: 978-1-60125-152-7

INFERNAL SORCERESS
BY GARY GYGAX
INTRODUCTION BY ERIK MONA

When the shadowy Ferret and the broad-shouldered mercenary Raker are framed for the one crime they didn't commit, the scoundrels are faced with a choice: bring the true culprits to justice, or dance a gallows jig. Can even this canny, ruthless duo prevail against the beautiful witch that plots their downfall?

ISBN: 978-1-60125-117-6

STEPPE
BY PIERS ANTHONY
INTRODUCTION BY CHRIS ROBERSON

After facing a brutal death at the hands of enemy tribesmen upon the Eurasian steppe, the 9th-century warrior-chieftain Alp awakes fifteen hundred years in the future only to find himself a pawn in a ruthless game that spans the stars.

ISBN: 978-1-60125-182-4

WORLDS OF THEIR OWN
EDITED BY JAMES LOWDER

From R. A. Salvatore and Ed Greenwood to Michael A. Stackpole and Elaine Cunningham, shared-world books have launched the careers of some of science fiction and fantasy's biggest names. Yet what happens when these authors break out and write tales in worlds entirely of their own devising, in which they have absolute control over every word? Contains 18 creator-owned stories by the genre's most prominent authors.

ISBN: 978-1-60125-118-3

ALMURIC
BY ROBERT E. HOWARD
INTRODUCTION BY JOE R. LANSDALE

From the creator of Conan, Almuric is a savage planet of crumbling stone ruins and debased, near-human inhabitants. Into this world comes Esau Cairn—Earthman, swordsman, murderer. Can one man overthrow the terrible devils that enslave Almuric?

ISBN: 978-1-60125-043-8

SOS THE ROPE
BY PIERS ANTHONY
INTRODUCTION BY ROBERT E. VARDEMAN

In a post-apocalyptic future where duels to the death are everyday occurrences, the exiled warrior Sos sets out to rebuild civilization—or destroy it.

ISBN: 978-1-60125-194-7

STRANGE ADVENTURES ON OTHER WORLDS

PLANET
stories

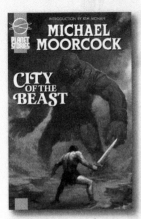

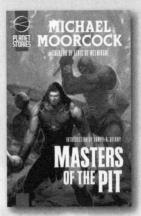
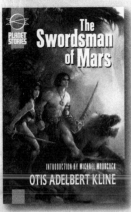

STRANGE ADVENTURES ON OTHER WORLDS

PLANET
stories

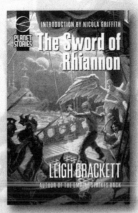

HIDDEN WORLDS AND ANCIENT MYSTERIES

PLANET
stories

SWORD & SORCERY LIVES!

Planet Stories is proud to present these classics of magic and perilous adventure from three unparalleled masters of heroic fantasy: Robert E. Howard, A. Merritt, and C. L. Moore.

•••

"Howard's writing is so highly charged with energy that it nearly gives off sparks."

Stephen King

"[A. Merritt] has a subtle command of a unique type of strangeness which no one else has been able to parallel."

H. P. Lovecraft

"C. L. Moore's shimmering, highly colored prose is unique in science fiction."

Greg Bear

THE UNIVERSE OF FUTURE CENTURIES

PLANET
stories

PLANET
stories

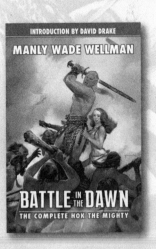

PATHFINDER
TALES™

For years, the award-winning Pathfinder campaign setting has provided fans of the Pathfinder Roleplaying Game with epic adventures, strange vistas, and unforgettable characters. Now the Pathfinder Tales line of novels introduces all-new stories by some of fantasy's hottest authors, bringing the world to life like never before! Each Pathfinder Tales novel is totally self-contained and suited for both dedicated Pathfinder fans and readers new to the world. From heroic quests to fantastic mysteries, Pathfinder Tales novels are everything you love about fantasy, plus a whole new world shared by thousands of other readers—all for just $9.99 paperback or $6.99 ebook. Are you ready for your next adventure?

A WORLD OF ADVENTURE!

PATHFINDER

TALES

The Future is Now!

Pathfinder Tales brings you sword-swinging and spell-blasting fantasy fiction set in the award-winning Pathfinder campaign setting. Now take your reading online for even more Pathfinder Tales adventures, in three different electronic categories!

FEATURING AUTHORS SUCH AS:

Elaine Cunningham
Dave Gross
Ed Greenwood
Monte Cook
Robin D. Laws
Howard Andrew Jones
Liane Merciel
Richard Lee Byers
...AND MANY MORE!